THE SPRING IN MY HEART

A LOVE FOR ALL SEASONS
BOOK 4

J L LORA

Larimar

For all the dedicated single Papis.
May the right love find you.
May you recognize and hold on to it with all your strength forever.

Especially you, Lenin.

DONE WITH THE FROST, READY FOR THE FLOURISH

By Bougie Girl

Winter is finally tapering off…at least down in the D.C. metro area. The tulip sprouts announce the shift in the seasons and not a minute too soon.

I'm so ready.

I spent the last few months in New York, and it was brutal. I've been cold to the bone, getting slapped by the frigid air every time I open the door, dreading every time I left the house but being forced to step out under gray skies and rain and snow showers anyway.

Store openings, winter galas, product debuts, and rooftop parties under the bright lights made bearable by patio heaters all blended together. I ended each day and night worn out and mentally tapped. If I had to smile at one more celebrity/influencer/reality star's "sexy" version of "Santa Baby" or the unboxing of freebies they got from desperate companies, I would have been rocking back and forth in a straight jacket on the sidewalks of Manhattan next to a steaming manhole cover.

When did I start hating the winter? It used to be my favorite season.

Probably when I left the warmth and joy of a good night to traipse back into the true definition of insanity: 'Doing the same thing over and over again and expecting different results.' Thank you, Einstein, for coining it.

Anyway, my skin is dryer than a Sangiovese pressed under the Tuscan sun. I lather on so much lotion daily that I could slide down a hill and into another galaxy. And I would welcome that so I don't have to feel the constant whining and moping of my heart.

The seasonal blues are definitely a thing—a thing I find myself fighting, though it feels like I'm swinging at an invisible target.

The thought of being out in public was enough to send me into the fetal position. The scrutiny of the past few months has been at an all-time high. My name has seen more tabloids than a Port Authority stand. I keep having to smile and put on that *nonchalant* face. Even though, deep down, I am *overly chalant* to the point of despair. Receiving the new Naked Blush palette by *Lash N' Gloss* didn't bring the usual makeup-wizard joy in me. Instead, it became a harbinger of anxiety. Me putting makeup on signaled going out, facing the sun, the stares, and the whispering. It meant stretching my cheeks, making my eyes widen and lashes flutter like a ~~happy girlfriend~~ sponsored mascara collab.

I would rather stay under the sheets *alone* than out in the streets.

Nope. Even two of my favorite brands could not make me excited. I practically had to pry myself off the couch to go to the Nidia X Thic-cletics fashion show.

But thank God, when I lacked the courage, Lauren delivered a swift, long-distance kick in the butt. That is what best friends do when you've mourned a heartbreak long enough. They put their foot down and kick you out into the world.

And I'm glad she did, or I wouldn't have forgiven myself.

Because, GIRL…the fashion show was *exquisite*.

Glam athleisure in cashmere is to die for. It slides over your body like a second skin that's luxurious, sexy, and amazingly fitting. The fitted tapered pants flatter any figure. The top whispers above the belly button, making the set playful but versatile. But the true star is the duster that teases my mid-calf, bringing it all together harmoniously. The collab brought back one of my favorite things in fashion: the three-piece set. Three matching pieces make you feel like you have your life together, and you're *that girl*. You know, the one that turns heads, always makes good decisions, and won't put herself back in a toxic situation. You won't find that girl at home mentally reliving the magical night where she felt understood only to fall back into a trap.

I digress, though.

After the Nidia X Thiccletics fashion show, I scored a couple of ensembles, the teal and emerald that play dramatically well with my eyes. Then, my brother Chase, who can be equal parts heaven's gift and hell's star minion, surprised me with the dusty-pink, berry-red, and black sets. I thought those were sold out.

I bet you're wondering what the lesson in all this is… Girl, me too. LOL.

I guess getting up and showing up, even when you don't want to, can pay off big. Because winter is long, but the promise of spring is in the little things, even if it's makeup and three-piece sets or friendships that force you to go out and live again. Maybe it's the small gifts that bring you delight and make you look forward to wearing colors again. I'm ready for the blooming and the blossoming. I'm ready for color to fill my life, first in blushes and pastels and then in a full, vivid spectrum. Bring. Spring. On.

Until then, stay warm and keep on slayin'.

Xoxo,

The Bougie One

1

Oliver

Mierda mano, when I think shit can't get any worse, it can. I have to face my one-night stand from *Noche Buena*.

The one I relive at least four to five times a day.

The one where I got left behind so she could run back to her ex.

The one that has me playing Aventura on a loop.

And it starts with her brother, my friend.

Coño

I pull out the wet wipes I always carry around and swipe the back of my neck, over my arms, and under my pits. I reapply deodorant and throw on the clean Henley I keep in my trunk for emergencies. I blow a breath into my palm and instinctively reach for the mouthwash in the glove compartment.

I need to put the long morning at work behind me—the fight with Lyssa, my girlfriend, over our canceled weekend trip, and my former mother-in-law's attitude because Ayla wants *me, not her,* to take her to the mall this weekend. Now, my day is turning into a latrine, but I need to make it look like it smells like roses.

Because Luciana Blake didn't cancel the appointment for a walk-through of her reno project like I've been praying she would.

I got a text from my friend Cam confirming his sister would meet me at two in front of the side-by-side properties she is looking to unite. My boy actually sounded happy, excited, hopeful...all the things he wouldn't be if he knew what happened the last time I saw Luciana.

We slept together.

And by slept, I mean *nos comimos*. Yeah, we ate each other up, rolled on the hardwood floor of my flip, and rode each other to exhaustion. Her scent clung to my nostrils for days. No matter how many times I bathed, I could still smell her on my skin. No matter what I ate or drank, I still tasted her tongue on mine.

Now Cam wants me to work with her and renovate her house like I don't wake up in cold sweats thinking about how well she fits in my arms. I would have to see her every day, look into her eyes, and remember how she held my hand as we traded stories from our pasts.

And relive how she ran back to New York, Mateo de la Cruz, and a life of parties, press, and riches. All that is the polar opposite of my world as a contractor, coach, and single dad.

When I tried to tell him I'm too busy, too booked, he hit me with, "Please make a space for her. Chase and I wouldn't trust anyone else."

Me lleva el diablo.

So I couldn't say no after that, not when I fully understand what it means to be protective of someone. Anyway, it will just be business with her. I can use the money to pad my savings, which is always a good thing. My *negrita*—my daughter, my life, my Ayla—wants more things as she grows up, and I'm determined to give them to her. She will never not have something because I don't have the means to provide them for her.

There's also no way I can say no without raising more questions from Cam or Chase of why I won't work on their sister's project.

Besides, if Lux has no problem with us, I won't be the one acting *despechado* over what happened between us. We did what we set out to do on *Noche Buena*. We gave each other an unforgettable night. Now, she's back with her famous ex, and I'm in a stable—*kinda*—relationship.

It's all good. Really good. Fantastic, really.

I finish freshening up and head to her house in Federal Hill, arriving thirty minutes ahead of our meeting. I barely remember driving up the steep hill lined with red brick rowhomes on Christmas morning when I brought her home. That day, I concentrated on the road ahead, the fallen snow, and the hole she carved in my chest. I ignored the park and, through the snow-covered trees, the view of the Inner Harbor. She has a picturesque view from her front windows and her rooftop. How many times have I seen this on magazine covers and photos on the internet?

This area is like Lux herself—something I watch from afar but never really reach. She is high-class and luxury. My beginnings are so low that humble looks down its nose at them. Every time I step into the shower spray, I thank God for running water inside my house. She'll never know what the opposite of that is. Just like she has siblings that love and care for her to the point of buying her a property and ensuring a trusted person to work on her renovations. *Mis hermanos* wouldn't spit on me if I was on fire.

I can't believe I let myself dream of the possibility. I shake the thought off and turn my head to what's at hand, like I've been doing for the past two months.

I examine the perimeter, walking around the leading property and then the one I'll be annexing to it. Both are a good size, but I can see why she needs double the space. Baltimore City row homes are famously narrow. Merged, these two will be a perfect-size masterpiece. I can already tell I'll need to draw permits from the city to merge the water pipelines and the electric panel.

I establish the horizontal width with my measuring tape, then I cross the street and pull out my phone to use the measuring app to get the correct height. I also take several photos and make notes. It will help me with visualizing the annexing point.

The satin-bronze Range Rover pulls up at five till two in front of the property. Through the glass, I can make out the shape of her slick bob. Luciana's hair, no longer blonde but now a soft brown, is straight today with none of *Noche Buena*'s bouncy waves. She pulls down the sun visor and applies lip gloss. I love glossy lips on a woman, but it's the meticulous taps at the corners with her fingertips that get to me.

My heart takes off, pounding away hard against my sternum. She's wrong for me, like high blood pressure. I rub my chest to thank him for the reminder. This already was all it was meant to be.

I take a breath to steady and brace myself as the door opens. When she steps out of the vehicle, she's wearing jeans that mold over her hips and that nice, round ass.

I fight against the flutter in my chest because she's not as beautiful as I remembered her. She looks even more like a flower that bloomed after the winter, from the jade-green top to the sky-high heels.

Heels? I hope she realizes how much walking we're about to do.

She smooths her hair and looks around but doesn't see me immediately. I don't call out to her but let her walk to her door. I want to see her walk. Looking ain't going to kill me.

At 1:58, I cross the street.

She turns around, and our gazes meet. Her eyes round for a second, and then her gaze slides over me like mine did over hers just minutes ago. "Hi. I didn't realize you were here already."

The itch to get closer to her is instant, but I squelch it and smile at her like none of this is a big deal.

"Hello, Luciana. I got here early to take photos so I could visualize the plan better in the design stage. I also want to anticipate any issues with the outdoor structure."

Yeah, get down to business quickly so we can get it over with.

She looks away for a brief moment, her gaze beyond the park, and then it's centered on me again. "Did you notice anything?"

"Some minor stuff. I'll have to draft permits for the outside as well. The city will have to come merge the pipelines."

She gnaws on the corner of her lip. "Is that going to be hard?"

I shake my head, trying to shake the memory of those lips against my mouth and my neck. "It's not too hard, but it will cost you."

"How much?"

4

"I'll have to calculate that and let you know." I don't know why she's worried. Cam has enough money to cover that. He and Chase knew it would cost a pretty penny to complete this project.

"Yeah. We'll have to discuss costs," she says.

"Yes, we can do that when we figure out everything you need done. Also, you have to tell me what your budget for this is."

She nods and gestures toward the front door. She unlocks it, and we go through it. We stand in a rectangular space with a set of stairs on the right-hand side and a door to a garage on the left.

"I have to talk to my financial advisor to nail down my final budget. I want to give myself a cap so I don't overspend like I always do."

She probably doesn't want to ask her brother for too much money. "Cam is pretty well aware of the costs. He has a good sound mind when it comes to this."

She snorts. "You mean Chase does. Cam knows about the quality of stuff. He has no sense of money. Chase does all the research and the legwork."

"Really?" It shouldn't surprise me. We had a long conversation about investments recently. "Chase is very good at that. He invests money for Ayla. I thought it was weird when he first brought up the idea, but after my conversation with him, my mind was blown."

"It's amazing, isn't it? When you're talking investment and money with him, he becomes Warren Buffett. That's why Cam trusts him so much."

And so do you. It's in her proud smile.

"You guys are lucky to have someone so conscious about the money who knows where to put it to make it grow."

She nods. "It's true. As annoying as he is, he would never steer us wrong. He's the most loyal person I know."

I wonder what it's like to trust a sibling so implicitly. Hell, I wonder what it is like to have siblings who not only acknowledge your existence but go out of their way to be protective of you and try to find ways to make your life easier. Does she, Cam, and Chase even realize what they have in each other? I shake the thought out of my head. It's none of my business what they do as a family. I need to stick to what I'm here for.

"So…tell me how you envision your place. And don't hold back. Give me the full picture of what you see when you close your eyes and think of your ideal space."

Her eyes drift closed, and she releases a long breath. "I'm thinking three functional floors. The first floor can have a receiving area, a couple of bedrooms, and a formal living room. I want the kitchen, a family room, and two bedrooms on the second floor. The master suite is one of them."

"I'm not prying into your life, but why do you need so many bedrooms? It's my job to make sure you get what you want with no regrets."

She chuckles. "I get it. I have an extended family. I have three nephews and a niece. If I want to have them over, I want to have enough space for all of them."

"I get it." She told me that night how much she loves her niece.

"And my niece is attached at the hip to her best friend. Whenever they want to come over to get away from their parents, I want them to have space here."

She's thinking of my Ayla hanging at her house with Bron, her niece. I instinctively start to lean toward her but catch myself.

Jesus. It hasn't even been five minutes, and I'm already trying to get closer.

Her eyes fly open, and she clears her throat. "I'm sorry. I hope that's not inappropriate because we…you know…"

The blush that stains her cheeks is so pretty, but her words land like a gut punch because she just ripped off the Band-Aid and kicked the elephant sitting quietly in the corner. Now, it's ready to stampede all over this meeting.

Only, I won't let it.

"No, not at all," I say like it's not burning a hole through my stomach. "We both went in with our eyes open, knowing what that was and moved on as soon as the night was over."

The second the words are out of my mouth, I regret them. It's all a fucking lie—at least for me. Her face is now darker as she examines a painting on the wall. I sounded like a *puerco*. My throat goes dry. This is the worst mistake of all. Neither of us is okay with this, but she has to be the one that calls it off.

Then, her gaze is back to mine. "Right." She points up. "On the third floor, I want my workspace. I need it arranged so I can film from different corners of it. It would have a dedicated office space, a sitting area, a luxury bathroom, and areas where I can do standing photoshoots or shoot objects in lightboxes. I also want a whole sound system."

I clear my throat, following her lead and moving past the moment. "Got it. But why on the third floor? Most people want their workspace on the first floor."

She shrugs. "I think I would get better lighting there than on the first two floors. There's a rooftop, so if I want to go shoot a video there, I can."

"I see. You're right. Light is one of the focal points for this. Have you thought of either skylights or a moonroof over your studio space?"

Her eyes grow wide, excitement creeping up in her voice. "Like the moonroof on my Range Rover?"

Her enthusiasm makes me smile. "Same concept, but you can make it as wide as you want. You can also have different skylights in strategic places."

She presses her hands together. "I love the sound of that. Natural light is everything. But will that ruin my patio space on the roof? I like to sit out there when I can."

"Not necessarily. We can work around it."

"God, I would love that. You can make that happen?"

The look she turns on me is soft, as if she is asking me if I could rope the moon and bring it to her fingertips so she can touch it.

"Yes, I can," I say, and my chest puffs up because I can wow her with this project. I can make this place look way beyond her imagination. "And remember, that's not necessarily too much of a problem because we have double the roof space now."

"Yes."

"You also have to remember, this will make the budget go up," I warn.

"But it will be worth it. It will increase the property value, and I can take on even more work. It's a write-off on my taxes."

I pull out my notebook. "Now that you know what you want, let's go floor by floor, and let's catalog what needs to be done."

We go through the townhouse she is already living in. The floors need immediate updating, but she used the décor to make the most out of it. The mixture of blue and green on the walls is classy and pleasing. I've had a couple of my clients ask for this. I know the color name by now, Venus Teal. Luciana has accomplished what they failed to do. She's made it work with other pieces like the gold, floor-to-ceiling mirror and without painting over the Baltimoresque exposed brick wall. Even her pink looks perfectly in harmony. *Shabby chic luxury* if that was a thing. If I were to stage this place for sale, I wouldn't change a thing.

She tells me what she wants, and we decide to discuss finishes later. When we get to the third floor, her face lights up.

"I can't wait to see what you do with this place. It's going be so inspiring. I can feel my creative juices flowing. I'll need a makeup counter with a built-in light, like what you did for the makeup areas in Autumn Lush. I want one of those in my bedroom too."

"Why don't you just get one and do your makeup in one place? Do you really need two?"

Why the fuck are you asking that? It's none of your business.

But she's non-plussed. "I want to keep work separate from my personal life. This is why I want a sitting area. I don't want my actual house and living room to show up in videos most times."

"I thought showing where and how you live is part of what you do."

She waves her hand back and forth. "It is, and it isn't. Mostly, you give the illusion of accessibility because social media can become too much. You can overshare, and I don't ever want to do that. I want to keep some things separate."

"That makes sense. I don't know much about what you do."

But you know how lonely she feels sometimes because everyone's watching her relationship ups and downs. You know how much her mother gives her the blues. You also know every inch of her body. You've kissed and sucked all of it.

She sighs. "As a vlogger, I take people on a journey. I tell them a story through what I'm experiencing and using the senses, especially visually. That creates an organic connection when you are genuine. While I want them to experience things with me, I want to keep some things to myself. People get confused and think they deserve full access to your life and your space. I plan to build my own brand and expand my reach and access. I don't want any blurred lines between Lux and Bougie Girl. Sometimes, people become obsessed. That is also why I will need an excellent security system all around the area."

Her words make me stop writing my notes. "Is someone bothering you?"

She blinks a few times, then her lips curve. "No, just in case. I'm Cam's sister, and people have tried to get close to get to him. I also have followers on social media. You never know."

"You can never be too careful." I seriously believe this. I'm constantly talking to Ay about the dark places on the internet and how you really don't know people like that.

"When do you think you can have this project complete? Six weeks?" she asks.

It's my turn to laugh. "I see you've been watching the twins on TV. It's probably going to take longer than that. We want this done right and following all codes."

"HGTV makes it seem so easy," she says.

There's a smile tugging at the corners of her mouth, but it's true. TV shows have managed to warp people's expectations and make it hard on us contractors. Everyone wants to use high-end materials, shiplap, and considers themselves experts after watching a few shows. "I don't have that large of a crew, a time jump machine, or the magic of editing."

She snaps her fingers once. "Damn. I was hoping you would be like a genie who can nod, and boom, my wishes come true."

"I can grant some insta-wishes. This one is not one of them. This is more of a long-term wish."

She toys with her fingers against her top. "What kind of insta-wishes do you grant?"

Then her eyes widen, and I could swear that, like me, she's reliving the memories of our *Noche Buena*, alone in an empty house like we are now. And without noticing, I'm a step closer to her.

Her phone goes off, and we both jump back. My skin is practically boiling.

Always her fucking phone.

She picks it up and turns away.

I take a breath. *This is not good.* I need to rein in the flirting.

"Oh. I'll be right there." She turns back to me. "I'm sorry, but I'm helping Chase and Lauren with the kids while they're out of town for the weekend. That was Felix's school. He has a stomachache."

"Do you need help?"

She shakes her head. "It's probably a bug or something."

"Do you mind if I stay to take some measurements?"

"So, you'll take the job?" Her voice is soft, but I can't sense anything from it.

I shrug like the gap in my chest is not widening with each moment that passes. "You need a good contractor to renovate your house. I'm the best. Is that going to be a problem for you?"

Seconds tick by. She swallows and reaches into her bag, handing me the key. "Not at all. Just lock up. Text me when you're done, and I can set the alarm."

"Will do. I'll call you once I have a proposal. We'll meet and go from there."

She steps toward me, pauses, and then climbs on her tiptoes and kisses my cheek. In that second, I'm surrounded by that sweet, expensive scent clinging to her skin— the one that lives in my psyche and sometimes won't let me sleep.

"Thank you for meeting me, Oliver. See you later."

And with that, she rushes away, and I'm left standing in her living room, praying this doesn't become my personal hell, but my skin has already started to burn.

———

Lux

Monday

Oh no, no, no, no, no. Damn you, Cam, for putting me in this position today.

My heart is trying to punch its way out of my chest.

We were so close. I could smell the sweet mint of his breath. I was engulfed in the smell of his cologne and his skin. The same scent that soothed me in the moments when panic threatened to take me down. I anchored my thoughts on it, remembering the touch of gentle yet rough hands.

And I push down on the gas, speeding away from my own house like a bat out of hell. My face is on fire, and I want nothing more than to call my brother and tell him how bad he just screwed me over. Seriously. He put me in the same room with the man I wanted to avoid. Thanks to Cam's meddling, Ollie and I are now in the most uncomfortable situation.

But instead of dialing Cam, I crank up the volume on Jhene Aiko. She's belting that we have to keep going. And I do.

Because me and Oliver working together spells disaster, and I can't put a stop to it because Cam and Chase wouldn't let this go. They would want to know why I won't work with the contractor who has created magic for Cam's house and Lauren's business, *Autumn Lush*.

There's no way I can tell them the magic he created for me in one night. The way he made me feel seen, heard, and fucked...*so good*.

Shit.

I run my hands over the bob I spent so much time perfecting today. Jhene is now going on and on about the angel that opened the window to her soul, and I smack the button to shut the radio down. I would rather ride in silence, listening to my own madness rather than her reasons for being.

For months, I've been in a relationship where I've been alone and surrounded by people like water on an island. And just one look at Ollie and he brought it all back. Christmas Eve, happiness, and smiles. Connections, sex, rejection. It was what it was, a night where we made each other happy, with no ties, and the full intention of reclaiming our lives once it was over.

Except, I let myself dream. I opened the doors, only for my mistakes to come stomping in and for Ollie to slink out of.

It's been the longest winter. My phone vibrates with a call.

Please don't let it be Mateo. I can't talk to him right now.

Chase's name appears on my dash. I breathe a long sigh of relief and hit the answer button.

"I'm almost at the school," I say before he can say anything.

"I figured," my brother says. "Just want to check that you got this and don't want us to head back early."

I put on my turn signal and switch lanes. "I got this. Felix probably just misses you. He cried this morning when I dropped him off."

"Oh man," he says. "We should probably head back."

"No, this is a good prep for the wedding. We had a great time last night. I think it hit him today how long you've been away. You're back tomorrow, anyway. How's it going over there?"

Chase took Lauren for a long weekend getaway to help ease her wedding jitters.

"Really good," he says way too enthusiastically.

"Ew."

"Not like that," he snaps, then adds, "well, yeah, just like that too."

"That's pretty gross," I shoot back.

"I thought this was the kind of thing you would want for your best friend."

"Stop." I yell.

He laughs so loud it's contagious. "How was your meeting with Coach?"

He means Ollie, and my stomach starts to churn.

"Good," I say.

"Just good? When does he start digging? Is he starting with your bottom?"

The image of Oliver's hands between my legs is instant and so quick it makes my stomach dip. "What the hell are you talking about?"

Chase sighs, and it's loaded and exasperated. "I'm asking where the reno is starting. Is he starting with the bottom floor? We want to know so we can clear the guest room in case you need to stay with us."

"Oh, I don't know. He's putting a proposal together." My face is burning, and I crack my car window to let the air in.

"You didn't bring that asshole to meet with Coach, did you?" His voice is tight and loaded with his hatred.

The asshole he is referring to is my boyfriend, Mateo. At times, this is the perfect description.

"No, I didn't. This is my house and my reno." My tone is harsher than I mean it.

"You don't sound excited, even though this is what you wanted."

I shake my head to clear it. "I am. It's just...there's going to be a lot to do, and I just want it to be done. I don't want to stay at your place or Cam's. I want to be in my own space."

He's silent for a few seconds. "I get that. Just stick it out, Lux. Don't go back to New York where you're miserable."

"I'm not—"

He cuts me off. "You hate it there. You hate being with him."

"Chase—"

"No, don't say anything. I'm not trying to pick a fight. I am just saying that you can use this time to build your life here. The life you want."

He's right.

"I know. And I am. You and Cam just need to let me do this my way."

He sighs again. "We just want you to be happy. And that douche..."

"He's trying..."

The other line beeps, and now Mateo's name pops on my screen. I need to answer since I've been ignoring him since last night.

"I have to go, Chase. I'll ping you once I pick up Felix."

I switch over to the other line.

"Finally," Mateo spits before I can even greet him.

"Hi," I say.

"Hi," he mimics. "I've been calling you since last night. Where have you been?"

"I watched a movie with Justin and Felix and fell asleep after putting them to bed. I texted you."

It's not a complete lie. I'm just not admitting to the part where I saw his messages and opted to put on a mud mask rather than answering.

"Luxxy, we haven't really talked in, like, a week." He's annoyed, and I get it, but I can't help how I feel. I just want time away.

From him.

"I know…" I trail off. "We'll see each other this weekend."

He's coming into town with the Emperors to play against the Orioles in their home opener."

"I'm staying with you."

Cold flashes over my stomach.

Staying with me? God no. Dread begins to spread through me.

"My house is not ready yet. I'm starting a renovation soon, and it wouldn't be as comfortable as a hotel. You're used to luxury, and I don't want you to be uncomfortable."

"Luxxy, you forget I used to be poor. It would be like traveling back in time. I just want to spend time with you. I'll still have the team hotel room, but I'll stay with you—unless there's a reason I shouldn't."

My stomach feels like lead, and I'm going to be sick. I just know it. *Fuck my life.* I need to either breakup with him or stop running.

"Fine. I'll see you on Friday."

Chickenshit.

He chuckles. "It will be sooner than that. We're getting in on Thursday morning."

I almost swerve at full speed into the school parking lot.

"Thursday," I choke out.

"Yeah. We have to do press in the afternoon, but we can spend all morning together. Can't wait to see you."

"Yeah." I clear my throat. "I'm picking up Felix, and I'm already at the school. We'll talk some more later."

I don't give myself time to think, or I'll go into a panic attack. Instead, I head inside and straight to the nurse's office.

Felix leaps out of his chair when he sees me and rushes to hug me.

"Titi Lux, my tummy aches."

I hug him back. "Mine too, baby. Let's go home."

Except, his tummy ache will go away... Mine will be here through the weekend.

2

Lux

Friday

Social media is a snake you raise with all the love, care, and attention in the world, but then it turns on you one day out of nowhere.
Even those who follow and adore you are quick to cut you down. It
happens so fast that it has a whiplash effect.

*And I'm still reeling so bad even the softness of my Mohair velvet
couch pisses me off.* I push to my feet, pelting it with my glare. The
peachy-pink vintage fabric with the gold-painted wood and tufted back
is now as offensive to me as my Twitter feed.

I started my morning with a reel, a short video, to my ten million
followers about the yoga position that helped me loosen my hips for
the best sleep. It was some of my best work, shot in front of my antique
gold mirror—the perfect complement to my couch. My makeup was
flawless in that full beat that looks so natural it makes people ask you
for your skin regimen. The telltale was the black eyeliner that
contrasted against my tanned skin and framed my green eyes. I
lowered myself to the floor in my seafoam ribbed jumpsuit. I was so
happy with the way it framed my D-girls and showcased my round ass

built on a squat regimen. I looked the fuck good. As I pulled my long hair into a high ponytail and pursed my glossy lips, I knew it would go viral. I never suspected it would be for all the wrong reasons.

Two hours later, my innocent video has become fodder for everyone to put me down, along with my relationship. Well, if I'm honest, the video didn't do it alone. You've got to have a cheating asshole of a boyfriend who can't keep his dick in his pants for five minutes and an idiot who keeps taking him back—me—to accomplish that.

The *Poor Luxxy* hashtag was just the beginning. The viral take-down has been nothing short of epic, using my video to feed comments and puns.

Maybe instead of reclining hero pose to sleep better, she should be working on her plow pose. Maybe that will keep Mateo from jumping in beds with raggedy hoes. #JustSayin #PoorLuxxy

She goes to the spa, wears posh clothing, and has ten million followers. But does it really matter when her man is slinging his peen on any #mid-influencer with less than 1,000 followers? #SorryButTrue #PoorLuxxy

Face beat to the gods. Body tighter than 1A1 drum. Can't keep Mateo from straying no matter how much yoga she does. It's just sad.

Maybe she should try #therapy instead of yoga because she always takes him back. #PoorLuxxy you're better than that.

The heat flashes up my body, turning my face into a boiling kettle. I fling my phone onto my couch, shove my eyes closed, and let the waves of hot shame wash over me. I don't breathe deep or count my breaths. I learned long ago not to fight it and just let the feeling do what it will. If I resist, I'll end up with a panic attack.

I'm not letting Mateo give me any more of those. I'm also not going to cry until my face swells. Nope. I stand still and repeat one of my mantras—*This is temporary, and I will prevail. It is what the fuck it is*—until my body cools again.

"Lux."

My heart stumbles down my chest, and my eyes fly open. Lauren is standing at the top of my stairs. Her black hair, shaped into perfect waves, tumbles down her shoulder and on to the Atelier blazer she let me borrow two months ago. Her naturally glowing skin is set in a pinched expression, a contrast to the chic outfit that screams bad bitch on a mission. Except, she's wearing flats, which means she ran out of her house in a hurry.

"How did you get in here?" I practically growl at her.

Her frown deepens. "I knocked. Chase gave me the spare key. When you didn't answer the phone, we got worried. I asked him to let me be the one to come by. As you can imagine, he's... I didn't want him to run into Mateo."

"Yeah, that's for the best. It's not worth a reaction," I say with as much carelessness as I can muster.

Lauren's shoulders dip. "He deserves it for what he's putting you through. Again."

I shrug in a not-a-big-deal kind of way and clear my throat. "I'm fine. It's not the first time he cheated on me."

Her hand shoots out.

I take an instinctive step back. "No, don't touch me."

She nods and stays where she is. "Your brothers are losing it. Cam is holding Chase back from going to look for Mateo."

"There's no point. That will do nothing but land Chase in jail."

"Wha—"

Fast footsteps up the stairs stop her mid-word.

A second later, Mateo's imposing 6'2" frame lands on the top step. His muscular frame towers over Lauren and me. His beautiful amber skin is flushed like he ran here from the stadium. He's wearing his brown-and-yellow baseball uniform, cleats, and regret all over his face. His eyes land on me, and he reaches out. "Luxxy, I left practice to come and explain. Nothing really happened with that girl. She was there when I was partying. You know I came home to you last night."

And jumped in the shower before getting into bed and didn't want to have sex.

The memory sinks my stomach even lower. At this point, it's going to drag me to hell. I take a step back and practically spit venom, "Get the fuck out of my house."

"You don't mean that, baby."

The word sends another surge of heat up my body. I turn around, grab the first thing I find, and fling it at him.

He ducks, and the mug shatters against the wall. He looks back at it. "Are you fucking crazy? You could've hurt me with that."

"Then get the fuck out, like she asked." Lauren yells, pointing toward the stairs.

"Mind your business."

"Or what?" she asks. "And before you answer, let me tell you something. I'm the only thing that stands between you and a career-ending beating from Chase."

He looks away from her and back to me. "Come on, Luxxy, let me explain. Just us. This is just between us. We love each other and have been through so much together. We understand each other."

"I understand you can't keep your dick in your pants. Fuck off. I want nothing to do with you."

"Luxxy—"

"Get out." I scream.

He doesn't move. "I won't leave."

"Fine." I reach for my phone in my pocket, but it's not there. Right, I threw it on the couch. "Lauren, call Chase and let's post the meeting on social media. I want to see what the press will say when the New York Emperors lose today because their cleanup hitter is in the hospital because he got beat for trespassing."

"That's ridiculous, Luxxy. I'm staying with you while I'm in town."

"You're no longer welcome. Get out of my house."

His face goes black with anger. And here goes one of his tantrums. Rage flares in his eyes, and then it's gone. He smiles. "Fine. Let me go get my stuff in the bedroom."

"No. You will never set foot in my bedroom or this house again. Go downstairs, and I'll bring it to you."

Mateo's fists clench. "Whatever. I'll wait till your friend is gone and you can think for yourself." He storms down the steps.

I go to the bedroom and grab his suitcase, dress jacket, and the watch on the nightstand. I come back to the living room and start moving toward the stairs.

Lauren grabs my arm. "Where the hell are you going?"

I look at her like she's stupid. "To give him his shit. I want him out of my life."

"Yeah, but you're not a fucking valet to bring his luggage down."

I'm so mad I'm seeing red. "Well, how the hell am I going to get it to him? Do I fling it out the window?"

I meant it sarcastically, but she looks at the window and then back at me and smiles, her lips stretching like the Cheshire cat.

It dawns on me what she's insinuating, and I shake my head. "I can't do that."

"Why? Are you planning on taking him back?"

The question makes my face burn because I'm ashamed that this has become my life routine. I take him back every time. It has to stop, because the embarrassment keeps escalating. God knows what he'll do next to humiliate me.

The surge of anger hits me so hard it blurs everything. At that moment, I don't care what the neighbors say or the destruction it could cause. I don't even care if it ends up on social media. He put my name in everyone's mouth, anyway.

"I'm done for good," I spit out.

She turns around, unlocks the window, and flings it open. "Okay, then." She tilts her head.

That's my cue. I stroll to the window, lift the suitcase, and fling it.

Lauren screams, "Watch out."

Mateo's eyes bulge out, and he scrambles out of the way like a cartoon character.

"What the fu—" The loud thud comes before the end of his sentence. "Are you crazy?"

Lauren is smiling. "That was fun. But you know what would be more satisfying?"

"What?" I'm seriously afraid to ask.

She points at what I'm still holding in my hand. "That watch hitting the ground. Do you think he would dive after it like a baseball in the outfield?"

I stare down at my hands wrapped around the rose-gold case with the black sapphire dial, the soft alligator straps draped over my palms. It's a beautiful piece. "Lauren, this is a Patek Phillipe."

Her smile is wicked. "I know."

And the urge hits me. I want to see him dive for his expensive watch. He's always shown his possessions more reverence than he's shown me. He doesn't let his watch face get smudged, but he cheats on me every chance he gets.

I look back down. Mateo and his driver are picking up clothes from the ground. His Versace silk shirt is soaked from falling on the curb. The yellow tinge tells me it's not dirty water.

"I forgot to lock the suitcase."

"Oops?" Lauren shrugs. "Too bad. So sad." Then, her gaze cuts through me like a freshly sharpened steak knife. "Make his day worse, Lux. Finish him."

I stick my face out the window. "You forgot this." When he looks up, I yell, "Catch." and send the watch flying past his head.

The shock on his face segues to him rushing to catch it, only for the Patek Phillipe piece to land on the roof of a car and bounce onto the asphalt. "You lost your fucking mind, Luxxy. You're going to pay for that."

"I'm already paying. Don't call me, and don't ever come back. We're done."

He starts to talk, but I can't hear him because my ears are buzzing, and my gaze lands on the red truck behind the limo and the man standing by it, watching the whole spectacle.

Oliver.

Mateo is yelling something, but my heart is beating too loud, too fast. And I'm mortified because Oliver probably thinks I'm a straight-up psycho bitch, and now he's a witness to this toxic dumpster fire that is Mateo and me.

Why is the earth not swallowing me whole?

I slam my window shut and sit on the couch. My hands are starting to shake, so I tuck them under me. I'm letting the emotions wash over me, but this time, the burning in my chest lingers.

Lauren is moving around, but I keep my eyes on the damaged wooden floor I haven't gotten around to having fixed.

The whole world is talking about me. Everyone is laughing at me. How many of these have I endured? I've lost count.

I can't do it anymore.

Lauren's footsteps grow closer. She stands before me, waiting.

I can't look at her. "You should go home. Chase is waiting for you, and the boys need you. I'm okay. Thank you for coming." My voice is strained. I can barely hold it together.

She doesn't leave. Instead, she sits close enough without touching me. "Here, take your wine." She thrusts the glass at me.

I'm forced to grab it. "Please go. I want to be alone."

"Bullshit."

My gaze shoots to hers. "Excuse me?"

She leans closer. "I said *bullshit*. You just dumped your cheating ex. No one wants to be alone after that. You want alcohol, greasy food, cake, and a friend to help you trash his worthless ass."

"I don't need a friend," I snap, making my voice as sharp as I can. I need psychotherapy, electric shocks, a lobotomy, or probably all of it. What I don't need is another witness to my shame.

Lauren sighs and puts her glass on the table. "That's good, because I'm not here to be your friend. I came to be so much more than that. I'm going to fast-forward the clock past my wedding and be your sister now."

The skin on my cheeks tingles, and I flinch like she sucker-punched me. I want to shake my head and tell her I don't need a sister. I just need to be alone and sort this out like I usually do. But I don't even recover before she throws her arms around me.

I don't hug her back. I can't.

But she holds onto me tight and rubs my back in a way that only Mateo has ever done. Because my mother never did, and my brothers were just as messed up as me. We are there for each other, but we don't manage emotions. The people who were supposed to teach us never did. We were never anything but pawns to them. Cam, who wasn't much older than Chase and me, was more of a father to us than Walter.

I don't hug her, but I cry with her like I do in silence every time. I cling to her warmth with everything I've got. I let it out until I have no more tears.

When we pull back, I'm surprised to find tears in her eyes.

Then, she smiles. "Now we eat and get drunk."

I sniffle. "I have nothing in my fridge."

She chuckles and points a finger at the bag on my counter. "I came prepared. Fuck Mateo."

"Yeah, fuck him. This is the last time I cry for him. He can go to hell and take his gender along with him. I'm done with them for a long time."

But I see Ollie looking up at me, the shock in his eyes—and probably the judgment.

3

Lux

Monday

My day is packed, and I wouldn't have it any other way. I have a meeting in New York at 11:00. It sucks, but I'll be rushing back to Baltimore for my five o'clock with Oliver.

I'm glad I got everything together last night because the Acela leaves at 7:30, and I need to be on it to make my meeting. I leave my G-Wagon at home and take an Uber to the train station. Thankfully, my train is on time.

On my way to New York, I work on the script for one of my next videos. I hate having to do this twice a week, but thankfully, I'm able to concentrate. This one is special. I'm featuring Lauren's new styling on-demand service. It's going to cater to women of all sizes at affordable prices. I'm going to help her style and showcase how the looks work. We'll even have a line with me as part of it.

It's going to be a *Bougie Girl X Autumn Lush* collaboration. I've never done that, and I'm super excited, so I just need to get to working on the video concept so I can tell Lauren about it when we meet formally next week.

I stop an hour into the trip and set it aside. I can work on it for another hour on the way back. I check my phone and find a message from Ollie. I eagerly check it.

OLLIE

I'll see you at five. Got great things to show you.

Butterflies rustle in my belly.

Stop being silly, Luciana. Remember, we swore off men and should stick to the cause no matter how lickable and tempting he is. That ship has sailed. He probably thinks you're a psycho after watching you throw your ex's shit out of the window. Besides, he's got a girlfriend.

He's talking about work, not how—*you know from experience*—he puts it down. I can't help it, though. I've been looking forward to seeing him all week. I've had to cancel our appointments twice because work had me drowning all week, and the fallout from the breakup has been taxing despite Maeven's artful handling. Somehow, the chick he was with ended up being cast for a reality show where the cast is sequestered away while they find love.

People now believe it was orchestrated and bought the story that Mateo came home straight from the party and just dropped her and her friend off.

I don't know how she did it, and who cares? Not my problem anymore. I am determined to put that chapter of my life behind me, so I force my attention on the notes for my meeting. They want to meet me to start this new series, and it's obviously important enough that they want to discuss it in person. This could have been a Zoom call, but you know what, they pay me well enough, and it's only an hour or so meeting. I should be out by noon. That should give me enough time to go to the Golden Door spa and get a facial or massage if they can fit me in.

When the train pulls into Port Authority, I hop on the subway and make it to *Big Apple Magazine* in twenty minutes. The security guard smiles and waves me into the elevators. At the top floor, the secretary practically leaps off her chair when she sees me. The textured two-piece suit is tailored to perfection.

She trades her signature smile for the frown crowning the top of her glasses. "Mimi is waiting for you and cleared her whole schedule to speak to you."

What now?

Mimi is our boss, the head editor for the life and style section of *Big Apple Magazine*. We all swear she's an Anna Wintour wannabe who has modeled herself after Meryl Streep's character in *The Devil Wears Prada*—from the big shades to the sometimes downright cutting way she prefers to handle every situation. I'm lucky to be in her good graces because she loves Mateo and lusts after Chase constantly.

The secretary ushers me into Mimi's office, and when I walk in, I'm immediately disconcerted.

My boss is surrounded by the editor-in-chief, the creative director, the marketing team, and three graphic designers.

And everyone is smiling at me like I'm Rosemary walking into the dinner party with the cult.

What did they get me into this time?

"Luxxy," Mimi, in her high chignon, hollow cheeks, cigarette pants, and five-inch heels, crosses the room and hugs me. "So glad you are here."

She towers over me on her platforms, looking down from what looks like a pedestal.

"I thought we were discussing a series." They've ambushed me, so I don't feel the need to be polite.

"Oh, it's more than that, darling. Come sit down." She leads me to a chair next to hers.

I sit and try not to cringe at the expectant way everyone is looking at me. "Why are you all smiling like that?"

Mimi frowns. "You didn't read my email from last night?"

No. I was watching *Justice League* with Bron and the boys. I saw the email come in, but I was in a *throuple* with Ray Fisher, Jason Mamoa, and Henry Cavill. No way I was going to check that. "Uh. No. I'm sorry I was taking care of some family business."

"That explains why you look so surprised to see everyone." She waves around the room. "Luxxy, we are starting a new lifestyle magazine."

I struggle with what to say, because this could be my way out. I am renovating my house and can go into business for myself. "That's... great?"

"It's more than great. It's wonderful. It's the most amazing thing that could've happened to all of us. Your influencer status is going to shoot out of the stratosphere."

"My influencer status?"

"You're going to be the star."

Where is this coming from? The last time I brought this up, they didn't entertain the idea.

"I'm sorry, what?"

"*Bougie Girl* is going to be more than a blogger. She will bigger than a vlogger. *You* are going to be a brand. Think of *Magnolia* by Joanna Gaines, but all things style. You can have more collaborations. We're thinking of your channel as more mainstream, treating it like a real TV channel with dedicated hours and shows."

I open my mouth but close it. I need to ask the right questions. This is something I've been thinking about. Lauren and I talked about this. She said I was already a brand but needed to own it.

"Why now?"

"It's not coming out of nowhere. I've thought of how we can use you more. Your column is our most popular one. You get millions of views on your YouTube videos. We've been doing research, and when you feature a product, sales shoot up. Not to mention that now you've gone past New York. That piece on Autumn Lush garnered so much attention and praise. Of course, the *Lash N' Gloss* nod makes it even more prestigious. I'm still waiting for you to do an unboxing of the huge box you got from Amelia Solis."

Ah. They're trying to ride my coattails. They want to use me and my connections.

"Thank you." I'm struggling with what to say.

"We can do more collaborations and celebrity interviews, like a peek behind the curtains, and feature some of their charity work. We will build you a studio here, and you can shoot more videos weekly."

My pulse quickens. A brand. They're building a brand around me. It's everything I've been wanting. I've dreamed of taking people on a journey, like Anthony Bourdain, letting them experience the world through my senses and inspiring them to go taste the world for themselves.

I've wanted to expand, and this is my chance.

But this has to be on my terms. I don't like that they sprang this on me without warning. They should have told me and my agent. Ruthy should have been invited. I also need to make sure they know I'm not staying in New York.

"This is not going to be an hour meeting, and I had other plans. Can you give me five minutes to make arrangements and call my agent?"

The smiles freeze in place as I step out of the room.

First, I call my agent. "Ruthy. I need you to drop everything and come meet me at *Big Apple*. They're trying to make me into a brand and center a digital magazine around me."

"Why was I not invited in the first place? You know what, I'll find out for myself. On my way," Ruthy says.

Next, I call my brother. "Hey, Cam, I'm stuck in my meeting. They want to turn me into a brand."

He doesn't miss a beat. "Don't talk to them without your agent, and don't sign anything without a lawyer. I'm sending you one of mine."

"I don't think that's necessary yet. I don't think we are signing anything today."

"I'll call them as soon as we hang up and tell them to be on standby. Make sure you send them any paperwork right away."

Always the big bro. "Will do. Thanks. Actually, I called because I need a favor. I'm supposed to meet with Ollie today to talk about the floor plans. Can you meet with him? I don't want to stand him up again. I'm going to send you an email with my thoughts. Please apologize for me."

"Okay. I'm supposed to see him after practice today."

"Great."

"Lux, listen. Play hard-ass ball when you go in there. You're a commodity. If they want to create a brand around you, it is because they recognize your worth, what you bring to the table, and your reach. Make sure you call the shots. You can ask for whatever you want. They won't say no."

I smile. "I will, thanks."

"I'm not just saying that because I'm your brother. I'm saying it because it's true. Don't go in there and let these people get the best of you."

I hang up and go to the bathroom to give myself five minutes to breathe. This is a good thing. No, a great thing. It's the next level in my career. And I can dictate the rules.

Because they want me, and it has to be on my turf, playing by my rules.

I walk back in the room with my shoulders squared.

"My agent is on her way, and I would like to wait for her to begin the discussion. After, I would like for it to be put in a contract so my lawyers can go over it. I will tell you right off the bat, Baltimore is where I live now, and I'm planning on staying there. Also, I want executive producer credits, and I want input and veto power in all concepts."

The editor-in-chief smiles in a way that goes as far as her perfect veneers but doesn't reach her bird-of-prey eyes. "Executive producer credits and veto power? That's a renegotiation tactic for a proven star."

I return her you-simple-bitch caliber smile. "Isn't that why I'm here? Because I have the followers, the selling power, and the status to back it up? I know what I bring to the table, and I know the money you'll make off me. I won't be treated any other way."

The air goes out of the room. Everyone is silent, and Mimi and the editor hold a silent conversation.

A drop of sweat skids down my back. *Did I overplay my hand?* I can breathe in the tension like August humidity. There's no way I can back down now. They'll never take me seriously. So, I push my chest out and dig into the silence like everyone else. I get started on a mental list of my next steps. If they walk away, I can always get started on my own. I have enough followers. I'll have to do way more organic content. I can even take my followers through my renovation series.

Mimi clears her throat. "I'm sure your agent will be here shortly, and we can begin. Would you like a mimosa in the meantime?"

———

Lux

After a five-hour meeting with *Big Apple*, a debrief with my agent, and conversations with the lawyers, I was left with tight muscles and a mound of stress weighing my neck down. I practically ran to the spa. The treatments did the trick with the relaxation, but I just want to be alone in my own space.

I stretch like a cat with my hands above my head, enjoying the liquid feel in every inch of my body. The heated massage bed cocoons me, cradling me like a baby. I don't want to leave. I want to lie here and nap. The spa would let me stay as long as I want, but I need to get off this bed. I'm going home tonight. I want to lie on my own bed and do nothing.

And see no one.

I need to see if I can catch a late train.

If push comes to shove, I'll rent a car and drive back. Maybe I'll go to Cam's and take one of the spare cars he keeps there. That's what I'll do. The drive will get my creative juices going. Now more than ever, I need those to flow so I can have fresh ideas for content since I'll have a whole new team, and I want to make sure I keep my own authenticity.

Bougie Girl is going to be a brand on its own. The Bougie Life was born today.

I smile and hop off the bed without bothering with the clothes I came in with. Instead, I get more comfortable and trade my heels for flats, my favorite fitted yoga pants, and a long cardigan.

The treatment left me feeling so good that I left my hair down and chose to go with no makeup. I don't feel like putting in the extra effort when I'm about to drive for over three hours to Maryland.

I add a fat tip in cash for the masseuse. When I get to the checkout, I'm glad I did because they comped my treatments, and they give me a full goody bag.

Love. My. Job.

I make my way to the mirrored doors and grab the handle when I catch the reflection behind me. Like a poltergeist in the mirror, my mother materializes behind me. And yes, it's like seeing Annabelle the doll or the horror nun staring at me. It roots me to the floor, so I can't obey my basic instinct to run, run, run. I school my face and brace myself.

Why did I fucking linger? If I had gotten off the massage table just two minutes earlier...

I almost had it.

The metal bar is still ensconced in my hand, and I'm still facing the glass. I take a breath and force my face muscles into something pleasant and not the very human version of the swearing emoji raging inside me.

Because...fuck this. I don't need this right now.

That's what makes it so sad. It's also what pumps twenty-nine years of guilt right through my whole body. She's my mother. I don't see her that often.

I turn around and smile. Marilyn is just a few feet away. She's wearing her signature Manolo Blahniks and Anna Wintour-at-a-clearance-sale type of disdain on her face. She rarely smiles to avoid getting wrinkles, and she's succeeded. Except that now her face looks rigid. There's also no joy in her, which scares me to this day. Since I was sixteen and found out who she and Walter really are, I've been in fear of turning into her.

"Hi," I say.

"Luciana." She closes the distance between us and hugs me.

"How are you, Marilyn?" I ask. After being around Adri and her mom, Victoria, it feels weird to call her by her name, but I can't bring myself to call the woman who birthed me anything but her name.

"Were you at the gym?" Marilyn asks. "You're all disheveled."

There's never a compliment or just the joy of seeing each other.

I don't let it ruffle me. "We're at a spa. I just got a treatment."

"So did I, but I made sure they did my makeup and hair."

"I'm not going to be out on the town. I'm driving back to Maryland."

"You're a Blake, Luciana, and someone notorious. People look up to you because of your style. You should always represent your brand."

Does she know about my meeting today?

"Brand?" I ask.

"Isn't that what influencers are considered? It's a status thing."

Jesus. It's not like I look like shit. I'm wearing Thiccletics, which are the hot item of the moment. My pointy flats were declared the item of the season by New York Flair. She makes it sound like I'm in rags and my hair is scraggly. I'm not going to explain that, though. I just need to get the hell out of here.

My therapist used to try to steel me against this. *You can't make her be the mother you need her to be, so you just need to remove yourself from the situation. She'll never change…but you have.*

"I need to go, Marilyn." Yes, her name is the appropriate one to use. *Always*. Because she was never the one that I could run to when I got hurt. I couldn't tell her about my fears or confide in her. I couldn't remember her reassuring me, telling me I was smart or brave, or even telling me my interests mattered. Even shopping sprees with Marilyn came with a laundry list of traumas for me to unpack with my therapist years later.

She doesn't even see my trepidation. She doesn't see me.

"We haven't spent any time together. Let's go grab tea and catch up. Tonight, you can stay at the brownstone with me."

Only if you shoot me with a horse tranquilizer and tie me down after.

"I'm headed back to Maryland."

Her lips go flat. "You are spending a lot of time there now."

"I live there."

"You're a fashion and style blogger. You are established here. All my friends and their daughters watch your blogs and read your articles. You can't abandon the city where you've become an icon."

"I can blog from anywhere. I come often for work…" I trail off, but it's too late. *Shit, I fucked up.* I see it in the cold glow in her eyes.

"Yes, you're here all the time. Yet, you never visit your mother. You never come see if I'm dead or alive."

Don't be dramatic or anything.

"I know you're okay. I talk to Eddha all the time, and we communicate."

"We text, Luciana. That's fast communication. I don't even know what's going on in your personal life. Mateo can't be happy that you're in Maryland all the time."

I clench my teeth so hard so I can keep my mouth shut. Why does she have to bring him up every time we talk?

"Mateo and I broke up for good this week. We are not getting back together, and that's final. I'm done letting him make a fool of me."

She waves a dismissive hand. "You always break up, and you always end up together. He's a good catch."

For me and half of New York.

I chuckle. "One I would gladly throw back in the Hudson River."

"No man is going to be perfect, Luciana. He's a good man, with a great profession and impeccable taste. You never hear anything salacious about him. He's handsome and well-known. You've always made a handsome couple."

Now I do laugh.

"Do you not read the papers? He's always with some chick—you know what, it doesn't matter. I am done. He seems to have accepted that. It's time for you to do the same."

I get the death stare, the one that used to keep me quiet as a mouse as a kid. She's always known how to make her disapproval known without many words. It's almost a relief because her next technique is to freeze me or my brothers out. Only, I'm not so lucky this time.

"Let's go have some tea."

I shake my head. "I really can't. Maybe next time—" The lie doesn't make it out of my mouth.

She follows the death stare with a grip on my wrist. "You can spare an hour to have tea with your mother."

Kill me now.

I could insist, but then she would get whiny and even more manipulative. "Okay. Let's go grab a cup of tea, and then I really have to get going."

We take a car service—no Uber or cabs for Marilyn Blake—and head to the *Baroque*, her favorite tearoom. I know better than to suggest a Starbucks. She needs bone china, chintz decor, and expensive prices for mediocre herbal blends you can find anywhere.

During the drive, I apply a little concealer, eyeshadow, and lipstick. I pull out a scarf from my tote and tie it into that elegant knot everyone's so crazy about. I put my earrings back on and prepare for inspection.

She looks at me, and her gaze softens. "You're so beautiful, Luciana. Like I was at your age. I had so many suitors come calling my mother didn't know what to do." Her laugh echoes of yesterday, turning her into someone different than the woman who shrieks and manipulates her children.

It's jarring because I know who she is. Her compliments are like an acid bath.

Just grin and bear it, Lux. Get this over with. "Thank you."

"This is the way you should always look."

Welcome back, Marilyn.

As we make it inside the tearoom, the weight of hanging out with her presses down my shoulders, popping out kinks the masseuse worked hard to smooth out. On the car ride, I concentrated on making myself ready by her standards. That kept me from internalizing this whole thing. Now we're alone in the sense that her attention will be solely on me, and I'll have to stay in the moment because there's no Chase or Cam to split the burden with.

My chest tightens as the doorman pulls the handle on the door and lets us in. The desire to spin and run spreads over my body. The red, brown, and gold wallpaper swallows us in, trapping me in with her.

Stop being a child. You can do this. You don't always need your big brothers.

"Mrs. Blake," the hostess beams, her eyes bright and dancing in the light. "We were waiting for you."

How the hell? She didn't know she was going to see me.

"I always have a standing reservation on Mondays," my mother says before following the hostess. I have no choice but to trail behind them. As we cross the threshold into one of the rooms, I look past the divider screen, and my gaze collides with Mateo who is standing up from a table. His eyes round, and then his lips curve.

My face begins to tingle. This is not happening to me. I shake my head because *hell no*.

"Mateo," my mom squeals.

"Marilyn," I say, my voice low but carrying the jagged edge that is knifing through my insides. I wait until she turns to me. "I'm leaving."

I turn to walk away, and her hand clamps on my wrist. "Don't make a scene, Luciana. If you storm off, everyone will be talking. Let's just head to our table."

"I don't care. People already talk about me anyway. Let me get out of here."

"Please, Luxxy." Mateo is suddenly in front of me in a raspberry-red shirt that seems to have bled out of the wallpaper pattern. "Don't go. Please. I don't expect your forgiveness or for us to get back together. I just want the chance to apologize to you. I don't want to end on bad terms."

I don't snort like I want to. "Consider your apology stamped, delivered, and in the past. I have a late train to catch."

My mother doesn't relinquish the grip. "But we were going to spend time together."

"It will have to be another time."

Mateo moves to block my exit.

"Look," he says, his olive skin flustered, his eyes liquid. "I know I messed up too many times. I squandered the biggest blessing of my life. I don't know what it is. We have everything I need, but I get so scared at times."

"You're a grown man, Mateo. This is a bullshit excuse," I grit out.

He looks down at his feet. "I know, and I'm sorry. Please let's talk.

I don't want that day to be the last memory you have of me. In the name of everything, we lived together. Please, Luxxy. It's just a conversation. I know you're over me, but I love you, and I need this closure. I can't move on without it."

I look at the door and back at him. I see the guy who always held me when I needed it most. I cried all night when my father got arrested and went to jail. The same person who dropped everything to come with me looking for Chase when he was on a destructive binge.

He's been a staple of so many moments when I needed someone. And he was there every time. He was all I had at times, because my brothers were as messed up as I was. Cam would close himself off to the world. Chase went running after thrills. I let myself get used by him so I could feel wanted. Mateo gave me that feeling. It's true he hurt me, but he's also been there for me. And he taught me what men are like. That's why I need to be done once and for all. I can't settle for what they have to offer anymore.

"Okay, let's talk. We'll have closure."

The smile splits his face. "Okay, go ahead and have tea with your mom. I'll pick you up tonight, and we'll go to dinner."

"Why? We're here. Let's get it over with."

He looks from Marilyn to me. "Your mom is here. It should be just us."

A group of older women, East Side Stepford wife types, approach us. "I'm sorry to interrupt you, but can we have a photo with you, Mateo?"

"Of course, ladies." His arms sweep out, spreading like an eagle, so they can move in on either side of him.

I'm left standing there with my mother, who wastes no time to advocate for him.

"He's right, Luciana. We can catch up, and then the two of you can go out." She turns to Mateo. "Pick her up from my house."

Oh no. I have to put my foot down. "No. I'll be at Cam's. I have clothes there."

He leans in and kisses my cheek. "See you tonight."

Mateo disappears through the door, and we sit at the table. My stomach knots. Not only do I have to deal with Marilyn now, but I have to deal with him later.

"You did the right thing." Marilyn smiles. "So glad the two of you are back together."

What the fuck.

"We are not back together, and we are not getting back together. It's a conversation, and we're done for good."

Her smile only brightens. "Of course."

I curse myself again for lingering at the spa.

4

Lux

It's not good.

No. Screw that. It's a colossal mistake. I shouldn't have listened to Marilyn. I cannot trust her decisions, because everything to her is about control, money, and status. Her pleas to talk, accompanied by Mateo's begging for a chance to just talk and his acceptance that it's over, did me in. Like always. I know I shouldn't be doing this and will regret it.

Yet, here I am, rummaging through my closet at Cam's brownstone. It doesn't bode well for me. After spending time with my mother, I'm never in a good mood, but I need to get out of here, or I'll fall into a funk. My eyes well, and if I don't get a move on, I'll cry. So, I grab the black high-necked shift lace dress and throw it on the bed.

I put my hair up in a tight ponytail at the top of my head and go to work on my makeup. I go soft-glam meets minimal. Just foundation, translucent powder, and peachy highlights on the cheeks. I go with a little rose gold on my eyelids and dark berry on my lips. I'm not spending a lot of time on this.

I get dressed in twenty minutes and walk down the stairs in my black patent-leather, pointy-toed Louboutin Mary Janes. I found these in the piled-up mail when I came in, and I'm in love with the T strap in the middle of my foot and the three by the ankle. It frames the foot in such a sexy way. It's the best when companies try to buy my love with gifts.

As I head toward the door, Marli is coming out of Cam's office.

My brother's assistant looks me up and down, her gaze lingering on my legs. "I didn't know you were here."

She's the cutest, from the bun in the shape of a bow at the top of her head and the bright pink sweatsuit she's wearing.

"Hi, Marli. I wasn't planning on being here tonight, but I missed my train and got trapped into going out."

"You look beautiful." She finally peels her gaze off my legs and looks at my face.

"Thanks, love. I'm headed out to meet Mateo."

Her face scrunches up. "Douche boy? I thought that was dead?"

I sigh. "It is, but he and my mother ambushed me—you know what, it's a long story. It's just a dinner. Depending on how I feel tomorrow, I may take one of Cam's cars and drive back to Baltimore."

She nods. "Okay, but whatever you do, don't take the Lambo."

"Oh, God. Never. I hate those dumb things. The only person in this family that drives that is Chase when he's in a mood."

"Cam is going to sell it. It's just collecting dust, but he doesn't want to put any more mileage on it."

"If I take anything, it will be one of the RRs."

Marli smiles. "Great choice."

My phone pings, but I don't look at it. "Gotta go. Next time I'm in town, I'll take you and Tessa to lunch at The Coven."

"She'll love that. She's been dying to check it out. We want to try the *Love Spell* together."

"You'll love it. It's yummy, and it hits the sexy spot."

I wave and head out the door. Mateo's fuck-boy car is right outside. I don't roll my eyes. I just sigh. I don't know much about cars. I only know the obscene amount of money he spent on it. *At least Cam's was a gift.* Mateo gets out of the car and comes around to pull up the door for me.

"Thank you."

"You look gorgeous, Luxxy," he says, leaning in and kissing my cheek.

I take my seat, and he comes around. We're cruising around Madison Ave. at thirty miles over the limit. He smells delicious as always, and I feel the familiar tug in my belly. I squelch it by remembering how he turned me into a hashtag. Thinking about it, I should've remembered #PoorLuxxy and told him to fuck off at the tea house.

I pull out my phone and check my messages. I have tons of texts. After the ambush, I didn't feel like talking, especially because I had agreed to dinner with Mateo. If I talked to anyone, I would hear a thousand lectures, and I just wanted to put this behind me properly.

God, what the hell am I even doing?

"Thank you so much for coming with me. I am grateful that you are giving me another chance."

I raise a hand and open my mouth to tell him not to confuse the situation, but he holds up a finger when the word Maeven appears on the dash.

"I'm sorry. I have to take this."

I nod, and he takes a call from Maeven, but he doesn't put her on the speaker like he normally would. The woman needs a raise for the bullshit she deals with. Thankfully, I was momentarily saved from the conversation. I concentrate on my texts. My agent and lawyers will hammer out the contract with *Big Apple*. I don't have to be here for that.

There's a message from Oliver, and my finger goes straight to it.

OLIVER

Met with your brother. He okayed everything I showed him. Want to talk to you before I start working, unless you are okay with a koi pond in the middle of your living room.

I chuckle.

Finding a koi pond in my living room would
be the highlight of my day.

"Who's that?"

I turn to look at Mateo. "What?"

"Who has you smiling like that?"

I could tell him it's my family texting, but I don't feel like it. "No one."

"It didn't seem like no one." His tone is cutting and at odds with the smile on his lips.

Here we fucking go. He was the one cheating but always throwing jealousy tantrums.

Thankfully, I don't have to put up with that shit anymore. "You know why we're going out tonight. That was clear, right?"

His smile turns sheepish. "You're right. This is going to be a great night. We are getting back together—"

I hold up a hand to the side of his face. "No. You said you wanted to talk. I'm giving us the chance of a conversation. That's all."

"Baby." His hand glides over my thigh.

I place my palm over it to still it and fling it away. "It's way too soon for you to be trying this."

His laugh is soft. "Later, then."

I don't correct him, because that's how we always fall into the same pattern. I explain too much, and he finds a way to weasel himself in. Not ever again. I'm going to stay light and do what I came to do. After we talk, I'm going straight home.

When we turn onto Madison Ave and pull in front of Central Park, I don't groan like I want to.

"We're going to Parlay on the Park?"

"Yes, you know how much I love the food here."

This motherfucker.

46

He doesn't seem to remember what happened last time we were here. I turn to remind him, but he flips the doors open, and immediately, there's a valet next to me, helping me out of the car. The second my foot hits the concrete, the shutters and flashes of cameras go off. I wish I could hide my face inside my jacket.

I hate that he brought us here where he knew the cameras would be. I walk fast around the car to meet him. He tries to hook an arm around my waist, but I move quickly, and his hand lands on my elbow.

"You guys together again?" someone yells.

I open my mouth to set him straight, but Mateo beats me to it.

"We always find our way back to each other."

Oh, for fuck's sake.

I smile at the paps over my shoulder. "Just two friends having dinner." I don't shove Mateo away like I want to, but when we're inside the elevator, I move as far away as I can.

"You okay?" he asks, leaning toward me, his hand reaching for my face.

I step back until my back is against the wall, and I'm out of his reach. "I'm not. You didn't have to say that. You know they're going to run with this."

He leans back against the wall. "No matter what we say, they will write what they want. That's what gossip rags do."

Unfortunately, he's right.

We are shown to our table on the top floor. The view is breathtaking, but it's just not worth the hassle of the media and paparazzi.

We order drinks. He insists on champagne. I plan to stick to sparkling water.

"You can't let me drink champagne alone." His voice is soft, cajoling, in that tone that used to get me to do anything he said.

Jesus, I was dumb.

"Please, go ahead. Don't deprive yourself on my behalf. You said you wanted to talk." I take a sip from my water.

He sips on his flute. "I miss you. I know I messed up before, but things are different now. I realized that I can't keep going the way I was. I don't want to be that guy that loses the girl he loves because he's immature and can't keep it in his pants."

I don't roll my eyes like I want to. "You know what's funny? You're always one hundred percent sure, and you always look the part. But we end up here every single time. It's exhausting."

"I know I make it hard for you to believe me…"

I scoff. "You don't make it hard. You make it impossible. And I don't care anymore. There's no point in belaboring that. No matter what you say or do today, we're done."

"You have to believe me. I've changed. I'm a hundred percent determined to be a one-woman man. I'll go to therapy. Whatever it takes to get us back—" His eyes round as he stares past me.

In the next second, a beautiful woman with olive skin and eyes greener than mine stands next to our table with her gaze peeled on him like a GoldVein knife.

"I guess this must be your agent." She hooks a finger toward me. "I guess I'm your publicist, then."

"Naomi, what are you doing here?"

She leans in. "I've been calling you for two weeks, and you seem to think you can ignore me. I'm six weeks late, Mateo. This…"—she points at her belly—"is not going away."

Shock takes over. *She's late.* He's here with me, begging for a chance, and she's pregnant.

I let out a giggle. They both turn to me.

Naomi looks like she wants to snatch me by the hair. In that moment, I realize everyone in the restaurant is looking at us.

I don't do scandals or scenes—at least I didn't before the other day. And with my new project starting today, I don't want my name associated with Mateo's bullshit anymore. There's only one way out of this.

I stand and throw my arms around her. "Naomi, long time no see."

She stiffens in my arms.

I talk fast, whispering in her ear, "Please don't make a scene. I don't want him. You can have him. If you sit at the table with us, I will leave in the next ten to fifteen minutes. The headline tomorrow will be how I went out with the two of you as a friend and gave you my blessing. If you make a scene, the three of us will be on the cover of every paper, and you'll look like a side chick because everyone knows he's always trying to get back with me."

Her arms go around my waist. "Fine, but you are leaving, right? Because I *will* make a scene if you don't."

"I give you my word and a Birkin bag."

We sit together.

"I love your blog," Naomi says. "I follow all your recommendations. That last piece on affordable meets high-end changed my shopping ways.

I chuckle. "My sister-in-law is an expert at putting together outfits that look expensive on a budget.

Mateo gulps down his champagne and mine, looking like he wants to barf the whole time.

"Aww. He must be feeling first-trimester sympathy nausea," I say to Naomi.

"I just know it will be a boy. Mateo Jr," she replies.

Exactly fifteen minutes later, I stand up to say goodbye. I lean in as if I'm about to kiss Mateo on the cheek. "You brought me to the same place the last chick you cheated on me with worked. This is where she told me you were sleeping together, and now you do this. You're a loser. Go fuck yourself."

I pull back and kiss Naomi on the cheek. "I hope you know he's screwing all the waitresses here."

As I'm walking, I press a hand to my mouth and say semi-discreetly but loud enough for others to hear. "Congratulations to you both again. I'm sorry I spilled the beans on the new Birkin bag Mateo bought for you."

I head out of the restaurant, not stopping to look back, but smile at the three men walking in. They're tall and built, forming a wall between me and the entrance. I recognize them immediately as the Yankees' shortstop, third baseman, and centerfielder. They're handsome and as famous as my ex. If I really wanted to get back at Mateo, I would sit with them. I don't know them, but I can talk my way to their table. Even as they smile at me, I'm not even tempted. It would be superficial. To be honest, I am tired of jocks and people in the lime-light. Somewhere, there has to be someone as driven as me who doesn't come with a ridiculous amount of baggage of side chicks and issues.

It's hitting me how I've wasted this time. I should've gone straight to my less-than-perfect rowhouse. Instead, I'm hit, yet again, with how much I've put up with. He embarrassed me, and I stayed. Never again. I won't ever date a guy like him again. I would rather be alone.

As a matter of fact, that's the plan I'm sticking to.

5

Ollie

"You had a long day, didn't you?"

I peel my eyes off my plate to stare up at my daughter. She's sitting across from me, in her pajamas, blinking at me as if she's been there for a while. What did she just ask me?

Oh yeah…

"I did. It was a lot of work. Why do you ask?"

She shrugs. "I've asked how your presentation for Lux went three times, *Papi*."

Her eyes are knit into a frown.

But I can't tell her that Lyssa spammed my texts with one angry message after another because I missed our time together because I had to wait for Lux, only for Cam to show up and ruin my good mood.

I didn't get to see her smile as she looked at my plans, or ooh and aah at the design for the sky boxes.

"I'm sorry, *negrita*. I guess I got lost in my thoughts. She had a meeting, so she sent Cam instead. How's my better-than-Chipotle burrito bowl?"

She puts a forkful into her mouth and smiles. "What is Chipotle?"

I chuckle. It's one of her favorite things and super easy to make. Since my day had run over, I had little time to prepare it. It consists of leftover rice and beans, corn, lettuce, tomato, a fresh steak, and avocado to top it off.

"How about you? How was your day?"

"It was good. Took my quizzes, B and I used our lunch hour to work on our new art projects, Suzie is still a big, dry-snitching pain, and I talked to *Abue*."

Abue, short for *abuela,* is what she calls her grandmother on her mother's side.

I shake my head. "Let's go in parts. How did you do on the quizzes?"

"Brilliantly. I'm your little genius. Remember?"

I don't smile like I want to. She's also my little smart-ass. "And what about this dry-snitching?"

She sighs. "You know how Suzie is. She's always hatin' about B and me. She loves tattling over any little thing."

"What is there to tattle about?" Suzie has always been jealous of Ayla and Bron and their friendship.

"She told Ms. Winter we stayed in the art classroom during lunch and how we are trying to get a leg up on everyone else. But we're not. We're just trying to work on our concepts for the project we are working for our private classes."

"Okay. You shouldn't be using the words dry-snitching."

She frowns. "Why? It's exactly what she does. She says passive-aggressive things, like, 'I would've done more for my assignment if I had extra time in the art room, like some people who sneak in there at lunchtime.'"

I can't come up with a single thing to say, because that's one of the best examples of dry-snitching I've heard. It's sad that Suzie is like that. All three girls have known each other since the early days of kindergarten.

"You and Bron could always invite her to hang out with you guys."

Disgust twists her pretty features. "Why would we want to do that? She's a hater."

"She probably just wants to be your friend." That little girl could probably use friends who are not as self-absorbed as she is.

"*Papi*, you know the history. B and I can't have that kind of negativity threatening our auras."

Como?

I shake my head. "Um. How's your grandmother doing?"

She smiles again. "Good. She wants me to come visit her on Saturday."

I nod. As much as there is no love lost between Mrs. Morales and I, she loves my Ayla and is always there for her.

We finish our dinner, tidy up, and settle in the family room. We turn on the TV, but I quickly lose Ay to her phone when she gets a call from Bron. I'm going over my blueprints to make some annotations and notes of what I need to check. I divide my staff so two of my strong workers can go over half the day to the Lucia—the Blake project.

I hope my disappointment didn't show in my face too much when Cam showed up instead of his sister today. I have not forgotten the talk he and I had about Luciana after the baby shower for his son, CJ. He asked me if I had any interest in his sister. He said she wasn't in a good place to date anyone.

I was struck by his and Chase's protective nature. I don't have a relationship with my siblings. I grew up as an only child—not by choice, but by rejection. But I get it. When Ay was born, every protective nerve and cell in my body activated. I would do anything to keep her from harm. I told them I would keep my distance.

And I did. *Until Noche Buena.*

And we didn't date. We just— Nope, not thinking about that.

And that's after I couldn't shake the image of Lux at the baby shower for months. She looked like a sexy nymph. I found her hanging out with my daughter by the swings decorated with roses. She was taking photos of A and Bron and laughing with them. She was being so kind to my girl, and when she turned to look at me, all I could think was—

"Wow, she looks so beautiful."

My thoughts come out of my daughter's mouth, but when I look at her, she's staring at the TV. I look at a woman getting out of a sports car. Not just any sports car, a Veneno Roadster, one of the most expensive cars, a true automotive jewel. And not just any woman, the one I was just thinking about.

Lux is strutting around the car in a little black dress that clings to her form like she does to my thoughts. Her steps are confident, like she's on a runway. Her smile says as much. On the other side, Mateo De La Cruz, home-run god, is waiting for her. The flashes of the camera illuminate her face, and she's smiling. His hand is proprietarily fastened around her elbow. They walk in, and the people are shouting questions at them.

Does this mean you're back together?

When did it happen?

"We always find our way back to each other," he says as they rush through the doors of the building.

"Awww. Isn't that sweet? He's trying to win her back."

I turn to look at my smiling daughter. Her big brown eyes are soft and dreamy, like there should be hearts instead of eyeballs. At that moment, it's like I don't even know her. Then I notice the phone in her hand.

"B, you're so right. It's super cute. They look so good together. Too bad he's a dog, but maybe he changed his ways. Look at his car. So sick. I can't believe your dad is going to sell the one the Emperors gave him. We have to talk to Lux. She has to show us how to make our ponytails look glam like that. And did you see her shoes? Gaggin'."

No, I'm gagging. It's sick.

Because it's true. Luciana looks beautiful and glamorous, and they do look great together. Like they belong. I guess it was more than a work meeting that kept her in New York today. Why would she rush back to meet with a little contractor about a place that would probably be the equivalent of a vacation home? I can't see her staying here now that she's back with Mateo.

"You okay, *Papi*?"

"Yeah, why?" I ask.

"You look like you ate some lemon."

I feel like I ate a lemon.

"It's nothing. I lost my train of thought."

I don't know why I'm mad. I never had a chance. That's why she ran back to him Christmas day and again today.

I go back to my blueprint. This is a good reminder. This is just a job. Treat it as so.

Don't fantasize about her. Stop remembering the flirting. It comes easy to everyone. You just need to concentrate on making things work with Lyssa.

6

Oliver

The Baltimore sun rages through the windshield of my car. Someone forgot to tell Mother Nature it's the first week of April, not the dog days of August. I'm okay with that, though. My Caribbean soul wouldn't have it any other way. These days remind me of being that little kid playing baseball with the neighbors in the yard, pretending I was Manny Ramirez at the plate.

"You're not going to be late, right?" Ayla asks. Her voice is soft, but the tentativeness is there. Her lucky socks, made from my old ones when I played pro baseball, are in my backseat.

"You know what I'll say to that, *señorita?*"

"*Oliver Amador is a punctual man of his word.*" She giggles at the end, sounding more like an eight-year-old than the thirteen-year-old who now wears lip gloss and takes forever to get ready in the mornings.

"That's right. Now, go warm up that arm, Ace. I'll see you soon." I hang up and turn right onto Divello Road to enter the newly built community, an oasis in the middle of downtown. The single-family brick homes are beautiful with their orange brick exterior, white frame steeple, and black shutters, bringing a stark contrast to the surrounding rowhome areas. These make excellent rental properties. I'm happy I followed my instinct and invested early on.

I pull into the only available space and park. I unlock my phone, but I don't get to go into the messages app. The flash of the red flowing dress catches my eyes, and I get caught in the curves, the jiggle of full breasts, the come-hither smile that activates the *sucio* in me.

The *sucio* is my alter ego, the entity that possesses me when I'm alone with the woman I'm seeing or want to be with. He's different than the good dad that's there for his daughter or the encouraging coach of a girls' baseball team.

Lyssa walks up to the driver's side and leans in, her lips grazing the side of my mouth. "Thank you for bringing my phone back."

"No problem," I say. My eyes glide over her brown skin, traveling from her wide-set eyes to her perfectly shaped mouth, and finally lingering on her chest. "I'm glad we got to have lunch together and clear the air."

She sighs and leans in, running her hand over my cheek. "I can't stay mad at you. You know, Robbie is at his dad's tonight. Maybe you can come by later, and we can *really* make up. Do it like last time where we got it on against the door 'cause we couldn't wait."

I remember that vividly, like her hands are still clawing at my back. I run my fingers over the back of her hand. "I can't tonight. Ay has a game, and I'm taking her to dinner after."

"Oh," she says, like I didn't tell her this earlier.

I take her face in my hand and press an open-mouthed kiss against her lips, searching her mouth with my tongue until she sighs. "I'll come back tomorrow. We'll make last time look like a quickie. Now I really have to go."

"Okay." Her eyes narrow, and she points to the backseat. "What's that?"

I follow the direction of her gaze to the garment bag hanging from the hook of the backseat. "My suit for Chase's wedding."

"Ayla's going to be a bridesmaid, right?" Her tone is light, and her lips curve lightly.

I nod, which reminds me that I need to ask Adri if she can take her to the last fitting in two weeks along with her and Bron.

"Who're you going with?" Lyssa asks, sounding a little disinterested, but hope echoes in the way she says it.

"By myself."

"Are you sure?" Her gaze narrows, bouncing back and forth between me and the garment bag.

Mierda mano.

I take her fingers in mine. "Yes, I'm sure, Lyssa. You're the only person I'm seeing."

"Yet, you never asked me to come with you. You don't have to go alone."

"We've been through this before. It's not time yet." I look at the car dashboard. "Look, I have to go. Ay's game starts in an hour, and I can't be late. I don't want to get caught in traffic."

"Sure, go." Lyssa steps back and crosses her arms.

"Don't be like that. We just made up."

"Like what? Like I'm good enough for you to plow me on every surface possible, but not good enough for you to take to your friend's wedding?"

"You know it's not that. I care about you. I want us to be on firm ground before we go public."

She shakes her head. "You mean before Ayla knows about me."

"Yes, before we meet each other's kids."

She rolls her eyes. "Don't bring my son into this. Robbie knows I date you."

This is getting out of hand, and I really need to go. "It's different with girls."

"It's not. Not really. You tell her you're dating me, and we move on from there."

The heat creeps up the back of my neck. Why is she bringing this up now? "Lyssa, what is this? We talked about this. You said you were okay with waiting."

"I was until I got to thinking…what the fuck are we waiting for? It's been three months, and we're not getting any closer. You're okay with fucking. You didn't want to wait for that."

Now that pisses me off. "What are you accusing me of? I didn't pressure you. If I remember well, you were just as eager."

"Of course I was. I'm a normal woman. I'm okay with just sex, but there comes a point where we get past doing just that, where things progress, unless we're just screwing. You swore up and down that we're more than that."

"We are. We spend quality time and talk about life, make plans—"

"From nine to three. This is like your part-time job."

"What are you talking about? We went to dinner a couple nights ago… Look, I don't have time for this right now. I need to go—"

"Yeah, you do. You're going to Ayla's game because a kid's baseball game trumps anything else in life."

God, I hate this. She doesn't get it. "I'm the coach, and she's the starting pitcher today."

"It's not even a championship, just a regular fucking game. You're acting like she's playing for the Yankees. Then again, anything to avoid talking about this. Mr. Unavailable will find any excuse to avoid conversation. He'll hide behind that little girl to keep stringing me along."

"What? When did I string you along? We are working toward something."

She laughs. "Working toward what? We fight more than we fuck. You give me money for the bills but don't want to put in the time, so it doesn't mean anything. I'm done with this. Go to your daughter's game and beat off at night. I'm tired of not being option one or two because Ayla is both."

That does it.

"Oh yeah, we're done. Just because you had a change of heart about what we have doesn't mean you can talk about my daughter that way. Since I seem to be wasting your time, let me free it up so you can find someone else who can give you what you want."

Her mouth drops open.

"You're breaking up with me?"

Is she *loca*? "You said we were done."

"What the fuck? That's your cue to fight for me, to course correct."

"It doesn't work like that with me. You need to choose your words better, because once they're out, you can't take them back. Now I know how you really feel, and I won't change the fact that my daughter will always be number one. You can't accept it, so we're done here."

She takes three steps back, the shock reflected on her face.

Maybe I was too quick to make this decision. I should talk this out with her. I reach for the handle, but my gaze lands on the clock, and the next thing I know, I am putting my truck in reverse.

Our gazes meet again. The shock in hers is palpable. She storms forward, and I hit the brake, hoping to salvage this.

We can work through this.

Then, she reaches the window and rears her arm back, and her hand crashes against my cheek. "Fuck you and go straight to hell."

My cheek stings, but I keep both hands on the wheel, gripping it hard. "You don't have to tell me twice. Goodbye, Lyssa."

I back out of the spot, and in the next minute, I'm back on the main road. The sting of her hand keeps my cheek tingling.

I don't know how that went wrong. We had an agreement. We were going to take it slow until we were sure and then tell our kids. As always, I'm learning that women never mean what they say. Whether you've been with them for a year, or three months like me and Lyssa, or even have a business agreement like I have with Lux, they rarely keep their word or intentions.

I should've known better. She's right in that we fight more than anything else. Anyway, this is Lux's fault. If she hadn't been stringing me along with appointments, I would've had the time to spend with Lyssa.

Or if you hadn't been so eager to see her again, you made her appointments a priority...

But this is for the best. It's better I found out now before I introduced her to Ayla. I don't ever want to explain to her again why someone who's supposed be in her life is now gone. Not when I can shield her from the pain.

"Hey, Siri, play *Dile al Amor* by Aventura."

Rome Santos is blasting Cupid for the bad job he's done in his love life when my subcontractor calls, cutting off the song. The crew at the new construction site has a cracked foundation. I deal with instructions as I continue to cruise down 695. The song continues with Romeo listing all the reasons why he doesn't need love in his live.

And I agree. We don't need that shit, and I count along with him all the chances love has failed me. Noris, Marcia, Lyssa, Lux…

No, that wasn't love. It was a lust match that is coming back to haunt me professionally. But I plan to make things clear with her. She's not going to toy with my time or my emotions.

Fortunately, I'm able to hit all the traffic pockets, and by the time I go into the LaSalle Academy parking lot, we have found a solution. All I have to do is call the vendors to let them know my people will pick up more materials.

I make it to the field five minutes before the game begins. In a sea of people I know, my eyes zero in on the girl standing in the middle with my assistant coach. She nods a few times, but when she spots me, Ayla begins to wave me in.

I cross the distance between us and give her a hug.

"Where are they?"

I pull the pair of old socks from my pocket and hand them to her.

She crouches down, takes off her cleats, puts on the socks, and then adds her regulation socks over it. When she stands again, she looks up at me, and her smile brightens everything around me. "Thanks, *Papi*." She turns to the pitching coach and tilts her head to the field. "I'm ready for them now."

She runs into the field to join her teammates.

Cam turns and points at me. "Dad of the year. Coach of the year."

I touch my cheek. It stopped stinging. And it's a good reminder: pain subsides, and pleasure is momentary. Women will come and go. I'll keep dealing with them the way I've been doing because the only woman that truly matters is the girl who just looked at me like I hung the moon and made it shine in the sky just for her.

My *niña* will always be my number one. Anyone else will always be miles behind. I really don't need anyone else to love me. She's the only one.

———

Lux

This phone call won't end, and it's getting on my nerves. *Big Apple* lawyers keep bringing up scenarios for my lawyer and agent to sort out. It's the last leg of the contract before we sign, but Jesus, this is taking a lot out of me. Ollie will be here any second, and I need to be off the phone. I already feel terrible for canceling meetings last minute with him.

"Well, you're worried about a proper studio to film. Lux is building one in her new home. It's only fair that we make the expense part of her package," my agent says. She's a shark. I never realized how much until we started negotiations.

"We are not in disagreement," Mimi says, adding, "but because there are certain lighting and creative elements we would want, we insist on hiring our own people—"

"No," I say, speaking for the first time. "I already hired a very competent contractor who has been sending me comps and finding innovative solutions for this. If you want to bring in a consultant to speak to him, you can, but I'm not dumping him when he's doing a merger of two row houses and has put in so much time."

"That's not what we're saying, Luxxy. We can work with him to make sure we have the appropriate lighting," Mimi offers.

"You can send a consultant, but Oliver is still in charge. Also, I don't want your decorators. I want to do my own decorating." My tone is definite. I'm not willing to compromise on this. He knows my vision, and I already hired him.

"No," the creative director snaps. "We have a vision and an idea of what we want this to be. We have experts in arranging visual appeal.

We need to make sure we send the message with every piece and to get the audience to make an emotional connection. They know what works and doesn't."

"Well, she's the talent, and these are her demands—"

I hold up a hand to stall my agent. "It's not only about that. I am going to be managing a lifestyle blogging channel. A lot is going to circle around me as the central figure."

"I'm not doing this if it doesn't look 100% authentic."

"It won't be organic if I'm in a fake homey environment that you create for me. I want to build this studio in a way the public feels it comes from me. When I sit on the couch and talk about the latest thing I want people to try, I want to do it from the place I built. When I have guests and sit to talk to them, I want it to be in the chairs I've chosen as they drink from the teacups I've selected for them. If I feel natural in my environment, that will translate."

Everyone is silent, and my phone buzzes with a text from my agent. *Well said.* Ruthie has been doing that through the whole meeting.

The doorbell rings. *Shit, Ollie is here.*

"Let's discuss this a little—"

I cut off the creative director with a hand in the air.

"Please, hold on. My contractor is here. I'll be right back."

With the meeting on mute, I rush out of the room, pausing in the hallway mirror to smooth my hair and apply the lip gloss I'm carrying in my pocket. By the time I get to the door, the excitement courses through me. I've been having to postpone this meeting all week, and I so love looking at him. I pause at the door, take a deep breath, then open it.

And drool.

He's standing there in a camel blazer, an olive-green shirt that plays beautifully against his skin, and jeans. The spicy notes of his cologne send currents of heat to pool past my belly, down my apex, and straight to my pussy. His gaze threatens to incinerate the clothes off my body.

"Hi," he says and leans in to kiss my cheek. When his lips connect with my skin, I am thinking of other traditions—the ones that have existed for men and women since the beginning of time.

Naked bodies. Garden of Eden. Sex in front of a fireplace on Christmas Eve.

God help me.

"Hi." I move out of the way. "Come in."

"I have a lot of stuff to show you and discuss. I want to briefly go over the blueprint to make sure you okay the plans and see if there are any minor adjustments you want to make. Also, I've made some arrangements and—" His gaze lands on my pressed lips. "Is something wrong?"

"Yes and no. I'm still in a meeting with *Big Apple* and my agent upstairs. Do you mind setting up over there at the dining table, and I'll finish my meeting?"

There's a fleeting frown, but he nods. "I just have somewhere to be in about two hours. I want to make sure we get through this."

I nod and smile at him. "I'm sorry. I'll be done soon. Don't worry. I won't take up that much of your time."

His lips flatten. "Okay, no problem."

"Be right back," I say and run back up the stairs.

I need to get back soon. I unmute my mic. "I'm back, but as I said at the beginning of the meeting, I have an appointment with the contractor, and I don't want to keep him waiting."

"We understand, but we need to iron this out so we are not doing double the work. I consulted with marketing and analytics while you were gone. They have an issue with this. They feel we need to be precise about the space, and while they understand your need for comfort, there's also the need for profitability."

"I'm not budging on this."

A text comes through.

RUTHY

Let's tread with caution here. You'll get your way, but let's not be downright antagonistic.

ME

> I'm not letting them bring in someone new,
> and I'm not going to let them pick the look.

Her reply is swift.

RUTHY

> Of course not. We just need to massage this
> for them.

I don't fucking have time for this. Ollie is downstairs, and I don't want to rush through the meeting. As it turns out, the massaging takes another hour. I get my way, but I'm pissed off beyond belief. We almost threatened to walk away.

Thank God Ruthie pulled an ace from her sleeve—the offer she is getting from *New York Style Magazine* for the same kind of project. She killed the argument with one sentence. "I'm sure they won't oppose her ideas for inbound marketing, as it's a proven formula."

I run downstairs, feeling triumphant and less annoyed.

Ollie is by the window, looking out to the street. He's keeping his voice down, but he's got in his AirPods, and his hands are gesturing. I almost call out his name, but his words stop me.

"Yeah, I'm sorry too. I hate that it went that way." His tone is a little too honeyed to be a client. Then he turns around, spots me, and his body tenses. "I'm sorry. I really have to go. I'll call you when I get out of here."

There's silence for a bit, and I am taken aback by the coldness of his stare.

He chuckles. "It's a matter of speech. Nothing like it sounds. We'll talk."

He's talking to a woman.

I recognize the cadence, the way he softens his voice. It's the same way Mateo used to talk to me when we weren't together. When he wouldn't say he loved me and didn't want me to know he was with someone else. Or maybe he didn't want the other person to know how important I was.

I'm keeping him from meeting someone. The pang of disappointment is instant. So is the shame. I'm messing with his time again. It's not my fault, though.

He taps his earbuds to hang up. I open my mouth to apologize but don't get to.

"Are you ready to get started?"

I nod. "I'm all yours now."

The second the joke is out of my mouth I regret it. He walks to the table and starts pointing at things.

"Here's where I left off from my meeting with Cam. I've sectioned off the bedrooms on the first floor as you asked."

He's going through it efficiently, and I can't argue with anything. I love the kitchen concept. It's big and airy and goes well with the family room and dining room areas. It reminds me a lot of Cam's brownstone in New York, but this would be laid out better and even more modern. Except, the finishes he's picked are a little dark.

"I want white quartz countertops with white cabinets."

"You're the client. Whatever you want is fine, but I want to let you know before we move on, that's going to be too much white on white." His tone is clipped. His voice is a little tight, and I can't blame him. I did take too long. He's been sitting here waiting.

I smile at him, trying to soften the situation. "I know it may seem that way, but it can be done really well. We can break up the white with hardware and a double farmhouse sink in matte gold stainless."

He pauses. "I thought we had already agreed on another kind. That's going to bring up your budget."

"Yeah, I know. Don't worry about the budget."

"Does Cam know?"

I frown. "Why would my brother need to know that? I got this."

"Changing the finishes and the type of cabinetry means I will need to make adjustments because I had measured on the spot."

"I'm sorry about that, but I want to go with this change. There are also changes to what we talked about in the studio. Just a few. I talked to my employer, and during today's meeting, some things came up. I've had to make a couple of concessions."

He straightens up and levels with me with a look. "It would've been nice to know this earlier in the week."

"Yeah, I'm sorry. It came up today."

"A lot of things seem to be changing in between the meetings that keep getting canceled." The edge in his voice makes my spine stiffen.

"I'm—"

"Sorry. Yes, I know. This is a big project, and it's not my only one. I am trying to deliver a great product in the time I promised, but between all the canceled, postponed, and delayed-by-the-hour meetings, it's really challenging."

"I didn't mean to take so long today, but my work meeting went over and—"

"I get that, but this is the third time this week that something has come up. How can I deliver the product if this keeps happening?"

"It's the last time. After the changes from today, nothing major will fluctuate."

"I hope so, but we'll have to wait till you consult with Cam and he approves it so we can order the materials. The stores don't carry these exclusive things you want to add. I also need to put a stop to what's already been ordered."

Damn, he's really pissed off. I need to fix this.

"I get that, and I apologize again. The delay is my fault, and I'm willing to assume the cost of it. Please hire more people if need be so we can finish this on the time agreed. Go ahead and put a stop to the old material and order the new one. You can also put a rush on it. If there's an extra fee, I'll pay it. No big deal."

His lips go flat. "Fine, but you explain to Cam about this."

For some reason, that sets me off. "Why do you keep bringing up my brother in this? This is none of his business. All he is doing is advising me when necessary."

"And footing the bill."

"Where the hell did you get the idea that Cam is paying? My brother may have asked you to take this job because I don't know any contractors in the area and am normally not into home renovations, but he's not paying you for this. I am. From *my* money. The only person you need to concern yourself with is me."

He seems taken aback for a few moments but recovers quickly. "I'm sorry for my assumption. He seems to be keen on the budget and keeping things within a certain amount."

I nod and try to temper my voice. "Because he knows the budget that Chase, as my financial advisor, and I allocated to this. Cam wants to keep me to it. But things have changed. I am no longer tied to that budget. I can move it around and double it if I see fit."

"It's nice that you're rich and can throw around money as you please, but there's also my time that you keep putting off. You cancel meetings to go to parties in New York, and I lose clients and opportunities while waiting for you. I can't get that time or the opportunities back because you decide this is not important enough." His tone is stern, like I'm a child who broke one of his precious rules.

And I see red. *Fuck this.* He's basically calling me spoiled, judging me, and chastising me. After what I went through last night, I'm not in the mood to put up with chauvinistic shit.

"You know what, Oliver? You no longer have to worry about this project and missing opportunities because of me. Please send me a bill me for the work you've done so far and make sure to include the hours you've *wasted* waiting on me."

His head rears back. "What?"

"We're done here. Please see yourself out."

———

Ollie

My whole fucking day has been one disaster after another after I left Luciana's house. She kept me waiting for an hour, then pissed me off even more by being flippant about my time and effort. She put the cherry on top by firing me when I wasn't catering to her rich-girl whims.

She fucking fired me.

I left there practically chewing on glass, only to find out a toilet erupted in Winter and Grayson's house because the neighbor down-stairs hired an unlicensed plumber who caused a backup in the pipes. I've had to go supervise it myself and make sure both the neighbor's and Winter and Grayson's pipes were working well—not without me and my crew getting doused by the excrement water. So, I came home smelling and feeling like literal shit.

I wasn't even able to go to practice or pick up Ayla from school. Cam had to do that for me. I don't ever miss my daughter's practices, or games, or anything.

I fumed all the way to his house, dreading having to see him because his sister already probably told him about firing me. I've never been fired before. I'm so embarrassed I don't know where to put my head. But when I got there, Cam was all smiles.

He couldn't stop gushing about A's arm and how he thinks she may be ready to learn the cutter. My heart grew so big it gave me my first smile all day since Luciana opened her door looking like a model in a reggaeton video.

I guess Cam hasn't spoken to her yet. He even invited me to dinner with them. Maybe he knows how his sister is.

No, he doesn't know.

I declined, and A and I headed home. We ordered bowls from our favorite Mediterranean restaurant.

Ayla was on her phone with Bron most of the time. Normally, this is our time on the drive home to catch up on each other's day. We do that over dinner every night, but today I'm grateful for how attached at the hip they are. I need to think. I can't get past the fired part. The churning in my stomach is hard to turn off.

We get home and go through our routine before dinner. We shower and eat in front of the TV. I let her watch an episode of *Vampire Chron-icles* and even move on to the next after dinner as I check on tomor-row's schedule.

"Are you going to tell me what's wrong?"

I take my gaze away from my planner to look at my daughter. She's scooted closer to me, and I didn't even realize it.

"Nothing, *corazón*. I'm making my to-do list for tomorrow. This project for Winter and Grayson is bigger than I'm used to, and I want to avoid another incident with the pipes."

She nods. "I know, *Papi,* but you've let me watch two episodes on a school night and written 'suggest upflush toilet' three times."

I look down at my list, and sure enough, there is the same entry separated by a few of the others.

I try to laugh it off. "I must be tired."

Her hand lands on my shoulder. "Tell me what's wrong. I know something is bothering you."

That fight with Lux is plaguing me, but I can't tell her about that. "It's nothing for you to worry about."

"If it was me hiding something, you would make tell you."

I would, because I can't stand to see her sad or worried. I would have to make whatever it is better. But this is different. I don't want to put her in the middle of this.

"It's an adult thing."

"Oh." She smiles in a way that's way too grown and makes me uncomfortable. "You mean it's about a woman."

I nod before I can think better of it but go back to the list.

Her eyes are burning a hole in my head, and when I look up again, she's still smiling and staring at me.

"It's about a female client."

"It's Lux, right?"

Coño.

"What makes you think that?"

She giggles. "You're working on her place, and you had a meeting with her today."

"How do you know that?"

Jesus, she probably already knows.

"It's on your calendar. I saw it when I went to write in my important events this week."

Oh.

"Yeah, I had a meeting with her, but it didn't go well." I need to fess up before she hears it from someone else. "I won't be working on her place anymore."

Her mouth forms into an O. "But why? She's really cool, and you're the best at renovating places. She won't find anyone better."

Her vote of confidence is so absolute it makes me smile. "*Gracias, mi vida,* but I don't think it's going to work out."

"Why?"

"It's complicated. We have different approaches to things."

She frowns. "You were so excited about working on the project. You even talked about how cool you could make her studio. And she's going to need it now that she has the good news about her channel."

"I was excited, but I messed up today."

"How?"

"I let my frustration speak for me and said things I shouldn't. I was rude."

She shakes her head in disbelief. "You're never rude. Not even to Mr. Elias."

Because of you and Bron and Cam. Otherwise, I would have told him *que se vaya pal carajo.*

"I was rude and assumed a bunch of things that weren't true. Now she's really upset."

I don't want to tell Ayla that Lux fired me. She likes Lux. I don't need to make things messy, especially because there are so many friendships in the middle of this. Bron and Ayla, Cam and me, Chase and me. There's too much riding on this, which is the reason why we both had agreed to keep things civil and work together. But anything involving Luciana is bound to be messy, and I can't do messy. Not with this.

"*Papi,*" my daughter yells.

"Huh?"

She shakes her head. "You really are feeling bad. I was saying you should apologize to her. Call her and ask her to meet you for coffee, and then you can tell her that you were frustrated and took it out on her."

It's funny how I didn't think about that, but it's such a simple concept. But how do I say that when she's the source of my frustration?

And that's when it hits me. *Jesus, I was jealous.*

"That's what you would tell me to do," Ayla continues when I say nothing.

"You think so?"

"Yes, sir. Because we don't do rudeness. You would tell me to apologize for my part in it without mentioning where they went wrong, because I need to stand up for my mistakes and not gaslight anyone."

"Gaslight? I've never used that word."

"Maybe I heard that on TV." She pushes herself onto my chest and hugs me. "We all make mistakes. Just apologize."

"What if she doesn't accept?"

"She will."

I kiss the top of her head. "What makes you so sure?"

"I know, sir. Trust me. And get her some macaroons from Citlali's. She's crazy about those."

I highly doubt this will work, but I'm going to try anyway. For my baby. I don't want her to ever be disappointed in me. And because I let jealousy that I had no right feeling get the best of me. And now I hate feeling like the biggest asshole in the world.

7

Lux

It's a beautiful morning. Fells Point is almost empty. The view beyond the water looks straight out of a tourism poster.

But I'm walking faster and faster, like I'm trying to outrun this picturesque scene. This is supposed to be relaxing. I love exercising, and most of all, I love walking outdoors. I used to walk forty or fifty blocks on the Upper West Side, get a walking breakfast, and then have the most endorphin-blessed day.

Today, I'm hungry, cranky, wound tighter than CJ's toy guitar—and getting more annoyed every time my phone pings. So, I walk as fast as I can without running until a hand clamps on my arm and stops me in my tracks.

"Slow down. This is supposed to be a stress buster not a *stressor*. I'm sweating like a horse that just passed the finish line at Pimlico. I'm out of breath, and you're red like a lobster. Are you trying to kill me and yourself?"

I blink a few times at Lauren. She does look a little worked up, sweat beginning to form near her hairline, hardly out of breath, though.

"Sorry. I have a lot on my mind, and *Big Apple* staff is either bending over backward to grant all my wishes or being downright petty. They text me to ask my opinion about everything, including the paper we'll be featuring on my desk. They hate how much they had to give in to keep me."

Lauren chuckles. "They should've known when they saw Cam's lawyer and your agent together."

"So true."

We resume walking—at a moderate pace this time.

"That's not all that's bugging you," Lauren asks. "I mean, the phone pinging constantly is annoying, but this is not the kind of stuff that bugs you. You would just ignore it."

"It's not. I didn't sleep well. I had to block Mateo and his sister this morning. Not to mention, I'm stressed out because I need to find a new contractor."

It's out of my mouth before I can control it, but I don't look at her. Maybe she'll latch on to the asshole ex talk and forget I said

"It was high time you blocked his ass and his number-one enabler —I'm sorry. Wait a second. Did you just say you need a new contractor? What the hell happened to Ollie?"

I shake my head. "I can't talk about it with you. He's your friend of many years, and I'm—"

"My sister." She doesn't add the word in-law and seems to have no plans to do so. "Now spill."

I smile anyway because who would've thought I would get another sister through Chase after all the friendships I lost because the girls were interested in him. "Ollie and I got into an argument. I've canceled a few appointments with him, and I know it was terrible, but I couldn't avoid it. Getting this contract ready has been a big thing. Then, I had him waiting for an hour, and he got pissed off. I don't blame him for that. I would've been too if someone kept me waiting."

I go through the story, and all she does is nod and listen.

"Two things set me off. One, he kept mentioning Cam's opinion and making insinuations that my brother's opinion would be valid because he was footing the bill."

"What?" She laughs.

"It's not funny. He basically called me a spoiled rich girl."

She presses a fist to her mouth. "Your brothers probably let him believe that."

"Why would they do that?"

She rolls her eyes. "Because they see the chemistry. Everyone does. The two of you sizzle." Lauren's finger touches the skin of my arm, and she pulls it back quickly like it burns her.

She's not wrong. We do sizzle.

We sizzle so bad my body feels hot, like I ran a 5K, when I'm in the same room with him. All my thoughts go to our night together—the one we promised each other wouldn't affect anything but changes so much. I yank my thoughts from the memories. He was such an asshole yesterday, and maybe we just need to stay away from each other. It's for the best, since we can't seem to keep it strictly professional.

"We have to fix this," Lauren says.

"Fix what?" I ask.

"This whole mess. Ollie is a great contractor, and he's a good guy. And he makes you all flustered. We all need a guy that makes us flustered by walking in a room or just talking." She pins me with a gaze. "It's just talking, right?"

I look at the water, but she steps into my line of vision and latches onto my arms. "What are you not telling me?"

I shove my eyes closed. "We slept together on Christmas Eve, and now things are super awkward."

Her mouth drops open. "And you didn't tell me?"

I shake my head. "We agreed to keep it to ourselves."

She gasps. "Oooh, secret great sex is the best...well no, engaged sex is the best. It was the best, right?"

I sigh. "The best I've ever had."

I go through an abbreviated version of the story of how we agreed to give each other the perfect *Noche Buena*, but then Mateo got injured, and I went to New York to be there for him, leaving Ollie behind."

Her slack jaw dissolves into a smile. "No wonder you've been so mopey even though you were back with Mateo. You should have dumped his ass and stayed with Ollie."

"I don't disagree, but that is not what he wanted. He had someone else in mind."

"How do we get a repeat of that?"

I gape at her. "Are you not listening, Lo? It's a disaster, and he's dating someone. Not to mention he's friends with everyone in my family. I'm not trying to get into anything messy. We can't repeat it, and this can't be fixed. I fired him."

"You fired him?" she yells, and I wince. I still can't believe those words came out of my mouth.

"It got nasty, I tell you. He pissed me off, and maybe this is too close to home. He's friends with my brothers, and he's Ayla's dad, and she's Bron's best friend. You all love him. He's a good friend to all of you."

"He is."

"Shouldn't there be boundaries?"

She nods. "You can establish them when you rehire him."

"Why would I do that? He hasn't even apologized or asked me to take him back."

She winks at me "He will."

"I doubt it. He was pissed off. You didn't see him."

She points at my phone. "Before we stop for breakfast, he will message you."

No way.

"What makes you so sure?"

She shrugs. "I know him. He's a nice guy and respectful. Plus, the way he looks at you…and he's had a taste too…"

My belly dips. No. I am not thinking about that.

"Stop it."

"His eyes bugged out when he saw you the first time at Cam and Adri's housewarming party…and the way he got so close at Winter's wedding… He is going to apologize. You have to decide what you'll do then."

What would I do if he calls?

"I don't know if I should entertain any of it."

She takes out her phone and looks at it. My brother's name is on the screen. "A conversation won't kill anyone."

Then she proceeds to answer.

It won't kill anyone, but I already have issues saying no. And not working with him would mean I don't have to see him—*which is for the best, Luciana, because he's not interested.* That was clear from the way he talked to me yesterday. And there's the woman he was on the phone with. He sounded extra cozy.

He may find me attractive, but he doesn't think much of me. And I can't make a fool out of myself again. This can't be Mateo part two.

"Your brother is something else." The smile on her face tells me she finds whatever he said endearing.

Poor soul.

"You're hopelessly in love."

"I am." Her tone is so firm, happiness vibrating off it. "Why were you just frowning like that?"

"I was thinking about how I won't ever go through another Mateo."

The smile slides off her face. "Where did that come from?"

"He could always worm his way back into my life."

She points her index finger at my chest. "But you're not going to let him anymore, right?"

I shake my head. "I said goodbye to him for good."

"Back to Ollie. You need a plan."

"For what? He's not going to call, and even if he did, he probably would just want the money for the time I wasted. I told him to bill me."

"He may not be as rich as your brothers, but he does very well in his business. He never lacks work. Trust me, he will call because he likes you, and knowing him, he's pissed at himself for losing his shit yesterday."

"I don't believe it, but you know him better. Either way, I'm ready to put this behind me."

Lauren taps her chin and smiles. "I'll tell you what. If he doesn't apologize, full spa day at Autumn Lush on me. If he does, you have to let me help you fix this."

"Deal," I say because I know he won't call. His type can't handle what they see as rejection.

We continue to walk, and Lauren begins humming. Less than a mile later, my phone pings, and this time, it's a phone call, and Oliver's name appears on my screen.

I flash the phone to Lauren, and she pushes it toward me. "Answer it."

I hit the answer button.

"Hi, Lux. It's Oliver." His voice sounds so warm, his name perfectly enunciated, like there's a bit of a smile in it.

It's not fair that he's so confident, and all of a sudden, I feel stupid, like the rich, spoiled girl who got reprimanded. *Fuck that.* He's not going to make me feel like something I'm not.

"Yeah, I know." My tone is dry as it would be with a telemarketer.

"Of course you do. I called your cell." He laughs again, and this time, it's a little off. "Uh. I was wondering if I could speak to you."

"He wants to talk," I whisper for Lauren's sake.

She shakes her head. "Tell him later."

"I'm out and about right now. This is not a good time."

"I didn't mean right this second. It can be later on today or whenever you're available. Could you give me fifteen minutes?"

I don't say anything. I don't know if this is a good idea. When I give a guy an inch, they take enough miles to build a county. Boundaries need to be a thing.

"Look, I know our last conversation wasn't very good, but I don't want to leave things like this. I don't have any expectations. I would just like you to hear me out and let me apologize."

I blink a few times. "Okay. You can call me around four today."

A couple of seconds pass. "Can you meet me for coffee instead?"

"Meet you for coffee?" I say for both Lauren's sake.

Is this really a good idea?

"Yes, please. When I offend someone in person, I apologize in person. Please allow me to do that."

Everything in me says yes, but I want to do this on my terms, and I'm not ready for that today. "Let's meet at four at Calliope's on Fed Hill."

There's a long breath on the other end, something that sounds a lot like relief. "Okay, great. Thank you."

————

Ollie

I pull up in front of Calliope's, the coffee house we agreed upon, and right away, I see Lux sitting by the window. Her head is bent, gaze on the screen of her computer. She's typing away. I don't know what her state of mind is. She didn't sound so sure she wanted to do this on the phone.

Can you blame her?

Prior to that day, you've been flirty and suave. Then one day, you get pissed because you see her all over the tabloids with her ex and you beast out on her.

She stood me up.

Yeah, but you didn't flip the hell out until you saw her with Mateo.

I've never done that with a client before. I pride myself in completing the job, in my professionalism, in not shitting where I eat.

And you really la cagaste this time.

I'm going in, apologizing, and heading back out. I don't want her to think I'm unprofessional or a jerk. I'm a *sucio, yes,* but never an asshole.

She looks up from her computer and out into the street. We lock eyes.

It's go time.

I grab my messenger bag from the backseat and the brown paper bag. I cross the street and am in front of her in the next thirty seconds. She runs her fingers through her hair, pushing it back behind her shoulder.

"Can I?" I say and then shake my head. "May I? I can never get those straight right away."

A hint of a smile ghosts over her mouth, and she nods. "Please."

I place the brown paper bag on the table between us.

She frowns. "What is this?"

"Peace offering."

She doesn't make a move to open it. "You didn't have to do that."

Coño. This is going to be tough.

"I know, but I am really sorry about the way I acted yesterday. I had no right to be like that with you. I should've handled myself better and voiced the issues without saying things that are none of my business or—"

"Assuming things you know nothing about."

She lands the blow seamlessly, and I can only wince. It's true. I assumed a lot. If she only knew the other things I worried about that are really none of my fucking business—like her fucking the night away with Mateo or his face buried between her...

You know what? That's not productive.

"You are a hundred percent correct. I want to apologize for that. It wasn't professional of me, and I pride myself on my work ethic. I can work with difficult people, even those who don't have any respect for me or the work that I do. I'm even more impressed because you have always been a nice person to me and my daughter. You are my friends' sister and that was uncalled for."

Not to mention we shared one of the best nights of my whole life.

She nods. "I did cancel a few times, and I didn't communicate the changes that are happening in my professional life that would affect the work."

"It doesn't excuse my behavior. I should've acted, and reacted, better. I apologize."

The way her eyes round reminds me of my two favorite marbles as a kid. Her lips drift apart, but she presses them together.

I reach inside my messenger bag and pull out the plans I had already worked on. "Anyway, that's want I wanted to tell you. I want to wish you luck with the project and give you these. This is what we had already talked about. I made the revisions you mentioned yesterday. You can show them to your next contractor, and they will get a good idea of what you want."

"Next contractor?"

"I already did some of the research and put in a couple of contracts with the city and can pass on the information and help them with the transition. I can also take a look at what they do if you ever need a second opinion—free of charge, of course."

She just stares at me and finally asks, "Why are you offering to do that?"

It's a good question. This is my chance to walk away clean from the situation. "Your employer may already have someone in mind that can do all of this. I want to facilitate the transfer and make it easy for you."

She tilts her head to the side. "You're doing it again, Oliver."

The way she says my name makes my spine stiffen. It's the way a schoolteacher would say it, something meant to correct you and put you in your place.

But my body doesn't know it. Instead, my cock stirs in my pants, like she woke him up.

"Doing what again?"

She leans on her elbows. "Assuming and acting like someone else, and not me, has the right to make decisions about my house and work-space. Yesterday, it was Cam. Today, it's my employer."

"That's not what I'm trying to do."

She sighs. "That's what you did, though."

Mierda, I can't win with her anymore. I should just bow out now. I open my mouth, but she beats me to it.

"I don't have another contractor in mind. Honestly, I was so pissed after our conversation I just wanted it out of my mind for a while. I went for a run instead. I was going to start looking today."

"I understand. I didn't feel good about yesterday either."

"Thank you for being honest and for admitting to your side of this. I should have been more mindful of your time. The truth is, I don't want to look for another contractor. It's annoying, and I'm not in the right mindset for it. Besides, you already know what this project needs, and your plans have me so excited. I would love to keep working with you."

My mind goes blank, and all I can do is stare at her.

"If you're still interested," she adds.

I stare at those sexy pink lips and warm eyes. *Fuck yes, I'm still interested.*

And then it clicks. She's talking about the project...if I'm still interested in being her contractor.

"Yeah, of course, I would love to stay on the project. I've never been fired before."

She grimaces. "I didn't like firing you. I felt so bad thinking about Ayla. I don't want her upset if she found out."

My little angel is my savior in all aspects of my life.

"Ayla knows I'm the one that messed up. She told me I should apologize, and she chose the peace offering."

Lux's pretty mouth falls open. Then, she digs into the bag and pulls out the box. The scripted title on the white box peeks at me, but I'm looking past it to the curving of Lux's lips. "God, I love her. She's so smart. Citlali's Macaroons are a new favorite thing since I moved down here."

"That's what A said."

"Thank you. Tell her I am going to enjoy these so much. And thank you for getting them." Excitement permeates the air.

I chuckle. "She's the boss."

Her smile widens. "The two of you are so cute together."

I have to look away. "Is Ayla the only reason you're taking me back? Because I could talk to her."

She shakes her head. "Not the only one. There's also your friend-ship with my family. Mostly, it's because you're qualified, and you apologized. I like that you took responsibility without putting it on me."

"That's just being a man, Lux."

She pushes her hair back. "Right. Um. So, we should probably establish some ground rules. I'm going to be more mindful of your time and let you know in advance. And you—"

"I'm going to be flexible, even if you have to cancel something, and not assume you blew me off to go party in New York with—"

Her eyes bulge.

Oh shit. Eres un imbecil, Oliver. You were both in a good place. Why would you bring this up?

She opens her mouth, but I hold up a hand. "I'm sorry. I shouldn't have said that. That's also none of my business, and you have—"

"Stop." Her tone is like a whip cracking between us. "I don't have to explain myself for that, because it's my private life, but I can see why you thought that. I did not blow you off to go hang out with Mateo."

I shake my head. "Seriously, you do not have to explain anything."

"I know, but I want you to know that I called Cam as soon as I knew my meeting would run over. I told him I would not make it to the train on time. That's the day *Big Apple* made the new offer that changed my career. It took too long, and I couldn't get back in time."

I nod. I don't know what else to say. She had a successful day. "You had to go out and celebrate that night."

She snorts. "The successful part of my day ended very shortly after I got out of my meeting. That wasn't a celebration, more like a burial of a carcass that had been laying out in the sun for too long."

"Como?" I frown.

She shakes her head. "That was over when you saw me throw his luggage out the window, which, by the way, I appreciate you not mentioning to anyone. Anyway, let's agree to have open dialogue and communicate with each other through this project. Deal?"

I offer my hand, and she pushes her smaller palm into it. Her skin is soft and warm, but it's the *come get me* look in her eyes that gives me pause and tightens my chest.

How can this stay professional when all she has to do is curve her lips and I want to devour her mouth? All she's doing is shaking my hand, and I can feel her fingers sliding over my cock like they did three months ago.

"Deal," she says and pulls her hand from mine.

Was she trying to let go of my hand for a while? *Jesus, I hope not.* "Great."

"Why don't we discuss the new additions and when we can get started?"

I nod, shutting the door on the *sucio* so professional Oliver can take over. "First, tell me what I can expect now that there are changes like you mentioned."

"Well, before, it was just going to be me making the videos and setting up my channel, but now, *Big Apple Magazine* will be sponsoring it, and the expenses are part of the contract."

"Oh. So, this is a big deal?"

She nods. "Oh yeah. It's everything I wanted but didn't know it—if that makes sense."

I shake my head.

She laughs. "It sounds a little confusing, but they're turning me into a brand with my own channel. I'll be doing more videos than I had planned. I'll have more blogs, celebrity guests, and more products."

Big deal is not even close. This sounds huge. "Congratulations. So now there will be more videos of you out there?"

I have to make a note to go watch them. Or maybe not. God only knows I ended up in the shower, beating my meat, the last time I watched her review of that hotel in Miami, shaking a dirty martini. I wanted to be on her like that skimpy white bikini.

"Thank you. I was hoping to make that happen, but it's good to have the backing of *Big Apple*. It will open even more doors."

"I'm sure. And now they get to pay for the reno since it's a work expense."

"Exactly. The only thing is that they'll want to send their guys to inspect some of the lighting to make sure it's optimal for recording. I'll make sure they always let you know when they're coming."

"No problem."

"Make sure to include any extra time you have to put in for them and charge full price for everything. No friends discount."

"I've never had a client tell me that."

"They have the money, and it's written in my contract that I get to pick the contractor. Now, tell me you can give me what I want."

I can give her whatever she wants. How and when she wants it. I could give it to her here in the middle of this coffee house. *Sin ningun tipo de verguenza.*

But she's not talking about my dick. And that's not going to happen anyway. This is going to stay strictly professional because there's too much at play. And if yesterday and today were any evidence, this could get way too messy.

I don't do messy...*anymore.*

FROM THE HEART

By Bougie Girl

Finding the perfect gift for a loved one is often a nightmare. I always have trouble identifying what is meaningful and will occupy space in their home or life as opposed to getting regifted or ending up in storage. I also like to see their faces when I give them something meaningful. I pride myself on putting way too much thought into it. For example, my brother is getting married, and I needed to think of a gift for him and one for my soon-to-be sister. They're both so special to me and so different from each other. A his-and-hers type of thing wouldn't work. Chase is a giant hulk of a guy who enjoys rough sports and stocks (gag). Lauren is all about beautifying people and the world around her (heart emoji). I've been searching and researching for months for something to convey the meaning of the occasion. My brother is marrying the love of his life — the first girl he ever loved and the one he never forgot no matter how far away from her he was — and that in itself is inspiring.

Can you imagine being loved so instantly and furiously that it conquers distance, hurt, and past trauma? Can you imagine a love so strong that it lived dormant for years only to awaken at first sight all over again? I couldn't if I had not seen it twice, with both of my brothers, and as someone who loves them, it means the whole world to me. It also gives me hope that someday it will happen for me too. Like Emily Dickinson's quote, "Not knowing when the Dawn will come, I open every Door."

I'm going to let the possibilities bloom like peonies in the spring.

Anyway, back to the presents for the bride and groom, I finally settled on two objects that I think represented their history, their present, and our hope as a family for the future. The two pieces capture my feelings and give us a new mantra as our family multiplies. As I wrapped my gifts today, I wondered if I was making too much of it, but when I thought of the symbolism, of what I'm going to say to them, my eyes welled up. And yes, it could be because I'm super sentimental, but it's also because the gifts feel right in my heart.

That's all for me today. I leave you with two questions:

Are you like me with special gifts, or do you just want to check the box of "I got you something," and they can feel free to return or regift it? We #listen and we #dontjudge if you're the latter.

Are you leaving every door open for the possibility of dawn?

XoXo

The Bougie One

8

Lux

I reread the words again and again, looking for places where I can improve or cut.

Is it too trivial? I don't want to say what I got Lauren and Chase. My brother's gift is obscenely expensive, and I would never want my readers to feel like they have to get something expensive for it to be meaningful.

The one I got Lauren is not as expensive right now, but it's a one-of-a-kind piece that I hope she will love. I had it designed especially for her. It's a fierce warrior, in head gear and glorious hair, but in heels.

I look up at the digital clock in my home office, and I'm shocked. It's almost time for me to go. The bridal party is supposed to meet at four so we can head to the venue together ahead of tomorrow's wedding. I hit save on my blog and send it to Mimi, my editor. She'll have lots of input. Mostly, she'll want me to share what I got them, but that's not the point of the article. She'll just have to be mad at me.

After ensuring the email is sent, I run to my bedroom, comb my hair into a messy bun, and slip into a $7 black bodysuit, $10 white joggers, and $50 pointy-toed pumps from *Autumn Lush*. I pair my outfit with teardrop faux-emerald earrings to stand out against my soft brown bob and bring out my eyes. The crown piece is my Chanel 19 Large Stitch Bag. It adds a touch of cohesiveness to the outfit. It also elevates the look.

I've just finished applying eyeliner, when my phone rings. I rush to it, thinking it may be Lauren needing me to pick up something, but it's not.

Marilyn's name appears on the screen, and my hand freezes halfway in the air. I can always let it go to voicemail, but with the wedding being tomorrow, I don't dare. You never know what's in my mother's head and when she decides to get scandalous, especially since she's not invited.

I sigh and answer.

"Luciana, I've been calling you all day."

I inspect the lining of my lips. "My phone was off. I was working."

"I could've been dead for all you know."

But you're not, because you're complaining on the phone.

"Did you need something, Marilyn?"

"Yes, I wanted to ask if everything is okay for tomorrow."

I stop applying my lipstick, the Coralberry gloss filling only one side of my upper lip. "Yes, why?"

Please don't throw another fit asking why you can't come.

"Just checking. I want Chase's day to be perfect. Do you have your dress ready?"

"Yes..."

This would be a normal conversation between any mother and daughter, but for me, it's a WTF moment.

"Who are you going with?" she asks.

"I'm going alone. I'm in the wedding party, and I get to escort Felix in."

"That's one of the kids Chase hangs around with, right?"

Jesus. And she wonders why she's not invited.

"Felix is his child, my nephew, and your grandchild, Marilyn. Look, I have to go—"

"You shouldn't be going alone to a wedding. Your followers will

96

probably look down upon that. Bougie Girl shouldn't be dateless like an old maid."

As always, her missile finds a landing spot and makes the heat explode in my chest.

"What?" I sputter. "I just want to celebrate Lauren and Chase's union and happiness. I'm not interested in men right now, like I told you the other day. I'm concentrating on my career and developing a business plan to market it better."

"And you think you're going to do that by going to a high-profile event alone when you're supposed to be influencing young women? Do you think they'll envy you if you don't even have a man by your side?"

"Marilyn, I don't want anyone to envy me. I want to show them where to find good things, affordable or not, so they can live their best life. You know, I really don't have time—"

My mother's exasperated breath fills the line. "Stop being prideful and call Mateo. He would be happy to escort you to the wedding."

So that's why she called.

"Uh...no. Wait, let me rephrase that. Hell no. I don't even want to hear his name. I only went out with him the other day for closure, and look where that got me. I'm done."

"He made a mistake, but he's New York's most eligible bachelor. He's like Derek Jeter used to be, only more famous and better looking. Think of all the photos you can post on Instagram. When you're with him, you're the envy of every girl."

And miserable like no other.

"No, thanks. I'm good, and he's about to be a father. Now I have to go because I have to meet the bridal party."

"I'm not finished with you—"

But I'm done with you.

I lean on the one thing I know will get her off the phone now. "Why don't I send you and Eddha a little something so you can go to the Ferragamo store before you head out to the Hamptons? You can buy yourself something pretty you can show off."

"That would be lovely."

"Consider it done. I'll call you soon, Marilyn."

I don't breathe until I'm able to hang up the phone, open my bank app, and shoot her and Eddha the money. I don't know what Cam, Chase, and I would do without Eddha, that saintly companion who takes care of our mother so we don't have to relive our traumas on an hourly basis. Every year, we raise her salary. It always feels like we don't pay her enough, though.

I finish applying my lipstick and head out the door, but unfortunately, I'm not alone. Marilyn's voice is with me as I hop into my Uber and the whole way there.

I'm going stag to a wedding where my brother is getting married to my closest friend, and everyone there is a couple except for the children. Now, in my family, everyone will be married after tomorrow, and I'm the single auntie with no prospects.

Maybe I should call someone to come with me. Lauren wouldn't mind. Fabian would be willing to fly to Baltimore. He's a safe choice, as we are not interested in each other. He would be *Instagrammable AF*, but that would be a scandal, as everyone knows he and Mateo hate each other. I don't care what Mateo thinks, but that's not a good look for me. It would look like I'm trying to get his attention.

No, I am staying the course because this is the kind of thinking that would have landed me in Mateo's bed or making some type of desperate decision.

Baltimore's Inner Harbor peeks in between buildings, giving me a view of the ships docked and people walking along. I smile at the people paddling on the pink swan boats. Brave souls.

As metropolitan as this city is, it's not New York. There's a bit of a small-town feel, and here I'm not depending on one person to make me feel less lonely.

You'll be with family. You don't need anyone else today.

I don't know why I'm letting Marilyn get in my head. It leads nowhere good. So, I go through one of my favorite mental exercises. I take Marilyn's words, put them in a box, and hurl them out the window into the harbor. The mental imagery makes me smile.

My Uber pulls up outside of Lauren's red brick rowhouse. The black door with its glass and iron paneling creates a wonderful contrast, as does the matching trim on the windows. It's so simple and elegant. A white stretch limo is parked outside, waiting for us. I thank my driver and rush out of the car.

Ayla's waiting outside the rowhouse door with her bag at her feet. She waves at me. "Hi."

Her smile is so warm you can't help but return it.

I hug her. "What are you doing outside by yourself?"

"I just got here. *Papi* is getting something for the boys from the car."

She points at something behind me, and when I turn, her dad walks toward us. When his gaze lands on me, the smile materializes on his face. All white teeth, full lips, and perfect. There's a little stubble over his cheeks and such heat in his eyes that he sets off sparks, igniting all my sensitive areas.

Yeah, I was right the first time I met him. *Total DILF*. And no matter how much time I get to spend around him, my body reacts the same way in his presence, like an overheated carburetor.

"Luciana, hi."

The sound of his voice brings me back to our last interaction at my place and sobers me up.

"Hi," I say.

We lean forward, and I catch a whiff of something so mouth-watering I have to squelch the urge to sniff him like a hound in her first heat. Our cheeks brush, and for a nanosecond, his stubble sears my skin in what feels like slow motion. The wave of need scratches through my insides.

"How are you?" he asks, and there goes the stir in my belly. Between his accent, his face and body, and the mouth-watering manliness of his cologne, I don't know what makes me more wet. I definitely have a type: him.

Down, girl. Remember you swore off men.

"I'm doing well, Ollie. How about you?" Yeah, that's good. Call him Ollie. He's just a family friend. You're not attracted to him.

But I am. Since the first time I saw him.

He was an ass to you the other day.

"*Papi*, can you take our photo?"

He blinks and fishes out his phone. "Sure, *negrita*."

"We're bridesmaids," Ayla says proudly.

I put my arm around her. "Yes, and we're going to have so much fun today and keep Lauren relaxed."

"B and I can't wait until you show us how you do your makeup. *Papi*, send me the pic."

She's giddy, but her dad looks pained.

Bron steps out, and she hugs me first and then says hi to Oliver. Then, the two girls hug like they haven't seen each other in years.

Oliver shakes his head. "I don't know what makes me more nervous, the fact that she's a bridesmaid so young or the makeup and heels part."

I chuckle. "Don't worry. She's a beautiful girl. She doesn't need much. But…" I lean in. "I'll preach my less-is-more gospel."

He leans a little closer too, his lips only a breath from mine. "I knew I could count on you. And coming from someone like you, she'll one hundred percent believe it."

I blink up at him. "Someone like me?"

"Beautiful and an expert at these things." His mouth is so close.

God, all I need to do is lean in a bit more. If I hadn't sworn off men, if the girls weren't right there, if it wouldn't ruin everything…

"I know a little and will happily share with her."

His smile deepens. "Thank you for including my *negrita* in all your plans. She was very excited for today, and as much as I try, this is the part where I'm a…fish out of water?"

I resist the urge to bite my lip. *Or his.*

"You've done a great job. She's a gem."

"Thank you, Luciana. How's life in Baltimore thus far?" he asks.

"Good, so far. Excited about what you can do with your hands."

His eyebrow rises, and I realize how that sounded.

I clear my throat. "Not like that."

I wish it was like that, though. A lot.

My cheeks are suddenly on fire.

"Yeah, your reno is going to look amazing," he says, but the light dancing in his eyes is too much. He's enjoying this.

I nod, powering through the blush. "Yeah, uh—"

The door flies open again, and Adri, my sister-in-law, steps out. Her eyes bounce back and forth between us. She smiles, missing nothing, but turns her attention to the teenagers. "Girls, come on. We're leaving."

Lauren steps out and zeroes in on us. "Your brother is trying to convince me to elope just hours before our wedding."

"I guess I'll see you all tomorrow," Ollie says, but his gaze is on me. He and Adri escort the girls to the car.

Lauren hooks my arm with hers. "He's going stag too. You should totally take advantage and kick it to him. Or get him alone in a corner for a Christmas do-over. I'm all for someone getting it on my day. I did after Winter's wedding, and it was so good. This would be my way of paying love forward."

"Stop, you know I—"

"Yeah, yeah, you swore off men. So did I, and then your brother came back into my life. Now, I don't know if you know…" She leans in and whispers in my ear, "I'm getting married to him tomorrow. It's a proven formula."

As she ducks into the limo, my gaze meets Oliver, and he waves. He's so fine I feel all tingly. I would totally be up for getting him in a corner.

Nope, not doing that. I'm going to stay the course.

But I can't help but take in all of him before I climb into the vehicle.

Lux

I take another sip of champagne and let the calming lavender scent wash over me. The excitement permeates the room, and I want to ensure I capture it all for the bride's memory book. The hotel manor is the perfect place for a wedding. This room is ideal for the bridesmaids to get ready. I snap a photo of the bride's ankle-strapped white sandals.

"I don't get tired of saying this. Her cheekbones are everything," Lauren says.

I follow her gaze to the vanity where the makeup artist is brushing a little highlighter onto Ayla's cheeks. It waves a rose-gold path over her brown skin like magic flowing from a wizard's wand.

"Don't forget her eyes and her mouth. It's so freaking perfect. She needs to model. That face should be in magazines," I say louder than I mean to.

Ayla's eyes fly open, and those brown orbs meet mine, blinking. Her shy smile spreads a little, making her skin glow a darker hue.

"You do look gorgeous, A," Bron says, pressing her hands together. The half-up, half-down hairstyle Lauren chose for her and Ayla allows her curls to brush over her shoulder. The knot at the top of her head gives it an edgier look.

"Thanks, B," Ayla replies, smiling at her. "You do too. We have to take lots of pics. Papi can make me a poster-size collage for my wall."

"I want one too," my niece tells her.

Lauren and I turn away from them, and she whispers, "Aww," close to my ear.

"They're the cutest together. And both look so beautiful." Lauren lays her hand on my arm.

And they are. They always make me want to post their photos on my Instagram with a hashtag of friendship goals. They're always so supportive of each other. It's everything Lauren and Adri had when we were growing up. What I always envied. I never had friends like they are to each other. The people who got close to me were always there for a reason.

I shake the thoughts. Today is not the day for this.

"Speaking of beautiful," I say to Lauren, "you are that word times a thousand. Your skin is glowing, and your makeup is amazing."

I'm so glad she decided on this two-day stay at the manor. It allowed her to relax and concentrate on getting ready for the wedding.

She laughs softly. "Haven't you heard? I'm getting married today."

"You are, and you look the part. I can't wait to see you in your dress."

Her eyes sparkle, and the smile turns enigmatic. Her dress is the most beautiful thing I've ever seen, but there's something about it no one has seen. Not even Adri. She says it's a surprise for my brother.

"The soft glam makeup was a great choice. Here, let me take some shots. I want to use them for my IG if you're okay with it."

She nods. "I'm marrying the love of my life. My forever one and only. I want people to see the photos on Mars if that's possible."

I laugh. "I don't know about Mars, but my twenty million followers —thanks to Mateo's fuckery—will surely love these."

Grabbing my phone, I snap pics of Lauren. She plays up for the camera in her big, fluffy white robe. The two-day stay at the venue has gone a long way to ease the bridal nerves. The massages and practice run for the bridesmaids were a great idea.

Winter walks closer to us and lays her daughter down on one of the couches. "This one is down for the count. Thank God."

"She's an angel," Lauren says.

I nod in agreement. Avelyn is such a happy baby.

"Yes," her mom agrees. "And now we can get the angel's shoes on, and since she's napping, she won't be cranky for her big moment ahead of the bride."

She winks at Lauren when she says it, but the bride swallows hard and presses one hand over the other.

"I need more champagne."

Here comes the jitters.

"It's going to be fine, Lauren," I tell her.

"I know, but..." She trails off and looks Ayla's way. "Oh, God. Your shoes are not here yet."

Winter and I share a look we've been perfecting since the engagement party disaster when my mother stomped in like Dumbo's mama into a fine china shop.

On that night, Winter, Adri, and I decided that whenever any stressful situation came up around the wedding, we would run to put out the fire by dividing and conquering whatever we had to. So, I grab the champagne bottle and pour Lauren another tall glass.

Winter touches her arm. "I spoke to Ollie. He is bringing them. I made sure he put them in his car while we were on the phone. He's on his way here to help Cam and Chase with the boys. You don't need to worry about anything."

Lauren nods, and Winter goes back to lay out her daughter's clothes.

I tag in with the glass of champagne.

"The wedding is going to be perfect. You're going to be the most beautiful bride. And then you'll be saddled with Chase for life. That's my gift to you. You're welcome."

The laughter bubbles out of her like the ones rising to the top of the champagne glass. "Yes, I'll be stuck to Chase forever. And thank you." The look in her eyes is so deep, the emotion so naked, it can only be love. She loves him so much.

My eyes fill so quick I can't fan myself fast enough.

She loves him.

And that makes me happy. He's waited for her love his whole life. And it's the same intense love he feels. I can see it in her eyes, in the way she says his name, in the way her voice drops after the word forever. I love the crazy way they love each other. It's not perfect, and it's been messy, painful, and dramatic, but it's so real and authentic.

"Lux, you're going to make me cry."

"No crying." The makeup artist doesn't even pause applying mascara on Ayla. "We don't have time to start over with both of you."

Bron is looking at us, smiling. "They always cry when we have girls' days."

"That's not true," I say, pressing the tip of my finger into the corners of my eyes to stop the tears.

"You do. You're always remembering stuff," Ayla chimes in, and I can't help but stare at her.

"Gosh, you look gorgeous. You both do."

I wave my hands for her to stand next to Bron. They look fifteen instead of barely thirteen, so I am pretty sure their parents will hate it. They're confident and not all mopey like when I was their age.

I start snapping photos, capturing how cute they look. I even step in, and we do selfies.

"You have to teach us how to smile like that," Ayla says.

"Like what?"

"Pretty and with your eyes," Bron adds.

"Ohh. It's going to be easy for the two of you because you're both already gorgeous." I step away and stand across from them again. "What you do is look at the camera, relax your eyes, and then think of something that makes you smile. I always pretend I know a secret that no one else knows about, and everyone wants to find out what it is. And it's like I'm not telling."

The girls' eyes widen.

"Let's try it. Bron, you can go first." My niece is less shy, and it will give Ayla more time to get used to the idea.

Bron's smile and look are perfect. It's so teen catalog. That face and smile would make you want to buy whatever she's selling.

"Perfect," I say.

She and Ayla high-five and switch places.

Ayla's shoulders shrink, her smile wavering. Her eyes are darting all over the room where everyone is looking at her.

"Look only at me, and remember, you have a secret, and I'm dying to know, but you're not going to tell me. So I look back then whirl around like this, and show me that face." I show her how to do it and wait.

She turns away from me, and it takes her a second, but when her body twists around and she looks straight at my phone, I freeze.

Her angelic face completely transforms, and her eyes embody it. I hold my finger over the click button and take a burst of photos as she angles her face in different ways.

"How was that?"

"Slayed," Bron says, and I can only nod.

I hit the photos app so I can look at all the shots. Both of them,

Lauren, and Winter come stand around me, and we look at their photos.

"This is so *Teen Vogue*," I whisper, and Lauren nods.

"We look like Chloe and Halle back in the day."

"Yes," Winter says. "God, you two are so beautiful."

"Thanks," they say in unison.

They're so cute.

I get a few shots of them together again. And then, I guide Lauren to stand by them. Then, I take some with just the bride in the middle with one arm around each girl.

The door flings open, and Adri walks in. "I'm sorry. It took CJ a while to go to sleep. The groom's area is not as—" Her mouth drops open as she looks at the girls. "You two look so grown up." Her hand flies to her chest. "You don't look like my baby."

"Mom," Bron says and comes to stand by her. "We talked about this. I'm a bridesmaid today, not your baby."

Adri nods and holds her hands up. "You're right. Sorry. Felix is way too excited and does not want to sleep. They need extra hands over there. I need to get my makeup done so I look like I belong with you all."

"Yeah, his excitement is way over the top. He can't wait to walk down the aisle." Lauren turns toward the door, and everyone's mouths —Adri, the makeup artist, Winter, even the young girls—open to speak at once.

I grab her arm. "Where do you think you're going, *Bride of Chucky*?"

The next second, we're all laughing.

"Sorry, I am so used to being the one that can calm him down."

"I'll go. You stay here. Be right back."

"Use something like a baby wipe or a wet cloth on him. Then, lay him down and sit with him for five minutes. Don't leave it up to Chase, they would end up playing a video game. If he gets an hour nap, he'll be recharged for the rest of the day."

I nod, grab the gift I brought my brother, and make my way down the hallway. I try for long, fast strides, but the heels and the tight-fitting dress keep me at a less-than-desired pace.

I knock on the door and am greeted with my oldest brother tossing a sock at Felix and the little boy tossing it back.

"Stop that. You're all going to be sweaty and gross. Cam, why are you not ready yet? The wedding is in two hours. At least put your clothes on."

"Hi, Aunt Lux," Justin says and comes to hug me. I love his hugs. They're so sweet. Felix comes by next. He's only wearing an undershirt and shorts.

Beyond the room, Chase's barber is giving him an extra touch-up.

I do as Lauren tells me and, with Justin's help, get Felix to lie down. CJ is on the couch across from him, sound asleep. I'm hoping Felix follows soon. But he doesn't sleep. Instead, he's asking tons of questions.

"Where is *Titi* Lo?"

I gently push him back on the couch. "She's in the bride's suite."

"How come she didn't come with you?"

Justin sits next to us. "Felix, don't you remember? *Titi* Adri just explained that the groom can't see the bride before the wedding?"

Felix frowns. "But he sees her all the time. They sleep in the same bed and in the same room and sometimes they shower together. And they lock the door."

"Felix, stop talking about that." Chase's voice doesn't even faze him.

Felix gets an impish smile on his face and moves his head closer to mine. "Chase says they're going to make a baby."

"I didn't say that to you," my brother says, not even moving from his spot under the clippers.

Felix's smile widens like Chase's when he's about to do something he shouldn't.

"Let's play a game," I say.

Felix's eyes light up. "I love games."

"This one is the *quiet and close your eyes* game. You count in your head as far as you can with your eyes closed. The person who does it the longest, gets the big prize."

His face tells me he's not buying it. "What's the big prize?"

I didn't think that far ahead. *Dang.*

"I'll let you wear my big watch," Chase says.

Felix's eyes widen. "The big-big one?"

Chase chuckles. "That one."

And now I'm happy because this plays into my gift.

Five minutes later, the room is in silence. Justin is playing his handheld game, and Cam goes to get dressed. Chase is all done with the barber, and I go up to him, handing him my gift.

"What's this?"

"Open it."

He frowns. "But what is it?"

"When people give you something wrapped in festive paper, it's called a present. Normal people get those on their birthday or Christmas or, in this case, their wedding day."

His face doesn't change. "Why would you give me a present? You should've given it to Lauren."

I don't let it bother me. "I gave her a present. This one is yours. And I want you to open it. Now."

I snap at the end, and it does the trick. He begins to tear through it until he gets to the leather, engraved box. I had the jeweler engrave: *Pass on the best of you.* He stares at it, not making any moves.

"The gift is inside," I whisper.

He nods and opens it. Then his gaze ping-pongs to mine.

"Because our family is so fucked up, we don't have good traditions. So, I wanted to create something we can pass on. I gave one to Cam on his wedding day. Now I give this one to you. You can pass it on to the boys on their wedding day."

His hand shoots out, and he bear hugs me, knocking the air out of my lungs. He lingers a few seconds and then clears his throat. "Thank you. Now go back to make sure Lauren is okay."

I fight back a smile and head back out. I'm happy my brothers are happy. Both chose the right people, the right women. They'd known them since high school, and that love was always there for both of them.

I'm the one who chose wrong and keeps perpetuating the same mistake.

9

Oliver

Coño, this is not happening to me.

Even as I cringe, I can't help but smile. My Ayla looks beautiful. Not just beautiful. She's always been the most beautiful girl around, but today...she's a young-woman type of beautiful. She's wearing makeup and heels, and I just can't fucking take it.

"*Papi*, I'm talking to you. Did you bring the protectors for the bottom of my heels?"

Heels. *Santo Dios.*

"*Si, mi niña.* I got the protectors. Here they are," I say, handing her the bag.

"Then why are you staring at me like that? Do I look bad?"

I shake my head. "*No, mi vida.* You look beautiful, *bellisima.* Too grown up for my heart. Your *Papi* is having a hard time with that."

She smiles, big and wide, in that Ayla way. "Thanks, *Papi.* It's just makeup, you know? Nothing about me has changed."

I pull her in for a hug. "How was your girls' night?"

Even as the words leave my mouth, I can't help but think how ludicrous they are. It feels like I was baby proofing the house for her just days ago.

"It was good. Lauren's squad came and pampered us. The grownups got champagne. Bron and I got sparkling juice. You should see my swag bag. We also got to practice walking in the heels some more. They thought we did really good."

I hate this so much but smile anyway. "You've been practicing a lot lately at home. I knew you would be impressive—as always."

"Yeah. I have to go back inside the room. Lauren is super nervous, and I don't want her to worry because she doesn't see me."

"I better go help out with the boys. I imagine Felix must be all over the place."

She stands on her tiptoes and kisses my cheek. "I'll see you later. Love you," she says before she dashes down the hallway and disappears into the bride's suite.

I turn around and head back to the groom's suite. The door swings open, and a woman steps out in a green dress that clings to her curves. Her face is away from me as she closes the door slowly. But I see all I need in that one step. Coke-bottle shape, a bounce-a-quarter-off-it firm and round ass, gorgeous legs, and dark-brown hair below the shoulders. It's the kind of hair that you wind around your hand when…

She turns around and freezes.

I freeze too.

Lux's mouth drifts open, then it curves up, giving way to that inviting smile I can't help but emulate. I close the distance between us in a few steps, stopping short of being inappropriately close. Nothing that would make her brothers want to have another talk with me.

"Luciana."

Her smile widens. "Oliver. How are you?"

"I'm well. I was bringing Ayla's shoes, and now I am going to see if I can help out with the boys."

"We got Felix to lie down for a nap. He's way too excited about the wedding."

"Oh good. How's Chase doing?"

"He's doing well. Frankly, I thought he would be a mess. I came to see if he and Cam needed anything. I'm proud of them. They actually have it all together," she laughs. It's soft and feminine, widening that kiss-me-suck-me-fuck-me mouth of hers.

God, I want to do all three again. Kiss her, suck her, then fuck her. Right here. I want to make her moans echo down this hallway.

"I guess they don't need my help, then."

"They will. Once—" Her gaze drifts past me, her lips flattening. "Shit, this is not good."

I turn and see a man is standing at the end of the hallway near the bride's suite. It's Elias Saunders, Cam's best friend. From my understanding, they've known each other forever, but it's clear by her face that he's not welcome.

She moves past me with determined steps.

I follow close behind just in case she needs my help.

"Hi, Elias. Can I help you?"

He takes her in, his gaze straying down her body, and he smiles wide. I know that smile. It's the same *sucio* look every man gets when he can picture a woman without her clothes. When he can see what he would be doing to that body. When he can practically hear the moans and gasps he can extract from her.

It raises a kink behind my neck. He's ogling is too obvious, bordering on disrespectful.

He finally looks into her eyes. "Hi, Lux. I need to talk to Lauren for a couple of minutes."

"It's her wedding day." Lux's tone is neutral, but there's a get-real snap to it at the end.

"I know, but she and I need to have a conversation. It's important," he insists.

"This is not a good time," Lux says, firmer this time.

He turns toward the bride suite. "I have to talk to her."

I unclench my teeth and move to stand in front of the door. "*Amigo,* she just told you this is not a good time."

He looks at me for the first time. "I am not your friend, and this is none of your business."

"You're right. We're not friends, but this is my business. Chase and Lauren are my friends. This is their wedding. You are not invited."

"How do you know that? On top of being the handyman, are you also the wedding coordinator?"

Electricity flows to my hands, and it takes all of me to control my fist from flying. I take a step forward, but Lux jumps in between us.

Her finger hovers in front of his face. "You're a complete asshole for that. Oliver is our friend. Chase and Lauren want him here. The same cannot be said for you. Get the hell out before I tell my brother you are here. He would love to pound your face in before getting married."

Elias's gaze flickers to the other end of the hallway. A smirk hovers, and his shoulders straighten.

He's a coward. On top of being a rich dick with his nose in the air, he's afraid of Chase.

Little does he know that he's about to have a bigger problem than Chase if he doesn't get the fuck out of here.

"She asked you to leave," I say. "Please go."

He smiles. "I'm leaving. Tell Lauren I need to talk to her, Lux," he says then moves closer and places a kiss on her cheek.

She swipes at it as if trying to undo the action. I should've placed myself between them.

"I'm sorry you had to go through that. He's an asshole," she tells me.

I shrug. "It's fine. I'm used to dealing with people like him."

Her chin juts out. "No, it's not fucking fine. He has no right to talk to you like that. No one does."

She's worked up with the color heightened in her face, with her eyes shooting sparks, and her hand in fists like she's ready to swing.

I love it.

It makes her look so beautiful and lethal, like I already know she can be.

"Don't let him ruin your day, Luciana."

And yes, my voice drops lower than I mean it to when I say her name.

And no, I don't miss the way her eyes darken or how the color in her face heightens.

And we stare into each other's eyes in a way that takes me back a few months and less than ten miles away to the flip I haven't been able to sell yet.

I want to press her against the wall behind her and kiss her breathless. She would be up to it too. I can tell by the way she's looking at me, by that quick swipe of her tongue across her bottom lip. It makes my cock stir in my pants, and it takes all of me to stay rooted and not back her into that wall.

But no, we're supposed to be only professional. So, shove the sucio in the closet and go about your business.

"Let me know if he comes back. We don't need to bother Chase with this."

She blinks a few times and clears her throat. "You're right. I need to go inside. I don't want to give Lauren any worries. Her bride anxiety is already at level ten."

She doesn't move.

I nod but don't move either. *Walk away, Oliver.*

She turns, taking two steps toward the door.

Good. This is really good. *Let her go.*

But I can't.

"Luciana…"

She turns to me again, and there are so many things on the tip of my tongue. I want to tell her that I would love to take her out sometime. That I have not forgotten what her lips taste like. That I still dream of the day when I can wake her up with my mouth, my fingers, and my dick.

Yet, as I look into her eyes, only one truth flows out of my lips. "You look *bella*, breathtaking."

———

Oliver

I lied, I realize as the organist plays the bridal march, and the wedding party walks in.

Lux doesn't look just breathtaking. She's like a wet dream, gliding down the aisle. Her smile is brighter than the chandelier lights. Her gaze alternates between her brother at the altar and Felix, whose hand she is holding. She's trying to pace their march, mindful of his height. Thankfully, he's not tugging at his bowtie like he was in the groomsmen's room. His hand is tight around hers, but a grin lights his face up. He's not bashful or nervous.

When they walk by me, I catch a whiff of the sweet notes of her perfume. Sweet and dark and mouth-wateringly sexy.

Like her.

Our gazes meet, and I'm caught up in those hazel eyes. We linger, and she quickly looks away.

You're going to have to let that go, Oliver.

She walks Felix to stand by her brothers, stopping briefly to kiss Chase's cheek. She whispers something in his ear. He blinks a few times then swallows and nods at her. I follow her trajectory as she joins Bron on the other side of the aisle.

I turn around fast, not wanting to miss the next entrance. My eyes may want to stare at Luciana Blake forever, but my baby is about to enter the room, and I can't miss that.

And here comes my Ayla, two inches taller in the heels I brought her earlier. She's holding onto Justin's hand. He's trying hard not to smile but failing. He can't hide the gigantic crush he has on my *niña*. Who could blame him? She's the most beautiful, sweet, and kind-hearted girl. Her smile widens when she looks at me, and I fish out my phone and take a burst of photos.

God, please slow down time. I'm not ready for how fast she's growing.

When she passes by me, I mouth how beautiful she looks. It makes her smile harder. She goes to stand by Bron, and I really need to let go of how grown-up they both look. I have to be the only person more worried about the young bridesmaids. But when I look at Cam on the stage, he's shaking his head.

Yeah, he's got it worse.

I've seen Ayla through the years. From our talks, I can tell it's hard for him that Bron is growing too fast, and he's already missed so much of her life.

In the next second, everyone is laughing and cooing as Spencer Grayson walks down the aisle holding his barely walking daughter's hand. Avy, in her princess white dress, is sprinkling rose petals as she goes along. She's giggling as she dumps them. My A was that small just yesterday. I hope Grayson is remembering every moment.

Avy takes her time, and the whole crowd is watching her, except for Chase, whose eyes widen, and there's this shocked look on his face. His eyes go warm and even a little wet before he swallows and smiles.

I follow the direction of his gaze, and my throat catches.

Lauren is standing in the back of the room, in her pristine silk and lace white dress, a black leather jacket, and a bouquet of white and pink flowers with huge orange and red hibiscuses. I don't know much about the other flowers, but Cayenas—hibiscuses—line the front porch of my *abuela's* house in Dominican Republic. When I was a kid, my friends and I would pick them and chew on the bottom of the bulb where it's sweet.

Lauren is looking at her husband-to-be with the most serene smile on her face. She always smiles like that around him. Over the past few months, I've learned how rough the road to today has been for both of them. He's a cool guy, and she's like a sister to me and has always been great to my A and me. She deserves the best. Chase doesn't know how lucky he is.

They found great people in each other.

I turn back to the altar, and most people are still looking at Avelyn.

Luciana is staring at Chase, but she doesn't react. Instead, she looks at me. At that moment, we share a secret. Other than Chase, we seem to be the only two people who know Lauren is back there.

And the moment goes on for a while. Our gazes hold for that long.

"She's here," someone whispers, and the crowd erupts in a collective gasp.

Our attention goes to the bride as she glides down the aisle like a dream. Women are dabbing at their eyes. Congressman Davis drapes an arm around his wife's shoulders. She dabs at her eyes like her daughters, Adrianna, and Winter in the front row—and all the other women. As Lauren reaches the altar, Cam steps down to help her up the steps and hands her up to his brother.

But the bride and groom only have eyes for each other.

"You look amazing," Chase says.

Lauren's smile is sweet, and her skin glows brighter. "Thank you."

I have to look away. It feels like I'm intruding. It wasn't like this when I got married. It didn't feel intimate and beautiful. No one in the room was dabbing at their eyes. The occasion was more somber than anything. My ex-wife and her father were the only ones happy. My side of the family tempered their emotion. My mom kept shaking her head at me. She knew it was a mistake.

Hell, I knew it was a mistake.

"I am so happy," Aunt Millie whispers next to me, pressing a tissue to the corners of her eyes. "My girl deserves it."

"She does," I say, touching her shoulder.

"Now we just got to find you a girl."

Ever since I started working on expanding Winter and Grayson's penthouse, Grayson's aunt has been on a kick about finding me some-one. "I don't think I have time for that, Aunt Millie. I'm always on the go with work and Ayla."

"Bah. Of course you do. You're a great guy, and you can find your-self a good woman and mom for Ayla."

A mom for Ayla…that would be a first. It's also the reason I can't be with anyone. It would have to be someone who loves her like I do. And I don't think anyone can.

Plus, I wouldn't put Ayla in the position to be rejected.

The ceremony is mostly traditional, but as soon as they finish kiss-ing, Justin and Felix break free. When they walk out of the room, Chase is holding Felix's hand, and Lauren is holding Justin's.

"You see? Chase loves those boys like they're his. They're going to adopt them together," Aunt Millie points out.

I frown at her. Everyone knows about the adoption process and what Lauren has had to deal with in the past year to get them. What happened to her sister is public. Why is she telling me this?

"There's someone out there for everyone. Someone that will love you and your little queen," Aunt Millie insists.

I would love to find that woman. I just don't know where to look.

An hour later, I'm sitting at the banquet table next to my Ayla. She's chatting away with Bron and eating. Cam, holding his son, CJ, is sitting next to me on the other side. Our daughters asked us to move so they could sit next to each other.

"Thank you for helping out Lux earlier," Cam says.

"Don't mention it. I didn't do much, but it helped that Elias thought I was working security."

"God, he's an asshole. How the hell didn't I know how bad he was? It's bad enough I have to hear 'I told you so' from Chase about him on a daily basis. I don't want to know what he would've done if he had seen Elias here today."

I have noticed that Chase hates the man. "That's what we're here for—to help the day go smoothly for him and Lauren."

I look at them at the main table, and by their faces, we've succeeded. They're happily staring into each other's eyes.

I turn to Cam, and baby CJ is staring at me. I poke at his belly, and he giggles. "There's going to be another one of you on the way soon."

Cam laughs. "According to Chase, that's his next goal. Meanwhile, I am trying to convince Adri on another one."

"Really? You want more kids?"

He steals a quick look at his wife. "Yeah. I told her three more, and she laughed at me, but I think I can get her on board for another one or two. Bron is growing so fast, and I want another before CJ gets much older."

"That's a teenager, a toddler, and a baby, Cam."

"It's a death wish, isn't it?" He chuckles, but his words don't erase the look of determination in his eyes. This must be what it's like when you have a real partner in your life.

I've never wanted another child. Ayla and I are a perfect unit.

"Excuse me, *Papi*." I turn, and Ayla is staring at me with a smile. "Come on."

"Where are we going?"

She points up and shakes her shoulders. "Merengue is playing. We have to show these people how it's done."

"Excuse me, Cam." I stand up and extend my hand in the way I'm hoping she expects every man to ask for a dance. She takes it, and we get to the middle of the floor.

On the other end, some members of Lauren's family are dancing. I take Ayla's right hand in mine and place my left one on her shoulder. We begin swaying to the fast beat of the music.

Ayla learned this really fast and has gotten so good at it. I'm proud that we dance at least once a week. A has always been proud of our culture, wanting to learn our ways and keep them present.

"You dance like an angel, *negrita*."

"Gracias, *Papi*. You have to dance with B too. We've been practicing, but Mr. Cam doesn't know Spanish music. He can't dance with her."

I nod. "Of course. Remember what I said, a good guy always dances with all the girls in a group. Even if he comes to the dance with one girl, he has to be attentive to all her friends. Because everyone should enjoy themselves. Don't ever expect any less than that."

She smiles a little, and I'm hoping that when she goes anywhere with a guy, it will be about twenty years from now. She looks over at the table and calls Bron over. Her friend shakes her head, but A waves her hand faster.

Soon, I'm dancing with both of them to Anthony Santos. I take turns turning them around.

We all laugh, and Adri is taking lots of pics of us. She and Winter join us, and at one point, I'm the one guy dancing with four girls. And that's just fine, because that's how it used to be growing up with my cousins. I was always the one guy who could dance and made sure they all got on the floor.

Lauren joins us with Justin and Felix, and it's not long before there's a big circle, and all the Latinos are in the middle, dancing and clapping. We take turns going into the center.

This wedding takes me back to growing up. Since I left Monte Cristi to come to the U.S. to play baseball, I haven't been to a wedding like this. Happy, beautiful, and full of life. Everything mine should have been but wasn't.

As my Ayla starts dancing in the middle of the circle, I smile. I didn't have all of this on my wedding day, but the very best thing in my life came six months later.

10

Lux

I thought he was hot the first time I saw him with that wide, mind-obliterating smile. His eyes devour and suggest things that only live in my head. Images of that hard, sexy body—with strong arms to hold you in—make me conjure, remember, and repeat.

But today, watching Oliver dance with his daughter and bringing our group of friends in…it takes my attraction to a new level. He's dancing with Ayla, Bron, Winter, Adri, and Lauren, managing to give them all his attention. He's about to make me combust.

But…think, Luciana. Where have you heard something like that before? Yeah, Mateo talking to his friend on the phone.

A real man can handle many ladies. I have enough to give all of them.

Except…Ollie is not Mateo. He's not creeping with groupies and z-listed reality starlets. *I think?*

He's dancing with his child, to whom he's totally devoted. God knows my panties slid a little down my leg watching the way he beamed with pride when Ayla walked down the aisle. Now, he's including her best friend, your niece, and all your friends. Because they're all like a big family.

You're the one on the outskirts.

Felix and Justin run up to me, zapping me out of my thoughts. "Come dance, *Titi* Lux."

Felix's little hand closes around mine, and Justin grabs my other hand, and now I'm getting pulled onto the dance floor.

Lauren turns to me first, and the smile on her face tells me she sent the boys for me.

"Why are you doing this to me?" I ask, leaning close to her.

"When Dominicans are happy, we dance. Now you're officially part of the family, in writing and everything." She takes my hand and lifts it over my head.

"Why don't you make Chase dance?"

"He's running now, but he married me. There's no avoiding." She doesn't stop smiling, and God, she's so happy with my idiot brother. I follow her gaze across the room, and he's watching us dance. He's always watching her. I've never seen him this happy, this full. Lauren will never know how grateful Cam and I are for the way she grounds him now.

She lets go of me, and next thing I know, I'm dancing with Bron for a few minutes, and then Adri takes my hands. I get the hang of the circle we are doing. Ayla is next, and she's smiling full, like her dad. She moves well, just like him.

"You're a great dancer."

"Thanks, Lux. You're doing really good."

"I don't know if I told you enough times, but you look beautiful."

She blinks a few times and then smiles again. "So do you. I can't wait to wear dresses like that."

"When you're both older, I'll take you and Bron shopping for stuff like this."

Ayla beams, let's go of my hand, twirls, and moves on to the next person. Oliver's scent reaches me first. I would recognize it anywhere because it lives with me. Sometimes, I wake up from dreams so vivid I could swear I smell him on me. I can't even explain it. It's a hint of warm body, spices, and nautical notes. It sneaks up my nose and invades my senses. The next thing I know, his hand is sliding into mine, and he's pulling me close.

I look up, and our mouths are so close. Then he spins me around very fast, and I brace a hand at his shoulder and follow his steps. And just as quick, we settle into the side-to-side sway.

"You're really good at following the lead," he says, his accent so thick and smooth. It's almost melodious.

I love the way he talks. *And the way he moves.*

"Only when it comes to dancing. Everyone will tell you I'm not good at listening to them."

"You dance merengue like you've always done it."

"I've danced a few times…" A lot of times. *I'm sure he can figure out with who.*

"It shows." He's staring into my eyes, and I don't know if the heat creeping up my face is because of the compliment, or the fast dancing, or because he remembers, like I do, when we moved together in sync before. Maybe all of it.

"How do you all dance and talk?" I ask, looking at Adri, Lauren, and Winter chat as they sway.

"Practice. We all get taught this when we're very young. It's like they drop us in a rhythm pool, and we have to dance our way out."

"Makes…sense?" The image makes me laugh, and he joins.

Then, he looks over my shoulder and back at me. "Your mother's here?"

My heart drops, and I snap my head around so fast I step on the train of my dress and lose balance. Oliver's arms fold around me, and I fall against his chest. It's hard as a rock, but I'm barely aware of it because my eyes have landed on the woman at the entrance of the ballroom.

My mother is standing there, flanked by Mateo at her side.

I swear the music stops playing—at least for me.

I look at Chase on the other side of the room, and he's in deep conversation with Grayson and playing with Avy. Then I find Lauren, near me. She's still dancing and laughing.

I turn into Ollie's arms, and his face is closer than I expected.

"I have to get her out of here before Chase realizes she's here. I don't want her to ruin their day."

Ollie frowns. "Do you think she's here to do that?"

I nod. "You don't know her. She will ruin this day if we let her. Do me a favor. Can you discreetly tell Cam? I'm going to take her out of the room."

I let go of Oliver and move in quick steps, intersecting my mother before the attendant shows her to a table. "Marilyn, can I see you for a second?"

She blinks at me. "Luciana, I just got here. I have not spoken to your brother yet."

"It won't take long."

"*Bella.*" Mateo smiles.

I hook one hand on my mother's elbow and the other on Mateo's and pull them both with me. We walk to the far end of the lobby.

"Where's Eddha?" I ask.

"I didn't need her today."

"What do you mean you didn't need her? You don't go anywhere without her. You're supposed to be in the Hamptons."

"I know, but I couldn't miss my son's wedding. Mateo was kind enough to do what you and Cameron should have done. He picked me up and brought me."

She couldn't miss the wedding, but we've been at the reception for two hours.

"Marilyn, you're not supposed to be here," I say, holding back the urge to scream." Neither you nor Mateo were invited."

"Don't be rude, Luciana. Mateo is a perfect gentleman. He's here because he cares for you enough to be with you on your brother's wedding day so you're not alone."

"I was never alone. The room is full of people in there, and soon-to-be *dad of the year* is not welcome. Anyway, the two of you have to go before Chase realizes you're here."

"What are you talking about? I'm his mother. Where else would I be on Chase's wedding day?"

Jesus, can she stop saying wedding day like she has a right to be here?

"Please, go home. Lauren and Chase have been through too much. It's their day. For once in your life, think of your son."

"Luxxy, that's a horrible thing to say. She's your mother. I'm sure Chase would be happy to see her. Weddings are best when the whole family is together." Mateo is frowning at me.

His words are horrifying. Marilyn in that ballroom with all of us? He's never understood the dynamic between Marilyn and me. He's always tried to get in good with her, and together, they've ganged up on me. Not anymore.

"All she does is cause strife. Chase won't appreciate it. No one here would."

"His wife will. A good partner knows the importance of getting along with the family. Also, it would look bad for Ms. Marilyn to be the only person missing today, especially since your dad can't be here."

Is the universe punking me right now? I guess he never was listening to me when I explained that both my parents were personas non-grata for my brothers and me.

Marilyn sighs. "Mateo, don't waste your breath. I'm going inside. I don't need an invitation to be at my son's wedding, even if he's not marrying the kind of woman I would have chosen for him. He and Cam never listen to me. I'm happy you are here, because Luciana still has time to make a good choice."

What the fuck?

The way she's looking at Mateo is downright cringe. This woman cannot think I am going to marry this fucking player. She must have forgotten about the times he's shown up on *Page Six* because he was creeping on me when we were together.

Why shouldn't she forget, Luciana? You did. You kept taking this douchebag in and ended up back in the sheets too many times.

"Let me escort you both back inside," Mateo offers.

He takes my mom's arm, and I jump in their path. "No. You are not escorting anyone in there. You're going to take Marilyn and go back the way you came."

My mother pelts me with her disapproving look. "Don't be ridiculous, Luciana. I'm going inside."

"You. Are. Not."

"What's going on here?" Cam asks from behind me, and in the next second, my brother is standing next to me with Ollie on the other side of him.

Marilyn smiles. "Cameron, tell your sister to move aside. I am going inside the ballroom."

I open my mouth, but my brother beats me to it. "You are not going in there, Marilyn. You're going home. I've already procured you a driver."

"I can't go home. My son is in there, and it would look terrible for me to miss his big day, even if he chose to marry—"

"Stop," Cam says. "We talked about this already. I told you not to come. Chase and Lauren are happy today. You're not going to ruin that like you tried to ruin the engagement party."

"All I did was show up like any supportive mother would."

"Yes, and you tried to insult her," I say, wishing I would've let Lauren's mother deal with Marilyn. Mrs. Guerrera was about to hit my mother, and none of us would've stopped her.

"If you don't get out of my way, I will make a scene."

Ladies and gentlemen, Marilyn Blake.

"Are you drunk?" Cam asks.

"Of course not. I had a gin and tonic in the car, but only one. You know flying makes me anxious."

I square on my ex. "You gave my alcoholic mother a drink, Mateo?"

"Stop yelling. You're going to embarrass me."

"You're embarrassing yourself by being here. You didn't even mention that you were thinking of coming yesterday when we spoke on the phone," I tell her.

"I wanted to surprise my son. Is that so wrong?"

Yeah, she's drunk. It's the only way. How is it that she's still acting like this would be a good surprise for Chase?

Cam takes her arm. "Let me talk to you for a minute." Then he shoots a look at Mateo and says, "Ollie, can you stay here with Lux, please?"

Ollie nods as Cam takes my mother outside.

I watch them go and breathe a sigh of relief. I know Cam will convince her to go. He will offer her money and whatever else so she'll go back to New York.

I close my eyes and breathe.

"Are you okay?" Ollie asks, putting a hand on my shoulder.

I shake my head. "No, but I will be."

"Who is this man?" Mateo asks.

And that's how I remember him. Marilyn needs to take the man who brought her here back to New York with her.

I turn around and point a finger at Mateo. "Cam is about to convince her to go home. You need to go back as well."

"You don't mean that. I came to be with you, to be your date."

I scoff. "I don't want you here. You didn't even ask me if it was okay? You thought showing up uninvited, with Marilyn, was the way to go? You know what my relationship is like with her. You saw me bring her home after the engagement party, where she made a damned fool of herself."

"All families go through stuff, Luxxy. When she called, I couldn't say no to her. She's your mom, and I have the utmost respect for her. I love you, and I wanted to show that by honoring her. She was in tears about coming. I couldn't say no."

I want to scream right now. "This has nothing to do with honoring her. She pushes me to be with you, even after everything you've put me through. And on the topic of honoring people, did you ever think of honoring me?"

He drapes a hand over my shoulder. "Come on, baby. Don't be like that. Let's talk this out." He turns to Ollie. "My man, give us a minute."

Heat flushes all parts of my body. How dare he? Oliver isn't the person I want leaving.

———

J L LORA

Ollie

I don't get offended easily. I can't. A bastard son—the result of an affair, with a mother everyone felt free to point a finger at—can't afford to take offenses to heart. That's why I didn't go crazy when my wife left me for another man.

Life has always looked to offend me.

So, I take the slights from people who look down upon me in stride. It's a regular thing. Hell, today it is apparently happening hourly, starting with Elias Saunders. But something just pricks at my patience about the way Mateo just dismissed me. He obviously doesn't remember me. Why should he? It wasn't like we were friends before, just prospects hoping to make it into the big leagues. The dismissing flicker of his hand is just something else.

Why does it surprise you?

He's Mateo De La Cruz, homerun god, hero to his hometown and our native country, and darling of New York baseball. His trade contract is one of the biggest in history.

Yet, he has no right to do this. I would never—no matter what my status was—dismiss someone like that.

People won't always handle things the way you would, Oliver. That's why you have to be prepared for when it happens.

This is none of my business, and I should let Luciana and Mateo handle this on their own. He's the ex-boyfriend, and I'm just the guy that caught her on the rebound when she let me in for just a night. The way his hand slides over her skin, I can tell he's been there too many times to count.

My jaw tenses, unsure of what Lux wants.

Then she shrugs Mateo's hands off her shoulders and shoves a finger into his chest. "Don't fucking tell Oliver to go. You have no right to do that. He's our friend. You will not treat him like you do your employees."

"That's not what I'm doing, *mi amor*. I was just asking him for a moment of privacy so we can talk."

"We"—she points at him and then herself—"have nothing to talk

130

about. Besides, it's my brother's wedding. You show up unannounced with—"

His hand shoots out to grab hers. "Forgive me. I just want you to make peace with your mom. I don't want you fighting. I would give anything in the world to be able to have my mom living so close."

She sighs. "I've explained before that Marilyn and I don't have the same relationship you have with your mom. This is not something that can be solved by you showing up and forcing her on me. Do you know the issues you are causing? If Chase finds out…"

Mateo moves in, and his arms close around her, pulling her into his chest. His hands tighten at her lower back, and his gaze lifts to meet mine. There's a tiny curve at the corner of his mouth, and his expression tells me everything I should know.

She is his, and he is making it known.

He bends to touch his lips to the side of her temple. "I'm sorry. Please forgive me. I just missed you so much. When she called, I jumped at the idea of seeing you. I want to make up, Luxxy. Let's go back to being us."

Now I really have to go.

Their relationship is famous for these breakup-to-makeup phases. I've heard Adri talk about it, and it's all over the internet. This is better, anyway. I shouldn't have any protective feelings toward her except the normal ones we should have about females we know.

I'm about to turn when she shoves herself away from him.

"I'm sorry you wasted a trip, coming all the way here. We are definitely not making up. I don't think you're a bad person, but you treated me like shit, and I don't want to be with you anymore."

"Come on, you don't mean that. After everything we've been through. You know what, I'll leave, but I will stay in town. We can have lunch and spend the day together tomorrow. I know everything you remember is the bad right now, but let me remind you of the good."

"What good? When you're not cheating, you're treating people around me like crap."

She turns to look at me. Her face is so troubled that I need to get her away.

"Let's go back inside," I say, holding out a hand for her.

She nods and hooks her delicate hand on my elbow.

"Wait a minute. Is this the fucking guy?" Mateo asks, his face scrunching up with his gaze peeled on me.

The adrenaline unleashes through my body, because I know exactly what he's referring to. *Noche Buena*. He must have heard my voice after he heard us. He stayed for the whole show, like it was one of my grandma's radio *novelas*.

Lux ignores him, and I do the same. We set out to walk, but then she tugs at my side. I stop and look at her and realize he has a hand on her.

My body tenses. He needs to take his hand off her.

"Luxxy, I'm asking you a question."

"One, stop calling me that. You know I fucking hate it. Two, I told you Ollie is a friend. Three, it's none of your fucking business. We are not together."

He tugs one more time. "It is my business. You're my girlfriend, and you cheated on me with this fucking guy. I forgave you. You still have the ring I gave you, right? We are not done for good."

"Let go of my arm, and are you fucking kidding? We are done for good. I donated the stupid thing. You gave it to me while you were screwing half of New York. And I never cheated on you. We were broken up. Wait, you know what? I don't owe you an explanation."

She tries to free herself from his hold, and I've had enough at this point.

"Let her go."

Luciana freezes, and so does Mateo, enough to let her go. I step in front of her.

"Bro, consider yourself lucky I don't fuck you up for what you did. Back off. This is none of your problem."

I don't move. "It is, because she told you to let her go, and you're still holding on. She's telling you it's over, but it's like you don't hear her. She asked you to leave, but you are still here, arguing."

"She doesn't really want me gone, *pariguayo*. She's just scorned, but we have something. *Dejame decirtelo en español para que lo entiendas bien. Because your English is not so good.*" He points at Lux. "*Ella es mia. Nadie la conoce como yo.* That's why she always comes back to me. I'm only explaining so you can stop meddling and avoid some trouble for yourself."

Lux moves closer to me. "I'm not yours. Get the fuck out of here."

"Luxxy," he says, moving in on her.

I step forward to block him from getting closer. "She said get out. If I have to tell you again, you're not going to like it."

His chest puffs out. "You wanna go, tough guy?"

It revs my blood, and I nod. "If you're ready to risk your season."

"*Te voy a matar, degraciao.*" He leans in.

Luciana tries to step between us. "Stop—"

I stop her with my hand. I don't want her getting hurt. But I lean in. "If that's how you want to do this."

"What the fuck is happening here?" Chase asks from behind.

He's next to us in one second, his gaze bouncing from Lux to Mateo and back to my hand on her in front of her chest.

"Chase." Mateo smiles. "Congratulations."

The smile is not reciprocated. Instead, Chase turns to his sister. "I didn't know you brought a date."

"I didn't."

Chase nods and looks at me. "You good, Coach?"

I look at Mateo. "Yeah."

"Oh. You know who this motherfuck—"

He cuts Mateo off. "If my sister didn't invite you, who did you come here with?"

Mateo stiffens and opens his mouth.

"No," Lux says.

Mateo's mouth curves a little. "I came with Miss Marilyn."

Chase's face hardens, and instinctively, I place myself closer to the middle, between the two men.

"You brought her here?" There's something telling about the way

Chase says the words. It hangs in the air, charging it with tension. It's the tone you hear before a fist hits your face.

"She called and asked me to escort her. She said Lux needed a date, and she wanted to see her son get married."

"Did you ask my sister about that?" Chase doesn't sound like he believes Mateo.

Mateo rolls his eyes. "I didn't need to. She's your mother. She has the right to be here."

Chase shifts ever so slightly, but I'm there with my hand on his shoulder.

"Cam is going to handle it. Marilyn is going back," Lux tells her brother.

"Who's going to drive her back? This douche?" Chase doesn't take his eyes off him.

"I'm not sure, but don't worry about it. Mateo, get out of here." She points at him and then in the direction of the entrance.

"Luxxy, we need to talk," Mateo says.

She sighs and turns to me. "Let me make sure Cam gets her out of here. I'll be right in there. Chase, you need to go inside before Lauren realizes Marilyn is around. We don't need that."

I pat his arm. "Come on. It's your wedding day. Let's go back inside."

We start to walk away then Chase stops and looks back. "Mess with Lux again, and I'm going to break your knees. You know she's the reason I haven't beat the bricks off of you. But you're not together anymore, and I'm tired of seeing you around my family. You better not be here when I come back out to check on her."

The way Mateo shifts on his feet, he believes him.

Shit, I believe him. Chase is a big dude who's not afraid of bumping against things. I guide him away.

"I don't think he'll be here," I say.

"He's not very smart, but it's been a while since I beat up anyone. This one will feel good." Everything in Chase's tone tells me he's not joking at all.

Before we go in, I look back one more time, and Lux is standing in front of Mateo with her arms crossed. "I'll come back to check on her if she doesn't return with Cam."

Chase nods. "He's not dumb enough to try anything. He knows Cam and I would castrate him like we've been wanting to—not physically, anyway."

"Does he hurt her in other ways?"

We are walking to the open bar. "He's fucked around on her too many times."

We order two shots. It's as much as I'll allow myself and only because we'll be here for a few hours. I have to drive Ayla home tonight. The bartender pours McCallan for both of us.

But my mind is still outside in the lobby. "Why does Lux go back to him? She's too good for that."

The question is out of my lips before I can stop it. Chase's eyes sharpen on me. I just made a big mistake.

"You like her, don't you?"

I'm not a coward. "I do, but she's your and Cam's sister."

He smiles, and I don't know what to make of that. Is he telling me to fuck off?

"She is, and I would break the balls of anyone who hurt her. God knows I'm dying to put my hands on that fucker out there. But she's a big girl." He rolls his eyes. "I just don't want to see her suffer. She needs some time alone to wash that asshole off her palate."

"I would feel the same if I had a sister." At least a sister who recognized me as a brother and wasn't ashamed that I had a different mother.

"You're a good man, Coach. Cam and I agree on that. Lux is not in a good place to get into a relationship. She needs to let that bullshit out there go for good." He hooks a thumb on the door.

"I get it. I do. I'm not making moves."

He nods. "You're by the book, and you've proven to be a good friend to me and my wife." He smiles wider as he says it. "Lauren is my wife now."

He tells me like I wasn't there when they walked down the aisle, when they took their vows, and when they danced together for the first time as husband and wife. I understand, though. He loves his girl.

Everything reflecting on his face is what a man should feel on his wedding day.

A man shouldn't feel tension or reproaching stares from family members at his wedding. A man shouldn't be wondering if he was making the biggest mistake of his life.

I did. Because I had.

"You're both going to be very happy."

They are, because there's an understanding. Because their love is palpable whenever they are in a room together. Because Chase is really a good guy who has taken her nephews as his own sons.

From the dance floor, Lauren and the boys are waving at him to come over.

"I can't hide from the dancing forever." Chase doesn't stop smiling.

"Go over there and shake your hips, but not too much. You shouldn't look like a girl." I laugh at the way the smile slides off his face. "Don't be scared. It's just bachata."

He smiles again and goes to join them. Ayla is holding Avelyn, and they're all dancing and passing the baby around.

I look to the door and head to find Luciana. I nearly bowl over Cam.

"Hey," I say.

He sighs. "It's taken care of. One of my drivers is taking Marilyn and Mateo back to the airport."

"Oh."

"Thanks for your help, Coach. I'm going to go see if Adri needs help."

I go out into the lobby, but Luciana is not where I left her. I walk to the end of the hallway and find her in one of the sitting rooms. It's a sunroom with a view of the backyard. She's looking down at her phone, but the screen is all dark.

"You okay?"

She looks up and pastes a smile on her face, one that doesn't reach her eyes. "Yeah. I just needed some time to breathe."

"How's the air?"

She laughs. "Good. I guess. Thank you for your help earlier."

"Don't mention it."

"Too bad it didn't work, and Chase found out anyway. I don't want his day ruined."

"Last time I saw him, he was headed to dance with his wife and sons. He had the biggest smile on his face. Nothing can ruin that man's day."

Her lips curve in that big wide smile of hers—the one that makes my mouth dry. I want to kiss her so bad. "He's so in love. Lauren is too. Before, she was more guarded about what she felt for him, but now it's so open. It's beautiful and uncomfortable to see."

I laugh. "Why uncomfortable?"

"He's my brother."

"I guess I get it." Then again, I don't.

"Do you have brothers?"

I hesitate, because how much should I really say? Then, I decide to go with the truth because I have nothing to be ashamed of. "I do. Three brothers and a sister, but I don't know them. They're from my dad's marriage. We have different mothers."

"Oh. I'm sorry."

I shake my head. "Don't be. It's all good."

"But they're your brothers. As annoying as mine are, I can't be without them for long. Do they know you exist?"

I nod. "They don't want to know me."

We fall into silence.

I want to ask her to go inside, but she's not ready. I sit on the chair across from her. There's a frown on her face, and she's looking out the window. Whatever went down with Mateo had to be heavy. She looks so lost.

She shakes her head a few times.

"Do you want to talk about it?" I ask.

She nods. "Yeah, because I don't get it. How can they not want to know you? You're a good guy and so loving with Ayla."

My jaw goes slack. She's talking about my siblings, and that look on her face is like she can't believe it. Like she can't accept that someone wouldn't want to know me.

"Is that what you were thinking about?"

She brushes her hair back with her hand. "Well…yeah. It's more perplexing than what I was thinking about before…my mother."

"I thought you were thinking about Mateo."

She scoffs. "Why would I be thinking about him?"

I shrug. "He's your ex, who came all the way here to see you. And he wants you back."

"He always wants me back, Ollie, but that's not about me. It's about his ego. I'm over him, and he can't handle that."

I'm not convinced. He's possessive with her. "Are you sure? He seems very determined."

"Every time he messes up and I cut him off, he's more set on getting back with me. I'm just status to him."

That is the most ridiculous thing I've heard. "Have you seen yourself? Have you seen the way he looks at you? The way every man who is not related to you looks at you? You're more than just status."

She chuckles. "Yeah, the most popular vlogger in New York and Cam's sister. I'm also a trophy."

"You're the prize, Lux."

There goes that smile again, that lip disappearing behind her teeth ever so briefly.

You just told Chase you weren't after her. Get the hell away from her before you break your word. "We should go back inside."

She nods before leaning in. Almost instinctively, I turn my head, and my lips drag across hers. I reach for her.

"Aunt Lux," Bron calls out.

We jump back.

"Coming," she answers and stands up. "Thanks, Oliver. I'm happy you're here. You totally saved the day today."

She rushes out, leaving me with a pounding heart and the sense that everything just took a different turn.

THE BOUGIE LIFE IS HERE

By Bougie Girl

You're used to seeing me as your regular blogger. Bougie Girl is the one that tells you what products to try, where to get the best massage to smooth the stress out of your body, and who to go to for a blowout that will have your hair flowing like a Mariah Carey meme. For years now, I've prided myself on finding gems for you, places that will have you feeling like a socialite on a budget.

But all good things must end...or transform into bigger platforms with more and better content!

I'm proud to tell you that I'm moving up—well, down since I'm now living in Maryland. Next week, I am launching my own YouTube channel as well as my own section in Big Apple Magazine.

What does the move mean?

I'll still be doing the trying, the finding, and the reviews, but now all of it will be on a bigger scale. The Bougie Life is coming to your phone, tablet, computer, or smart TV. It's a chance for you to get to know more about me. I'll be doing more videos and featuring the content you've been asking me for.

I'll go live with you to show you my morning and evening routines.

I'll also be following the products you suggest for me and trying them along with you. You can go through my house renovation journey. If I take a weekend trip, I'm taking you with me—because we're besties, you and me. We're growing and changing together.

If there's something we all need to learn, it is not to be afraid to tweak, flip, change something for a new version of it that can be better, more passionate, and more satisfying than the way it is now. Risk is part of the game. When you risk nothing, you gain nothing, and every-thing is in peril. That which doesn't grow dies. So, let's go after the unknown and exciting together.

How do we start this new journey?

In the most personal of ways, of course.

My first video will be in my new studio at home. I can't wait for you to see it.

The next one will be an afternoon with a stylist, featuring my sister, Lauren, the founder of Autumn Lush. I don't even have to tell you what it is, but in case you've been living off the grid, Autumn Lush is an exclusive, stylish store located in Baltimore. It recently launched its own on-demand styling line, mixing high-end, low-end, and mid-range priced pieces. In my first piece for The Bougie Life, let's do a day in the life of a stylist and see a concept from beginning to end.

Are you coming along for the ride? You're as bougie as I am. I know you want to.

Xoxo,

The Bougie One

11

Three Months Later

Lux

I love the new facade of the house. The door was already relocated to the center, and the new entrance system was installed. I take a second to pause, adjust my earbuds, and take a photo. The new windows look wonderful, definitely worth the extra money so nothing can break them from the outside.

I'm recording the first video for the channel in the new space. Only half the area is finished, but that's all we need to record a video sitting at my desk. The next one will be at Autumn Lush, and I can't wait for that one either. Lauren has so many fun things to do there.

Nothing can blur the excitement I feel today—not even the conversation I'm having with my mother right now. She's like background noise or elevator music. It's happening, but it's not touching any part of me.

"Thank you for my Manolos. When I got the exclusive newsletter the other day, it was love at first sight," Marilyn gushes. Her excitement is so palpable I shift my gaze to my phone screen. Her face is glowing in a way I haven't seen in a long time.

It's a clean glow that triggers a smile of my own. I know this kind of giddy happiness. Every girl should get a pair of their favorite shoes on her birthday. It brings joy to us like nothing else. "Happy birthday. I hope you wear them often."

"I will. I'm going shopping for the perfect outfit for them. They don't do enough pieces in baby blue these days. Magazines are also not giving the classic designers enough promotion. That's something you can do when your new channel comes out."

Tension rings like a bell at the base of my spine. I haven't really talked to her much about the new channel. I haven't talked to her at all since the New York episode, and I don't want to make the call longer than it needs to be. I don't want to have to explain what this means to me. "I'll think about it, Marilyn. I really have to go now. I need to get some things in place before the crew gets there. We're recording an episode today."

"Oh. That's exciting. I read the announcement *Big Apple* made. I'm really proud of you, Luciana."

Proud.

I'm stuck on the word. She never says she is proud of us, except when Cam is getting a lot of press for his games or when the magazines feature him. Because those are tangibles in her world. She can brag about that.

"Thank you."

"You're going to be even more famous now and make more money. Did you know that Libby Emerson told me the other day that her daughters wait until you review products before they use them? I found out that your endorsement of the Golden Spa got them so overbooked there's a long waiting list."

I'm on her radar. That's the only place I don't want to be.

"Thank you for that. If you need me to make you an appointment, I can make a call and get you in. But I really have to g—"

"I would love an appointment, but before you go, I want you to do me a favor."

Whatever it takes to get you off the phone and your attention off me.

"Sure. What is it?"

"Can you please call your father?"

My stomach sinks. "What? No."

"He's not doing well, Luciana. He's been sick, and he told Elias he wants to talk to you. I know the three of you don't believe he has changed, but he's working on himself. He's going to church in there. Give him a chance. Oh. Eddha, someone's at the door. I have to go, Luciana."

She hangs up, leaving me frozen outside my door. I'm floored for a second. It's like she threw a grenade and ran.

Well, don't stand there and let it blow up in your face. Open the door and get out of the way.

I head upstairs to my bedroom to take out some of the stuff that I'll need to film. We're filming on the far side of the room where Ollie's crew has already finished the wall. *Big Apple* staff was here earlier, arranging the area and decorating that side of the room with everything we need.

I grab a few things from my dresser so I can put them on the desk. These are things I bought to decorate with.

My phone pings.

> **ELIAS**
>
> Your mom told me to contact you. Your dad really wants to see you.

I text back.

> **ME**
>
> She told me.
>
> Do you know what that's about?

> **ELIAS**
>
> He's been sick and really down. He's sad because you never call. The doctor said it would be good for him to hear from you.

I send two words back and dump my phone in the tote in front of me.

LUX

Thank you

Walter wants to see me. Why the hell? Why now? I went with Marilyn last time she visited him. I try to call every couple of months. Why a visit?

I stand in the middle of the room, looking around. *What else do I need?*

It would help to talk this out. Except, with who?

It would be awkward to talk to Cam. How do I tell my big brother that our father, the man who kidnapped his daughter, wants to talk to me? And forget talking to Chase. Walter made his life miserable and treated him like shit—something that really didn't hit home until he told us Chase is not his biological son. Chase has every right to hate him.

That day, Walter changed so many things in my life.

I used to love my daddy. He was my reprieve from Marilyn. I was his little girl. But that all changed when I grew up. When I saw how cruel he was with my brother, I couldn't believe he was the same dad who used to carry me on his shoulders. Then, the incident happened, and I was done with him.

The image sneaks in my head so quicky. Walter walking out of the room. His friend smiling so wide and sitting next to me. Then, me running and him right behind me. Locking myself in the bathroom and calling Chase while panicking.

My heart quickens. No, I won't think about that day.

I can't let myself remember how my father was angry at my brother for coming to my rescue instead of at the man who tried to touch me.

It still burns and hurts because Walter is my dad. I envy that Chase can say he's not related to him, that Walter's blood is not running through his veins. Cam and I are stuck, but my older brother has found his way out. He's cut him off, because he's made a family that has nothing to do with Walter. And he's keeping Marilyn at bay.

I try, but I can only run so much from her. She's never far behind, though.

I swallow the lump in my throat and swat at the tears that force themselves to the corners of my eyes. I can't conjure those memories without triggering myself. *Today is not the day to cry, Luciana.*

I run upstairs to the third floor. I've learned that if I want to keep the tears away, I need to keep busy. Let me go arrange stuff the way I want it before the crew comes back. Here, by myself, I can self-soothe and get emotionally prepared to film. I can cry myself to sleep tonight. For now, I just need to hold on and work.

I make it up the stairs and stop dead in my tracks as I look to the back of the room.

Wow.

It looks amazing. The desk is set, the lights are off, but the walls are pristine, showcasing canvases of New York. The big desk I chose to match the one in Cam's office, except in blue-green wood, reigns in the middle of the space.

Ollie's crew has already installed one of the sky boxes. It looks exactly the way I dreamed it would. And for some reason I can't explain, that makes the tears spill. I should be happy. My dream is coming true, but the mere mention of Walter's name, the simple implication that he wants to see me, brings me down like a boulder. It's the memories. They darken a day full of beauty.

"If it's wrong, we can fix it."

My blood freezes in my veins, and I whip around so fast I drop my bag. My hand goes straight to my chest. Oliver is on the unfinished side of the room. He's kneeling on the floor.

"I didn't know you were going to be here. We're filming."

He stands slowly. "You told me I could come and do some inspection."

My heart is still hammering in my chest, and I keep thinking. I did tell him to come by yesterday. I forgot after talking to Marilyn, because that is what she does, upends my world.

"I'm sorry. You're right. I guess I forgot for a minute."

I run my hand through my hair and bend to pick up the tote. Some of the things I brought up spilled out.

The make-up palette I wanted to wear cracked.

"Oh no."

Ollie is by my side in my next breath. "Are you okay?"

I shake my head but then nod. "I'm fine. I need to arrange some of these things on the desk. I want this stuff to look authentic, and I wanted to feature that eyeshadow palette but dropped it like an idiot."

I reach down, but he grabs my hand in his. "There's glass. Let me get it. I'm sure you have more makeup."

My gaze snaps to his. The look on his face tells me he doesn't understand.

"This palette comes from a small business. It's this young woman who created her own makeup line to support her family. If I talk about her, it could help her sales. Now I can't do that because it's ruined."

"Oh. I'm sorry. I don't understand a lot about this," he says.

"It's okay. It's not your fault."

"I can go out and buy you another."

It's the nicest thing to say, and I have to swat at my tears some more. "She sent it to me in the mail. The stores don't carry her yet. Oh wait. Lauren has one. I'll text her and have the crew pick it up from her."

I fire up a text to Lauren and another to the make-up artist that's coming.

Ollie is on the floor, picking up the stuff, and I'm just standing there, watching. The pretty turquoise eyeshadow spilled everywhere. He grabs a hand vacuum and sucks it up.

"All clean."

"Thank you," is all I can say.

He puts the vacuum away and comes back. "Why don't you go sit over there and catch your breath?"

I shake my head. "I'll be sitting soon when they come to do my makeup. Right now, I need to set my stuff up. I don't want them to do this for me. It's important that this is my design."

"Let me help you, then," he offers.

I don't get to say no. He lifts the tote and puts it on the desk.

"Thank you," I say again like the idiot that I feel.

He begins taking things out of the bag. "Don't thank me anymore. Put me to work. What do I do?"

"I'm sure you have stuff to do. You don't have to help me with this."

He smiles. It's that megawatt smile that disarms me and loosens my underwear. "It's no biggie, and I want to."

My insides shiver a little, and I'm leaning slightly toward him. *Remember, this is just professional.* I straighten up and rummage through the bag. "Why are you being so nice?"

"Because I think you're having a bad day, and this is your first video. You're probably nervous, so I want to help in any way I can."

I didn't expect that.

"I'm not nervous. I've done this many times. I'm excited."

His gaze stays on my face, like he zooms in on me closer. "You don't seem excited. You look...sad."

"It's nothing. I talked to my mom...you've met her," I say like that explains everything, and it should. He's seen her cause a scene before.

"Did you fight with her?"

I shake my head and place the statue of the female Buddha on the corner of my desk. "With her, it's never a fight. God, I need to get a hold of myself before the crew gets here."

"Why don't you postpone it for a day when you feel better?"

I shake my head. "No, they all came here to work from New York and probably want to get back home. It wouldn't be fair. This will pass. I just need to breathe this out."

"Do you want to tell me about it?"

I shake my head. I don't need to get more emotional than I am, but I find myself opening my mouth anyway.

"You know about Walter, right?" I blurt out.

"That's your father?"

I nod. "He's in jail."

His gaze is slightly strained. "I know. Cam told me he took Bron."

It's so embarrassing. "He did. I don't have a relationship with him. It's a long story, but my mom asked me to call him. He wants to see me."

"And you don't want to?"

I pause and do a gut check. *Do I want to see him? Am I intrigued? Why am I letting this bother me so much?* "I don't know. He's horrible. They both are. They messed us up so bad. But Elias told my mom he's been sick and that he wants to talk to me."

"How does Elias know?"

"He's always been friends with my dad."

"Friends? I thought he was Cam's best friend."

I nod. "He used to be. It's complicated. Everything about this has too many layers. Anyway, I was having a great day. I didn't even mind talking to my mom on her birthday until she brought this up. She said he's sick. All I can think about is how bad things were with him. How bad he treated Chase. He treated us like objects he could use. He didn't protect me—"

Stop.

Don't say anything else.

Oliver's gaze narrows. "What do you mean he didn't protect you?"

"Nothing." I shake my head. "It's old, and I'm over it."

He takes my shoulders in his hands. "I don't think you are, and you can trust me."

His hands are so strong and warm. So reaffirming is the look in his eyes that I can't help but believe him.

"One of Walter's friends got handsy with me. Wouldn't take no for an answer. Walter didn't believe me and sided with the man. He tried to get Chase arrested for stomping on him."

Emotions flash through his face like a slide show on 2X speed. His jaw clenches, and his hands tighten around me. "Did that man hurt you?"

A flash of fear blows over me. I've never seen this look on Oliver's face.

"No, I locked myself in the closet and called my brother. Chase did a number on him. I don't think he'll ever bother a woman again."

Oliver bobs his head up and down, easing his grip a little. But he pulls me closer and wraps his arms around me. I let myself feel his warmth, the way our bodies mold to each other. It's comforting and triggers the instinct to bring myself closer.

I open my mouth only to close it and open it again. It takes two more tries before I can find my voice. "If we keep hugging like this, I'm going to cry, and I can't do that right now. I can't let the crew see me like this."

He pulls back but doesn't drop his arms. "You shouldn't have gone through that. Your father should have believed you. I'm glad Chase was there."

"Thank you. I don't think Walter knew he would try that, but it hurt me that he would stand up for that guy. He would've pressed charges against Chase if Cam had not threatened to cut him off financially. Anyway, you see why it's so complicated?"

"Yes. But let me say this: you have the right to your feelings. You have the right to say you never want to see him again. He should have protected you."

"Shouldn't I at least want to see what he wants? Or what he needs?"

He shakes his head. "Only if it doesn't bring you down. You have to take care of yourself too."

"I know, but now I feel like—"

"A traitor," he finishes.

I can only nod.

"Don't. Remember I told you about my dad and my siblings once? He only wanted something to do with me when I got the MLB contract. He was calling me *son* and coming to see me in Chicago. I was dumb enough to fall for it. When I walked away from it, it was like I didn't exist again."

It makes me sad for him, but I understand. "Sounds like Walter. He was only happy with us when we did things that brought him money.

He and my mother are all about the money and prestige we can bring them."

"Is he on his deathbed?"

I frown. "I don't think so. They didn't say it was an emergency."

"Then put it out of your mind for now. Can you do that?"

The doorbell rings.

I turn to him. "I have no choice."

12

Ollie

Her emotions flip like a light switch. The doorbell rings. Lux unlocks the door with her phone. She hands me the other items for her desk, and I place them where she points. She dabs at the corners of her eyes, and by the time her coworkers reach the third floor, she's pasted a smile on her face.

"Hello," she says, hugging and kissing each person on the cheek.

"Mimi is downstairs. She's taking a phone call," the guy dressed all in black says.

Lux straightens up and sucks in a breath, but seconds later, a tall skinny brunette comes up the stairs.

She beelines for Lux and hugs her like she's an old friend. "Are you ready for your big moment?"

Lux nods. "Yes. I didn't know you were coming."

"I wanted to be here for the first one. I'm sure you'll be your usual gorgeous, extroverted, sexy, and genuine self. And that will make the video perfect. I'm just here to make sure the adornments, lighting, makeup, and angles all play up to you."

Lux's smile wavers, but Mimi doesn't seem to notice. Instead, she turns around and looks at me. There's a catch in her eyes, that widening I can't miss even though my attention is only mildly on her.

My gaze is here only for Lux, especially after her confession. I hate that she has to do this even though she's not feeling up to it.

Mimi is oblivious as she walks up to me and blocks Lux from my view. She's almost as tall as me. "And you are?"

I extend my hand. "I'm Oliver. I'm Lux's contractor—"

"Oliver is my friend," Lux says behind her. "I wouldn't just trust any contractor in my personal space."

The word trust hits me straight in the chest, first her confession about what happened with her father's friend and now this. I don't even get to recover from that, because Mimi squeezes my hand and smiles into my face like the Cheshire Cat, just a little more cunning and a lot more polished.

"No wonder she fought to keep you. I must admit, I would have fought too."

"Excuse me?" *Lux fought to keep me?*

"Mimi, he's really just a friend."

"I'm sure he is." She winks at me and squeezes my hand a little too tight.

I know women like her. She's friendly with Lux and suspects there's something going on between us, but I am sure she would press herself against me and run those overly lined lips over my jaw the second we were alone in a room.

I extricate my hand as gently as I can. "I'll go finish my measurements and plans adjustments on the other side of the room. I'll be very quiet so I don't bother you."

"You're not a bother at all. Right, Luxxy?"

Lux is saved from answering because she's already sitting in a chair, and the make-up artist is spraying something on her face. She has her eyes closed.

I go about my duties, examining the new walls. There's supposed to be an exact number of wall plugs and connection points for all the electric devices—lighting, sound connectivity, the wiring for the heated floor. I'm only barely paying attention to what's going on, but from time to time, I look up and watch.

They're using too much makeup. Lux is already gorgeous. Her skin is glowing, and her lips are edible. She's perfect the way she is, but they keep drawing lines on her face. I hope Ayla doesn't ever start doing all this stuff.

Lux is still not smiling, and her eyes look liquid, like she may cry any minute, but no one seems to notice. They're testing the lighting and ooh and ahh over my light boxes. Lux goes to the bathroom, and Mimi starts directing people to move things around. She also has them add other products with labels I don't recognize in those same spots that Lux asked me to place her things.

I open my mouth to say something, but Lux returns, and my eyes almost fall out of my head.

She's wearing a green blouse that leaves her shoulders bare and molds itself to her waist. It makes her eyes look greener. She looks edible, delicious, and fuckable from every angle. But there's still no smile in sight. Then her gaze shifts to the desk, and color breaks out on her cheeks. She takes her place behind the desk and begins to shift things back.

"Luxxy, I had them change those to be more aesthetically pleasing. The desk needs to be the focal point," Mimi says.

"I want them where they were because it's more feng shui that way. I want the Green Tara in my right hand for a reason," Lux argues. "It was a gift from a friend. Also, I don't want anything directly in front of me because I'll be facing the camera, and from what I understand that's the best spot to shoot."

The camera man agrees. "She's right, Mimi. We need a clean shot of Lux instead of the knick-knacks."

It earns him a snap of Mimi's head. "These are products we are sponsoring."

"Yeah, this is just in bad taste. I don't want to sponsor things blatantly. I'm not against doing a soft placing, but everyone knows this is not me." Lux points at the stuff on the desk. "I have not vetted these products. I don't want my audience thinking I'm giving them the okay when I don't know what these even do." Her voice is strong and her tone firm.

"Luxxy, you're a brand now, and you're going to have your own channel. You won't have the time to review everything before it makes it to a video."

"Yes, I get that, but I don't want to make false advertising a norm. We talked about this."

Mimi's lips form into a flat line. "I know we did, but we need to find a compromise."

"We are. I'm not banning all of them from my desk. I'm keeping the ones that make sense. The other ones will have to go somewhere else. Nobody keeps a tin of tea on their desk. That belongs in a kitchen. If it was a mug, I wouldn't mind, but just a bag tea I haven't tried? That's a firm no from me. They can send me that pink gold-rimmed mug that they have on their website. It has the company name, but on the other side, it has an inspirational quote. I would definitely feature that."

They stare at each other for a tense moment.

Mimi sighs. "I think I have one of those in my car. I'll go get it."

The minute she is out of the room, the makeup artist high-fives Lux while the rest cover their laughs with their hands.

Our gazes meet, and her lips part.

"You look beautiful," I mouth, and her smile spreads.

It pulls at a string in my chest, and my body warms ups, like she touched me, like she's still wrapped in my arms.

She sits, and they start testing the lights with her, drawing the blinds, and playing with the light boxes set up around the room.

By the time Mimi gets back, they're ready to shoot. She hands Lux the mug, and she places it near her.

I get back to my work and only look up when they start counting down.

Five…four…three…two…

The smile materializes again on her lips, like she's almost happy.

"Hi, Gorgeous. It's Bougie Girl. If you follow my videos for *Big Apple* and my blogs, hi again. If you've never heard of me, I'm Lux, and I welcome you to my channel. I experience the bougie life so I can tell you the best places to go and what products to try. You can then make the best decisions for you. If you're bougie like me, then come on aboard.

"Hit that *like* button and subscribe to get notifications any time I upload a new video, which between you and me..."—she inches forward as if telling a secret to the camera—"it's going to be almost every day."

The teasing in her eyes is soft and sexy. I can definitely see why they hired her for this. She's a natural with the camera. She's so good it almost fools me. But when they break, there's a tiredness in her eyes, and her shoulders droop like she's been weighed down.

The minute the camera is back on, she brightens up like they shot her with adrenaline or something that just makes you happy and bright-eyed.

"I'm so excited we're on this journey together. New channel, new home, new life. I'll be showing you the rooms as they finish them. My next video is going to be a super special one. I'm going to be doing a series from Autumn Lush and follow its owner, Lauren Guerrera, as she styles a bride, shows us how she puts together outfits for her personal styling service and the online version. She's going to let me tag along and help her. Drop a note in the comments about what occasions you would like to see us style, and we'll choose the most popular ones."

I finish what I need to do, but I stay there, watching her, enthralled by how good she is at this. My phone vibrates, and it's a message from Ayla.

Shit, I need to go pick her up.

I stand with the phone in my hand.

> AYLA
>
> B and I need to work on our presentation for English. Can I go home with her, and you can pick me up from there?

I fire back a quick response.

I'll check to see if it's okay with her parents.

I send a text to Cam, explaining and asking if that is okay. His reply is immediate.

CAM

Of course it is. Love having her over. Adri is picking them up. Hey, you at Lux's? How is she doing in her first shoot?

Your sister looks sexy and fuckable, and she's like light in a dark room. I want to bend her over on that desk and knock Mimi's tea mug on the floor. That's what I want to say. Instead, I text back.

Me

She's doing great and is a natural at this.

All true things—just not my truth.
He replies.

CAM

Good to know. This is a big step for her.

When they wrap up, they take photos of her. She plays up for the camera with different kinds of smile. There's a shy one, then she switches up to surprise, like she didn't know anyone was in the room. Then she hits them with my favorite: that extra-wide one that begs me to taste her lips and eat her up.

"God, these promotional shots are going to be such a hit," Mimi says. "We'll also choose one for the video thumbnail. Once the graphic department has done their magic, we'll pass it on for your approval."

"Thanks for coming, Mimi. Having you here was really good."

It's the right thing to say, because Mimi preens. "Bah. You are a pro, Luxxy. You would have nailed this all on your own."

"I loved having your support."

Mimi hugs her. "I'll take the whole team to dinner tonight to celebrate. I'm sending a limo for you."

No one seems to notice the cloud that ghosts over her face, but she blinks it away. "That will be fun. See you all tonight." Lux excuses herself to go downstairs.

Everyone goes around the room, picking up everything and putting it away. I tape the tarp to protect the finished side of the room and slide the doors to close off the section.

Mimi grabs her purse and comes to shake my hand. "It was great to meet you. You're doing a great job with her studio. I can't wait to see the finished version. If it's as good as this side, we'll have to hire you for more stuff."

"Thank you," I stammer because that could be huge for me too.

"I'm so glad she insisted on having you as part of her package deal."

My face must be as blank as my thoughts, because Mimi laughs. "Oh. She didn't tell you that she demanded we keep you as her contractor. It's written into the contract and everything, but let's keep it our secret, then." She winks, adding, "Do you have a business card? We have other projects you may be able to help with."

I nod and fish one out of my wallet.

"Bye, Oliver," she says and walks away.

The makeup artist comes to shake my hand. "Be careful. She's a succubus. Nice to meet you, man."

I finish up and then head downstairs ten minutes later. Lux is in her kitchen, in joggers, a sweatshirt, and a freshly scrubbed face.

How can she be so pretty with makeup or without?

How can she be so hot in this plain sweatsuit?

I need to check my hormones. I'm acting like a teenage boy.

"Are you okay?" I ask.

She nods. "Glad it's freaking over. Just hope it all turned out well."

"Are you kidding? You were great. You're going to get a lot of likes."

She pauses in front of a cabinet. "Really? You think so?"

I nod. "You're a natural."

"Thanks. I'm making hot chocolate. Would you like some?"

I nod. "Thank you, but shouldn't you be drinking champagne?"

She snorts. "I'll be doing that tonight apparently."

"You don't seem enthusiastic about that."

"I would rather celebrate with those closest to me. But the crew deserves this. They worked really hard." She sets a kettle with water on the stove and takes out a fancy tin of chocolate.

She's going to mess it up.

She catches me staring. "You make your hot chocolate with milk, don't you?"

"How did you know?"

"You have that same look on your face that Lauren and Adri do when we go to a restaurant and it's made with water."

"We, Dominicans, are really particular about our hot chocolate. When it's made with water, there's a science to it and a specific type of chocolate. With milk, it is easier to get it right for others."

She steps back and waves me in. "Be my guest."

I smile at her. "Do you have evaporated milk, sugar, ginger, and cinnamon?"

She goes to grab them. Then, I wave her to the chair.

She chuckles and sits. "It better be as good as Lauren and Adri's."

"Listen, Ayla loves my hot chocolate, and kids are the worst when it comes to stuff. They never like anything."

"Okay. I'll let you know."

I mix everything and serve it in the mugs. She sits on her couch, and I take one of the armchairs across from her. I don't trust myself to be closer, not when she's blowing over the steam ever so slowly. Her puckered lips should look cute, but it's just uncomfortable for me. It brings back memories.

I shift on my seat. "How come you said yes when you don't want to go tonight? Just because of the crew?"

She nods. "If it were just Mimi, I would probably find a way to say no, but I like my glam squad." She takes a sip, and her eyes close, her expression turning into pure bliss.

My mouth dries, but I find my voice. If I keep talking, it won't be awkward. "Good, isn't it?"

Her eyes are bottomless, like a green tunnel, as she looks at me. "So good. I need this recipe."

I shake my head. "We can only pass it on to other Dominicans."

"Then you just need to make me come every time I want it."

I freeze for a second, and then my cock twitches. *Did I hear her right?*

"I'm sorry. What did you say?"

She frowns. "I said you'll have to come and make it for me every time I want it."

"Oh. I'm sorry I didn't hear you right."

She pushes a strand of hair behind her ear. "I'm sorry. It was a joke. I didn't mean to make you uncomfortable."

"You didn't. I just didn't hear you."

She tilts her head. "You seem uncomfortable."

"No. Just disappointed."

Oh fuck.

"Why?"

"No reason. I didn't mean to say that. I should probably go." I stand and grab my bag.

She intercepts me at the stairs. "I'll walk you out."

I shake my head. "You don't have to."

Then she smiles. It's soft and stretches her lips. "Are you nervous?"

Nervous? Me? No, just horny and dying to kiss you. "No. I just need to get going."

"Ah, okay. I'm sorry." She takes a step toward me, and it takes all of me to not to step back. "I just want to thank you for being there for me earlier."

"I didn't do anything, just helped you arrange stuff."

"Not only that part but for listening and for this hot chocolate. I can't believe I told you all of that. I don't even like talking about it. It meant a lot how understanding and great you were, and it helped more than you know."

I lean a little toward her. I can't help it. It's the smile, the eyes, the way her body calls out to me. "I like that you trust me. That's what friends are for."

"Friends." She offers me her hand, and I grab it in mine.

She moves a step closer, climbing on her toes and pressing a kiss against my cheek, way too close to the corner of my mouth. The contact is electric, and the feel of her lips travels all over my skin, my left hand resting at her waist.

And she hums.

Because she must feel it like I do.

Let her go, Oliver.

She pulls back a little, pressing another kiss, this time on the corner of my lips. My reflex is to pull her against my chest.

And we are facing each other, her breath fanning my lower lip.

I need to let her go.

I need to go. Get away fast before it's impossible for me to go.

But she inches up more and brushes her mouth to mine, her tongue sliding over my lips.

This is not good.

It's soft, sweet, and sexy.

It's fucking heaven.

I let go of her hand so I can hold her at the base of her neck and caress her back as my mouth opens, and I take control of the kiss.

She doesn't taste like I remember. Her mouth is more potent, wetter, hotter.

Her hands are grabbing onto my sweater, and she's pressing herself tighter to me. I can feel her tits, the pebbles of her nipples through her sweater.

She hums again, and I need to feel the skin of her back, so my hand sneaks under her top.

"Lux. What the fuck? You left the door open."

We both freeze.

It's Chase.

Shit.

She pulls back, looking to the stairs and then back at me. "I'll be back."

She darts off and disappears into the hallway. I cross the room to sit in my vacant chair. The last thing I need is for him to catch me with a woody in his sister's family room. My butt hits the seat just as Chase reaches the upstairs.

Her brother is big, like a tight end. Even with a bouquet of flowers in one hand and a gift bag in the other, he looks menacing. And if he had walked upstairs a few minutes earlier, he probably would have beat my ass and then made me eat all those roses and the peonies too.

"Coach." His smile is unsure. If 'what the fuck are you doing here?' was a facial expression, it would look just like him right now.

I manage a smile of my own. "I was inspecting the work today and got caught in the middle of the taping. I thought I mentioned yesterday that I was coming to do work here."

He frowns and then smiles again, more assured this time. "You're right. I'm sorry. You know I have two kids now. A lot of stuff to remember."

He looks over to the hot chocolate mugs.

Yeah, I'm going to have to fight him.

"I get that. I stayed until the end because they were taping her video. Lux offered me some hot chocolate."

"Oh." Chase nods. "Did it go okay?"

"I don't know much about that stuff, but I thought she did great. Mimi thought so too."

"Oh, God. Mimi was here? Thank God I missed that," Chase says, moving to the couch. He takes Lux's mug and takes a sip. "This tastes like Lauren's hot chocolate."

"Yeah, it's really good." I start to push off the chair.

He points at the chair I left vacant. "Stay a little, Coach."

I nod. "Only for a bit. I have to go get Ayla."

"She's at Cam's. I just spoke to Bron on the phone."

"Yeah, but I don't want to abuse the friendship and leave her there for too long."

He chuckles. "You're kidding, right? She helps out with CJ. If it was up to Bron, she would move in today."

I laugh. "Yeah, I know how that goes. She loves to remind me they're going to college together. I hope they stay best friends forever."

"They will. Look at Lauren and Adri."

I nod. Adri and Lauren are great friends. *Fuck, where is Lux?*

"You okay there, Coach?"

He's going to punch me in the face, and this is going to cause a mess. "Yeah. It's been a long day."

"Lauren was telling me you have a few jobs going. You work too hard."

But not as hard as my dick is right now…

Lux's footsteps click on the hardwood floor. She's wearing flip-flops, and her face looks a little different.

She's got makeup and lipstick on.

"Ollie, I'm sorry. I was answering a call from—" Her gaze lands on her brother as if she didn't know he was there. "Hi, Chase."

He smiles at her. "You're so rude. You left Coach alone here, and your door was wide open. Anyone could walk in. You know better than that. Where are your New York instincts?"

"I'm sorry, Ollie. I had to answer that." She turns back to her brother. "What are you doing here?"

He hands her the flowers and the gift bag. "I brought you these."

She blinks a few times. "Are these from Lauren?"

"No. They're from me. I guess this is what I get for being nice."

She goes up to him and puts her arm around him. "Thank you."

As they share the tender moment, I see my opportunity to get out of here.

I stand and cross the room. "Well, I really have to go. I need to stop by Winter's house to pick up a plan I need to file with the city tomorrow before I go get Ayla."

It's not a lie. I was planning on picking that up tomorrow, but now there's enough time to do it.

"Thank you for everything, Ollie."

"We'll talk later, Coach," Chase says.

I make myself walk down the stairs at an even step. There's no way he didn't realize something was going on. The way he smiled... I've had enough talks with Chase to know the man is really smart.

I make it all the way to my car when a message comes through.

The first one is from

LUX

I'm sorry. I didn't know he was stopping by.
We need to talk later.

I hope she wants to do more than talk. I hope she wants to repeat it. *And go much further.*

Jesus, so much for staying professional.

I drive away, and three minutes later, my phone pings a second time. I wait until I'm at a light to look at it.

This one is from her brother.

CHASE

We need to have a drink and a chat, Coach.
Name the time and the place.

13

Lux

I find a vase for my flowers, lock the screen of my phone, and straighten up. I place the objects on my countertop and dig up some scissors from the drawer.

Chase is typing on his phone, probably with Lauren. I still think it was her idea for him to bring me flowers.

"These are beautiful."

He eyes the peonies and nods. "I figured you would like them. You always bought them in the spring for the house."

I blink at him a few times. It's true. "You did get these for me."

He shrugs like it's no big deal.

"I'm hungry. Can I have some more of the hot chocolate?"

Shit. I don't know how to make it.

"It's all gone. I'll make you a sandwich."

"Just like that? You're not going to make me beg or tell me to do it myself. You're just going to make me a sandwich?"

Oh no. I was too nice too fast.

"Well, you were nice enough to bring me flowers…"

He leans forward on the counter. "And a bracelet."

I run back to the living room, thankful for the distraction, and grab the bag he gave me. I tear through it and find the box. It's a tennis bracelet with charms of a purse, a heel, and a heart.

I run back and hug him again. "Thank you, Chase. It's beautiful and thoughtful. I'm so grateful."

He hugs me back. "Because you think that now I won't ask you about you and Coach."

My heart plummets straight into my belly, and I push away from him. "What are you talking about?"

He points to my living room. "I obviously interrupted something."

"Are you crazy?" I laugh. It's desperate and louder than I meant. But I can't quit. I need to commit to the lie.

"I'm not crazy. Both of you were acting, as Bron would say, *sus*. Like you got caught in the middle of something."

I take my place behind the counter again but offer him my wrist so he can help me put on the bracelet. "And, according to you, what did we get caught doing?"

"I'm not sure how far you got." He clasps the bracelet.

Far enough for my lips to still be burning from the kiss and my body humming from Oliver's big strong hands.

I shake my wrist. "You have an active imagination, Chase."

"Yes, but you can never lie well, Lux. You also can't kiss anyone without it showing all over your face. That's why you had to go touch up your makeup."

He got me.

"I wasn't touching up my makeup." *I was putting makeup on.* There's a difference.

Chase smiles at me. "I'm not mad."

"No?"

He shakes his head. "Coach is a good guy. I like him. So does Cam. But I worry because he's a friend, and you're my sister. I know Ollie— the dad, the coach, the friend. I don't know how he treats the women he dates. And you're a good girl, Lux. If it doesn't work out, I don't want you running back to Captain Dickhead."

He means Mateo.

It makes me smile because it's sweet that he worries. "Thanks, Chase, but I'm not dating Oliver. We've never even had that conversation. We're just—"

"Oh, God. Don't tell me."

I shoot him the dirtiest look I can muster and turn to the fridge. "We're not doing that either, dummy."

"Good." The relief in his voice is unmistakable. "If you do go into anything, you both need to be sure. You have too many people in common."

It's the same thing I've been telling myself since the day I met him. Since we met in the garden, and he smiled like we were naked, and he was about to throw me on top of the bouquet we were working on.

"I know that. I don't want Bron or Ayla hurt over this. Plus, again, we are not there."

He shrugs. "You like him, and he likes you. It's only a matter of time."

"I can't talk to you about this."

His face twists. "Why not?"

"You're my brother."

"And? You gave me advice once, and I let you. I didn't even hold it against you that it was shitty advice that almost got me canned by Lauren."

I close the fridge door and begin to assemble his sandwich. "My advice was great. You were probably not smart enough to execute it."

"I'm not smart enough to execute it? I'm married to her now."

He is. No one can take that from him.

"Anyway, like I said, you don't have to worry about anything."

"I have a lot to worry about, but it's fine. You're a big girl, and you can make your own decisions, but just tread carefully. You know Coach has Ayla. The kid is number one, and we all know how needy you are."

What the fuck.

The slice of ham lands square on his face, and he looks as stupid as he deserves. He peels it off his face and begins eating it.

"It's the truth. You always want people to pay attention to you."

"I hate you."

He shakes his head. "You do not. You're making me food. I just want to make sure you are okay. You've been dating Mateo way too long. I don't ever want anyone to treat you like he did, and I don't ever want you to take that from anyone again."

My chest squeezes. No matter how many times I call him my idiot brother, it's never far from my mind how I can count on him. How he's saved me before. How I can always run to him with anything.

"Thanks, Chase."

"I know I tease you a lot, but you're the whole package. You're smart, beautiful, and a good girl. Don't settle, and don't let anyone treat you less than that. But if you want to have fun, you can go ahead. Just don't ever talk about it to me or mention you're doing the nasty around me. And lock your fucking doors."

My face is burning, and all I can do is nod.

"And for fuck's sake, don't tell anyone that we had this conversation. I have a reputation to keep."

I laugh, and the embarrassment evaporates. "That was shot the moment you started running after Lauren like a lost puppy. Also, anyone who sees you with Felix and Justin knows you're a softie."

"Don't be nasty, Luciana."

I got to him. He and Cam never use my full name unless I get to them.

"I'm just saying." I put together his sandwich and put it in the panini maker. "Do you want chips?"

"Why would I want a sandwich without chips?"

"Don't be sour." I grab some chips and put them in front of him. "At the risk of ruining this tender moment, did you talk to Marilyn today?"

He sighs. "I did. Even I can't avoid her on her birthday."

"Did she mention anything about Walter?"

His hand pauses on a chip, his back going ramrod straight, his gaze zooming in on me. "No, why?"

Tension inches up my neck. "She mentioned him during our call today."

"She didn't mention him to me. Maybe she didn't want to rock the boat and risk pissing me off when I was feeling generous."

"Oh, yeah. She wouldn't want that. So that's why she sounded so happy when she spoke to me. She had already hit you up."

He grunts. "And Cam. She made out like a bandit. What did she tell you about Walter?"

His demeanor doesn't change, and he looks disinterested at best, but like everything with my brother, the underlying care is in there.

I'm most worried about him when he's silent, because in the past, that's when things went wrong. And though Lauren and the boys have stabilized him, Walter is still the sorest of subjects.

For all three of us.

"He's sick, apparently." I stop there, looking into my brother's face.

His reaction is swift. "He'll be fine. Not even the devil wants him. Just don't get caught up, Lux. If you want to put money in his commissary account, do it, but don't let Marilyn drag you into it. You don't need to take a dip into the cesspool."

The finality in his voice is unmistakable. I can't talk to him about this. Because he's right. It's a cesspool, but the bacteria is my dad.

Chase is the really lucky one. He doesn't have Walter in his genes. I can't do anything about that. That's why I envy him and sometimes hate Marilyn.

Why couldn't I have a different dad?

"Lux?"

I blink. "What?"

"I asked for more juice."

"Oh. Okay." I go to the fridge and serve him some.

My phone is blinking on the other side of the counter. It's Ollie.

I give Chase his juice and turn back to check the text.

> OLLIE
>
> Let me know when it's a good time to talk.

I don't answer right away. Instead, I turn around, and Chase is watching me.

"What is it?"

I shrug and look for something that's not a lie. "I'm going to celebrate with Mimi and the crew tonight. Want to come?"

He shakes his head so forcefully that it could probably detach from his shoulders. "Like the kids like to say, *hell no to the no, no, no.*"

I chuckle at his song but can't help but tease him. "Chase, she just thinks you're attractive. You don't have to be scared of her."

"No one's scared, but still hell no. I don't want to be anywhere close to her. But you can take Lauren. It will be good exposure for her and Autumn Lush."

"You're so smart."

"Obviously," he says.

That's what I'll do. Lauren can serve as a buffer for Mimi, and I can get her opinion about Oliver.

———

Lux

Mimi set up the celebration dinner at Innuendo, a 20s-inspired luxury spot in the heart of downtown. It's Baltimore's hottest and most exclusive restaurant/bar/lounge. Here's where you catch NFL and baseball players after the games, not to mention celebrities from the DC/Maryland/Virginia area.

And we dressed to give them a show. Lauren had the idea to covertly style ourselves in 20s fashion. I don't know where the hell she got me this velvet pink cocoon top with the long split all the way to my belly. We paired it with exact-fit, tapered tuxedo pants. For herself, she found a scoop-necked jumpsuit in the same material as my pants. We chose a pearl choker and necklace for her. For me, we found tassel earrings.

"Thank you for indulging me. It's such an ego boost that you trust me with fashion."

I look away from my Instagram feed to stare at her. "Are you fishing for compliments? Because this is the hottest idea. We are going to start a trend." I sweep a hand back and forth between us. "This is viral material."

She half smiles, half chews on her glossy lips. "Maybe I am, because I think we look sexy and fab, vintage but understated, like old money."

I nod. "We're flapper-non-flappin'."

She laughs. "That's a good way to put it. We need to coin this style so it flows naturally when we tell people."

She's right.

"I can't believe we were able to find all these pieces in such little time."

She shrugs. "According to your brother, I'm a fashion hoarder."

"Ignore him. He says the same thing about me. That reminds me, I need to have all my stuff shipped from Cam's apartment."

She taps her chin. "Or you can convince your new kissing buddy to help you bring it down."

My pulse picks up. "I've been trying not to think about it"—the kiss, that is, but I don't have to explain it—"but failing miserably." I can't get his lips out of my mind, the tender but firm way they settled against mine. "I'm so glad Chase didn't run him off."

"Ollie's a man, not a fuckboy. But you need to be ready because I think Chase is going to try something. He was all secretive on the phone with Cam. Adri noticed it too."

And there it is again. I've been trying not to think about my brother's reaction, because I don't think Chase is that open. Neither is Cam. Something's coming, but I'm so excited about seeing Ollie again, I'm trying not to freak out.

"Chase's reaction was too...well-adapted? He was always a few breaths from beating Mateo. The only thing that stopped him is that I got him to make me a promise."

Lauren purses her lips. "I believe it. He hates that guy. Mateo hurt you."

"He did," I agree. *And God how dumb can someone be?* "It's like I never learned."

"Forgiving ourselves is the hardest part. I never asked: how did you ever get Chase to promise not to hurt Mateo?"

I wince. "He owed me from a time he made me cry when he risked his life. I am really good at saving my bargaining chips for when I need them."

"You should've let him get Mateo one good time."

"The pain goes away, but now he doesn't have me, and that's going to hurt way more." And I love that I can say that with my whole heart.

Lauren smiles. "I love that. And you know what? Game's over for him, and you have a better prospect for the next one."

"A baseball pun?"

She chuckles. "Because Ollie used to play and was very good."

"Yes, I heard—"

Our car comes to a full stop, and flashes start going off. There are photographers outside taking photos, and annoyance has my eyes rolling. I turn to Lauren. "This is Mimi's doing."

She looks surprised, but her smile is a little tentative. "You're used to this."

And she's not.

I push my shoulders back and smile at her. "We look gorgeous, and your idea is genius. Let's go have fun with it. When you look at the camera, picture my idiot brother's eyes. You know, the one that makes you happy."

She smiles again. "I can do that."

I walk out of the limo first and hold out my hand for her. We pose, giving the photographers some fun shots.

"Bougie Girl, do you have a date tonight?"

I look at Lauren and say, "Yes, my sister. Isn't she gorgeous?"

We walk inside the building and head for the elevators.

"That was fun," Lauren says.

Five minutes later, we're on the top floor and walk into Innuendo. The place is beautifully done in 20s-style decor paired with lush plants and oversized chandeliers, but as we're shown to our table, my gaze is beyond the glass walls onto the view of the city. Baltimore is lighting up the beautiful night. The city is beautiful and vibrant tonight.

Mimi stands as soon as we approach, leaving someone mid-sentence. She runs to hug me like we haven't seen each other in years.

"Look who's here. The woman of the hour."

Everyone smiles, and she moves closer and presses her cheek to mine. A man two tables away takes a picture of us.

Ah, fuck. I need to warn Lauren, but before I can move, Mimi kisses both her cheeks and guide us to sit down.

"Lauren, I want you to know. I'm not holding a grudge. I'm just green with envy," Mimi says, the pageant smile frozen in place.

The crew laughs.

I lean over. "She means because you married Chase."

Lauren's smile is soft, but there's pleasure in her eyes. "Thank you, Mimi. He's high maintenance, trust me."

"What kind?" my makeup artist says. "Because I could be his repairman, his mechanic...I would even do floors—whatever he or his brother needs."

She throws her head back and laughs.

"This is so gross," I say and take my place, leaning to whisper in Lauren's ear. "Mimi's got someone taking photos of us and the whole table."

"Is that why she's smiling with her full mouth, but her eyes are dead?"

I look at Mimi, and that's the most accurate description I've ever heard. "Yes, and because she's really jealous of you. Why do women like Chase?"

Lauren smirks in a way that makes me roll my eyes.

"I don't mind anyone taking photos when we're out in public, but she really shouldn't do that without your—" Her gaze is on something over my shoulder, her eyes going wide and then narrowing.

I whip around as he approaches. Elias is smiling at us.

I don't let my head hang back like I want to. *Does this man have no kind of awareness?*

"Let's play nice. I don't want to cause a scene on your big day," Lauren says.

I turn back to her. "I'm going to be nice enough to tell him to fuck off."

I'll never forget he is Felix and Justin's father and the games he played with those sweet boys. Not to mention how he talked to Ollie on Lauren's wedding day.

Lauren grasps my hand. "No, please be really nice. I'll explain later."

Her eyes are pleading, so I relent.

"Good evening." His voice is grating, like dragging the top cap of your umbrella against asphalt.

I turn around and smile. "Hi, Elias."

His eyes dart between Lauren and me. "How are you, Lux? Hello, Lauren."

His voice drops when he says her name, as if he's fully expecting her to embarrass him.

"Hello." Her voice is a few degrees away from freezing.

"Is there any way I can get a minute of your time, Lauren?"

Her hand is still tightly wrapped around mine, so I can feel the stiffening of her body.

"I'm sorry, I can't. We are in the middle of a celebration for Lux right now."

His mouth opens like he's about to say something, but then he presses his lips together into a flat line.

Everyone at the table is watching us with interest, so I jump in. "I'll call you."

He nods. "So, you had time to think about our conversation earlier?"

Fuck.

Lauren doesn't react, but I'm now on the radar.

"Yes, we can talk about that too."

"Well, I will let you enjoy your evening, then," he says but makes no move to leave.

"You can always join us," Mimi offers.

My stomach drops at the thought, and the way Lauren squeezes my hand, I know she's about to jump over the table and choke her too.

"Mimi, Elias is here with other people. That would be rude. We will catch up with him later."

I turn a pointed look at him, and thankfully, he understands.

"Correct. I will call—" His face dissolves into a smile, the smoldering in his eye unmistakable. Without turning, I know there's a woman behind us.

"I'm sorry I'm late. Mila insisted I finish my end of the project before heading out," someone says behind me. Her voice is feminine and warm.

"It's okay. Let me introduce you to some friends. Lauren, Lux, this is Madison."

The woman comes into view, and I can't help but look at her from head to toe. Slick-cut blonde hair, Lanvin silk blouse, and pointed-toe Anouk heels lean closer to him. She's beautiful.

She opens her mouth, but it turns into a bit of a surprised laugh. "I know you. I mean, who doesn't? Bougie Girl." She shakes my hand and then moves over to Lauren. "And you own Autumn Lush. Your video together months ago and the article was nothing short of amazing."

"And there's more to come," I say of our collaboration. "It's great to meet you, Madison."

"We should go," Elias says, pointing at their table. "They're waiting for us."

Madison looks over and nods. "Oh, yes. And I'm starving too."

They wave at us and walk away toward their table where a woman and two other men wait.

I lean toward Lauren. "She seems so nice. What the hell is she doing with him?"

She nods. "I know. The whole time, I wanted to be like the lady from *Ghost* and say, 'You're in danger, girl.'"

"Can you imagine if he had accepted the invitation to sit with us?"

I then turn a raging stare on Mimi, who conveniently is paying more attention to her wine glass.

I pull out my phone and fire a text to Mimi.

ME

I better not see photos of that man, or of our interaction, anywhere on social media tomorrow.

179

"I guess we both have things we need to tell each other later. Because I'm dying to know what he asked you to think about," Lauren whispers in my ear.

I turn back to her and sigh. "Okay, but you can't tell Chase."

Lauren nods. "Neither can you about what I'll tell you later."

Now I'm intrigued, but Mimi texts back.

> MIMI
>
> Of course not. Never.

I reply right away, adding a side-eye emoji.

> ME
>
> I can see the guy taking photos with his iPhone. 🐼

14

Ollie

Al mal tiempo, buena cara.

I also like to get things over quickly. There's no need to dwell, especially when there are friendships—of all ages—at play here. I drop Ayla and Bron off at *Mi Tesoro* so they can have dinner. Adrianna smiled and chit-chatted with me like there was nothing amiss. Cam probably didn't tell her what's going on. I just wonder how this is going to play out because, no matter what happens today, and if I have to fight with her brothers, Lux gave me an opening.

She told me she wants to talk, and if that talk leads to a little something more, I'm running with it.

When I make it to The Birthmark, a woman greets me at the door. She smiles. "Do you have a reservation?"

"I'm meeting someone here."

Her smile widens. "You must be looking for Chase." She points to the far end of the room. "He's in the last booth."

I find him with a beer in hand and his gaze on the spring training game on the screen.

His gaze shifts to me, and he lets out one of those good-natured chuckles. "Emperors' pitching isn't looking so good this season. No wonder they can't stop begging Cam for help. Have a beer."

He points to the ice bucket with four more.

"I don't think they'll have any luck with getting Cam back," I say, taking the seat across from him and helping myself to a bottle.

"Nope. He traded all that for the sexy bright lights of fatherhood."

I laugh at the dryness in his voice. "Didn't you just get lured in too?"

His head bobs up and down. "Yeah, and everything's been great…until I had to talk to Felix about the birds and the bees today."

"What?" He's too young.

"One of his little friends from school had a video on his iPad. Kid's older brother had been using it. Anyway, I had to explain it to him, and unlike when I had the talk with Justin, this one had tons of freaking questions. I can talk about sex with anyone, Coach. I felt sick when I had to talk to that kid today."

I nod. Who understands better than me? "Wait till you have a daughter and have to tell her about her body, her period, and that she needs to watch out for asshole boys all while reassuring her that if she meets a little asshole, she can come to you."

Of course, my situation doesn't have to be his. Lauren will be there as well.

Chase stares at me for a few seconds, the struggle in his features clear as day. "You win."

"It wasn't a contest." I chuckle and lean back against the booth. "Let's talk, Chase."

He stills, an eyebrow rising, but he doesn't talk right away. "That's why I like you, Coach."

Well, that's unexpected.

"But that's not why I'm here today."

"No, you're here 'cause you're messing around with my sister."

My spine stiffens, and I push back. "Wait a minute. I'm not messing with her. We haven't—"

His hand shoots out and stops between us. "I don't need details. Ever. Plus, I know it hasn't gone far. We need to make some things clear before it does. The first is your intentions."

Kiss her. Hold her. Eat her. Fuck her in as many positions as I can.

"I'm not Mateo," I blurt out, *and why the fuck would I even say that?*

You know why, because you're not trying to toy with her.

Chase bobs his head up and down and takes a sip of his beer. "If you were, you would be in a hospital getting a cast on."

Laughter would be a normal reaction here, but I don't laugh, because something tells me he's not joking. And a man who fights because he likes it tends to be dangerous. They fight like they have nothing to lose.

I'm not a punk. "That's assuming you would win."

He shrugs. "Either way. The only reason that asshole is still walking is that she finagled a promise not to touch him out of me. But she's all out of promises now." Then he laughs. "It won't come to that because I respect you, Coach, and you don't strike me as a douche that would hurt my sister on purpose."

"I wouldn't."

He nods. "But I don't know what your style with women is. There are few things I need to say."

I lean in so he can continue.

"Treat her well, and we're good. If the time comes when you don't like her anymore, or it's not working out, tell her straight out. Don't play games with her. Don't go fucking around and hurt her. I mess with her a lot, but that's because I'm her brother. I taught her to be tough. That's why she can punch as hard as a man and knows exactly when and where to hit, verbally and physically, but she's girlie and won't hit unless she has to."

I press my palms against the edge of the table. "Look, I know what's at play. I know when relationships get messy, it can bring down families and break up friendships. And I don't want Ayla to lose more people in her life. This is why I never made a move before."

"What changed now?"

Her smile makes my day. I wake up excited at the prospect of seeing her. For the first time, I see someone I can introduce to my A when we're ready. I've had a taste of her lips and her tongue. I've had her naked body pressed against mine. Her hum of pleasure still echoes in my ears. The look in her eyes as we traded hurt stories lives in my head. I can't stay away from her anymore.

"I've gotten to know her better, and it's not just attraction. I like the person she is the more I get to know her."

That blank mask stays over his face, so I continue.

"She's a good person. She's good to my Ay and loving with her friends and family. There was a hiccup between us with the work, and I know there's some steel in her. I learned that she's also hardworking, and we share that in common. I think if we take it slow and are sure of the steps we're taking, we can avoid confusion."

He nods, but there's no expression on his face. A couple of breaths later, he finally nods. "Like I said, I like you. Cam does too. It's the reason why I'm here and not both of us."

"He could've come too, Chase."

He smiles this time. "It's not an ambush. We just want you to understand. Yeah, she's a woman who can take care of herself. But we're not allowing anyone to pick up where Mateo left off." He holds up a stalling hand. "I'm not saying that's what you're doing, but sometimes even with the best intentions, we, as men, tend to fuck up."

"Yes," I say, because he's right. All I can do is try, but how many times did I hurt someone without meaning to? "That's a possibility. But just know that if it doesn't work out, it's not going to be because I disrespected her."

He sighs. "I get that, and I believe you, but relationships can be a bitch. God knows it took forever for Lauren and me to see eye to eye."

"But now you do, and you're married."

"My point is that it only takes one misstep, and it all goes to shit. It happened to me a few times. That's not what I'll hold against you. But if you embarrass or humiliate her, friend or not, I'm going to beat your face in."

"If I fuck up, I won't fight back."

"It's not going to matter anyway, but it won't come to that. You came here and faced me like a man. You didn't delay it. I appreciate that." He takes a swig of his beer, but his gaze never leaves my face.

"I *am* a man, and I have a lot more to lose than anyone if this goes to shit."

But I'm not stopping. I have to see this through with her.

15

Oliver

Traffic on the beltway was a goddamn nightmare, the crew got here before I did, and Lux has been downstairs in a conference call since before I got here. No time to talk but a whole morning to stew over what she's going to say.

Is she going to greenlight me to keep going where I left off, with my hands on her ass and my mouth all over her? Maybe she'll say there is too much conflict of interest for us to go forward with this.

What would I tell her if she says that? Do I quit because I wouldn't be able to keep my mind off her?

I adjust and push the heavy weight up toward the mount. The built-in light reflectors are hard to install. It takes all the crew members, and even I need to climb up a ladder to help install them at the right angle. It was a great hunch to raise the ceiling in the studio. It has made it possible to place them at the highest angle possible. It's also hell to get it in place, but when it clicks, the audible yes echoes throughout the room.

That other end of her studio is now a full light box, and she'll be able to get the best lighting with the least amount of hassle.

I get down the ladder, step back, and pull out my phone to take a photo of the crew tidying up the space. It's bright. This is exactly what I wanted.

A whiff of her sweet berry scent reaches me first. All the chatter stops, and their gazes dart past me. There's thirst in their eyes, and one of the guys licks his lips.

I turn around, and there's Lux, dressed in dark red, like ripened fruit plucked out of the tree, waiting to be devoured.

"That's amazing work. I can't wait to see how it looks in photos and videos."

I hand her my phone. "You tell me."

She looks at it, and her smile brightens the room more than the lighting. "It's perfect. The video quality is going to be out of this world. You're amazing." She looks around the room and then the crew. "You all are."

I hate that she added that. I don't want to share her praises with any of them.

"Good morning, Luciana."

Her gaze is back to me. "Good morning, Oliver."

"Let me show you around." We go through the new additions, careful not to get to informal, even when I take a test photo of her so she can keep on checking the quality. I'm not doing anything that could cause the crew to think they can get too comfortable with her. It's something you always want to be careful about because it's easy for lines to blur in men's crews sometimes. I don't want them ever to slip and disrespect her.

"I think we are ready to move on to the downstairs renovations. I want to show you the specs I worked out with Mimi and the team. I don't necessarily want to use my own kitchen commercially but building a kitchen here might be a little much. Plus, I wouldn't do kitchen videos often, and it's added to the budget. It wouldn't require many adjustments to your proposal. We'll need this kind of lighting if possible."

"I understand. We can make the lighting and reflectors tailored to the room so nothing looks out of place," I say. I like that she's all professional at the moment. It's also a little confusing because I don't know what she's really thinking. "Lead the way."

She thanks the crew again, and I swear their tongues are half out. Her phone rings, and she gives me the one-minute signal before she walks downstairs.

I hand out cleaning specifications and instructions on what to do next and follow her. Ayla texts me that she wants Chinese for dinner and a new pair of rose-gold high tops.

I'm still shaking my head when I hit the second floor and get yanked by the arm. Lux pulls me into her office. I don't even get a chance to react before she throws her hands around my neck and pushes up on her feet.

I bend, obliging, and her lips crash against mine.

Her mouth is sweet, but her tongue is bold and inviting. As my hands circle around her, all my questions are answered. We are back to where we left off yesterday—pressed against each other and kissing like the world hinges on our lips and tongues.

And just as quick, she pulls away.

"I know you were trying to be professional, but we needed this break. I needed to confirm yesterday was real." She's a little out of breath, and she tries to move away, but I grab her again and move us out of the way so we won't be seen.

I press her against the wall, plastering my body against her softer one. I kiss her again, this time with our bodies engaged, until she moans and writhes against me, and I thrust my hips against hers. Because I can't help it. Because she wants it. Because we both need it.

"It's more than real," I whisper.

"The question is, where do we go from here?"

"I think we both know. We need to decide how deep."

She presses even tighter against me.

"God, all the way in," she says, and then her jaw drops.

And in that moment, I see it. Me, deep inside her. Her body arching in front of me. Her lips lifting for my every thrust. The surge of desire that flashes through my body is violent, and I force a laugh. "I meant—"

"Oh, God." She lets her head fall against my chest, but the skin on her neck is red.

I tilt her face up. "No shame. I think we're both in tune with what we want."

She nods. She wants my dick, and she will get it, every fucking inch, so she can ride it to her heart's content.

I want to push her on top of that small, feminine desk, and make us both happy, but we need to clarify before we get dirty and decide if fucking is the first thing we'll do.

"Let's talk."

She laughs. "Aren't you tired of talking? You talked to Chase last night."

"He told you?"

She shakes her head and steps away to the other side of the desk. She lowers herself to the chair, so dainty and graceful. "He wouldn't tell me that, but I know him too well. He and Cam can't help themselves. I wondered if he would spook you away."

It's my turn to shake my head as I take the chair across from her. "Nothing he said would keep me away from you, Luciana."

The catch in her eyes and the heat that flows from them is enough to have me planting my feet firmer against the floor. I want to grab her again.

"Chase can be very convincing." Now she's coy, but I get it. She needs to hear the words from me.

"He can be, but this is not the first time I have had a talk with one of your brothers about you. Last time, I was willing to stay away because I didn't know where you stood. Now, we are on the same page."

"Physically, anyway." Her gaze sharpens as if she's weighing my reactions and responses.

"Yes, physically, but I think it's more than that. Don't you?"

She nods. "I just wonder what more means to you, Ollie."

"It won't be just sex with us. I like you more than that."

"Me too, but we have to talk about Ayla."

My stomach drops because this is where the recipe typically falls apart. "What do you feel about her?"

She frowns. "She's the sweetest and smartest girl I know, along with my niece. There's not a drop of malice in her. Who wouldn't love her to pieces? I know I have since the moment I met her."

And God, there's nothing else she could have said to make my heart feel this way. "Is there a *but*?"

She shakes her head and smiles. "Just that I don't want to hurt her or Bron."

The relief is so fast I smile. "Then we see eye to eye. How about we take it slow to see how things go at first, and when we are finally ready, we can tell her and everyone that we are seeing each other?"

She doesn't say anything in the beginning but then nods. "What do we tell her in the meantime? Won't she notice we are hanging out?"

"We don't have to say anything. We can just see each other and get to know each other better and get her familiarized."

"How is she supposed to get to know me better if she's not spending time with me?"

And this is where I'm stumped, because normally, women are so relieved not to have to deal with her up front, but Lux is different. *I want her to be different.*

"We can hang out with her and Bron, and you can keep seeing her like you do."

She says nothing, but I can almost see her thoughts clicking. "Yeah, that's a good way, and I also don't want the world to know I'm seeing anyone for a bit. After last time, I'm so sick of everyone knowing all there is to know about my relationships."

"I need to know, Lux. Are you still hung up on Mateo?"

Her eyes lock on mine as she answers, "No. That's been over for a long time. I want to give myself a new chance with you."

Something shifts in my chest. "Yeah?"

She smiles, this time brighter than the sun itself. Then, it vanishes as a cloud passes over her eyes. "What about you? Are you still hung up on Ayla's mom?"

"No."

"What about any other woman? You were talking to someone on the phone at one point. The day I fired you."

She didn't miss that.

"Not talking to that person anymore. We broke up, and she was regretting how things ended. There's no baggage from that brief relationship."

Her face is impassive. She's studying me, trying to gauge if I'm being honest. Her gaze stays on me, and I don't move, flinch, or break eye contact.

She nods. "Okay, then, let's give ourselves a chance."

I push up to stand. I need to kiss her senseless until the color is all over her face like yesterday.

The clomping of feet down the stairs keeps me rooted, and she turns to her laptop screen.

"So, we will need really good lighting over the stove and counter-tops. Have you seen those QVC kitchen spaces?"

I love her quick mind. "Yes."

"I want that." But this time, her eyes are on me, and my whole body stirs all over again for her.

OVERTHINKING CAN DERAIL THE BEST LAID PLANS, BUT THERE'S ALWAYS AN UPSIDE

By Bougie Girl

Being excited is as natural as breathing. We can all remember the jitters of the night before Christmas, waiting to get those presents. Or being ready to jump out of your skin waiting for the start of the Hermès show at New York Fashion Week. When the lights go on, our blood pressure is ready to drop. And who can forget the erratic beating of our hearts at a sports game? Make that to the 10th power if you watched your older brother pitch a no-hitter—three of the longest hours of my life.

If we zoom in even closer, we've all gotten ready for a nerve-wracking and fluttery first date.

It's always about the guy or the girl. Will they like us enough? Will we like them enough? What if lettuce gets stuck in my teeth? What if we run into my mother in a restaurant?

Shudders.

Because there's so much uncertainty, we like to fixate on what we can actually control, like choosing the heels that will enhance our legs more, practicing our hellos to sound casual, or picking the right restaurant. We want to look hip, chic, sexy, smart, desirable, confident, edible, and just the right amount of vulnerable.

With such small goals, what can possibly go wrong?

We overthink, overdo, and over-prepare ourselves into a state where we forget the most important thing: have fun, enjoy the experience, and live in the moment. If it goes wrong, it will be the anecdote you tell your friends over drinks for a long time. But if it goes right… you'll spend a long time reliving this moment and committing it to the vault of the kind of memory that fades the hurt from the past. And the minor things won't matter.

16

Lux

I'm ready for him.

God knows I've never prepared for a date like today. The table is set with the fine china that got delivered this morning.

I placed the utensils in the right order—in the obnoxious way Marilyn Blake would browbeat our employees into learning. My mother is a stickler for etiquette and the "right" way of doing things. Of course, all that fades back when it comes to people of a different class, those she sees as inferior.

Stop thinking about her, Luciana. Nothing kills a mood like Marilyn Blake's presence, even if it's in spirit.

Tonight, I need to be softer and fresher than the bamboo sheets at Marble House Spa, not only on the outside but on the inside. The only way to achieve that is to scrub my mother—and father—from my mind. I also must wipe the conversation I overheard between Ayla and Bron.

I rub a hand over my jittery stomach. The last thing I want in the world is to cause problems for Ollie, or even worse, for that little girl who's had so much turmoil in her life.

Grandma told her friend that Papi shouldn't bring any of his women around me until he knows it will last. She says he should dedicate himself to raising me. But I want him to be happy, you know?

At any other time, I wouldn't have cared what anyone thought. That lady doesn't know about me, so her opinion doesn't matter. Like Mateo's mother's opinion never mattered. She hated me on the spot because I didn't want to fetch things for her son. She wanted me to cook and make sure his clothes were pristine and fulfill her dream of the perfect wife for her fuckboy son.

That was a hell no.

But it's different now. Ollie is different. He loves his daughter so much. It's so special watching them together. I used to feel like that with Walter when I was younger, but that all changed when I was sixteen.

No, no, no. Don't think about him now.

Concentrate on the fact that Ayla says she likes you and thinks you're awesome.

I fluff my pillows one more time and head to the bedroom to get ready. The FoodRnr delivery guy rings the doorbell just as I finish getting ready. He hands me the delivery bag, and I wave him away, sending him the tip through my phone app. In the kitchen, I place everything in its proper serving dish.

When the doorbell rings, my heart jumps, and I press my palm to it as I make my way to the door.

Calm the fuck down, Luciana. You have everything set. Your hands are softer than Mongolian cashmere, and your skin couldn't glow more if you used Windex as a toner. Your maxi dress molds to your body, clinging to the right places. No heels because you're at home, and it would look like you're trying too hard. You look like the absolute doll the Autumn Lush staff said you were when you left. You got the correct date food you can feed to each other with your fingers. There's chilled wine and chocolate mousse, decadent and creamy, in case he wants to lick it off your skin. The mood lighting is set to a soft warm orange and you're wearing easy-to-slide-off, lace panties.

But my stomach is still in knots.

I go downstairs to let him in, pausing in front of the door. I need to be Bougie Girl, the fearless one, not Lux, for a minute—at least until he comes in.

I fling the door open to find him there, looking not like a snack but a delicious brunch with a little of everything—sweet, salt, spice, and richness. The white V-neck Henley under his jacket exposes just the right amount of chest skin. In his hands, he holds a bouquet of blush-pink daisies. They're beautiful, vibrant, and sweet. *I've never gotten daisies before.*

"Hi. These are for you," he says in a low timbre. His voice and that smile make my panties slip down a little of their own accord.

"Hi," I say, fighting the butterflies in my belly.

He leans forward and presses a kiss on my cheek. The softness of his lips pressing and lingering on my cheek makes my skin tingle all the way to my nipples.

"Come in, please." I'm breathless.

We make our way to the second floor. He looks around and turns back to me with a smile. "It looks great in here."

I shake my head. "I only added the furniture. You made it great with all the renovations." I look down at the flowers. "By the way, these are beautiful."

His smile widens, and there's the familiar tugging in my belly. "I told Ayla I was going on a date, and she helped me pick them out. I wanted to bring you roses. She said it was cliché. That probably every guy has gotten you roses. She said I should go with these daisies."

I nod. "She's right and so smart. She wanted to make sure you made the best impression."

He leans forward a little. "Did it work?"

Well, my panties are tugged and wet against my freshly waxed skin.

I nod. "It definitely worked."

"Good."

We stand there, looking at each other, and if I don't get a move on this dinner, it will get cold because I think my clothes may come off.

"Sit down, or you can come with me to the kitchen so I can find a vase."

"I'll come with you. You can tell me how your day went."

My day?

"It was good. I had to go check out a place and make notes for my next review. I also had to hand in a couple of assignments to the magazine, and then I shot a video."

"Sounds like a busy day."

"Eh. My job is charmed. How did your day go?"

"It was good. I had to go do some work for Winter and Grayson today. If you think this was hard to do, the renovation on their penthouse keeps getting larger and larger."

I pour some wine and hand it to him. "It's still a great gig, right? Two penthouses in that building."

He nods. "Yeah. It's going to be bigger than any house. Winter wants her own painting space so she doesn't disturb the baby or vice versa. Grayson doesn't want anyone else on their floor. I don't blame him. He needs to keep their family secure. And she needs her space, kind of like you, to make sure her creativity stays flowing."

"I imagine it can be hard to concentrate with a baby yelling for your attention."

"Yes, it is. When Ayla was about two, I was getting my construction management degree and working. It was just her and me. She was a chatterbox who didn't want to sleep. And we lived in a one-bedroom apartment." His eyes glow so strong when he talks about her.

"How did you manage that?"

He laughs. "I started teaching her how to read and write. I would buy her books and put on teaching videos. I made it as if it was study time for both of us."

His gaze grows warm.

"That was smart of you."

"It didn't work all the time. A lot of times, I would have to wait for her to go to sleep." He laughs again, the sound so penetrating and contagious I smile.

"Didn't that cut into your sleep time?" I grab a vase and scissors from the drawer.

"What sleep time? It was hard as hell, but I don't sleep much anyway. My uncle used to say you get to sleep a lot when you're dead."

It's my turn to laugh. "That sounds like an exhausting way of living. Doesn't your body ever protest?" My gaze drifts over said body, and nothing seems to be hurting. It's strong, tight, and well-kept.

"It's protesting a little now. Can I kiss you now, or do we need to wait for dessert?"

"We're never going to get to dinner this way," I say, tucking the flowers into the vase and walking around the island.

"We will." He puts his arms around me. "I'm not letting all this effort go to waste."

Does he mean my body or the plates set out? His lips crash over mine, and I don't think. I just open my mouth and let him take charge.

He pulls back. "Maybe I'll just eat you for dinner. I'm hungrier for you, anyway."

"I'm okay with that." I grab a handful of his shirt and pull him to me.

His hands slide down my back, tilting me up against him until we are flush again. With his mouth on mine and one hand on the back of my neck, he walks me back toward my bedroom.

I'm lost in the taste of his tongue, in the spicy notes of his cologne sneaking through my nostrils, overwhelming my senses. I'm barely aware of the hallway walls until I find myself pressed against one, the cold brick a bizarre contrast to the heat of his body pressed against mine.

Not until the backs of my legs touch the bed, and I feel the softness of the bamboo sheets against my calves, do I realize we are here.

Oliver's eyes reflect the soft candle-flickering effect of the lights. I raise a hand to his cheek. He kisses the inside of my palm and runs his thumb over my lips, swollen for his kiss, craving more bruising. I slide my hand to his chest. Is his heart beating as fast as mine? He traps it there with both of his, looking at me like the world has faded away, and we are on an island together, alone.

My throat goes dry.

Still, he says nothing. And I'm rattled. So, I reach for the hem of his shirt and push it up, sliding it over his head, letting it land on the floor.

He doesn't break eye contact, not even when I unbuckle his belt or when I pull his pants down. His thumbs hook on his underwear, and he discards them along with his pants and shoes, kicking all of it away from him.

I get my first glance at his thick, long cock. I wasn't dreaming. It's exactly what I remember, what I conjure when we're pressed against each other. My mouth waters, almost feeling as it fills my mouth, dying for him to slide down my throat.

I find him smiling like he can read my thoughts. And his lips are on mine again.

I start inching toward the hem of my dress, but he stills me with his hands.

"No."

His tone is soft, but it still booms against the silence.

I should've put music on. The silence is unnerving me. All I hear are our breaths.

I open my mouth to tell him that I need noise because the silence is making me nervous. He quiets me with his mouth near my ear.

"*Cierra los ojos y solo siente.*"

I want to tell him that I can't just close my eyes and feel. I need to see it happen. He flicks his tongue on my earlobe, and the sensation bursts and flashes all over my body, heating my belly, making my nipples hard against his chest.

Ollie's hands slide over my shoulders and down my arm as he kisses his way down my jaw. His lips brush mine, and he turns me so my back is to him, and his erection presses on my ass. I gasp at how hard he is and grind against him. His hand rustles over my dress, drawing circles with his fingers over my aching tits.

I moan.

He hooks me to him with his forearm while his other hand slides over my thigh and settles at my apex. He pets me over the dress like I'm a good girl about to get her reward.

I buck against his fingers.

"Kneel on the bed."

I do as he asks, and he rolls the dress up, hiking it over my ass.

"I love your ass. It's so good." He smacks it lightly, sending a twist of desire through my system. "It's so firm."

"Harder," I pant, shocking myself.

"*Es un placer* to indulge you." And his hand crashes hard on my ass cheek, rocking me. The wave of stinging pain mixed with pleasure makes me heady, and my knees buckle under me.

He's there to steady me, bending over, blowing over the sting. Then he presses a kiss and slides off my panties down to my knees. The cool air in the room hits my sensitive spots, and I'm trembling.

I look back at him, standing behind me, ready to fuck me, and I'll never forget this moment. I've never wanted anything more than that thick dick stretching me and pounding me until I lose consciousness.

"Come on. Fuck me. I don't want to wait anymore."

He smiles, but it's not his regular sexy Oliver smile. No, this is a smirk. It's devious. It's a promise. "Maybe later."

Then he pushes me onto the bed and kneels behind me. His wet kisses against my lower back, one followed by another as he inches toward my ass, titillate and make me desperate.

I almost come off the bed when his tongue slides between my crack, but I don't have time to moan before he is spreading me with his hands and drawing swirls between my cheeks. The waves of sensation that wash over me make me tremble.

He's sucking me and tongue-fucking me, and I can't brace anymore, so I lower my torso and lean on my elbows.

"That's a good girl," he whispers, tilting me up. His mouth slides to my pussy.

He licks, fingers, and sucks. The sensation is so potent my body breaks out in tingles, and my skin begins to expand like a balloon. I can't take it anymore, and I bury my face in the mattress as I come and fall limp against the bed.

My pussy is pulsating fast, but he's not done with me. He flips me on my back and lies at my side. His hand goes between my legs, and he lifts one over his thighs. I'm like a rag doll as his cock sneaks between my folds and pulls another moan as he fills me in a way I've only fantasized about before.

"Ollie, God," I gasp.

Then he begins to rock his hips up, one hand at my waist while the other strokes my clit. And I'm expanding again.

"The aftershocks are my favorite. *Besame, Luciana.*"

I contort my body to meet his lips, and I get lost in him again. In the rhythmic rocking of his hips, the stroke of his fingers, the way his cock moves inside me. But it's the darkness in his eyes and how good he makes me feel. The orgasm rips out of me, and my fingers fly to still his, but it's to no avail. I feel like I'm falling, and when he comes, we go down together.

———

Ollie

"Great thing we waited to eat, because the food is mediocre at best. I'm glad we jumped right into dessert," Lux says, putting her fork down.

It's bland, but I shake my head. "Don't say that. You put a lot of effort into this. It looks so nice."

She snorts. "I ordered this."

"Why?"

"I wanted everything to be perfect for tonight."

I look her over. Her hair is disheveled, her lips red from my kisses, her skin glowing. "I think it was perfect. The food doesn't change that."

She moves closer to peck me on my lips. "You don't have to eat that. We can have dessert, or we can make sandwiches. I don't really cook."

"Lucky for you, I do." I pull her to straddle my lap.

"A man of numerous talents."

"Did I tell you I make magic too?"

"I believe you, but you should show me."

I slide my fingers down her lower back, over her ass, until I find the wet trail and circle the entrance.

"Ollie…"

I lift my head up and capture her bottom lip between my teeth, sucking on it as I slip two fingers inside her. Her walls flex around my digits.

"You should let me…"

I silence her with my lips. "Shhhh."

"Wait." She stops grinding on my hand, and I pause. "Do you not like talking during…"

She's frowning now.

I shake my head. "I want to do a different type of talking."

I resume my stroking of her insides.

"I want your body to talk to me, to tell me how it feels when I do this." I crook my finger inside her, and she arches, offering me her bare tits.

"I want your body to let me know what it likes." I suck a nipple into my mouth, and she trembles against my hand.

I suck her harder, and her legs fly open. She begins to circle her hips around my fingers, and I get so hard it hurts.

"You hear that?"

Her, "No," segues into a moan.

"Your body is telling me it's ready for my cock."

"Yes."

"Show me with your body, Luciana. Don't tell me with your voice."

She bends, pressing her tits on my face and rocking her hips faster and more purposefully. She's trying to extract the orgasm, not let it come to her. I pull my finger out of her and impale her on my dick, extracting a guttural sound that threatens to make me come. I hold, suck, and lick her nipple, and let her fuck herself on me until the quickening begins, and she comes undone.

I close my eyes and let myself get swept in the pleasure with her hair all over us like a soft curtain.

We lie in silence, and I listen to her body once again. The breath that goes from ragged to even. The pounding heart settles into a murmur and then regulates. The skin that goes from boiling to warm and comforting. All of it tells me she's sated, like me. This was better than I could have ever hoped.

She snuggles against me, her face on my neck, and I stroke her. She's completely relaxed, half on top of my body. I'm relaxed too. I like being tangled up with her on her floor. I need to get up soon, but instead, I kiss her forehead.

"I know you have to go," she murmurs.

"You had your way with me, and now you're kicking me out?"

Her fingers trail up my ribcage. "No, but you have to pick up A."

I smile, loving that she's thinking about my baby girl. I tilt my head up and kiss her. She clings to me, digging her nails into my back, making my dick stir again.

I press her on her back, and I'm right back to our happy spot.

She opens her legs wider, pushing from her heels to meet my thrusts.

I stare into her eyes and pump into her until she's clawing and moaning. I take her face in my hands. "Tell me your pussy is mine."

"It's…yours."

"*Solo mio?*"

She nods hard. "Yes, all yours."

"Tell me you're mine, Luciana."

"I'm—" She shoves her head back and moans as her walls pulsate around me. The pleasure washes over her face, morphing it into a smile. I thrust and stare, and when I come, I collapse over her. Her arms and legs tighten around me, and now she's the one stroking my back.

"I'm yours," she whispers.

I don't move.

I just think about us. This moment is perfect in every way, and I don't want to leave. I want to stay here with her, inside her.

"Let's go out this weekend. We can start easing into it with A."

She shifts quickly so she's looking into my eyes. "Really?"

"Maybe you can bring Bron."

She thinks it over and then nods. "That's a good idea. It would look like a play date between them."

"They're a little old for that, but same concept."

She smiles, her eyes lighting up, and she lies back down on my shoulder.

My chest tightens because I see the happiness in her face. I feel it in the way her hand squeezes my bicep and how tightly her body presses against mine. My pulse speeds up in a different way than before. It's paired with a sudden urge to run, like danger is near.

Her fingers slide over my chest. "Wow, your heart is really pounding. I think—"

I tilt her head and kiss her quickly.

"I have to go before I'm late."

A cloud crosses over her eyes, but she blinks it away. "Oh. Okay."

I get up quickly, go to the bathroom, and get dressed.

She doesn't ask anything, even as she walks me to the door. But the WTF is broadcasted in her eyes.

"Thank you for a great evening," I say standing at the door, for some reason feeling insecure, like I'm asking her out for the first time.

Her smile is a little strained, like it pains her to quirk the muscles. "Yeah, I had a good time too. Drive safely."

I can't blame her. I've seen this look before in other women. She knows something is off. I could kick myself.

I thought too much and messed up the moment.

As I wait at the light, I send her a text.

ME

I can't wait to see you again.

Her reply doesn't come in until about two in the morning.

LUX

Me too

And I was wide awake and ready to like it when it disappeared.
She unsent it.

17

Lux

It's four in the morning, and I'm wide awake. My brain is firing on all cylinders because my thoughts have been everywhere at once. That's what woke me up at two. I left something sticking out of a mental drawer, and it came back to haunt me. The something was whatever happened at the end of my date with Oliver.

I was so tired from the sex and the whole day of moving around that I went to sleep as soon as he left. I didn't want to think about the last minutes of our time together. I purposefully didn't answer his text. I planned to do it in the morning, but when I opened my eyes and smelled him on my pillow, I reached for my phone. A couple of times, the typing dots came on, like he debated saying something but didn't dare.

I knew something was wrong and should've called it out, but I didn't dare either.

I am not sure what changed. I didn't push for anything. He offered to hang out with Ayla and me. All I did was say yes, but that seemed to make him uncomfortable. His message about wanting to see me again should have warmed me up. Instead, it felt awkward and as forced as my politeness when I walked him to the door. I didn't just want to leave him on read. I shot him a text.

Me too.

Then, I regretted it immediately, so I unsent it. I regretted that too. *Am I doing too much? Overthinking it?* My skin got jittery, and I hopped off the bed, knowing sleep wouldn't come. I ran up the stairs and began working on a blog and an idea for a video, which I started on right away.

7 Non-Cliche Ways to Nurture Yourself.

I jot down the full skeleton of my idea. I even do a practice shoot. Tomorrow, I'll call that tranquility coach that Winter told us about. She can guide me into better breathing and shutting off my thoughts. I haven't been able to meditate like I used to.

I go downstairs after I'm done and drop into child pose in my living room. I change into a reclining hero pose, and my stomach begins to burn, my breath stalling. My last breakup ruined the pose for me. It now induces anxiety, conjuring things that make me uncomfortable, like all the signs I missed during my relationship with Mateo and social media using me as a bullseye.

All I can see is Ollie's awkward retreat from me, getting dressed quickly, and leaving in a hurry like I was a drunk college hookup he needed to put behind him. My cheeks are burning with embarrassment. He couldn't wait to leave me. I quickly switch into a plank and torture my belly muscles. I let them burn until I can't hold it anymore, and I collapse on the floor.

As I pant, I wonder what's truly bugging me. I close my eyes for a second, and music blares while my heart bruises my sternum. Cardi is screaming that no bitch is gonna front on her while I massage a hand over my chest.

Who's calling me at this time? I pat around for my phone but can't find it. There's a bright light in my eyes and drool in the corner of my mouth. I look around and am still on the floor, in my underwear and tank top. It's bright daylight. *I fell asleep after the plank.* My phone doesn't stop ringing. I find it a few steps away and answer without looking.

"Hello."

"Oh, so it was a good date. You sound exhausted." The laughter is in Lauren's voice.

"I *am* exhausted. I fell asleep on the floor."

"Oh my. Better than I thought. You baptized the whole place…"

"Shut up. Why are you calling me this early?"

"Lux, it's ten in the morning."

Oh shit. I sit up fast. "I need to go get ready. The workers come at eleven today."

"So, he's coming back for seconds?"

"No," I practically yell. "He's at Winter's today."

"Why are you so touchy? Don't tell me nothing happened," she says.

"It did."

"And it was bad?"

My eyes roll to the back of my head with the memory.

"No. God. It was *good*." I think of the way he ate me with his open mouth and the pressure from his tongue on my clit. My nipples begin to tingle. "So good."

"Why are you so touchy, then?"

I sigh. "I dunno. Things got weird."

"Things?" she asks.

"*Oliver* got weird. He asked me to hang out with Ayla and him, and we can bring Bron so it's not so obvious, and I said okay. He got odd, like I'm clingy."

"He said that?"

I lean my head against the same hallway wall he had pressed me against. I can still feel his dick pressed against my apex. "No. It's how I interpreted it. He had that body language, like when you get clingy, and they need to make an exit."

"Running doesn't sound like him."

"I dunno. It's just a feeling, and it wasn't my idea. If it was, I would have been like okay, I made him uncomfortable. But he came up with it."

"Maybe you're both still learning your way around each other. This is also new and big for him."

"Or maybe it's something else."

"Like what?"

"I don't know, Lo." My tone is testy and bothered.

"Okay, let's go in parts." How is her voice so soothing right now? "How was the evening before that?"

"Yum," I say in a whisper, remembering the way we tore at each other and riding him on the floor of my family room. The way he held me after, the tender way he stroked my back. And our conversation.

"Why don't you give it more time, then? This is a big step for you both, and you need to get used to it."

"Is that what you would tell yourself?"

She's silent for a bit. "No, but I didn't use to give men much of a chance. I was hung up on your brother mostly."

"But he was hung up on you too." My voice is softer than I mean it, and maybe that's the issue. "What if he's hung up on his ex-wife or that other woman he was dating before and can't give himself a true chance?"

"I don't think so. Not when he looks at you the way he does, and he's making plans to let you hang out with Ayla."

"Maybe."

"Lux?" she asks.

"Yeah?"

"You know the best way to find out what happened with him?" I don't get to answer her because she starts talking right away again. "Ask him. You're not shy. Put him on the spot, make him talk."

"I don't want him to think I'm a stage-six clinger."

"No, you're a woman and have every right to ask. One thing I've learned is that not asking the right questions breeds insecurity that will doom any relationship."

She's right. I know it is. All the time I could have spoken up for myself with Mateo, and I let shit go because of dumb reasons. I could've saved myself so much heartache.

We hang up a few minutes later, and I jump in the shower. When the hot water hits my skin, all memories of him flood me and my senses, and I end up against the wall with my hands sliding over my breasts, down my belly, picturing his face between my legs as he laps me into an orgasm that makes my skin shrink around my body.

I sigh and lather, thinking of when I'll see him again. But if I am, I need to clear up last night. I need to talk to him.

I step out of the shower and call his phone. He answers on the first ring.

"Hi."

"Can you talk?" I ask.

"Yeah, I'm in the car. I had to leave my crew at Grayson's to come meet another client. Did you sleep well?"

"Not really," I say. "Did you?"

"Me neither. Was I the cause of your lack of sleep?"

I didn't expect him to bring it up so fast, but it's better this way. "Yes. Something obviously went wrong, and it was awkward."

"I'm sorry. I got in my own head and ruined our evening."

"You didn't ruin the whole evening. It was odd. Tell me why you got in your own head. What happened?"

He pauses. "It felt like too much all of a sudden. We're taking a big step to go out with A, and it got to me."

I flinch like he is in front of me. "I didn't ask for that."

"I know. That was all me. You were perfect. You are perfect. Everything was. I didn't know how to react. I'm bound to do stupid things. You know?"

And there's the thought that maybe he's not ready for this.

I chew on the inside of my cheek. "Yeah. If it's too much too fast, we can always table it for later. If it's not a good time, we can pump the brakes on this whole thing."

"No," he says quickly. "I think—no, *I know*, that it wasn't really about Ayla. It was that I wanted to stay with you. I wanted to hold you all night, to make love to you again, to wake you up with my mouth, stroking you with my tongue until your body shook."

His honesty disarms me and sends my body into a twister of raw need for him.

"All that would have been okay with me," I say even softer than before. God knows how much I want that. Now that I picture it, I can almost see us like a warm mirage, cocooned in my bed. I want that more than anything.

"I know. It's just…"

"You have Ayla."

"Does that make you mad?" he asks.

I frown. "That you have her? Of course not. I met you as her dad. I know the time may come for us to get there…"

Maybe?

"It will, Lux. I wouldn't have taken this step with you if I wasn't planning on following through."

"Okay, then," I say, not knowing what else to say.

"Oh, by the way, the crew should be there in an hour. We're running late. I sent you a message."

"I didn't see it. Lauren woke me up, like, twenty minutes ago, and I jumped in the shower."

"So, you just showered?" His voice drops.

"Yeah, I'm about to get dressed."

My phone begins to beep with the universal FaceTime tune.

I pick up, and his gorgeous smile fills my screen.

"Hello there," I say, trying not to swallow my tongue.

"There's where I want to be."

I shoot him a little smile. "We have an hour, right?"

"I'm near D.C. right now. I'm in Travilah."

"That's too bad."

The dimples appear at his cheeks. "I'm about to tell these people to shove their offer and delay the crew."

"You would do that?"

"To go over there and make you come all over my mouth, I would risk it all." He shoots me an *are-you-kidding* type of smile.

I chuckle. "Don't do that. We'll have more chances."

"I can make you come from here, then?"

I freeze. "What?"

But I know what he's saying, and *I want it*. Badly.

"Let me make you come, Lux."

I bite my lip. "You already did today…in the shower."

"*Diablo*, I'm good."

"Mmm-hmmm."

"*Dejame hacerte venir otra vez*. Prop your phone against a pillow and let me see."

My skin begins to tingle, and I don't even question it. I prop my phone.

"Lux," he groans. "I need you to be a really good girl for me. Do you know how to do that?"

I nod.

"*Asi, cierra los ojos*."

I do as he says and close my eyes.

"Your left hand is my hand. Put it on your tits." His voice vibrates through my body as I do what he says.

"Good girl. Now, your right hand is my mouth and your middle finger my tongue. Let me flick your clit, slow, easy. I have all the time in the world, and my only job is to get you off. *Nada mas sientelo*."

18

Oliver

"We should be there in ten minutes." I don't know why I say it. Ay is buried in her phone. She doesn't care what's going on.

I hate that both Lux and I have been so busy this week. I haven't been able to see her since our FaceTime session. We've texted. It's been flirty but not as light as I would want. Despite the FaceTime sex, I sense hesitation on her part. Now, we're going to hang out with Ayla without having a face-to-face talk about what happened the other night. I didn't want to cancel or postpone this outing. It wouldn't look good after my freakout the other night.

"Well, thank God we're almost there, because your anxious tapping is too much."

"Huh?"

She sighs. "*Papi*, you're, like, stressed out or something. You keep tapping on the steering wheel, and you're not listening to me."

"I'm sorry, *reina*. I didn't realize you were saying something. I've been caught up in my thoughts."

"No kidding. I know work has been really busy this week. You have way too many projects. Like you always tell me, *el que mucho abarca, poco aprieta.*"

It's my mom's saying. *He who tries to hoard too much seldom can keep a hold of all of it together.*

I laugh. "Are we at that point when you are now throwing wisdom words at me?"

I stop at the light and look at her. She's smiling more than usual, and her eyes are fixed on me. I pinch her cheek, and we keep going.

We park near the entrance to the complex and go out to stand in the front and wait. They're not here yet, but as I'm about to turn to my daughter, the champagne color Ranger Rover parks next to my Tahoe. I don't take my eyes off it. I don't want to miss the moment she steps out. She doesn't make me wait. She steps out in a green matching suit, the pants painted over her beautiful legs, illustrating every curve. She smiles and waves. And it's like we're alone. I exhale.

"She looks like a Thiccletics commercial."

I blink and turn to A. "Are you okay with this?"

She laughs. "Am I okay with hanging out with Bron and her Aunt Lux, who is probably the coolest person ever? That's not a weird question at all, *Papi*..."

I catch myself then. *Coño, get it together.*

Lux reaches us with Bron by her side this time. The girls hug, she gives me a chaste kiss on the cheek, and then she goes to embrace my baby girl. I get caught in A's big smile.

"I was telling *Papi* you look like a post sponsored by Thiccletics."

"Thanks, Ayla. I'm a little hurt the two of you didn't tell me the color of the day was blue."

And that's how I notice A and Bron are dressed almost the same.

The three of them are watching me with smiles, like I'm not in on the joke. "Are the two of you ready for us?"

Bron shakes her head. "Are you and Aunt Lux ready for me and A?"

"I thought we were a team?" I say to my daughter.

She shakes her head. "You're with Lux. A&B against L&O. Sorry, *Papi*."

The girls link arms and start going in.

Lux's smile brightens, and she shrugs. "You're stuck with me."

"We are…again." I whisper the last word for her ears only.

I can't help it. My brain jumps to our night when we were really stuck together, tangled up in her bed and then her floor with our mouths and bodies.

But I need to swipe that away. Today, we're with A and Bron. Those are not thoughts for this outing, so I shove the *sucio* back in the closet for the day.

We go inside, and I pay for the game. We get our jackets.

"Aunt Lux, A and I need a matching suit like yours."

"Economy price, please," Ayla adds.

"Actually, I can get you both this same exact one. I'll ask, and they will send them to me." She turns to me. "I'm sorry. Is that okay with you?"

I look from her to Ayla, who is trying to appear calm, but her eyes are practically begging me. I think it's a nice gesture. "It's okay. But I can also give you the money for it."

She shakes her head. "They sponsor some of my videos. Trust me, they'll happily give them to me."

"Must be nice."

"Her job is the coolest," my daughter sighs.

"I thought my job was the coolest."

She shakes her head. "No, you just build the coolest things."

"No lies detected," says Lux. "He's good with his hands…at building things."

She looks away, and my chest puffs.

"Oh, *Papi* is the best contractor. He has a 4.5-star rating on Amy's List. Some lady was mad and gave him a one-star review, even though her project was flawless."

That's what I get for getting involved with a client. It was one time, but *never again.*

"I'll have to go in and give him five stars so we can make that rating go higher," Lux says over her shoulder.

Except, this time. Lux is the exception to my rule.

"Thank you. I appreciate that."

The girls giggle, and we turn to look at them, but they're in their own world, whispering.

We get suited up and head toward the game room entrance. The tall gangly kid with the laser guns doesn't know where to look. He can't even look Lux in the eyes, but his eyes do a double-take on Ayla and then Bron. He's mumbling his words and not looking any of them in the face, and that's for the best, because I would shove that laser gun up his skinny ass.

The girls are too young, and Lux is mine...

Jesus, that's how I think about her now?

I don't get time to muse on that, because the doors open, and he mumbles good luck to the girls but not me.

The girls take off running, I'm sure trying to find a good place to get us.

It's dark inside, except for the neon lights marking the path.

I spot the corner, and the plan immediately comes together quickly. Lux is super serious with her laser gun ready.

"You've done this before."

She scoffs. "Chase is my brother. My whole life has been a manhunt. We've even played in the woods at night. That psycho used to delight in scaring the bejesus out of me."

We duck and make it to the corner, and I turn around, trapping her in, swelling her gasp of surprise with my lips on hers. "You look gorgeous, as always. I can't believe I held out for this long."

"I can't wait until you can kiss me in public."

"Soon."

She sighs into my mouth. "I shouldn't have said that. There's no pressure—"

Footsteps grow closer, and I jump back. She shoves me aside and shoots her laser at the kid before he can get me.

"You're welcome," she says and starts down the maze with me following behind.

"*Papi.*" I turn as I do every time I hear my baby's voice and get tagged in the chest.

She and Bron run away, giggling. "Later."

I don't see Lux for the rest of the game as I get kicked out. The pimply kid doesn't even thank me as I return the equipment.

An hour later, we are sitting in the food court, eating burgers and milkshakes. Of course, the two girls are sitting together, and the two of us are on the other side. I rub my leg against Lux's, and she sometimes makes it like she's looking for something and runs her hand down mine.

"Lux, what is your next video about?" Ayla asks.

"The people from *Feeding Charm City* are coming to show me how to cook some recipes. We are donating the proceeds from the viewing to the foundation. Lauren is sponsoring with Autumn Lush."

Bron laughs. "It's going to be great. Daddy is doing something with them too."

"*Papi*, you have to participate."

"What can I do? Donate? I'll definitely do that."

Lux shakes her head. "Actually, I think there's probably something you can do at their location. It's better if you donate your services. They can use that more, and they'll publicize you."

"I wouldn't feel right profiting."

"You're not profiting, *Papi*. They like to give credit, and that's to your benefit."

Bron takes a sip of her milkshake. "Yeah, you did a good deed, and it's like a side benefit."

Lux puts her hand on my forearm. "Sometimes these things are symbiotic. And the more you help and get clients, the more you can continue lending a hand."

I look at her hand, loving the feel of it, but she yanks it away.

"Sorry."

"No need." And I almost reach for her hand again but remember the teens. They're not even looking at us. They're looking at something on their phones. "You guys are teaching me a lot."

Bron looks up and smiles. "This is a good photo of us."

She turns her phone around, and it's the photo the dumb kid took of us when we got out. I look at Lux, and she's smiling. She held my hand behind the girls' backs. She also has her other hand on Ayla's shoulder. I like that they get along so well.

Ayla can be shy with people she doesn't know, but she is comfortable with Lux. I just need to see this through some more.

"Send me that photo, please," Lux asks Bron.

"Me too," I say.

I want a chance to talk to her and think it will have to wait until later in the week, but the doors of opportunity open when the girls stand up to go to the bathroom.

As they disappear around the corner, I turn to Lux. "We haven't had much time to talk this week."

She nods. "We've both been busy."

"True. I just wondered if there wasn't anything more."

"You mean me staying away from you like how you ran off the other night?"

Damn. She doesn't mince words.

"Yeah. I didn't mean to make things awkward. I just…"

"Got scared?" she asks.

"It's a big step. For me."

Her eyes go warm. "I know."

"But it still upset you. I'm sorry about that. That's the last thing I want."

She nods. "It didn't upset me, per se. It just gave me red-flag vibes."

My stomach tightens. "Red-flag vibes? What do you mean?"

She shrugs a little. "After we got off FaceTime…and as good as that was…" Her smile is fleeting. "Once I came off the high, I had time to think. I wondered if a close moment like that makes you so uncomfortable, how can we get to the next level?"

The itch breaks out on the back of my neck. "Well, we are just getting started, and I didn't cancel today. This scares me, but I'm here. We're here."

Her hand goes to my leg. "I know. It's just, at that moment…we were connecting, and we just had some mind-blowing…" She looks away in the direction the girls disappeared and then back at me. "It was really good."

"It was," I say, covering her hand with mine. "I just need a little more time. We will get there. I promise."

She nods. "I think it would be better if we talked things out if this happens again. Don't run, just talk to me."

"I can do that. Thank you for understanding."

She gives me a small smile. "I like communication and transparency. If there comes a point where this is not working for either of us, I want us to be free to be honest."

I press down on her hand and lean closer. "I like what we have. I won't clam up again."

"Okay," she says.

I look over her shoulder as the girls walk out of the bathroom.

When our gazes meet again, Lux removes her hand. I try to give her a reassuring smile, but she reaches for her phone.

And I swear that I won't make her doubt again.

19

Oliver

Two months later

The glow in Lux's cheeks is like a sun of its own. Her skin is rosy and warm. I love putting this heightened color on her skin, that smile that stretches her mouth. I have to get up soon, but I don't want to move. I want to stay here, with her wrapped up around me, enjoying the way her back arches against the palm of my hand, pressing her tits against my chest with each stroke.

"How long will you be gone?" she says with that lazy, sated tone that always stays with me long after I leave her.

"Two days." I hate how that sounds, even to my ears. Two days away from Ayla. From my job. *From you.*

"That sounds like a long time right now." She's echoing my thoughts. Her voice is clearer now, sobriety filtering through.

God knows I'm there too. We've had so many bumps, never seeing completely eye to eye. But this...this is a good time. Since we did laser tag, things have been cool for a while.

"I know. I wish this had not come up right now, but it's a great opportunity. I shouldn't turn it down."

I wouldn't have wanted to before. More money, bigger chances, more savings to give her the things she's used to.

Lux's forehead wrinkles. "You shouldn't turn it down. It's a good thing for you professionally. If anyone understands, it's me. Opportunities don't always present themselves this easily."

I kiss her forehead. "I know you get it. Thank you, especially because this opportunity came through you. Building another set for a *Big Apple* project is the dream. I just wish it was on this side of the country."

"It's all on merit." She leans in, and I peck her lips. Then she pulls back. "Wait. But doesn't Ayla have a game tomorrow? If you want, I can—"

"Yeah, she does. I asked Cam and Adri if she could stay at their house. You know she's more than excited about spending that much time with Bron. They're planning all sorts of teenage things. She even said something to the effect of this being practice for when they go away to college and study abroad. She took five years off my life with that statement."

She chuckles. "Aww. I can't imagine. Does she have other activities? If you need help—"

I squeeze her ass, pressing her closer to me.

"Winter will pick her and Bron up for their painting lesson, and Lauren has agreed to take them out to hang out or if she wants to go somewhere. I don't want to overload Adri and Cam since they have CJ."

"Oh. That's good."

There's a lapse in our conversation, and I want to take advantage of that. I dip my head to her neck, pushing her on her back, but she tilts away and throws the covers back. My face lands on her pillow.

"I have to go to the bathroom."

She gets up, and I get to stare at her while she walks away, her hips swaying. It's seriously her best look. When she's dressed, I spend so much time picturing her like this. Thank you, squat workouts. I wait a few minutes then throw my side of the covers back. A shower quickie before I have to head out, watching the water slide down her chest as I pound her, is even better.

When the door swings open, she's got her robe tightly wrapped around her.

"I was coming to get you." My finger sneaks through the folds of her robe.

Her lips curve into the tightest smile I've seen on her yet. "I'm going to make us some coffee. You'll need it for the road, and I need it to get back to work."

She strolls past me and goes downstairs.

I'm left standing on the bathroom door with a hard-on and the impression that everything just changed in the time she went to the bathroom.

I take two steps to follow her, but my phone flashes with the time alert. Shit, I have to get going so I can stop by the bistro to drop off A's favorite blanket and overnight bag after I get out of here.

I can take a quick shower at home, but first, I need to talk to Lux and see what the hell just happened. It couldn't have been something I said, because we've barely talked.

Is she mad because I didn't invite her on the trip?

I mean, I won't be available, but who knows? Maybe she wanted to come and spend time alone. She's a blogger who could probably keep herself entertained during the day.

But that's ridiculous. She's very direct, so she would've said that.

I'm on the stairs as soon as my shoes are tied and get downstairs in quick steps. She's in the kitchen, pouring the coffee. Her shoulders are squared back, and she's got that blank look I've seen before when I was rude to her. It's never a good thing because she's blacked out on me right after wearing that look.

She points at the cup she left for me.

I smile. "Thank you."

"You're welcome." Her lips do that ridiculous strained curve I didn't know I hated until I saw it on her. It's unnatural and unnerving —because she's ticked about something.

"What's wrong?"

"Nothing," she says.

Yeah, right.

Nothing says *something* louder like a woman's *nothing.*

"Are you sure? I could swear something is bothering you."

Her face remains impassive. "Nothing is bothering me."

So much for being transparent with each other.

I force a breath. "Lux, I have to take Ayla's bag to Adri's before I head to the airport. I don't have much time. I can't sit here and have a dragged-out conversation. If you tell me what's wrong, we can fix it so it doesn't fester."

Her gaze cools enough to freeze me in place.

"One, I did not ask for a long conversation, and two, nothing should be bothering me, because it's been clear as day from the beginning. I just see it better now, and I'll adjust accordingly—"

Her sharp tone makes my eye twitch. "What the hell are you talking about?"

"If you let me finish my sentences, you would know what I'm trying to say."

Jesus. What the fuck is this? "Fine, go on."

"I'll make it quick because you have to go, but isn't it funny you're rushing now when, just a few minutes ago, you were getting ready to climb all over me?" She waves a hand. "But I digress. How come you didn't ask me to drop off Ayla's bag for you?"

My mind goes blank, and then it clicks. She's pissed because I could have asked her for this favor, and I didn't. I almost smile with relief.

"You have a fair point. I guess I was trying to maximize our time together. As far as the bag, I don't want to bother you. You have things to do."

She leans on the counter. "But Winter doesn't? She has a baby, a full-time job, painting, charities with her husband, and a house reno going on. Lauren has a business, raising two boys, and a husband. Adri and Cam have two kids, businesses, and coaching. Be honest, Oliver. I believe you have bigger reasons for not asking me. And I am not okay with those." Her voice quivers in the end, but her gaze tells me she's dead serious.

I don't need this right now.

———

Lux

I have to stop talking and catch my breath. I am not handling this the right way. I came downstairs hoping he would take his coffee and run out. A big emotional scene wasn't in the plans. I didn't want to do this right now...or ever. But it's out in the open.

You can't take it back, Luciana.

My skin doesn't need to burn like this. My heart doesn't need to try to shove itself out of my chest like it's doing now. He literally thought of *everyone* in his circle but me.

"I didn't want to bother you. You never mentioned that you wanted to be that kind of help," he says.

The flash of heat over my face is so fast and so strong I'm like a kettle at boiling point.

Yeah, he's going to take me there.

"Are you fucking with me? I get that today you didn't realize I was offering, because you kept interrupting to tell me your plans. But how many times have I said how much I would love the chance to spend time with Ayla, just me and her. That could help speed up the process for us."

His hands press against the marble countertop. "Lux, we agreed to go slow with that."

"Yes, and I am okay with that. But I'm seriously starting to think it's something else. Maybe you think I'm going to hurt your baby girl, or you think I'm not someone you expect will last more than a little while."

His face goes dark. "I've never said that."

"You don't have to. Your actions do all the talking for you."

Shut up, Luciana. You're going to say something you regret.

I may have already said too much. He's looking at me like I'm some crazy bitch. But I'm so angry even the tapping on my arm is not working. My gaze lands on the wall behind him to the letters I had carved and sprayed in gold. It's my mantra. VYOEWINC.

Voice your opinion even when it's not comfortable.

It's a sign, and I can't even stop my mouth from opening and saying what's on the tip of my tongue. No matter the consequences. Silence never leads to a good place.

"You know, Mateo may be a monumental lying, cheating asshole, but he never tried to keep me as his dirty little secret. He still begs to spend time with me and be seen with me. He's proud to have me on his arm. You, the nice guy, want to keep what we have locked in a room with the curtains drawn, out of the light so your amazing daughter—and maybe the entire world—doesn't find out."

He takes a step forward then stops. "You're jumping to these far-reaching conclusions over me not asking you to do me one favor?"

"No," I scream louder than I meant. "It's not just one favor. You've left me out of all the plans, like I'm your booty call and not your girl-friend. And it's not just today. It's everything. You act as if I'm not worthy of introducing to everyone or even letting people know that we're together."

"We talked about this. We were going to build—"

"Yeah, build, not hide."

We're so close I can feel his breath on my face, and the warmth of it reaches me fast, like the implications of this moment. Understanding hits me with brutal force. *This may be it.* I can't compromise anymore.

"Luciana—"

I shake my head. "I'm sorry, Oliver, but this is not working for me. I won't be anyone's dirty secret. I may not be the most knowledgeable person when it comes to what's best for kids or relationships, but I know this is not right for Ayla or me."

He reaches for me. "You're not my dirty secret or hidden relation-ship. I just want—"

I step back. "To cover all your bases."

His head bobs up and down. "When you have a child, you can't risk hurting them."

My throat thickens, and there's that familiar tingle in my nose. I'm going to cry soon, but I am not going to do it in front of him. I breathe slow and measured, channeling the way I have to speak to my mother, who doesn't tolerate anyone else's meltdowns.

"I understand that. But in relationships with other humans, there's no possible way to cover all your bases. I understand these are your rules, but this is not fair to me. As much as I love Ayla and care for you, I'm not going to shortchange myself. I can't keep making you a priority if all I am to you is a comfortable hidden option."

There, you said it.

20

Oliver

This baby has been crying for the last two of the flight's five hours and six minutes. Between his wailing, the plane engine noise, and his mother's anxious fretting, my head has been pounding to no end. I can't say I blame him. The woman has been making me nervous and fussy. I can't blame her either. She's a new mom with—from what she tells me—an asshole for a husband.

I was just trying to help when I start talking to her. I know what it's like to get the pissed-off looks from everyone around you because your baby won't stop crying. I'm so grateful Ayla and I are over a decade past that stage.

"Can you fucking believe he chose to go to work overtime while I'm here struggling with this baby on a flight?" She swatted at the tears on her face. "I have a stranger holding our baby—no offense—because he puked all over me, and I'm shaking so bad."

She was so anxious that the flight attendant came by a few times. I took one look at the mom, and it took me back to my first flight with Ayla to Dominican Republic.

"Listen," I said, touching her forearm lightly and in a way that couldn't be misinterpreted. "He's going to be more agitated because you are. Right now, the flight is uncomfortable for him. His ears popped, and you need to be relaxed so you can help him get through it."

She blinked fast enough to send tears rolling down her cheeks. "But how? I feel like nothing I do calms him down."

I extended my hands. "Let me hold him for a bit."

Her hands flexed around the baby's back, making him scream.

Good. She's not so far gone she's not protective of him.

I smile. "It's okay. I'll be right here, and you can watch me. I have a daughter, and when she was little, she wasn't the best flier. She would rage and annoy everyone if I didn't keep her calm and entertained."

Her eyes narrowed on my face, and just then, the baby let out a big wail, and she practically shoved him at me. "Connor. You're going to annoy everyone on the plane."

I shift my gaze from her to the baby. "Connor? That's your name?"

The baby stops crying to look up at me with wide eyes.

I take advantage of his surprise to get acquainted with him. "I'm Ollie."

I extend a hand to his mother as well then proceed to hold the baby high against my shoulder and place timed pats on his bottom. He snuggles up.

"He likes you."

"I think he likes that I bounce him."

She laughs a little. It's a croaky sound but better than the sniffling and tears from earlier. Still, she's watching me like a hawk, just like I would if I was her. You should only let a stranger hold your baby in emergency situations or when you're at a breaking point and not doing either of you any good.

"How old is your daughter now?"

"She's thirteen."

"Oh, wow. I can't wait to get there."

I laugh. "You say that now, but times flies by, and you'll miss this time."

Her hand flies to her mouth. "*OhmyGod.* I don't mean to make it sound like I don't appreciate or love him. It's just hard."

"Hey, no judgment here. The first year is really tough, especially when you're alone."

"Where was your wife?"

There's a sharp pinch on my neck at the thought of Noris. I hate that she never entirely goes away, that I can't erase her memory from our lives. "We were going through a divorce."

Correction. I was going through a divorce. There was no we about it. She had left the relationship long before.

"I'm sorry."

"No worries. So, I had Ayla—that's my daughter's name—and she was awful on planes. I had to learn how to keep her from screaming. She got so much better. So don't despair with Connor."

She smiles and lifts a hand to the sky. "From your mouth to God's ears. And let me tell you, this is the last fucking time Paul leaves me alone to fly."

"It's hard when you have to work—"

She rolls her eyes. "He chose to. He could've said no. I keep noticing he always chooses to work when the difficult stuff comes up. I bet you tomorrow he shows up, fresh as a daisy, to his mother's house, after I get there looking like a truck ran me over. For the rest of the day, I'll have to put up with her snide comments about me not being a proper wife and mother."

"Yikes. I don't miss that."

She leans closer. "Was your mother-in-law a witch with b not a w like mine? This woman swears her son is the best brand of sliced bread, and I'm the grocery store brand of butter. She treats me like I'm a dirty rug outside a men's bathroom."

I nod. "Yes, I can relate. It took something earth-shattering to make my former mother-in-law see that I'm not the bad guy."

It's true. Mrs. Morales used to love looking down her nose at me. Her daughter could do much better than a jock that was probably going to cheat on her with girls in every city. And then her precious jewel left her new family for a married surgeon to the stars.

"How did you explain the divorce to your daughter when she was older?" Her voice carries a certain heaviness—one I can understand well.

She's weighing her options.

"I had ample time to prepare her. It was just her and me, so when she would ask, I made sure I told her the truth but buffered it according to the age."

She nods. "That's good. Is her mother still around?"

I push down the anger at the thought of Noris coming back. I still can't wrap my head around her leaving Ayla. "No."

"Jesus. That's terrible. How can you leave your little one?"

Yeah, that's the twelve-and-a-half-year question.

"Did you remarry?" She yawns. Her words are a bit slurry.

"No."

Her eyes take a warm tone. "Oh. How does a handsome guy like you stay single? You have to be a great guy to help me like you are."

I chuckle. "Thank you. I think it has mostly been by choice. I don't think I ever found someone who would love my baby girl like I do."

She frowns, but her head drifts back against the seat. "Maybe you're dating the wrong kind of woman, because if they loved you, how could they not love her? The right woman would want to be there for her like she is for you."

"I didn't—" I catch myself before I can say I didn't introduce any women to her. "You should nap. I'll entertain Connor so you can catch a few minutes."

Her eyes drift closed, and I'm left alone with a three-month-old. *Again.* I know what to do with this one, though. I rock him until he follows his mother's example and goes to sleep.

And now I'm left with my thoughts.

In a way, it was a blessing to be distracted by this woman and her problems. But she's made me think about mine. I have a pissed off… girlfriend?…at home—if she still wants to have anything to do with me. I couldn't tell my fellow passenger why another woman would never love my A like I do. Because her question hit too close to home…and because I never trusted anyone around Ayla, other than Adri, Lauren, and Winter, who pose no threat.

I never wanted my baby to experience any rejection or slight. I couldn't bear it if someone did to her what my father's wife or their kids did to me that one time we met.

I never gave anyone the chance.

I'm not even giving Lux the chance. She's there for me. I finally feel like I have someone I can talk to. And she's always loving and kind to my girl.

I love her, but I'm not giving her a chance, not giving us a chance.

My chest rattles as the words sink into my head. *I love Lux.*

No, I can't. It's too fast, isn't it? When could it have happened? We've only been together a few months.

But it's enough to have me waking up happier than I've ever been. She's filled that emptiness. She's become a partner, and she didn't run when I freaked out. Yeah, she was cautious, but she voiced her opinion, and we worked it out.

Jesus, I love her...*and you're about to lose her.*

"Ladies and gentlemen, we are beginning our descent into Los Angeles International Airport. Please turn off all portable electronic devices and stow them until we have arrived at the gate..."

The flight attendant's voice fades out to Connor's screams. I bounce him, buying his mother a few more minutes.

Fifteen minutes later, we're on the ground. I check my phone. I have one message. It's a selfie of Ayla with a sad face and bunny ears.

AYLA

I miss you already.

It's the only text I've needed before, but I can't help but feel like I'm missing out on another text, one I would've had if I had kept my mouth shut. The one I didn't know, hours ago, would matter so much after this flight.

I need to fix this. No, I'm going to fix it.

21

Lux

I planned to spend the day in bed, nursing my feelings with Netflix, a big cupcake from Market Fresh, and pitcher of pineapple-pomegranate mimosas. It's the proper segue after spending one hour mad at myself and two hours sleeping. But I can't waste a whole day on my feelings. At eleven, I dust myself off, get out of bed, and sit in front of my laptop. Thank God, once I know all I need to say, my job is pretty easy for me. All my research was done; I just needed to put it into words. I finished my blog entry in thirty minutes and am feeling so proud of myself that I'm ready to go back to my bed.

My phone buzzes with Lauren's name. It's a text: ***Come to Autumn Lush. Let's have lunch together and chill while I work.***

It's tempting. I can lose myself in her work, play dress up with real dolls, and Autumn Lush is one of my favorite places. I should've asked her to go there to write my post, but I'm not in the mood. I am not fit to be seen or to be in anyone's company.

ME

I'm a little tired and don't want to leave my bed.

The three little dots appear on my screen, and her reply comes right after.

> LAUREN
>
> I need you...I'm working on an official collection...

> ME
>
> Huh

And then it hits me.

> ME
>
> Wait, THE collection?

> LAUREN
>
> Mm-hmm. So come on.

She can't say, but I know she's working on Mrs. Davis's campaign outfits. She's hitting all the campaign stops, and she doesn't trust anyone but Lauren, because my sister makes her look appropriately bold, sexy, and sophisticated. I'm dying to see what she has planned.

That perks me up, and before I really make up my mind to go, I find myself in front of my closet. I jump into ripped jeans, a tight t-shirt, and a double-breasted jacket. I match it with pointy flats and dangling earrings. I add a little makeup around the eyes to hide the swelling.

I wish my stupid skin didn't show when I've been crying. Twenty minutes later, I am walking through the doors of Autumn Lush. The scent of lemongrass hangs in the air, and in the waiting area past reception, a group of women chat and giggle.

The receptionist points me in the direction of the back. One of the women gasps, and then her voices drop to a whisper, "Is that *Bougie Girl*?"

Thank God for the huge shades that hide my eyes, because the next thing one of them would've asked is what the hell happened to my face.

The relief doesn't last long because Lauren frowns the second I take my glasses off. "What's wrong?"

I shake my head. "Nothing. It's just one of those days."

She puts the pen down and leans forward in her chair. "One of those days when you cry?"

"I'll be fine."

"You should tell me what it is," she says. "If it's a who, I'll take my heels off, and we can go whoop them together."

I laugh, but I'm touched. She's a warrior for her people. This is why my brother worships the ground she walks on. "It's no one. I put myself in situations, make dumb decisions, then wonder why it blows up in my face."

"It's called *you're a human being.* How did Ollie mess up this time?"

I blink a couple of times, but she shakes her head.

"Don't bother lying to me. Once we talk about putting ourselves in situations and decision making, it's always about a man."

I sigh. She's right, and she knows what's up, so there's no point in denying it. "I'm starting to feel like his fallback girl."

Her eyes round, then she stands and comes around the desk. "Don't even joke about that. You're definitely not that."

"Think about it. I keep trying to pursue relationships with men who are definitely emotionally unavailable. Mateo, because he wanted to screw every girl that crossed his path. Now Ollie, because he doesn't think I'm worth having on his arm."

Her mouth goes agape. "Did he say that? Because if he did, he doesn't need to worry about Chase. I can handle him on my own."

I shake my head. "No. He doesn't have to say it. I can tell this is going nowhere I want to be part of. I wouldn't have been opposed to being friends with benefits, but that should have been worked out from the beginning. It's too late for that now."

"Tell me exactly what he did," Lauren asks.

"He didn't do anything wrong, really. The issue is...what he didn't do."

"Explain," she demands.

"It's in his actions, his words, and us. Everything is secretive. We can't hang alone with Ayla because he's afraid that if something goes wrong, then it will affect her. He doesn't tell her anything about us. He's not even gradually bringing us together. I don't think he has the intention to."

"Lux—"

I can't stop now that I got started. "Don't you notice it? He went on this trip and asked everyone, including you, to help with Ayla. Everyone but me. This would have been the perfect chance for her and me to spend time together and build on our relationship. She could've even stayed with me. You trusted me with Felix and Justin, but it's like he thinks I'm going to damage the person he loves more than anyone."

"Adri, Winter, and I have always noticed he's overly cautious with Ayla, and we commended him for it. That said, you're not just anyone. You two are dating, and he has to approach things differently now."

"He's not. But he did warn me about how much he guards her. He's been consistent with that. I'm the one who keeps trying to change things that have already been agreed upon. I just didn't realize it would drag on this long. And I can't do this. I can't be his secret. So, I got pissed this morning, and that's never good because I get cold and emotional."

She sighs. "And you blew up. Well, I can't say I blame you, but I do say you should've spoken up sooner. Sometimes, we don't speak up until we're ready to blow, and shit just goes wrong. How did he react?"

I roll my eyes. "Defensive. He wants to protect his Ayla, and honestly, I get that. I just hate that it's an excuse not to go deeper with me. We're not even going places, Lauren. He works all day, as do I, and in the evenings, he's home. As inventive as I can get, I want to go out and do things. I don't want to feel like we're just fucking."

Lauren nods. "Yeah, but he may not even notice that's what he's doing."

I open my mouth, but she raises a hand.

"However, you pointed this out to him. The ball is in his court. Let's see what his reaction is. While we wait, you need to decide what you want. If he comes back and says he can't do what you want right now…"

"I'll tell him let's revisit this when he can, but I'm putting myself out there."

"Yes, that's fair. You don't need to shelf yourself for anyone. You're too valuable. But Ollie is a smart guy. I'm betting he comes back after reanalyzing, and things will change."

"Lauren, Ayla's way too important to him. He's not going to do that." I shrug like the last sentence isn't burning a hole in my stomach.

She smiles. "Want to bet? You always lose to me."

———

My nephew's wailing is loud enough to reach me, but I know better now than to rush inside in a panic. Because nothing's wrong. He hasn't been dropped. Cam and Adri are not being robbed or kidnapped. Cam's junior version is just a crier, which, according to Adri, is exactly how Bron was as a baby.

It's hard to imagine, though. My niece is pretty much sunshine and love all the time.

That's why I smile and linger in my car, checking out the views on my latest video. Soon, I'll be inside, hugging and kissing on him until he stops crying. My video has already reached six million views. I can't believe my impromptu video with Lauren is getting this kind of attention.

After Mrs. Davies left, we were so hyped on what we had just achieved that we went live on Instagram, talking about our favorite pampering items and trying some of Autumn Lush's new gift set products. We also recorded it, and I posted it to my YouTube channel. It's better I snagged the video and posted it than some random person. I benefited from my organic content and unique views.

I'm watching the part where we hit the champagne for what we internally called a wink celebration, because the collection was ready to go to her seamstress for production. Chase had to pick us up and take us home. But the content is some of my best. I fell asleep fast and didn't have time to think of my possible breakup.

My phone goes off, and my heart skips a beat at the unknown number. Could it be Ollie from his hotel room?

I answer, half knowing I'm being ridiculous, half too excited to contain.

"Hello. You have a call from an inmate at Jessup Correctional Facility. Do you accept the charges?"

The robotic voice echoes in my ears, and I stare at my phone. The skin on my cheeks feels like it's been peeled back. *It's Walter.* My finger hovers over the red icon. *Do I hang up?*

The message repeats again, and I don't think. I answer, "Yes."

The line connects.

"Luciana?"

How can a voice so low bring so many memories?

"It's me, Walter. How are you?"

"There's my girl." His words are color in a smile, and the memory hits me hard.

I'm four years old, and we're playing in the pool. Cam and Chase are racing to the other side. Walter swings me in the air and lets me fall into the water, but quickly, his hands slip under my arm, and I only go waist deep.

My laughter rings out, and I beg, "Again, Daddy. Again."

He swings me up again, and I'm free-falling.

"Luciana? Are you there?" The memory comes crashing down.

I clear my throat. "I'm here, Walter. What do you need?"

His sigh fills the line. "I need to see my daughter. Come see me."

My stomach churns because I wish he had asked me anything, just not this. "I can't right now, but maybe in a couple of weeks."

There's silence.

"I know I shouldn't have taken Bron. I'm already paying for it. Don't let me die alone here."

The squeeze in my belly is so tight it hurts. "You're not going to die."

"Do I need to beg?"

Beg? I've never heard this tone of his.

"No. I'll come see you. I'm just busy right now."

"Cam has the right to be angry with me. The mutt does too. But I was a good dad to you, Luciana. You have no excuses."

The nausea rising up my throat is eclipsed by the rage.

"Don't call him a mutt. Chase had no fault. You and Marilyn made the choice to— You know what? I can't do this. I'll talk to you some other time." I hang up and take a couple of minutes to compose myself.

CJ is still screaming. The clock on my phone tells me it has only been two minutes, but God, that felt so long.

How can he be so evil? So horrible.

He and Marilyn decided to pay a debt with her body. She got pregnant with Chase from that night and chose not to terminate and not tell Walter until it was too late. He took it out on Chase when he was the innocent. They're lower than dirt for what they did and how he treated my brother.

I open my messages app and text my brother.

ME

I love you.

His reply is quick.

CHASE

Well duh. Are you drunk again, or do you want me to take you shopping?

I laugh out loud, and the nasty energy leaves my body. I head inside because I need to put Walter out of my mind. Bron is rocking CJ, and Cam is hovering around, trying to soothe him. Adri is in the kitchen, cooking something. Ayla is helping her out.

I say hi to everyone and go kiss the crying boy, but he doesn't want to come to me. He holds on tighter to his sister. I go back to the kitchen.

"What's my role here?" I ask Adri.

She turns around and hooks a thumb to the fridge. "Salad." She turns to Cam. "You and Bron take CJ for a walk around the house. Ayla, do you want to go with them? I can handle things here."

"I'll stay and help you, Lux." Ayla appears at my side. Her smile is contagious as she grabs the knife.

I hold up a hand. "Wait, should you handle that?"

She laughs. "I'm thirteen." She takes one of the cucumbers and begins to slice it in perfect wheels. She's better at it than I could ever be.

Adri is staring at us with a smile. She and Lauren are convinced that this is what I need to get to know Ayla better. It shouldn't be like this. Her father should be brokering this. I'm not looking forward to telling Adri that things may be kaput with Ollie.

I wash the lettuce and add the cucumbers on one side. Ayla has started on the tomatoes. "I can make my dad's dressing."

"At this point, you'll end up doing all the work. Wait, you know how to make dressing?" I ask, shocked she knows that much.

She giggles. "It's super easy. Papi says all Dominicans know how to make this one."

Adri chimes in. "Not me. I always get the wrong salt-to-vinegar ratio."

"I can show you."

She grabs salt, vinegar, and olive oil from the cupboards. She gets started telling us what to add and in what order, and in that moment, it hits me again how eloquent she is, how she transforms when she's instructing something or in front of the camera. If she decides to get her own channel, she would be a force. She could be a vlogger easily. The camera loves her.

I wonder if her dad would let her do a video with me. She, Bron, and I could do a recipe for my channel. Maybe I can ask him later.

When, Luciana? You're almost ninety-nine percent sure you'll be breaking up with him.

"Why are you looking at me like that?" Ayla's voice shakes me off my thoughts.

"Because you're so good at that stuff. You could easily do instructional videos for a living. You're such a natural at explaining and being on film."

"Thank you," she says. "I like processes and steps. It's easier for me to follow, so that's how I explain it. Like when you told me how to pose."

Processes? Steps?

"Next time, I'll try to make the salad, and you help me."

She brightens. "Deal. Can you do a makeup tutorial with us? B and I really want to learn so we don't look like clowns, like some of the girls in school."

Adri doesn't stop stirring. "I know who you mean. It's because their mothers let them wear too much makeup. You are all natural beauties at your age. Makeup should look as natural as possible. I'll be back. It's too quiet. Let me make sure they're all okay."

Adri walks away, and I lean closer to Ayla. "Makeup should definitely be as natural as possible—except for eyeshadow and lashes. But you want schoolgirl style and not to look like a fan."

Ayla laughs. "My lashes already get in the way of pitching if I don't comb them."

"It's because yours are naturally long. You're so lucky. Natural schoolgirl lashes and skin so gorgeous it should be in moisturizer commercials. I would kill for all that."

She tilts her head like she doesn't full believe me. "Really? I love your style. Your makeup is always great."

"I wear it to make my skin look smooth, but yours already is even and silky. Always take care of it so it will continue to be that way. Make sure you're doing three things. One, using a good cleanser. Two, moisturizing every day. And three, when you're out on the field, wear sunscreen to protect from the UV rays."

She nods. "Thank you. I'll follow one, two, and three. Ohh, B and I saw your video yesterday about the trendy tops."

"What did you think?"

"It was really good. Not everything has to be a crop top. *Papi* won't let me wear them."

"I can understand. You and Bron are still young. Honestly, there are so many ways to look pretty and sexy without showing so much. One of the primary rules of fashion is don't show skin everywhere. If you're showing shoulder, wear long bottoms. If you wear shorts, don't show your stomach too—unless you're at the beach."

She nods like it makes sense. "I wish you could come shopping with us one day. You're always great, and I sometimes don't know what to get."

"You should get things that you love, look good on you, and feel comfortable in," I say, and I can't explain why I'm so touched that she wants to go shopping with me.

"Do you ever get intimidated?" she asks, reminding me so much of me at that age.

"Of course I get intimidated."

She shakes her head. "But you never show it."

I shrug. "I've just learned to hide it well. I used to get super self-conscious, so I taught myself some tips and tricks to get through it."

"Can you show me?"

I nod. "The first thing is, the world doesn't have to know when you're not feeling 100%."

She blinks a few times. "How do you hide it? I get so nervous when I have to speak in public or with people I don't know."

"Sometimes, a little mystery is a good thing. I smile and don't talk if I don't have to, but I don't completely shut down. Also, I'm not overly bubbly, and if I have to walk into a room I don't know anyone in, I like to think about a situation where I feel completely comfortable, like when I'm bossing around Chase."

Her laughter rings out. "You're funny. *Papi* always tells me something like that when I'm pitching a big game, but as long as I have my lucky socks, I don't get intimidated by that."

I frown. "You don't?"

She shakes her head. "No, sometimes you strike the batter out, and sometimes they get the best of you. I just go out there and run through my arsenal. We always prepare well before games. You know? We watch videos. Mr. Cam and *Papi* always have footage of the batters, and they both give me advice. I figure with that and all the practice and skill I put in, if I get lit up, that's just the game."

I don't think I've ever heard her talk so much in one breath. It's so mature. "That's a really good way to look at it, Ay." I pause. "I'm sorry, Ayla."

Her smile is so earnest. "You can call me Ay. We're really close, right?"

My heart drips down my chest like butter melting over popcorn. "We definitely are."

"And I like it. Only Bron and *Papi* call me Ay."

"I'm honored, and I'll do that." I put my hand on her shoulder but squelch the urge to hug her. I don't want her to think I'm weird.

Why can't he see how good she and I are together? I sigh and swipe the thought left. It won't do me any good to think about it. It'll just upset me all over again.

"You should come out with *Papi* and me again."

My stomach clenches. "Yeah…that would be fun."

Even though I'm not sure…because I may have to dump her father.

———

I hold CJ up until we're face to face, and he smiles, his hands reaching for my face. He looks so much like Cam and Bron it makes me smile. "Stop being so cute."

"Yes, please. Because it makes his dad forget about all the screaming he does at night and then he wants another one of him running around."

I snort. "It won't matter to Cam. He's decided he wants many more of him and Bron."

"Tell me about it," she says, and her tone is soft.

I turn to her, and she's looking at us with a soft smile.

"You want another one too?"

"Yes. He's growing up so fast, and if we want to get a move on it, this is the time. So…we're trying."

My eyes fill before I can help it. "That's so nice."

She nods. "Winter and I will be pregnant together again. We couldn't get Lauren on board for this one. Now the two of you will have to go together."

My mouth falls open. "Um. I am not. We're not… This is too new for me to be thinking about kids."

"The time will come. I already know you'll be a great mom. You're awesome with Ayla."

And that's when I remember her, and my heart drops. I look around.

"They're in Bron's room, doing teenage things. I wouldn't put you in that position."

I sigh because I haven't mustered the courage to tell her that things may be dead between Ollie and me. "I know. It's just that Ollie is super careful with her, and I don't want anything to get in the way of that."

"You see? You already put her first. Very mommy of you. Now, give me my son, and go get the teens so we can eat."

I laugh and hand CJ to her.

I zap her words straight out of my mind. If going out in public is this much of a hassle, I don't even want to know what he would say about something like that.

Does he even want more kids?

I've never actually given it much thought. When I was with Mateo, we talked about it—well, in the beginning, anyway. That was the time when he called me the perfect wife material, and I listened. Worst of all, I believed it. The first time he cheated on me, he claimed it was out of fear. I was the perfect girlfriend, the dream wife-to-be. It supposedly scared him because his father had been a player who left scattered children everywhere. Everyone expected Mateo to do the same. Instead of doing better, he set out to fulfill the prophecy that plagued him his whole life.

"How did it feel to talk to her?" Bron's words slash through my memory as I turn the corner.

"It was…weird. But she's so nice, you know?" Ayla says. "She called me her *princesa*."

"Aww, that's what mama calls me sometimes." My niece's sweet response makes it all clear in my head.

Ayla's been talking to her mom. Ollie never mentioned anything, though. He normally gets very tense when his ex is mentioned. He would have said something.

"Are you going to keep talking to her?"

I can't see Ayla's response, and I move closer to the door.

"I want to. She said I could come spend some time with her in Cali. She wants to take me to the beach and shopping."

"That's so cool, Ay. I am so happy for you. You're getting your mom back. I've been so happy since I met Daddy." Bron's voice is so dreamy. She's a kid. She doesn't realize how different their situations are. Cam never knew about Bron, and when he found her, nothing could have kept him from her.

Noris has known all along where Ayla is. She walked away on purpose. I don't judge her, but she could've come back anytime. She chose not to.

"I've always wanted my mom, but I'm scared. I don't know what *Papi* will say. I don't want him to hate me."

My heart drops down my chest. She's doing this behind his back. *Oh God.*

"When are you going to tell—"

Bron swings the door open, and her mouth drops, stalling mid-sentence when she sees me standing there. Next to her, Ayla's face goes ghostly white.

We stare at each other, frozen on the spot. I don't know what to say to her.

Bron breaks our frozen state by stepping closer to Ayla. She's a little between us and, God, if I don't love the way they're so fiercely protective of each other. But I can't let that stop me from saying what needs to be said.

"I wasn't eavesdropping. I was coming to get you for dinner when I heard what you said. Ay, you need to tell your dad immediately. He needs to know you are talking to your mom."

Ayla's mouth opens, but nothing comes out. She only shakes her head.

"She has the right to see her mom," my niece says instead. "She hasn't seen her for thirteen years, and she wants to get to know her."

By her mother's own choice.

Ayla doesn't understand that, and she shouldn't have to, but still, she needs to tell her dad.

"I understand, but Ayla lives with her dad, and they should not keep any secrets from each other."

"He keeps secrets from me. He's had girlfriends…" She trails off, but it's the fire in her eyes that calls out to me.

"It's true, Aunt Lux." Bron is on A's side all the way.

Jesus. "I am sure he has his reasons. This is not the same. Your dad needs to know. He has custody of you, but if you tell him, he wouldn't oppose you talking to her."

Ayla shakes her head but finds her voice. "You don't understand. *Papi* is still hurt that she went away. I heard him talking to my *abuela* one day when she tried to talk about my mom. *Abuela* said Noris got scared, but Papi didn't want to listen."

"I understand, but keeping this from him is not right."

Ayla steps up and grabs my hands. "I just want to get to know her. I'm talking to her. I'm not doing anything else. I told them no when *abuela* wanted me to go with her on a cruise, and Mom would join us there. I didn't want to lie like that to my dad."

My stomach roils.

"A, that was the right thing to do. You cannot go behind Ollie's back and do that. Your grandma should have never suggested that. It's not cool, and your dad is going to hate hearing about that."

Her eyes threaten to come out of her head. "Lux, please. Don't tell him. I know I have to tell him, but I don't need to tell him about that. He would keep me from my grandma. I love my *abuela*. I just want to talk to my mom from time to time. I know she left, but she told me she was scared. I don't want *Papi* taking her away from me."

Her eyes fill quickly, spilling just as fast. My heart bends.

How can she think he would do that to her? Doesn't she know he would cut off his arm to make her happy? "He wouldn't do that, Ay. Never."

She shakes her head again. "She hurt him, and she left us. He wouldn't understand how I want to keep in touch with someone who hurt us."

Pain explodes in my chest because I do understand. This is how I feel about Walter. No matter what, I sometimes want to talk to him. Chase and Cam don't understand. They've cut him off for good.

"Okay, I won't say anything today, but you need to."

"Aunt Lux, don't be mean—"

I shake my head at my niece. "I'm not being mean. She should not lie to her dad. Neither of you should lie to your parents. Ayla has to come clean. I think your dad will appreciate it more if you tell him and you explain it to him like you're explaining it to me. He won't like to find out from someone else."

When Ayla says nothing, I tighten my grip on her hands and make her look at me once more.

"Ollie loves you more than anything in the world. He will do anything to make you happy. Promise me you'll tell him."

I need to help her make the right decision. I tug at her hands.

Finally, she nods. "I'll do it tomorrow night when he comes back."

She starts sobbing. I pull her into a tight hug. My niece starts crying behind her, and I pull her into a hug with us.

I wish life could be simpler, that I could guarantee that this will go well, but the little voice in the back of my head whispers of how bad this could get. Ollie tenses when he talks about Noris. The longer it goes, the worse it will be.

Maybe I should tell him so he's ready.

You just promised Ayla that you would let her tell him.

Yeah, she needs to be the one to tell him. It's her mom and his ex-wife. If you tell him, she won't trust you again.

The last thing I want is to cause division between Ayla and Ollie. I'll give her the chance to tell her dad tomorrow. That way, I will be keeping my word, and if she doesn't, I will be the one to tell him.

And then what? Dump him?
Fuck my life.

22

Oliver

I rub a hand over my neck to quell the kink. I'm tired, even though I slept through the flight.

My *negrita* spots me right away, her smile brightening the day as she hugs Bron and heads my way. I hug her so tight. She clings to me.

"I've missed you so much, *Papi*."

"Me too."

We get in the car, and she's telling me about the last three days. In between baseball practice and shopping, she lets it slip that she spent time with Luciana at Cam and Adri's. I'm nervous as hell about what I have to do. I pull up to the diner, and we go in.

"I want to talk to you about something that's been going on for a while," she says.

Oh god. She knows.

"*Yeah, negrita*, I want to talk to you about that too."

She's looking out the window. "You're mad at me."

"What? No."

She frowns at me. "Why are you using your serious tone?"

I shake my head. "I want to talk to you about something serious."

"Okay…"

"I want to talk to you about Luciana and me…"

"You like her—a lot—and you think she can do better than Mateo."

"I do like her a lot." There's no reason to lie about that.

"She likes you too."

"Why do you say that?"

She rolls her eyes. "It's so obvi."

"Obvi? We're just cutting words now?"

"Don't change the topic. I'm not a child, *Papi*. I'm thirteen."

JesuCristo. I hate it when she says things like that. "I know you're thirteen. I was there when you were born. But you're right, I do like Lux. Actually, I more than like her."

"Then you should ask her out."

"Would you be okay with that?"

"Duh. I like Lux. She's so cool. We get to do fun things, and she's not stuck up. Even though I'm not her niece, she makes sure I get the same treatments as her and Bron at the spa. She's also teaching Bron and me how to develop our own styles so we don't look like everyone else."

That makes me smile. "That's good you feel that way. *Como te digo*, Luciana and I have been getting to know each other more."

I let the words hang in the air.

Her eyes round a little. "You're talking to her."

"Well, yeah, we've been having conversations."

"No, *Papi*. I meant *talking*. You know? Like when two people are seeing each other, but it's not official."

Oh. "Yeah…"

"You didn't tell me." Her tone is soft, and there's something jagged in it.

"I wanted to be sure we were compatible before I said anything. You do understand, right?"

"I thought we didn't keep secrets from each other." Her voice is even lower now.

There's a dip in my stomach. "We don't, but my first priority is to protect you. I want to make sure something is going to work out before I involve you."

"Because of Marcia?"

Yes.

"You remember her?"

She nods. "She didn't call me again after you broke up with her."

"And you got hurt."

"I got over it. People break up. Look at Mateo and Lux…" She winces. "Sorry, *Papi.*"

"For what?"

"You're talking to her now. Nobody wants to hear about the famous ex."

Jesus. "I'm not insecure, but, Ay…Lux and I are more than talking. We've gotten to care for each other."

Her eyes round like saucers, and she lets out a small gasp. "She's your girlfriend?"

She looks down at her menu for a while and then back at me.

My skin begins to tingle, but I don't say anything else. I need to let her make up her mind and react to it.

"Okay, then. So how does this work?" Her face is a bit unreadable.

"What do you mean?" I ask.

"Are you going to propose?"

"We are not there yet, *negrita.* We have to get to know each other some more. And we have to get to know each other more with you. I want to make sure we spend time together and that we're a good family fit."

"Why with me? If two people like each other, then that's it."

I shake my head. "No, it's not. You're my world, my life, my number one, the person I love the most in the world. I want to make sure you are comfortable."

She glows with her Ayla smile.

"Thank you, *Papi.*"

"You don't ever have to thank me for loving you or for putting you first. That's a *papi's* job. I just happen to love that job."

She nods and looks back down at the menu.
Oh God.

———

Lux

OLLIE

Can I stop by your house? It won't take long.
I just have something I really need to say
to you.

I stare at the text from Ollie for a while and think of saying no, of saying maybe another time, but I don't see the need to drag things out.

ME

Sure.

I don't change out of my favorite athleisure pant set. It's so comfy, and the fabric is soft. The perfect stay-at-home or go-out set. But I add cyeliner and put on lip gloss. It's my way of not trying too hard but not being a bum either.

The doorbell rings fifteen minutes later, and I take my time going down. When I open the door, he's standing there looking so hot I want to jump on him like I did in my dream last night. He's just perfectly made, and only a fool would let him go, even if it's just as friends with benefits.

This fool values herself, though.

Ugh, stop referring to yourself as a fool.

"Hi, Lux," he says, not walking in.

"Hi, Ollie. I hope you had a great trip."

He nods. "I did, thank you. Uh, I wanted to stop by and see you."

Yet, you've been back in town all day...

When I say nothing, he continues, "But I needed to do something first, and now that I've done it, I—"

I put a hand up. "Listen, you don't have to—"

He stops me with his hand over mine. "Please, let me finish. You were right about everything you said the other day. That's why I wanted to formally introduce you to someone."

He moves back, extends his hand, and opens his car door. I didn't even notice Ayla was sitting in there.

She comes up to stand by him.

"Lux, I want to introduce you formally to my daughter."

"Hi, Lux," Ayla laughs and hugs me.

"Ayla, as I told you, Lux and I—"

"She's your girlfriend," she finishes.

I feel like I'm in a wind tunnel, and everything is happening around me, but I can't catch up. My breath is stuck in my throat. Is this really happening?

"She's my girlfriend," Ollie says, and now I'm really speechless because I don't know what I could possibly say. This is what I've wanted, but I don't know how to react.

As it turns out, I don't need to say anything. Ollie hugs me, and I hold onto him because I need a minute, but then I remember she is there, and this is the first time I'm the girlfriend to her dad, so I push away from him.

Ayla's smile gets wider. "I kinda knew."

"You did?" I ask.

"Apparently, it was *obvi* that I like you," Ollie says.

The smile slides off her face. "*Papi*, you can't use that word."

"Do you guys want to come in?"

He shakes his head. "We don't want to impose. I know you were not expecting us."

"I was just prepping to record tomorrow. Maybe I can get Ayla's take on my review?"

"Yes, and I want to see your studio."

We go upstairs, and Ayla immediately begins commenting on all the things she likes. I show her my place first, and then we go to the studio. She loves it, and I get her take on the pieces I'm reviewing.

"I've been asked to do a clothing haul for Thiccletics' new spring line."

"The colors are to gag for," she whispers, looking at the pieces.

"Aren't they? I think this fuchsia would look amazing on you."

She nods. "I really like it. Fuchsia is one of the colors you said would look really good on my skin."

Ollie is watching us, not saying much. He's in the back of the room under the pretense of taking notes and making sure everything is working well.

"I'll meet you ladies downstairs. I know nothing about fuchsia or videos."

We continue going through the pieces, but my heart goes out to him because I know how big of a step this is for him. And this is huge for us.

Us.

"Are you really okay with your dad and I being friends?"

"You mean boyfriend and girlfriend." She giggles, and it's really so cute.

"Yes."

"I love it. My dad is a great guy, and you're awesome. B and I always thought you two would make a cute couple."

"You never said anything," I say to her.

"You guys are like Carla and the Hybrid, hiding your feelings so others don't notice. Super cute."

I laugh. I've learned to love *Vampire Chronicles* with Bron. I couldn't wait for Carla and the Hybrid to become a couple.

"You like us being together. It means the world to me that you do."

"*Papi* said the same thing."

"You are the most important person to him, and I'm not here to change that. I couldn't change it, and I wouldn't want to either. I love you, and I'm getting to know your dad. If there's something I do that bothers you, please tell me."

"Okay. Thank you for not telling him. I'm going to talk to him tomorrow."

She can't be this easygoing about it, can she? But I don't want to make it weird by asking all these questions.

"Ayla, if your dad agrees and you do too, I want us to get to know each other better too. Like, we can go out, just us, and talk more often. I want us to be a unit too."

Her smile is slow, but there's something there that twists my insides. It was the same as when she asked me if we were close.

She gets a call from Bron, and I go downstairs to give her some privacy. I sense she has lots to say. I find Ollie in my family room.

"She's talking to Bron."

He shakes his head. "She'll be there for a while."

"Okay, then," I say and beeline straight for him, throwing my arms around his neck and crushing my lips to his.

I can't believe how much I missed his body and his mouth. He pulls me tight against him, and I'm reminded of other things I missed. I pull back.

"I don't want her walking in on this. We are not there yet," I say.

He presses his lips against my cheek. "I'm not kidding. When she's on the phone with Bron, you have to pry her away. I love that you're considerate."

He takes my hand and leads me to the couch. We sit a little apart. "What changed your mind?"

"I had time to reflect. You were right. I wasn't really giving us a chance, and you deserve better. I deserve better. Being a dad doesn't stop me from being a man. I also like you too much to let you go, Luciana. I can't remember the last time I felt this strongly about someone."

It's the right thing to say because I go all warm, and I'm almost leaning forward. Instead, I squeeze his hand.

"I wasn't trying to force you. I just wanted a real chance. I didn't think you would do this."

He frowns. "What did you think I would do?"

My gaze holds his. "Phase us out."

"That wouldn't be easy. What would you have done if that was my attitude?"

I look him straight in the eye. "I would've let you go."

"Just like that?" he asks.

"I couldn't deal with the down-low thing anymore. I think we are so much more than that."

He nods. "We are. It was never a down-low thing. I was scared because I've been living with this hole in my heart. It's where I carry my pain and my fear, and you filled it with everything about you, and like the light that you are, you drove away the darkness."

My mouth goes slack, and I don't know what to say to him.

He takes my hand in his. "I lied. I don't just like you. I've never felt something this deep for someone. Lux, I love you."

My pulse races, and I'm a little lightheaded. My heart is beating against my chest, and I'm in shock. It's only me, him, his words. His *I love you.*

I take his face in my hands and kiss his lips with all my energy, my heart, all the things I feel.

We pull away smiling.

"Ollie, I…"

Ayla's steps ring down the stairs.

I begin to scoot away, but he tugs at my hand, stopping me. Our bodies are not touching, but we're close enough.

The second she steps back in the room, Ayla's gaze goes to our interlocked hands. Her smile loses the megawatt energy that makes it so much like his.

My skin burns, and I try to extract my hand from Ollie's as gently as I can, but he holds onto it. His fingers intertwine with mine.

"You're already done talking to Bron? That's got to be a record." His voice is affable as always, but the nerves that he can't hide, no matter how hard he tries, edge themselves to it.

I'm glad I'm not the only one.

Ayla shrugs, her gaze on our interlaced hands. "I didn't want to be rude." She looks back at my face for the first time. "Your house is really beautiful."

"It's all your dad's work." My voice comes out like a loud whisper.

She goes to sit in the chair across from us, and for the first time, I'm uncomfortable around her. I never expected it to be weird between us. Maybe the handholding is too much, but Ollie is not budging.

"Would you like something to drink?" I ask. The silence is killing me.

She nods. "May I have some water?"

"I'll get it." Ollie lets go of my hand and stands.

Oh no.

He smiles at me, and I get what he's doing.

He wants us to be able to swim out of this awkwardness.

"Are you okay, Lux?" Ayla asks.

I should ask her the same thing or maybe put her mind at ease. Instead, I decide to go with the truth. "I guess I'm not doing a good job of hiding how nervous I am right now."

She blinks a few times. "You are? Why?"

"Because you seem uncomfortable, and that's the last thing I would ever want. Your dad and I..."

She leans back a little in her chair. "I'm okay with you guys dating."

"Does our holding hands bother you?" I ask.

"It's a little weird...he's my dad." Her face scrunches up a little in the most adorable of ways. "I'm getting used to it."

"We can stop," I say.

She shakes her head. "No, he likes it. I want him to be happy."

I lean a little forward. "I like it too, but I want you to be happy, A. You're part of us. You know that, right?"

She smiles. It's sweet, but I'm not convinced that she is okay with this.

Ollie comes back with the water and brings one for me as well. He tells us about his trip.

They leave an hour later. At the door, she hugs me. "Would you like to come to my game on Saturday?"

It feels like I've been holding my breath until that moment. So, I exhale and say, "I wouldn't miss it."

Oliver

Saturday

"She walks in her heels like she's barefoot, and she looks at the camera like she's looking in a mirror," Ayla says, and I pause my stirring to look over my shoulder into the family room where she and Lux are watching a red-carpet show. They look so comfortable, like they do this all the time.

"That's because she's comfortable in her own skin. When you've done something enough times and you've mastered it, it shows even in the way you pose," Lux tells her.

My *negrita* looks at her. "Like you in your videos."

Lux shrugs. "Maybe…but you know who's the better example?"

"Who?" Ayla asks.

Lux tilts her head toward her. "You in the pitcher's box today." She taps Ay's shoulder with her finger and yanks it back like it burnt her. "Talk about girl on fire. It reminded me of watching Cam pitch. You weren't nervous or self conscious. Even with that ten pitches at-bat. You kept going after that hitter until she got overanxious and struck out."

Heat explodes over my chest, and I have to turn my head away. I don't want them to catch me looking or eavesdropping, but I'm listening to everything.

"Thanks, Lux."

I know my baby is blushing. And I'm blushing because this is seriously the best compliment Lux could have given her. From the moment she showed up to the game this afternoon, the day has been nothing but idyllic. Though the moms and teenage girls tried to make something of her being there, Lux's attention was on Ayla and Bron.

She was supportive, and cheered for the team, and took more photos than anyone, but she didn't post any of them. And I know because I follow her, and I set up my alerts for whenever she posts anything. Instead of pizza after the game, we did milkshakes, and she integrated to the conversations easily.

Then she came home with us, and Ay has been showing her around while I cook.

"Oh no. Is that awkward? He's your ex."

I turn around quickly, and Mateo is on our screen. He's in a tux and smiling.

Lux snorts. "Not at all. Our relationship has been over for a while."

"But don't you feel anything? You were together not long ago."

Lux shrugs again. "Sometimes you care about someone, and you stay for that reason, but you shouldn't be together. It's hard to explain, but it's one of those lessons that we as girls and women need to learn early."

"Because he cheated on you."

"Ayla, maybe we shouldn't talk about this," I blurt out.

Both of them turn to look at me, but it's Lux who says, "It's okay. She's been respectful, and I don't mind sharing."

"I can stop if it makes you uncomfortable."

Lux shakes her head, but my daughter's eyes are on me.

I shake my head. "I have a pot to stir. Dinner is almost ready. Ay, can you set the table?"

The minute I turn around, they giggle, and then they gasp.

"Is that Miss Sadya? She looks amazing."

"She does," Lux agrees. "Lauren always styles her to perfection. I love the draping in her gown. It's the perfect ratio with the skirt split stopping at the knee. Remember what I told you about that?"

"Yes, if you show leg, don't show too much cleavage and vice-versa."

"Exactly."

Twenty minutes later, we sit to eat.

"I'm so excited," Lux says, looking around at the food. "I've heard awesome things about your rice bowl."

I chuckle. "My *negrita* is biased."

"I'm not," Ay says, digging in.

Lux smiles at me. "I actually heard it from Bron too." She tastes a spoonful and closes her eyes. "They were both right. This so good."

My throat goes dry because I've seen that expression, and it has nothing to do with food.

"Thank you," I say.

"I'll need cooking lessons."

"Next time, you cook, and we supervise."

Lux frowns. "That's advanced."

Ay laughs. "We'll have to record it for your channel."

After dinner, Ay heads to her room to watch a movie with Bron over FaceTime, and Lux and I get to be alone.

"This was a great day," she says as we finish washing the dishes.

"It was. I love how good the two of you are together. Thank you for proving me wrong." I reach for her, pulling her against me and trapping her by the fridge.

"You got it." She climbs onto her toes and kisses me.

I plunge my tongue in her mouth, and she flicks it with hers. Then she pulls away, her gaze snapping toward the bedrooms.

"She won't come out. They're in a world of their own." I switch us sideways so we can keep our eyes on the hallway.

I plunge back into her mouth, my hands pressing her tighter against me. She tastes sweet, like the ice cream and macaroons she brought for dessert. I rain kisses on her lips, and we end up back deep, mouth on mouth, with my hips rubbing against hers, my cock impossibly hard, trying to find his way in.

She moans low, bucking back, giving me the greenlight for my fingers to cup her ass and press her against me. My eyes shove closed, the need coating my body.

A door flings open, and my heart slams against my chest while Lux freezes in my arms.

"I'm grabbing some water. I can't believe she's still torn between them. Ansel seriously loves her, and Dylan is a total dog. Why do these girls always make the wrong choice when it's so clear?" Ayla walks out of her room with her phone in her hand.

I raise my arms from Lux's ass to her back, and we pull apart. Lux's mouth has drifted open, her lips red from our kisses.

Ayla stops to look at us, and a couple of seconds tick by. "I need some water," she finally says.

And now the three of us are staring at each other.

"Sure. We were just talking." And I could slap myself because that is the most ridiculous thing I could have said. My face heats up, and to make it worse, my daughter smiles as she walks past us to the fridge.

Then she grabs a bottle of water and heads back to her room. In front of her door, she turns around, still smiling. "Good night."

I'm frozen, watching the door. Lux drops her head on my chest.

And that's when we hear giggling.

"Oh my god. I want to die."

My heart is pounding, but one thing is clear to me: Ayla is not upset. "I don't think she knows…"

"She watches TV. Of course she knows what we were doing. You want to go talk to her?" Lux insists.

I shake my head. "We were just kissing. All she saw was when we were hugging."

"And on the way to more." Lux runs a hand through her hair. Her color is heightened, and she looks stressed and worried, and for some reason, it's the most endearing thing I've ever seen.

She's the one, the right person for me. And that frees me to want to go further with her.

"Want to spend the night? We can go to my room and continue where we left off?"

Her mouth drops open. Her eyes are impossibly wide as they bounce between the hallway and my face, her silent question louder than my heartbeat.

"Let's take a chance." I take her hand and lead her to my room, turning out the lights as we walk down the hallway.

We open the door, step in, and close it. I lock it while she's standing in place.

"Are you sure?" she asks.

And there's something about her being in my bedroom—where she is sometimes the last thought before I fall asleep—that makes my whole body stir.

I can picture her naked, without the jeans and white top, and I crave the feeling of her skin against mine. My mouth thirsts for her.

I don't answer. Instead, I pounce, taking her in my arms, kissing her again. She clings to me, and we end up on my mattress, tangled up.

The sound of our kisses is the soundtrack, revving my blood until she hums, and we break apart, breathless.

"We're too loud," Lux says.

I reach for the remote and turn on my TV to an action movie where the explosions begin right away. Our eyes on each other, we shrug our clothes off, setting a record for how fast we get naked. She's standing in front of me in a pink matching boy shorts and bra set. Nothing's hotter than that because she knows how much I like to peel her undies off.

And it flashes before my eyes how I want to fuck her first. I pull her to my bathroom and close the door, and I bring her to the vanity, facing the mirror.

"I want to see your tits bounce in the mirror while I make you come."

She nods, her darkened eyes staring at me over the mirror. I see my own need reflected in her. Her mouth tilts to meet mine. My hands roam her belly to cup her tits, and she pulls her mouth from mine to watch.

"I want to see everything you do to me."

My dick gets harder, and I rub it against her ass.

She moans softly and lets her head drift back against my chest, and her mouth meets mine again. I sneak a hand between her legs and pet her pussy.

"I'm ready," she whispers, bending forward and bracing her hands on my sink.

I'm grateful for the invitation as I tug her panties down and spread her legs a little more. My cock is in my hand, ready to storm her body. When the head grazes her, Lux shudders.

The jolt courses through me too, and instead of going in right away, I begin to brush her pussy with my dick, like I'm painting pleasure over her with up and down and circular strokes. Her mouth flies open, and when I don't think I can hold on anymore, I push past her folds all the way in and begin to pound her until we burst together.

My heart is erratic, not just because of what we just did, but because of so many things. I am finally in love with someone that matches me in every way, and I'm able to live this freely. I turn her around and hug her.

"*Te amo tanto.*" The words fall from my lips, and they don't want to make me run.

Her hands tighten on my back. "I love you too."

When we come down from the high, I take her by the hand and lay her in my bed, where I bury my face in her pussy, and we start all over again.

23

Oliver

I hate Wednesdays. It's my administrative day. This is the day when I go through bills and take care of anything that deals with paperwork. I keep things neatly organized because I hate scrambling when tax season comes around.

I pull out the credit card bill to make sure all the charges are correct. I go through the data and am not surprised to see how often my daughter has visited the accessories store or the shoe store.

I chuckle. The last couple of years have brought such a difference into our lives. She is more clothing and shoes conscious—well, the type of clothing and shoes. She doesn't like little girl things anymore. And the accessories have definitely been a new addition. We spend money on earrings, headbands, and, God help me, lip gloss.

I shake my head and look over the phone bill. I expect to see Bron's number all the way down with mine sprinkled throughout, but more recently, all her texting with Lux has increased and become part of the roster. They talk a lot. I try not to pry, but I've peeked in on it. They exchange outfit ideas, and she asks Lux what she thinks of her "fits," as she calls her looks.

Lux has been so gentle with her, and her advice is solid. She often discourages things that I would also veto. But she tells her what would be flattering on Ayla's figure.

I almost screamed when she told her about maximizing her beautiful legs. I held myself back because it was followed by advice on not showing too much because leaving a little to the imagination is always classier and more appropriate for her age. She advised Ayla to develop styles that are purely fashion to make her mark instead of trying to be sexy. That will come naturally from her confidence.

Then, the 510 area code grabs my attention. It's also sprinkled throughout. It appears fifteen times in the past two weeks. It shows up in the mornings after 8:30, when she's already in school, and in the afternoons. It's there late at night, when my daughter should be asleep.

I start to pull out my phone but think better of it. This may be all that talk about boys we had a while back. But what boy does she know with this area code?

What if it's some predator she met online, trying to lure my baby?

I open my phone and look through the parental guidance to find all her texts. I don't get to see the number because there's a thread that stops me cold. It's labeled *Mommy*.

My stomach dives, plunging to the floor.

I'm almost reluctant as I go into the conversation.

> MOMMY
>
> I'm going to send you a pair of those rose-gold high-tops you liked so much. You can consider them a late birthday present.

> AYLA
>
> Really? 😶 Thank you.

She's talking to Noris.

I ignore the twisting in my guts and follow the thread back. My phone pings text messages from Lux and my crew chief, but I dismiss all of them. I go all the way back to two weeks ago and start reading from there.

Two fucking weeks. Noris has been talking to Ayla for two weeks, and I didn't know about it. Why didn't A say anything?

> **AYLA**
>
> I can't believe we're talking.

> **MOMMY**
>
> Me either. You're so beautiful. You look like your dad.

> **AYLA**
>
> Thanks. That's what everyone says. (Blushing emoji)

> **MOMMY**
>
> You could be a model. You have that gorgeous face and the body for it. I bet the boys in school are crazy about you.

I don't know if I'm more sickened by this or the conversations about her knowing what Ayla's hobbies are or them talking about baseball and how good my daughter is. *That's our thing.*

I shove my eyes closed, bracing against the red wave that floods my eyelids. My pulse is out of control, and my hands are balled into fists, but I place them over my thighs. The way that woman is talking to Ayla is so familiar, so casual. Like she didn't leave her as a baby. How dare she think she can do this. That she can waltz back in and buy pink high-tops and talk about boys like that's going to erase all the time she wasn't here.

Maybe it has for Ayla.

There are a lot of emojis, and I can picture my daughter's big smile as she talks to this woman she shouldn't trust because all she does is destroy you once she's gotten what she wants from you.

My alarm goes off, taking me out of the text messages, and I have to look at my phone to remember that I need to check on my crew and head to Lux's. I get up from my desk, grab my bag, and head out.

I get in my car and drive away, but I'm not going to the work site. I find myself driving to Noris's mother's house. That woman and I have a conversation pending. I know she brokered this behind my back.

I'm halfway there when I realize I don't have a plan, and showing up at her house and screaming at a decorated veteran without all the facts is definitely not the way. I need the full story, and for that, I need to talk to my daughter. Ayla has the answers I need, and I need her to come clean with me. But I can't pull her out of school for this. And I need to calm down first. I head to the site, making annotations and ordering corrections on the tilling. It's all a blur. I text Lux to tell her I'm on my way.

And that lets me breathe a little. I can talk to her. She can help me sort this out. She knows Ayla and has been such a good influence on her.

I'm so glad she's in my life, that I have someone to sort this out with. I'm not alone.

I need to sort some of this out before I talk to my daughter. I know she has the right to know her mother, but why did she feel the need to lie to me? That is what's so hard for me to believe. I speed my way through the city. I need to get to Lux.

I need to talk this out, or I will burst. Why did Noris have to come back into our lives now? Ayla has been doing well as always. I'm finally in a good relationship with a good woman who loves Ayla. I'm finally in love with someone who checks all the boxes. The last thing I need is to deal with Noris, because if there's one thing I know, it is that woman ruins everything she touches.

And she has now touched Ayla.

But like hell I will let that happen. She will not hurt my baby again. She turned her back on her, and I'm not letting her do it a second time. I will protect her from her own mother. My gaze drifts to the dash-board, and I'm going too fast.

I force myself to slow down, breathe, and focus on getting to my girlfriend's house. Lux will help me calm down and put this into perspective.

———

Lux

"Are you serious? Hell no, Mimi. I am not doing it."

I push away from my desk and pace to the other side of my studio.

"Luxxy, please calm down. This is business." Her voice is calm, and that grates me as much as her news.

"I am not going to calm down, and I am not doing an interview with Mateo or host his dumb-ass gala. Are you crazy? Did you forget my history with him?"

"I didn't, Luxxy. It's just that the CEO has asked for this. He had dinner with the owner of the Emperors, and they want to generate good PR for the event, and this would be great for *Big Apple* and for you. They're going to give you 300K to host."

I want to scream.

"I don't want the money. Give it to someone else. Get a sports-writer to do the interview. Is Lucetta busy? He loves to bury his face in Mateo's ass."

I look down onto my street, and I need to wrap this up. Ollie is coming soon, and I can't imagine having this conversation with him.

"Luxxy, they don't want Lucetta or anyone else, only you."

I close my eyes and revel on the red behind my eyelids. *Fuck no. Never.*

"They can't have me. I refuse to do it. I have to go. I'm waiting for someone."

"Don't hang up, Luxxy." She sighs. "Look, we all have to do things we don't like. You get to hang out with your gorgeous ex for an after-noon, and all you have to do is be your beautiful self. That doesn't sound so bad to me."

"What? I said no—"

"Hold on." She cuts me off. "This is not an ask. We've given you a lot of control, but this is nonnegotiable. We've already promised the Emperors and the Cross Foundation. Be here tomorrow for the inter-view and the gala."

Rage blows through me like a supercell twister.

"What if I don't?"

"Well," her voice drops, "the next call will be from legal for breach of contract."

I have to hold on to the windowsill.

"Did you just threaten me?"

She sighs again. "No, Luxxy. I'm just stating the facts. This is not personal, and we will only resort to that if you shake your responsibility on this."

I blow out a mouthful of air. Because fuck her, Mateo, and everyone else.

"First of all, it's Lux. Second, I'll be there, but I hope you know this changes everything."

I cut off the call and email my agent and Cam's head lawyer.

Ruthy,

Big Apple *is forcing me to do an interview I'm uncomfortable doing. They want me to spend the day with Mateo and have insinuated legal action if I don't. I will fulfill my obligations, but I want out of this contract. Please find a way to get me out. We can schedule a call to talk about it later on today.*

I'm shaking with rage, but I drop to the floor in lotus position and breathe. I chant until the rage has left my body, and I'm calm again. I'll do the interview and gala, and then I will be done with him and *Big Apple* forever. I can do this on my own. I'll start my channel and take my audience. Maybe I can ask Ollie to come with me tomorrow.

My phone chimes, and it's him. The time stamp says eleven.

OLLIE
I'm on my way.

Oh shit. He's not going to like this at all. I need to be ready for when he gets here, distract him, and sweeten the pot, then tell him. Maybe he can come with me. We can definitely tackle this together.

Fuck. Why did this happen now? No man wants to deal with an ex.

I rush downstairs and into the shower. I choose the rose shower gel Ollie loves and lather my body in the matching lotion while still wet. I use fast and quick strokes, concentrating on him, putting my morning on the backburner. I let myself feel him, touching my body, stimulating and stroking, until I'm ready for him.

I want his hands to be the ones that roam and explore my body. I need my body soft and smelling like a bouquet as he sucks and kisses every inch of me like he promised me.

It's only been two days, but I'm starving for his touch.

I choose the white set of undies I bought a few days ago. I got them for him. It's the first time I got undies especially for him. I can't wait to see his face when he sees me in them. Heat pools in my belly just imagining his eyes flaming over my body, making me ache deep in my pussy. I run my fingers over my nipples, needing contact and a little friction.

My phone pings, alerting me that someone is at the door. I run down the stairs just as it opens.

Ollie steps through the door in a cloud of tension that weighs down the air in the room. There's no playfulness in his eyes, no flashing over my body or even acknowledgment of the white thong I put on specifically for him. He runs a hand over his face, evaporating all promises of a hot, sweaty morning.

I reach for the belt of my robe, securing it around me.

He stands in the middle of the room, like he doesn't know where to go.

I cross the room and place a hand on his cheek. "What happened?"

He shakes his head, his cloudy gaze on mine. "My ex-wife is in town. She's been talking to Ayla for weeks now. Can you believe that? Ay never said a thing. She's been lying."

She didn't tell him. I need to help her fix this.

I hug him tight. "She wasn't trying to lie to you. It was just hard for her to talk to you about it."

He pulls back from me, his eyes pinning me in a way that makes the hairs on my skin soldier up in attention. *Oh no.*

"You knew." His words are soft but reverberate like thunder in the middle of the night.

My hands are still around him, clinging to the backs of his arms. I let them drop. Yeah, this was a mistake.

"Let me explain."

His shoulders go up slowly as his eyebrows draw together. His gaze focuses deeper, magnifying me. The temperature in the room shifts again, rolling in intervals of hot and cold.

"You knew," he repeats.

The booming in his voice dries all the moisture in my throat, but I manage to nod.

"You knew Ayla was in contact with that irresponsible, cruel, bi—" He pauses, as if struggling. He looks around, as if trying to find something, but his eyes return to me. "I trusted you, Lux. I…she's my child, the most important thing in my life. *She's* my life."

My stomach drops, my hand flying to hold it in place. And the cramping begins. "I know. I was going to tell you. I was giving A the chance to talk to you first. She begged me to let her be the one to tell you."

"She's a child. You're an adult. Children have no secrets. *You* should have no secrets from me when it comes to my daughter. That woman is trying to take her from me." His face goes blank, all the emotion evaporating from his face like the blood from my body.

I hurt him.

"Did you do this on purpose?"

"What?" The single word flies out of my mouth in a painful croak.

"I don't know. You've been fighting for us to be a couple in public. You don't tell me her mother has been calling her, asking her to come stay with her. Why would you keep something this big from me? Did you think this may be a way for us to gain time without her?"

The flash of pain breaks over my chest, making me stumble back while he stands still, six feet away, like he didn't strike me with his words.

"No." My throat clogs, and I'm struggling for air because I can't believe he would even think that. I clear my throat. "Don't ever say that. I love Ayla. I would never hurt her in any way."

He doesn't move, just stares at me with those cold, enraged eyes. "Your actions say different, Luciana."

My name on his lips holds the softness of sandstone.

"I'm sorry. I made a mistake. I thought she should be the one to tell you. She just wanted to talk to her mom, Ollie…"

As if possible, his eyes grow colder, and I wrap my arms around my body, bracing against the chill.

"The mother who abandoned her, the one that walked away, not looking back, to go after some man she met online. The one who didn't even wait for me to get home but called to tell me I needed to get there because the baby was alone. The one who didn't care when I texted her to tell her Ayla had a fever. The cold-hearted bitch that didn't answer me even as I begged her to come back, not for me but for our sick kid. That's the woman you think Ayla should be talking to?"

Another wave of pain rushes through me. I made a huge mistake. He won't forgive me. I don't know what to say to make this better. *I'm sorry* sticks in my throat.

"Make me understand what the fuck you were thinking. Tell me how you can justify the damage you've caused."

I rear back, my chin tilting up. I'm not going to cry or beg for forgiveness. It's obvious the time for that has passed, but I need him to understand. "I walked in on the conversation between Ayla and Bron. She just wanted to talk to her and was afraid you wouldn't let her. She said you tighten up when Noris's name is mentioned. I've seen that myself. She promised me she was going to tell you. I couldn't say no when she begged me while crying."

"Children beg for all sorts of things, most of the time for stuff that's not good for them. You are the adult. You should know better than to hide things from her father that could potentially damage her, but that's on me. I should've known better."

My back stiffens. "Known better how?"

He turns his back on me and starts for the door. "Since her mother left, I led my life a certain way, with Ayla at the center of it, with no one else between us, on purpose."

"Ollie, stop." I hold up my hands, pleading, begging, asking. "I'm sorry I made the wrong choice, but that doesn't mean you shouldn't have opened up to me or let Ayla spend time with me."

He turns back to look at me. "Then how do I explain to myself that

I opened us up for this, and now my relationship with my daughter is damaged?" He shakes his head. "Ayla looked into my eyes day after day and lied, not about some dumb kid stuff, but about this. We were a unit, and now…it's like I don't even know who she is. She keeps secrets, and you helped her lie to me."

Each word is like a slash over my flesh, cutting down and deepening the already gaping wound. I want to tell him no, but it's true. I did help her lie, even if it was just giving her time to tell the truth.

"I'm sorry."

"Yeah, me too." He turns away again.

"Please don't go."

"There's no need to stay. All is said and done. No need to harp on it. I need to repair the damage…"

"That I've caused," I finish for him.

He doesn't look at me. "Goodbye, Luciana."

He walks down the stairs, leaving me frozen to stare after him. When the door clicks closed, pain peaks in my belly, and I double over, leaning against the banister. He dumped me. He walked away. I was only trying to help.

My gaze goes to the door. I have to go after him. I need to talk to him. I take a step forward, and then it hits me. I'm not dressed.

He dumped me. Because I made the wrong decision. I lost him.

Panic sets in, and I run down the stairs and engage the security lock enforcer and the deadbolt.

I crumble onto the floor and bury my face in my knees. I don't cry. I just will myself to breathe and let the waves pass. The last thing I wanted was to damage their relationship. He trusted me not to hurt Ayla, and that's exactly what I did.

Then how do I explain to myself that I opened us up for this, and now my relationship with my daughter is damaged?

The wave of nausea rises up my chest, and my hand shoots to clutch my throat. I shoot to my feet and run to one of the bedrooms on the ground floor. I barely make it to the bathroom. I empty out my stomach and, with it, all my energy and strength. There's a migraine looming in the back of my head. I rinse my mouth and collapse on the guest bed. The pain begins to set in, and I almost welcome it. It won't let me think about anything else. My eyes well, but I fall asleep before the tears come.

———

Oliver

I go to the bathroom and wash my face. It's been burning all day, like my blood, like my stomach, like everything I once thought to be true. Ayla is a liar, Lux was her accomplice, and Noris is back in my life once again, destroying my world as I know it.

Three times, she's done this.

It's different now. She broke me in a different way. I can't focus on feeding, changing, and holding Ayla, because she's now a teenager that keeps secrets from me. I don't have the option of throwing myself into my work because I need to have tough conversations about how she conspired with the woman who left us and never looked back.

Noris is her mother. A mother's love is the only thing I have not been able to give Ayla. I felt I was so close this time. Lux, God. Why did she ruin everything?

I swipe away the thought and step out of my bathroom. My daughter sits at the table, doing her homework, her pretty face down staring at her book, making annotations to remember the material. *God, why can't time just stand still and let me forget this?* I would give anything to go back to last night, where confronting my kid wasn't in the plans and I had a girlfriend with whom I could see a future.

I take a deep breath and tell myself I can do this rationally. She's a child. I can forgive her. Who I can't forgive is the adults who knew and conspired to keep this from me. *Noris. Her grandmother. Lux.*

Ayla's phone pings, and she reaches for it. She looks at the screen, smiles, types something, and returns to her homework.

And I see red.

Is that Noris on the other end? Is that why she's smiling that brightly? She's been acting like this for weeks. All I can think about is how she's been lying this whole time.

"Who is that?" I ask.

Ayla jumps in her chair, her eyes rounding as she looks at me. I've never used this tone with her.

"It's Bron. She said something funny and—"

"Ayla Amada, do you have something to tell me?"

She swallows, understanding dawning in her eyes. "Lux told you. I was going to tell you. I spoke to Noris."

"Don't you mean *mommy*? Isn't that how you have her in your phone?"

Her face falls.

"And no, Lux didn't tell me. She also lied to me."

She shakes her head. "I didn't mean to lie to you—"

"But you did. For weeks now. You sat here and pretended, all while talking to Noris behind my back. Why would you do that?"

"*Papi*—"

I hold a hand up to stall her words. Her eyes are so impossibly wide, and this is when I would normally back off her. She's so small, and I don't want to terrify her. I've never wanted her to know what fear of any man is. I take a step back and breathe, but I can't control the pain that courses through me like acid eating its way inside my veins. I can't make it hurt less.

"You lied so well…" I clamp my lips together so I don't finish the sentence with the words on the tip of my tongue.

Like your mother.

She recoils, her eyes filling quickly with tears, like Noris used to do. And I have to stop. *God, I need to stop.* I can't keep seeing her in my baby girl's face. No matter how much this moment takes me back to those days when I would catch her mother lying, and she would cry and make excuses. Ayla is different.

Is she, though?

She takes a step toward me, and I take another one back. I need space.

"You'll never lie to me again, Ayla."

She shakes her head. "I wanted to tell you, but I was scared. Grandma called—"

The flash of pure anger that courses through me has me raising my hand again. *Grandma*. The woman who knows the piece of work her daughter is, how she left us behind without a look back. She facilitated all of this. She's the one that brought Ayla together with Noris.

Is this the first time?

"How many times have you seen her?"

"Only once, *Papi*. It was two days ago."

"How long have you been talking to her?"

"Since Grandma's birthday." Her voice is so low, and it breaks me. And in this one second, my love for her is not more potent than the pain in my chest.

"Have you ever talked to her before?"

She shakes her head. "I always asked grandma why I don't ever see her, and I asked her if she ever thinks about me. Then Noris called on her birthday, and Grandma let me talk to her."

I believe her.

"From now on, I want you to tell me every time you speak to her." In truth, what I want is to tell her she's not to speak to her again, but I am not going to traumatize my daughter.

Ayla nods.

"I mean it, Ayla. Don't break my trust again."

"I'm sorry."

I nod. "I know you are, but I've always told you that actions and decisions have consequences. You decided to lie. Now I can't trust you."

The way her face crumbles is too much for me to take.

"I have a phone call to make." I turn and head back to my room.

"Tell Lux I'm sorry."

"Lux and I are done. She lied to me too, and I can't forgive her for that." I go inside my room and close the door. I stand in the middle of the room, unsure what to do next. My throat is clogged, and no matter how many shaky breaths I release one after the other, I can't loosen the knot.

The tears that sting my eyes come fast and spill. I quickly swat them away. I haven't cried since the day I took Ayla as a newborn to the hospital, and they hooked her up to oxygen and an IV. She was so tiny and helpless. I thought I would lose her. Her little hands were so cold, even though the rest of her body was burning. I still feel them between mine as I rubbed them to warm them up. I cried so hard that day.

I can survive anything, but I can't survive losing my girl.

That's when the tears come faster, and my hands ball into fists. Ayla is talking to someone on the phone, and I do what I never have before today: I open the app to confirm it's Bron she's talking to.

And there's relief and disgust because I don't trust her now, and that shatters my heart.

I lie in my bed, my face buried in a pillow. I want to pick up the phone, but who can I call? Lux is no longer an option. Our relationship is gone, and the thought that it won't ever be the same between us, that I won't get to smile with her and hold her, chokes me in a way that hurts more than anything.

I can't call Cam or Chase because I just dumped their sister. Our friendship is probably dead too. That's something I'll have to deal with tomorrow.

So, I close my eyes and force myself to sleep. I don't need anyone. I can always work it out by myself. But tomorrow, I'm going to the source. Noris and I will talk.

24

Oliver

"I'll see you at the game this afternoon," I say as we get to the front of the drop-off line.

Ayla doesn't look at me, but she nods, unbuckles her seatbelt, and steps out of the truck. Her bag in hand, she begins to walk away but stops and half turns her head, stops, and then keeps on walking to the entrance.

I'm frozen in place. There's so much I want to yell out my window. There's never a day where I let her go to school without telling her I love her and cheering her on. Today, I can't find the words.

She walks fast, disappearing through the back of the courtyard.

I breathe out.

This was the most uncomfortable commute of my life. The silence between us was deafening and gritting. She was buried in her phone, and I was lost in my thoughts. I put the car in drive again and head for the highway. I reach for my phone and unlock my screen. My finger hovers over Lux's name, but everything hits me at once again.

I don't have her. She lied to me. I broke up with her. Now I have no one I can talk to about this Ayla thing. If she and Ayla had not lied to me, I wouldn't be in this situation.

And I'm pissed all over again. I've been feeling like shit this morning when I did nothing wrong.

My phone rings, and it's my tile guy.

"Ollie, there's a leak in the main bathroom. We opened the hole to see if we could fix it, and part of the ceiling on the floor below came crashing down."

"Shit. How did that happen?"

"The pipe joints were not tightened properly. We shut off the water supply and cleaned around it. You'll have to tell the customer."

I bob my head up and down. "I will. They already warned me that everything wasn't up to code and some of the people who worked on this project were unlicensed. Get some photos and start prepping the area. I should be there in twenty. I'll call the client and let them know."

I disconnect the call and exhale. This is bad news for the client but a good distraction for me, so I dial their number before I leave thoughts of my current situation.

Twenty minutes later, we settle on replacing the pipelines and adding a new Sheetrock ceiling below. I call the warehouse and order a new, standing bathtub. I'm on the phone as I walk into the building and inspect the damage. I head out right after giving my crew further instructions on insulation. I need to return the bathtub we originally bought and pick up the new one along with some other materials. When I get there, they don't have what I need, which prompts another series of calls with the client.

It's eleven in the morning before I know it, and I just finished paying for the materials when I look at my texts. Some are from my crew, but I zero in on the ones at the top of my inbox.

WINTER

Hey, is there something I should know? Ayla doesn't seem like herself.

I asked her if something was bothering her. She says no.

Bron is also hovering over her like a mother hen. And Suzie has been super nice to her...

I scrub a hand over my face.

ME

Yeah, we had a difficult conversation.

Her reply comes through quickly.

WINTER

Ah, okay. Can I help? Hate seeing her like this.

I drive back to the construction site to deliver the new tub and the additional tiles. Then, I decide to stay to lend in some elbow grease. The damage had spread, and we had to remove the plaster and reframe the ceiling. I end up sweaty and dirty. I run out at two to head home and take a quick shower so I can make it to the game this afternoon. There's no telling if the water that fell on us was from the tub or came from the toilet tank, so I want to be safe and clean. I throw the clothes in the washer and notice Ayla's lucky socks on top of the dryer. I take them with me and put them on the bed then go jump in the shower.

I rush to the school, but I get stuck behind three school buses. The texts from Winter and Adri about Ayla light up my phone.

WINTER

I think she must also have a bug or something. She looks a little green, but she begged me not to call you.

ADRI

She doesn't have a fever or anything, but her demeanor is definitely off.

I weave my way through traffic, but by the time I make it to the field, the team is already walking in.

I pat my pocket and realize that I left her lucky socks on top of my bed. *Me cago en ná.*

"It's the perfect day for a game," the school principal calls out.

I'll take her word for it, because even with the warming weather and the bright sun, this day is bleak at best. I go stand next to Cam, who acknowledges me with a nod.

Twenty minutes of hell later, we stare at the field and back at each other.

In front of me, Ayla's back is ramrod straight. She hasn't looked at me directly once. And she's getting lit up like the Rockefeller Center Christmas tree.

My ace, who always strikes out anything moving, has allowed four runs and has loaded the bases.

She winds up, her shoulder impossibly rigid. When she steps, her back leg barely leaves the ground. The ball shoots straight down the middle, a jumbo meatball the kid at the plate somehow manages to foul back.

Next to me, Cam wheezes out a breath. We look at each other. I've never seen this kind of strain between his eyes. The man who pitched a no-hitter, making it look like no-sweat, is sporting his anxiety heavily on his face.

"We need to pull her. She doesn't have it today."

I take one look onto the field, at the way A is twisting the ball in her hand, waiting for Cam's nod to continue. And my chest squeezes when I shake my head at her, letting her know she won't continue to pitch today. Her eyes don't even widen, and her shoulders barely slump. She's been expecting it. The hand holding the ball lowers. Yet, her chin shoots up.

And my heart shatters. Because she's ready for me to pull her. She expects me to do it.

Is it because she thinks I want to? Does she realize how bad she's pitched today? Does she think I don't care? Worse, does she think I take pleasure in this? *Or that it's part of her punishment.*

My stomach roils. *Fuck this whole week.*

"I can do it," Cam offers.

I could let him. He's the pitching coach. But no, I'm not going to cower. I need to look her in the eye. I need to tell her I'm proud of her and that this is only one day. It will pass.

I shake my head and start to walk to the mound.

The other girls on the team come closer. Bron steps in front of her like she's trying to protect her from me. That would make me smile if my baby wasn't looking green in the face. I extend one hand for the ball and the other for her shoulder. I'm going to pat her back and tell her to go shake off this bad day. She places the ball in my hand and shrugs away from my touch, walking quickly toward the dugout. My fingers only get to skim over her shoulder.

The rest of the team barely reacts as I give them instructions. I could swear Suzie sneers at me as she makes her way back to the mound. Bron's glare is the most hostile thing I've seen.

By the time I get back to the dugout, Ayla is on the far end, talking to Cam. He has one hand on her shoulder. She nods a few times. Then, she disappears into the locker room.

Cam comes back to join me, a half-smile on his face. "She's the real deal, you know that?"

My eyes are still glued to the door where she disappeared. "What did she say?"

"She said she didn't have it today. That she knew earlier on, but she didn't want to let the team down. She's upset she hurt the team by trying to be a hero."

"*Coño*." I swipe a hand over my face.

"Are you going to talk to me? You're only half here, Ayla is a mess for the first time since I've met her, my sister is not picking up the phone, and my daughter looks like she hates both of us right now."

I glance at the field and find Bron glaring at us as she and Ayla usually do with Suzie.

"I broke up with Lux."

His face remains impassive. "That much, I figured. Lux hides when she's hurt. Is that why Ayla's been sick all day?"

"I don't want to talk about this with you. That's your sister."

"And you're my friend, and I love that kid." He hooks a thumb to the door of the locker room. "I need to know what's going on. Unlike Chase, I'm not going to punch you before I find out why you hurt her."

I pinch the bridge of my nose. "You can punch me if you want to. It's not like he didn't warn me."

"Just come clean," Cam snaps.

"Ayla's been talking to her mother behind my back for weeks. Lux knew and didn't tell me that the woman who abandoned us is now back in A's life."

His jaw goes slack. "What the fuck?"

His voice is louder than he intends, and thankfully, our relief pitcher strikes out the batter to end the inning.

She jogs back to the dugout, smiling. We both high-five her.

Behind her, Bron bypasses the two of us, like we're not there, and heads to find Ayla.

I don't tell Cam anything else. Once the game is over and we do the ceremonial shaking of hands, I set off to find A. She's sitting patiently by Adri, who stands as soon as she sees me.

She rushes my way. Ay follows Bron inside so she can change.

"Let me take her home with us," Adri asks.

I shake my head. "We need to go to our home and talk."

"Please. I think you both need a little time before you talk. She needs Bron. She's really down about the game."

"Did you know too?" I brace myself because, at this point, I'm expecting everyone to have betrayed me.

She shakes her head. "I wouldn't have kept that from you."

"It wouldn't surprise me."

Her eyes glaze with sadness. "I'm a mom, but I didn't see Ayla's face when she asked Lux to let her tell you. When you see someone so sad and hurting, it's really hard to say no."

"Adults should know better," I say, and she's not going to convince me otherwise.

"Knowing better sometimes is not that easy when you love someone and when you understand where they're coming from, like Lux does."

"You think I should let her see Noris? You think that woman has a right to see her?"

Adri shakes her head. "I don't know what you should do about that. What I do know is that Lux wasn't thinking about anything but Ayla."

"I'm not going to talk about her. It's not fair. She's your family."

"So are you and Ayla. Don't let this ruin everything…" She shakes her head again. "I won't tell you what to do. Just let Ayla spend some time with Bron. I'll bring her home after dinner."

I remind myself that she cares, and this frees up my time to do what needs to be done. I nod. "Okay, I need to go see Noris and her mother. After what I witnessed today, I don't think I should put A through that confrontation."

"You're right. She shouldn't be in the middle. I don't think she can handle it."

I wait until our daughters come out and stand before us. Bron is almost openly glaring at me. My daughter doesn't come near me. I can't even put into words how much that stings. It's like I've already lost her in a way. "Adri and Bron are inviting you to their house. I'll see you at home tonight."

She nods but doesn't look at me.

I place a hand on her shoulder. "It's just a game. You'll win many more."

"Yeah, thanks," she whispers. The emotion in her voice stirs up the same pain that twisted my insides all night and didn't let me sleep.

I need to handle her mother so I can fix things with Ay.

HAVE YOU EVER WANTED SOMETHING SO BAD, YOU SOMETIMES DAYDREAMED ABOUT IT?

By Bougie Girl

When I was little, my mother had a pair of patent-leather peep-toe Mary Janes. It was the most beautiful pair of shoes I had ever seen in my life. I've always had a love affair with classic heels. I would look through old magazines and cut out the pages with the heels I loved and kept them in a binder. I collected stilettos photos like other women collected pictures of wedding dresses and venues.

Yes, I had my own type of Pinterest before pinning was a thing.

On one of the worst days of my life, my brother took me to a vintage warehouse for my birthday, and I saw those same shoes my mother had. I wanted them immediately. I gasped and grabbed them with the intention of never letting go. Unfortunately, when I tried them on, they were uncomfortable to walk in, and they hurt my toes.

I was willing to risk it to keep them.

We've all suffered for beauty at some time or another. I walked a little more in them, and the heel was wobbly and folded, causing major pain in my ankle. I put them back, walking away with a broken heart.

Chase, being the man that he is, teased me about being sad about a pair of shoes in a warehouse full of them. I remember saying, "But those are the ones that I always wanted."

He rolled his eyes and said, "I am sure there are better shoes than that here. Shoes that won't hurt you or break your ankle."

I almost hit him with a pair of platforms nearby. I kept walking instead, and not even fifty steps later, my gasp echoed against the walls of the Meatpacking District warehouse. I saw a pair of patent-leather, red T-strap stilettos with a light shining above them as if anointed by the angels. I swear to you, I heard music. These shoes were godsent, and they changed my perception. Because beauty like that doesn't hurt. These shoes were gentle on my feet, gave me the added height any woman would want, and kept every eye on my legs. Mostly, they made me feel beautiful, like an Amazonian goddess.

One day, I made the grave mistake of placing them next to my vanity as I was doing my nails. I knocked over the nail polish remover, and it splashed over the front of the shoes. I won't lie to you, I cried. I couldn't think about how I would replace them. I thought about the irony of how I found them. I had been looking for something else that didn't end up being good for me.

Great things come when and where you least expect them. They're sometimes only fifty feet away, but you can't see them because you're focused on another thing.

This morning, because life struck again, I woke up thinking about those shoes and had to remind myself that there's also fun in looking and evaluating my options. I will find the one...pair again. I got addicted to the feeling my T-straps brought me—the smiles, the way they slid against my skin, how I felt invincible in them—and I'm unwilling to go without it again.

I can search in New York, in Baltimore, or online. The places to look are unlimited, as is the style and the type...of shoes. That gives me a little bit of comfort because the search is the hardest part, but I refuse to go into it scared.

Let the search begin...again.

25

Lux

I'm exhausted.

It's 8:00 in the morning, and my heart continues to race. My belly keeps dipping, and if I don't do something, I'll go into a full-blown anxiety attack.

I couldn't sleep last night after I slept most of the day yesterday. I cleaned my studio, mocked up some video ideas, and when I couldn't think of anything else to do, I got in the car at four in the morning and drove to New York.

The sun rose as I strained my eyes while coasting through the New Jersey Turnpike with the music blaring. I couldn't say what songs played, except when the DJ played an oldie but goodie and "I hate you so much right now" rang out from the speakers, I sang it at the top of my lungs and then turned the radio off and rode in silence the rest of the way.

As much as I wanted to go straight to Cam's this morning, take a hot bath, and relax before my hell starts, I decided against it. After the tongue-lashing I got from him and Chase, I don't want to thank them for anything.

I park my car at *Big Apple* and take the subway to 96ᵗʰ St. I walk to the park and head to the JKO trail in Central Park. It's so cold the skin of my face feels like it's shrinking. My pores are clinging to each other for body heat. Thankfully, I was smart enough to pack my goose-down jacket. The second I pass the entrance, I take off running like I have hellhounds on my tail. I want to put this week behind me and obliterate it from my memory.

Maybe it should be from the minute I heard Ayla talk about her mom. I wish I had stayed my ass in CJ's room. I should have probably stayed home that day. I should've told Ollie what I heard. I should…

My brain goes blank because all the *should'ves, would'ves, and could'ves* are a byway into Anxietyville. It's too late, anyway. The damage is done.

I run, harder than before, my breathing shallow, pushing my already tired body until I feel like I'm going to faceplant, but this is the best feeling. Right now, my sole worry is to survive this run. I have a new goal that has nothing to do with regrets about Ollie, guilt about failing Ayla, or annoyance about spending the day with Mateo.

I push myself to run harder than before, but I gasp for air, and my side begins to hurt. I'm not running in the correct posture, so the cold sneaks into my lungs, forcing me to slow and finally stop on my fourth lap around the trail like a car that ran out of gas on an incline. Luckily, I can lean on the rails of the Reservoir Bridge and gulp breaths of air.

Walkers and runners slow down and half-frown with that New Yorker's aloof concern. They're worried you may be in trouble, but at the same time, they want to mind their own business.

I mouth, "I'm okay," and turn away, choosing a focal point over the water across from me into the city view. I use the mantra I wrote in one of my worst moments last night, and start chanting it in my head in an almost manic way.

Anxiety is a lying bitch.
I feel the fear and still persist.
I won't dwell.
I choose to move on.

I lose myself in the view and the repetition until my alarm goes off.

I look at my watch. It's ten. It's time to head back to *Big Apple Mag*. I walk back to the entrance and catch the subway. I check my phone, and there are new texts: Lauren, Chase, Adri, Cam, Ayla, my agent, and Mimi. I don't even let myself savor the disappointment that none of them are from Ollie.

I go to the closest person to him.

> AYLA
>
> I'm so sorry.
>
> I know you're mad at me.
>
> Papi won't even look at me.
>
> I really messed up.
>
> I'm sorry I hurt you.
>
> Don't hate me. Pls.

My stomach twists, my heart tripping and landing 187 miles away in Baltimore. She is going through hell.

> ME
>
> He's mad, but he loves you.
>
> You will both get the chance to work it out.
>
> Hang in there and try talking to him.

I start typing another message, telling her I love her, but my phone rings, and it's Chase. I send it straight to voicemail.

It rings again. I sigh and answer.

"I don't want to talk to you right now."

"Yet, here we are," Chase says. "I guess you made it okay to New York."

"Yes, thank you. I just finished a run in Central Park."

"Keep your wits about you. Don't fucking daydream in the city, for God's sake."

I almost smile. "I have to go to work. Can we hang up now?"

"Yeah, but before we do, I have something to say."

I sigh. "Go ahead. It's not like I can stop you." I could hang up, but I won't do that to him.

"This is not the time for you to pull a Lux and go back to the old bullshit just because you're heartbroken."

Heat storms my face, and this time, it has nothing to do with how much I've run. He means Mateo. *What a fucking ass.*

"What the fuck is that supposed to mean?" I say. I hate that he's judging me while I'm fighting for my sanity.

"You know damn well. I heard you're working with Mateo—" He dares say the name.

And the red-hot-anger dam breaks. He's not going to throw my fuckups in my face. Not today.

"You know what, Chase? I don't take every opportunity I get to keep reminding you about the *many, many, many* times you screwed up in the past. I don't go pointing a finger and tell you not to go get in street races or fights until you almost die. Or go get punched in the face until you black out. Just because I messed up doesn't give you a right to throw Mateo in my face every chance you get. So kindly fuck off, and take your brother with you." I hang up on him and shove my phone into my coat pocket.

It keeps ringing until I go into the subway station. I put it on airplane mode. Unfortunately, you have to be alert on the subway, and I can't go back to meditating. So, I find a more constructive meditation that allows me to be aware and channel my anger.

Fuck you, Chase.
Fuck you, Cam.
Fuck you, Noris.
Fuck you to hell, Mateo.
Fuck you, Ollie.

I repeat it over and over and over through my subway ride, when I get to *Big Apple*, as I shower in their bathroom, as I sit in the makeup chair. I barely talk to the glam team. Everyone must sense how annoyed I am, because no one says anything but pleasantries and leaves me to my thoughts.

They bring me coffee, and I even eat a croissant and a piece of cheese—hangry on top of pissed is not a good combination.

I'm fully dressed in the clothes I chose for today: Valentino tweed jacket, $5 fitted red top that whispers above the waistline of my dark-blue, $14 jeans, and burgundy patent-leather Aquazzura pumps with cutouts on the sides. My lips are lined and painted in *Boss Bitchy* dark berry from *Lash N' Gloss*. It's a sleek "going to war" look that fits my mood. I send a test shot to Lauren. Her husband is on my shit list, but she's still my go-to.

LAUREN

Long live my boss queen.

It makes me smile for the first time today. I'm still doing so when footsteps echo on the carpeted floor, and then Mimi, Mateo, and his publicist, Maeven, walk in the room. And the rage levels on my *bitch-o-meter* spike to dangerous.

Mimi is smart enough to stay back. The smile on her face is luke-warm, but there's a deep strain in her eyes. She knows she has burned the bridge between us when she forced me to do this, and as my agent assures me, she's desperate to win me back over.

Good luck with that, bitch.

Mateo, on the other hand, is not that aware and takes four steps toward me.

"Let's get this over with." I walk over to one of the chairs in front of the green screen.

He looks around the room and back between Mimi and Maeven. No one else in the room will look at me.

Mimi releases an audible breath and goes to sit in the chair across from me. "Luxxy—"

I freeze her with a look.

She clears her throat. "I'm sorry. Lux. It's good to see you. You look absolutely gorgeous."

"Mimi, I don't want to be rude, but I'm not in the mood for pleas-antries. I want to get this over with, do tonight's event as mandated, and I'm done. I want to go home and—"

I almost say *spend the evening with Ollie.*

Fuck. My. Life.

Mimi takes advantage of my silence. "I understand. We want to make this as comfortable as we can for you—"

A haze of red floods my eye. The venom rises up my throat, and despite my best efforts to contain it, I spit it right at her. "If you wanted me to be comfortable, you wouldn't have forced me to do this, given what you already know about my history with him." I hook a thumb toward Mateo. "If you wanted pleasant, you would've gotten one of your sports bloggers to do the piece. But *you* didn't want pleasant, Mimi. *You* wanted drama. *You* wanted viewers. *You* wanted ratings. So, *you're* forcing *me* to help him clean up one of his usual and well-advertised media shitstorms. And now you got it because *this* is how I do drama."

My voice is loud enough for all eyes to be on us.

Mimi's face is passive, but the blotchy red spots break out all over the skin of her neck and face.

I'm almost sorry for her, but don't let myself feel bad. I'm nothing but a ratings machine to her, and she cares nothing about my feelings.

"Luxxy, don't be like that," Mateo says.

I don't even look at Mateo when I yell, "If the camera is not on, don't fucking talk to me."

A hush falls over the room, followed by the clicking of power heels.

Maeven stands in front of me, and my gaze immediately goes to her feet. Her Aminah bow pump heels are the most gorgeous thing I've seen in a long time, but I don't let them sway me. Instead, I meet her gaze with the same hostility I do Mimi's.

Her face is impassive, as it always is when she's dealing with one of Mateo's fuckups. She never lets emotions get the best of her.

I'm so jealous about that as I chew on glass after tearing my boss a new asshole.

"Let's go have a drink in the green room," she says.

I cross my legs and lean back on my chair, wallowing in my resentment. "Do you think it's a good idea to give me alcohol when I have to work with your client? If I have nothing good to say to him now, can you imagine..." I trail off.

The quick and small twitch of her lips tells me she would, indeed, like to see that. Too many times, she's been his fixer. He has charmed me on his own, and she has designed ways to smooth over his fuckups so we both come out clean.

"I'm not the person I was before, Maeven. I'm not going to play his girlfriend this time."

"I don't expect you to." Her voice is soft, and the look in her eyes is earnest. "Let's talk, because I think you and I can come to an agreement."

I debate. I don't know if I should trust her or not. She's going to do what is best for him. But I also know she was always cool with me. She was the one who once told me I needed to do what was best for me and if that was walking away, then it is what it is. I should've listened to her.

"Okay." I stand and walk out of the room and into the green room without looking at anyone.

Maeven follows me and closes the door, beelining for the fridge. She pulls out a bottle of Ace of Spades vintage. "He brought this so you can both drink it during the interview."

"Are you fucking serious?"

The disgust must show on my face, because she smiles. "Very. The whole world knows he has a woman pregnant. They live together, and she's not going away, but if there's one thing about Mateo, he's still going to shoot his shot." Her voice is drier than the champagne could ever be.

She's right. I frown at her, wondering why she's telling me this.

As if she can read my thoughts, she says, "It's my last day on the job."

My jaw hits my chest as the cork pops from the bottle.

"You're leaving him?"

"Yes." She pours us glasses and hands one to me. "And since this is also your last day on the job with him, why don't we make a pact?

Let's get through it together. Tonight, after it's over, we fuck up the town. Wait, you may want to get back to your boyfriend."

My gaze dips to the floor.

"Oh." She sighs. "You're going through a breakup. And we're putting you through this shit. No wonder you're pissed."

I refuse to let her pity me. "I'll be okay."

"Of course you will. So will I, even though I've been through the wringer the past few months. I'm doing a palette cleanse after this shit. You can join me in Positano. House on the hill, the beach, and no Mateo or the ex in sight. Plus, plenty of hotties to help you cleanse your palate too."

I think of how, for the first time since Cam moved to Baltimore, I don't want to go back there, even though all the people I love are there. I need to get away. I need to figure out how to live in the townhouse Ollie made beautiful for me.

The last thing I want right now is the memory of us everywhere I look. I can work from anywhere. And Maeven has always been cool. Even though she's on Mateo's payroll, she has always taken care of me too. She made sure to divert attention from the media and kept his side chicks away from me at events.

"Best offer I've ever had."

"You can play this interview in whatever way you want, as long as you're cordial. Tonight, you can host the ball and ignore him in your revenge, fuck-me dress. I have a contact at Clotho who will find you a number that will leave their tongues wagging. After that, you're done, all while making your Baltimore bae so jealous he'll want to throw himself headfirst into the Inner Harbor. I will make sure my media contacts show the world how happy, beautiful, and desired you are."

That's what I want. I don't want anyone to pity me. Even if I die inside, I want it to look like I'm on top of the world.

We shake hands and throw back our glasses. She pours refills, and we throw them back.

"Let's put this asshole to bed, for the last time," I say, wishing I could do the same with the ache in my heart and my love for Ollie.

———

Oliver

The sky opens on my way to Mrs. Morales's house. The raindrops splat on my windshield. It's raining hard, but I swear if I stood under it, I wouldn't get wet. It would sizzle off my skin. Because on the way to this suburb, all I can see is my baby's face and hear Adri's words. *Maybe Lux lied because she couldn't stand to see Ayla in pain.* But still, it bends me that she kept this from me. I can't forgive her.

Because here I am, standing outside this fucking house, looking for Noris.

Again.

The last time I came looking for her, she had walked out of the house and left Ayla alone while I was on my way from work. She called to tell me she was leaving and that I needed to come home.

That day, her mother had stood at the door and told me she needed time. She asked me to come back in the morning. She felt I needed to give her daughter some time. She thought it was postpartum depression. The next day, I had to stand there as she told me, with red-rimmed eyes, that her daughter had left and handed me the envelope with divorce papers.

I loosen my grip on the steering wheel and throw the door open, the rain immediately making its way inside my truck. As it turns out, I was wrong. The drops fall over my head and start drenching my clothes. I make up my mind quickly, pushing off the seat and slamming the door shut. I'm in front of the suburban house within minutes, knocking on the door.

Mrs. Morales's eyes widen when she sees me, her mouth slack.

"Ma'am, you know why I'm here. Please tell your daughter to come out."

She recovers fast, clearing her throat. "Oliver, it's pouring. You should—"

I shake my head. "I'm not coming back another day. I'm here to speak to Noris. I know she's here. Please call her."

She nods. "Come on in, then." She turns away from me. "I'll go get her."

"Wait," I say, waiting until she stops. "I trusted you. I never kept Ayla away from you. I let you have access to her without restrictions, and here you were, letting your daughter talk to the child she left behind."

"She's my daughter, Oliver." She says my name now like she used to prior to Noris leaving me—with soft disdain.

"I know she is. And Ayla is mine. You had no right to do that to me. I know you've always hated me, but I've always shown you respect, even when you treated me like gum on the bottom of your slippers. I'm the one who kept my promises. I'm the one who was a good father and kind to you, despite the fact that your *hot house flower* walked out on our marriage and her child."

Her face reddens. "You don't think I know that, Oliver? Do you know what it's like to see your child marry someone you don't approve of, only for her to do to you and your child everything I told her you would do to her?"

Her confession rocks me, rooting me on the spot. Her eyes are full of tears, but I swat away at the shock like I do any empathy that threatens to flow through me.

I'm so fucking tired of her and her daughter's tears. I'm done with her, like I want to be done with her spawn.

"Please tell Noris I want to see her."

She opens her mouth and then closes it, only to open it again. "I am sorry, Oliver. I know you don't deserve the lies, but she has the right to see Ayla. No matter what, she is her mother. She made a mistake, but she has all the right in the world to change her mind."

"Says who? She didn't make a mistake. She planned it. A mistake is what a friend of mine made. She got overwhelmed and hit with post-partum depression. She left her baby for a day but was right back. She was tormented, but the love she felt for her child was too strong. She didn't plot. She didn't get on fucking Tinder and meet some rich doctor. She didn't go see a divorce lawyer and get the paperwork drafted. She didn't leave her child home alone and call her husband to come home while she ran away."

I don't realize how loud I'm yelling until my words echo against the white walls.

"I'm still her mother." The voice thunders loud enough to still all my muscles.

I whip around to face her.

Noris Morales is standing six feet away from me. I take her in like I did the first time, all of her at the same time. She's staring at me, eye to eye, in her impossibly high heels. Her skin still glows like brown porcelain. She has always had the kind of body women would pay for and those beautifully angelic features I see reflected on my Ayla's face every day.

I chose to forget how much my baby looks like her. Noris is where she gets the statuesque grace and elegance. But that's where the similarities end.

Ayla is good, sweet, and beautiful inside as well. Her mother is like a doll. Beautiful on the outside but hollow inside. She feels nothing unless there is money involved, and the only time she shows emotion is when she needs to manipulate to get her way. Her last name, like her beauty, is nothing but a ruse.

Morales. Morals.

Her mother may have strong morals, but she didn't pass them along.

"You're not her mother. A mother is there for you, loves you, nurtures you. You've never done that for her. Hell, you don't even call."

"It's not like you have welcomed that. I knew you would block me from seeing her. That's why I waited until she was older and could make her own decision. As it turns out, Ayla does want me. She wants a relationship with me." She smiles like she's the MVP of the World Series, holding the Commissioner's Trophy, lording it over my head.

It hurts because it's true. Ayla has always wanted a mom.

I chuckle, though. "Nothing anyone could do or say could ever keep me away from Ayla. No matter how bad I fucked up, if the shoe were on the other foot, I would have never allowed you to keep me away from her. But that's the thing, right? I never kept her from you. I begged you to come back, and if you had, I would have never stood in your way. "You know why, Noris?" I walk closer to her.

She doesn't even flinch when I come close. She merely looks me up and down, her eyes traveling over my body, lingering on my chest. But that look stopped working on me when I realized how much of a manipulator she is.

"I'll tell you why. I would have let you come back because of Ayla. My daughter is the most important person in my life. She is the only thing I'm indebted to you for. She's the greatest gift and more than I deserve. I don't even know how an angel like her could come from inside someone like you."

She rears back like I slapped her.

"I forgot how cruel you can be."

"How cruel *I* can be?"

"Yes, I was nothing to you. Once I got big with pregnancy, you stopped caring about me. All you cared about was the pregnancy. *Te llenas la boca hablando de mi.* You love to talk about how bad I was, but what about you? I gave myself to you. I loved you, flaws and all, even though you were a player. You said you loved every bit of me and my soul. But you were using me. You didn't show me any kindness."

"You got pregnant on purpose. You orchestrated everything so I would have to marry you. If you hadn't done that, I wouldn't have gotten hurt. I quit baseball to provide for you. To be there for Ayla."

She laughs. "Yes, you quit baseball. But not for me. You could've gone back, but you were afraid, so you decided not to try at all. Once you saw Mateo, Fabian, and all the others rising, you acted like you couldn't measure up. So, you gave it all up to be poor. You were a good player. You could've made millions. We could've had a good life, and you could have still played."

"I had lost the love for it. We were having a baby. That was more important to me."

She sucks her teeth. "Por favor. You got *pendejo* and started taking handyman jobs like you were not meant for the big stage. You were not born to lay drywall. You were meant to break records."

It bugs me but doesn't sting as much as it should. Not her disdain, not the words that haunted me for years. Maybe it's because she already did her worst to me. Three times.

I shrug. "I'm not going to argue with you. It's not worth my time, and frankly, I don't give a fuck what you think anymore. If it weren't for you being Ayla's mother, I would gladly send you *pal carajo*."

She flinches back, her eyes widening.

I take advantage and continue. "Don't ever get close to Ayla without my permission again. Yeah, you're her biological mother, but I have sole custody of her. I can prove you left her alone and walked away from us. I also have evidence of your neglect and of all the times I asked you to come back and how you could've contacted her at any point. You chose now, and you chose to do it on the down-low."

"Wow, look at what a little education and your white girl have done for you."

White girl?

I freeze. Lux. That's who she's talking about.

"Leave her out of this."

"She's not *mami* material, you know that, right? She's like me. She is used to having a baller on her arm. Don't you see how TMZ follows her around in New York? She's all about expensive hotels and designer clothes. Mateo can give her a lot of things you can't. After these months with you, she's probably missing that and the glitz and glam of New York. Do you think she'll be happy being a soccer mom and washing your dirty work clothes?"

My muscles crumple together. *Damn*, she still knows how and where to hit. Noris has always been an expert at that. This time, she lands the blow easily to my chest, knocking my ego six hundred feet out the door and into the yard. Because this is what the small voice in my head has been telling me. That Lux will find herself a baller in no time.

I swipe away at the thought. I need to deal with what's at hand.

"I don't care what he can give her or if she goes back to him.

That's her business. But what I can say is that Lux cares about her family. She wouldn't walk away from them without a thought. She cares about Ayla's feelings and doesn't just use and discard her when convenient."

"I came back because I love my daughter."

"Do you, Noris?" I step toward her and then force myself not to move anymore. I need to think of the position I'm putting myself in. She's evil, so she would think nothing of saying I threatened her. But that's not going to stop me from telling her what I think. "You love Ayla so much that you came back in a sneaky way. You came back to teach her how to lie and keep things from me."

"She wouldn't have kept it from you if—"

"You had not asked her. I saw the text messages. All of them. My baby didn't lie constantly until you came around. You came to do what you always do: destroy. It's not my fault that you didn't have a relationship with her. I'm not the one that kicked you out. But if you ever ask her to lie to me again, I'm going to get a restraining order against you, and you'll never see her again."

Her mother gasps behind us.

I don't even glance her way.

Noris goes pale. Her hand presses against her throat. She knows, like I do, I have ammunition to do that. "You'll hurt Ayla."

I know that. I wouldn't do it, but I need Noris to know I mean business. "I've been raising a good person. You're not going to ruin that with your bullshit. I won't get in your way if you want to see her but only under the supervision of me or someone I trust."

"So, you can send you little girlfriend?"

She's not going to bait me.

"I can send whoever *me de mi maldita gana*. Yes, whoever the fuck I want, and you're not in a position to argue about it." I turn toward the door but stop and whip around again. "You are not to tell Ayla about this arrangement until I've had a chance to talk to her. Neither of you." I look from Noris to her mother.

Mrs. Morales nods.

I look at Noris, and she tilts her head, pushing her chin up.

I shake my head at her. "Don't try me. I'm not the guy that begged you to come back, but I'm the one that can keep you away for good."

I walk out of the house, walking quickly toward my car. The rain has let up, and Chase is leaning on my car.

Fuck. Cam must have told him.

He tilts his head to his car. "Follow me."

I nod. I'll go and deal with this and then head home to talk to Ayla.

26

Lux

The ballroom is a dream. The elegant Art Deco design with bold geometric patterns, rich colors, and stunning crystal chandeliers are everything I would have loved for my wedding years ago. Younger Lux would have swooned, imagining photos of myself in my white, long-sleeve gown against the fancy wall coverings or dancing in the middle while four hundred people watched me and my husband.

The thought makes my stomach dip now.

One, because I wouldn't want that many people. Only those who love me and are truly happy for me. Two, because I don't give a rat's ass what all those people think, so I wouldn't entertain them and share my happiest moment. Three, and most important, I don't have a husband, fiancé, or even a boyfriend.

I take a swig of champagne to quell the bitterness on my tongue. I catch a glimpse of myself in the mirror behind the punch table. This is such a great look. Maeven made good on her promise. Clotho sent this gorgeous peacock-inspired gown with gradient panels of blue, emerald, turquoise, gold, and bronze, which fade into a spectrum. Lauren jumped on the phone and guided the makeup artist to achieve the perfect eye to match my outfit while ensuring my face makeup was minimal but enhanced. I look like a polished million bucks, but I feel sharp like a five-dollar box cutter.

"It's time to present Mateo with the foundation's award," someone says behind me.

I turn to face Mateo's sister, Wandy. I wasn't surprised to learn she's the event coordinator. She's sporting a pink gown and a worried look. I heard she doesn't think having me here is a good idea after she heard what happened this morning. I don't give a fuck and smile, letting my eyes linger over her face as I take the speech from her hand.

"Thank you," I say and walk away from her. The timer on my phone lets me know I have five contractual minutes left. I head to the stage, catching Maeven in her white fitted gown. *The color of freedom*, as she called it earlier. I smile at her, and she winks at me.

I climb the steps to the stage and step up to the microphone, pasting on a smile as I face the audience.

"Well, it's been a whirlwind of a night, and I think we have done a fantastic job for the Cross Foundation. While we are still waiting on the final amount raised, the foundation wanted to take a moment to recognize its founder."

I pause as people begin to applaud, and I see Mateo getting ready to walk to the stage once I'm done, and a fire begins to roar in my belly because I shouldn't be here. I shouldn't be in the position to toast him. I try to force myself to read the speech, but I can't. No, I'm going to wing this my way.

"All of New York knows Mateo—from rabid baseball fans, the children who attend the Cross Foundation camps, to his groupies, and of course…the waitresses at Parlay in the Park."

The audience gasps, and I press my lips together playfully. Then everyone laughs.

"Hey, it's on the paper right here." I hold up the speech, and more laughter ensues. "We are all grateful for his dedication to the children. When he makes a promise to the Cross Foundation, he keeps it. He doesn't divide his loyalties with other charities or allocate the money to something else. Nope, he's loyal…to the kids. That's how I know he will be a great dad. He told me earlier how he cannot wait until his baby is born to give him or her the world. As a friend, I am happy to hear that and wish him the best of luck and more success to the Cross Foundation. It will continue to make a great difference in the lives of children, like Mateo has done with many young women here in New York."

Laughter ensues again, and it drowns out the beeping of my phone.

"Well, it's my time to stop talking and invite the man of the hour on stage."

The audience claps, and Mateo approaches. His face is a little pale. When he leans to hug me, he keeps his distance.

"Luxxy—"

"Go to hell," I whisper and walk off the stage.

His sister meets me at the bottom of the steps.

"Lux, why would you do that? You ruined the night for him."

I smiled at her. "He ruined my whole day. Now, kindly step out of my way."

I move forward, and she has no choice. I wave at Maeven and Fabian but don't stop walking until I am out of the ballroom. I am almost free, and I can taste it. I hand my ticket to one of the attendants who goes to fetch my car and jacket.

"Luciana."

I don't swear like I want to. For two hours, I've avoided contact with Marilyn, but I turn around to face her now. She's wearing a baby-blue satin gown that stops at her calf and the Manolos I got her for her birthday. She looks beautiful, except for the deep frown marring her face.

"Hi, Marilyn."

"Are you okay?" she asks.

"Better than ever, but on my way out."

"You got your digs in at Mateo back there." The reproach is in her words and the dry tone she wields like a sword.

It doesn't land like it usually does. "I could've said a lot worse. But I don't expect you to understand. You're always on his side."

She reaches out, but I step back.

"He loves you, and I know you love him. I've only tried to salvage your relationship because I don't want you to regret it. You kept taking him back, and I knew you would again. That's why I helped him."

She did help him. All the time.

I look at her, and something dawns on me. Months ago, at the tearoom… *She set me up.*

"Marilyn, I don't love Mateo. I don't think I ever did. He was just someone who showed me affection like you never did. He wanted me around, unlike Walter, who had no use for me and walked away emotionally. Mateo fed my mommy and daddy issues. He followed the pattern of the people who were supposed to love me but hurt me instead. And I continued to let him do it while you enabled his behavior and kept giving him access to me. And I'm not blaming you alone. I had a lot of say in it but never took control. Toxicity was all I ever knew. That's where I blame you."

She flinches. "He can give you everything you want," she insists.

"He can't. I want love and security. I want to be able to trust the man I'm with. I want to know that I'm not something for a man to keep on a shelf, like a doll, and discard me when his interests go somewhere else. He can't give me any of that."

Her eyes fill with tears. "Come with me, Luciana. I want to talk."

"No. I have nothing to say to you that I haven't already said."

"Please. I never meant to hurt you," she begs.

I scoff. "But you did. You forever hurt all of us."

Footsteps echo, and the attendant comes back with a long blazer and my keys.

I turn to look at my mother. "Goodbye, Marilyn."

"Luciana, please."

But I'm crossing the lobby to the door.

———

Oliver

I stare from the thick wooden door to the hulking man in front. The rain let up on the drive here. Yet, I'm still baffled. I expected us to drive to a park, not to a bar.

"This is where you want to fight?"

Chase's face shows no emotion. "I'm not here to fight you, Coach. I want to talk."

He turns and heads inside The Birthmark, not giving me the chance to tell him I don't have time for this. The owner, Saona, is at the hostess booth tonight. She smiles at us, stretching the mark on her lip. "Welcome back. Your usual table is ready for you, Chase. *Y Lauren?*"

"She's good."

We head to the booth in the bar area where I had drinks with him a while ago. There's already an ice bucket with beers in the middle. He must have called in ahead of time.

"I imagine we're here to talk about Lux." *Coño.* I wish her name didn't feel like hot sand on my tongue.

"Have a beer, Ollie. Relax."

I shake my head. "I need to go home to my kid. If you want to hit me, let's get it over with, but the one thing I don't want to do is make pleasantries or talk about your sister."

He shrugs, unperturbed. "We don't have to do either. I think you need a friend."

"You can't be my friend in this. I broke up with your sister."

The slight flare of his nostrils is instant. "I know. I spoke to her already, and she tore me a shiny new asshole. She made a mistake. It wasn't malicious. Lux doesn't have an ounce of malice in her bones. That said, I'm not here to talk about it. It's between the two of you. I'm here to see how you're holding up with this Ayla thing...and to make sure you don't do anything dumb."

I don't know what to make of that. I rub two fingers on my wet forehead and sigh. "I'm pissed off but fine. I have a good head on my shoulders and a kid to think about. I'm not going to do anything insane. Like always, I have too much to lose."

Chase levels me with a look. "I know you're a good guy who would never physically hurt a woman, let alone Ay's mom. But...you just went to talk to that woman and her mother alone. The whole world knows you're angry. Do you know what easy prey you could've been today?"

A cold wave blows through my stomach. My hand freezes with the beer halfway to my mouth. He's right. I went in there angry, and if she wanted to, Noris could make up some shit. I'd be in real trouble. I could lose Ayla.

"I was watching the whole time. You didn't move far from the door." Chase's voice is soft. His eyes are anything but.

"How did you know I would be there?"

"Adri told Lauren. We talked about it and decided to divide and conquer. I headed here…"

And Lauren went to his sister.

He nods like he can read my thoughts. "They're probably trashing you real good right now."

His lips twitch at the end, and I snort.

"Probably." I clear my throat. "Thank you, Chase. I don't think Noris or her mother would ever go that far, but I appreciate you having my back."

He bobs his head up and down. "Let's eat something."

"I should go home."

He pushes a menu my way. "You should eat and then drink something. Let Ayla spend the night with Bron. Take this time to sort your head out."

I open my mouth to tell him I can do that at home, but the waiter comes to take our order. We order and settle into silence after he leaves, with Noris's words swimming around in my head.

As it turns out, Ayla does want me. She wants a relationship with me.

My stomach is burning all over again. It's been almost thirteen years without a smoke signal from that woman. Now that we were headed in the right direction…

"Why did she have to come back now?"

Chase regards me over his beer. "That's the way shit works. When things are going really well, there's always that demon from your past that shows up."

I couldn't have said it better myself. He speaks from experience. I can tell. "Who was your demon?"

"The man that raised me mostly. Then, my mother. Last time, my bad decisions after I became impatient and listened to the past that always pushed me to self-destruct one way or another."

"Damn, that's deep."

"It is. Almost got me killed. I could've lost everything that was already in the plans for me. You know what I mean?"

I nod, remembering the bad accident he was in over a year ago, how it shook Lauren and his family, and how hard he worked in rehab to get back to normal.

"It's been a hard road for you," I say.

"Yeah. For you too, Coach. You're raising one of the greatest kids I've ever met. You've done such an amazing job by yourself. I don't want you to throw it all away because of a moment."

He's right. I have everything to lose if I don't handle this right.

"The one thing I've never been able to do is make it so Ayla doesn't miss having a mother. Noris has been looming in our background like a tidal wave that could flood us at any moment. I've always known that, and she still caught me with my pants down. She still flooded my life and destroyed what I treasure the most, how I see my Ayla, my relationship with Lu—"

I clamp my teeth together because that's the thing neither of us wants to talk about.

Chase leans back in the booth. "Noris can only destroy what you let her. It's your choice how you'll handle things with Lux. But I'll just say that you'll never find someone as loving or loyal. Trust me, she did not give up on me no matter how much I tried."

The burn in my chest intensifies, and I can't find a response in me.

He continues, "But when it comes to Ayla, your ex shouldn't have the power to change anything. The two of you are a unit, and Ay is an amazing kid because of you. Don't let Noris take that away from you. She doesn't have that power unless you give it to her."

"How do I deal with it? How do I overlook what happened?"

He grimaces. "I'm the worst person in the world to tell anyone how

325

to deal with hurt. As Lu—someone—reminded me today, I used to deal with it by doing something destructive, like racing, street fighting, or gambling. I went to therapy for years and still turned to those things. It took the accident and facing some truths to realize that being destructive was never going to fill the void."

You lied so well...

My words to Ayla echo in my head and bring a fresh wave of pain. The thought that she is like her mother makes my stomach turn.

It's not true.

I turned my trauma on my kid.

This is not about her or Lux. They made mistakes, but it was me who did the real damage here.

"Do you get the urge to go back to that?" I wait for his nod before I ask. "What do you do not to relapse?"

"I look at what I have. I constantly remind myself that if I want to be happy and whole, I have to focus on what truly matters. I keep my attention on Lauren, my boys, Lux, and Cam and his family. My advice is to keep your eyes on what's most important to you."

I see my Ayla, and I never want to repeat what we've been through the last two days. And then, Lux sneaks into my thoughts.

In my mind's eye, I see Lux and Ayla together in the living room, watching that red-carpet show and laughing together. The pressure in my chest inflates like a bubble.

"I didn't handle this well, Chase."

"If I-didn't-handle-it-well was a person, I would be the embodiment of it. Take it from me, life doesn't come with a manual, and you're human."

I sigh. "I knew this day would come. I should've been more ready. I blasted my kid for something that's normal."

"She shouldn't have lied. She had no reason to, and it made you react to something you were not prepared for."

I shake my head. "Yeah, but did I make it safe enough for her to talk about her mom? Did I teach her she could come to me about that?"

"I don't know, but what are you going to do about it?"

I press my thumbs to my forehead. "I don't know. How do I move us past this?"

I'm talking about Ayla, but I'm also thinking about Lux. I hate the way we left things.

I walked away from her.

"Be honest and be raw. Don't concentrate on Noris but on you and what you feel. Speak from your heart."

We're silent after that because the food comes, and I'm alone with my thoughts. I'm going to talk to A and fix things between us.

Then, I'm going to talk to Lux, because even if nothing comes out of it, I need to clear the air with her.

I finish my drink and head home. I get a text from Adri, asking if Ayla can spend the night.

Adri: She's more relaxed now. Bron and CJ are love-bombing her.

She sends me a photo of CJ with his mouth all over Ayla's cheek. She's smiling, and I know when she comes home, she won't be that happy. And that hurts my heart. And that is what makes me say yes.

———

Lux

We pull up outside Adri and Cam's, and Lauren undoes her seat buckle.

"What are we doing here?" My voice is sharp but louder than I mean it.

She's nonplussed as she opens her door. "I'm violating friendship boundaries with one person, but I'm also being a good auntie and sister to you. Get out."

"Lauren, I know you all mean well, but the last thing I want is another lecture from Cam or Chase. I couldn't take another 'you were stupid and didn't act like an adult moment.'"

She pauses, her eyes glowing like burning charcoal. "First of all, neither of those two are here. Second, did Chase say that? Did those fucking words come out of his mouth?"

I shake my head. "But that's what I heard."

Her features relax. "You need to clarify. Don't get me tearing your brother a new asshole for things he actually didn't say."

I chuckle. "Thank you."

"Don't fucking thank me. It's about time you and everyone else stop beating on you. You didn't do anything maliciously. Ollie will see it differently—"

My insides twist, and I throw the door open. "Don't say his name. That's the last thing I want is to talk about him. I'm just going to go in there and spend some time with Bron and CJ before I go on my trip."

I walk around the car, and Lauren's sharp gaze is all over me. "I'm going to shut up for now, but we'll talk about him again."

"Let's get drunk instead after we leave here. It will be my bon voyage celebration because you'll miss me so much."

"Deal," she laughs.

We make our way inside the house and walk through the family room, but no one is in sight. I follow her until we get to Bron's room. We pause outside.

"Go in. I'll be in Adri's room."

I frown, but she tilts her head to the door and walks away. I guess Bron and I are just talking alone. I knock and open the door. My niece is not in there.

Ayla is sitting on her bed and springs up when she sees me. Her face crumples, and so do my insides. My heart splits into pieces at the anguish in her face.

"I'm so sorry," she says and takes two steps toward me but stops. "You probably hate me."

I cross the distance between us and throw my arms around her. "No, I could never hate you. I love you too much."

"*Papi* is so disappointed in me. I don't think he'll ever forgive me or love me again."

Her arms go around me, and she squeezes me with so much strength, like CJ when he's in need of comfort, so I hug her tight and rub my hand in circles on her back. "Ay, your father loves you more than anything and anyone in the world. When you love someone that much, there's no way you can stop, no matter what."

She shakes her head. "He doesn't look at me anymore. Just…does everything…"

Her sobs are more than I can take. I hate that she feels like this. I hate that I could have prevented this if I had told him what I overheard.

"Your dad is upset, but that has nothing to do with loving someone. You can be mad at a person, but nothing has changed between you. You know? Come on, let's get a sip of water." I pull her to the seating area. There's a water bottle, and I hand it to her.

She takes a sip and breathes.

"I ruined everything. *Papi* and I were like best friends, almost like me and B, but now we're not talking, and he broke up with you, and he really loves you, and I do too."

Her words knife over my skin, and I feel them deep within. "I love you too. And that's never going to stop. Your dad and I just don't see eye to eye, and that happens with relationships. Sometimes, even though you love people, you can't be with them. I really should have told him earlier."

"It doesn't matter when you told him. He was always going to be mad. I should have told him, but I just didn't think he would want me to talk to Mom. She left us, and he hates her, but…"

"She's your mom. And he doesn't hate her either. She just hurt him. He doesn't want her to hurt you."

She nods. "I know. But I betrayed him. He's not going to forgive me, like he doesn't forgive her."

"Ayla, you didn't betray him, and it's not the same. You are his world. Your dad is a wonderful guy. But I also understand you want to see and talk to your mom. Our parents are our parents. Walter is not a good person, but I remember a time when we were so close, and I was his little girl. I can't help missing that sometimes. He's…"

"Your *papi*."

The tears slide down my face one after the next. I try swiping, but they won't stop. "He's more like a biological father. *Papi* is someone who is everything your dad is with you. Someone who loves you, puts your best interests above everything, and makes you his whole world."

"I'm sorry," she says and leans against me. "I wish your dad was like mine."

"Me too." I sniffle and wipe my face again. "That's why you have to talk to him, tell him why you talked to her, how you really feel."

She shakes her head and my whole body with it. "He will never understand. My mom says I need to give him time, so I should just go live with her."

Her words are like hacks with an ax, each making the splinter wider. I pull back to tell her she can't do that. She'll break her father's heart forever. I can already see the hurt in his eyes. But I need to be careful not to push her too far.

"Ay, is that what you really want? Do you want to go live with someone else other than your dad?"

The tears are back, cascading down her cheeks. "No. I want things how they used to be. I want to be with *Papi*. I love him more than anything. I only want to talk to Noris sometimes."

"Then you need to fix things with him. You don't walk away because it's hard. You fight for it."

She tilts her head to look at me. "Are you going to fight to stay with him?"

This conversation is breaking me all over again. "It's different. You two are each other's everything. We are just not compatible."

"But he's been the happiest with you."

The pain flashes over my chest, and it almost doubles me. "I was the happiest with him too, but you know what, that doesn't matter. You and he matter. I want you guys to be happy and together like you belong."

"It does matter. I loved having you with us. It was really cool. I wanted you to be my *Mami*... I shouldn't say that, right?" Her eyes are so wide and earnest.

It takes all of me not to scream. *I want to be your mom. I want to be with you.*

"I love our relationship more than anything. I love you and that you see me like that. It doesn't have to change. We can still be this close. You can call me whenever you need me, and I'll always be there for you."

Her shoulders droop, but I tug at her hand.

"You can give your mom a chance, but she needs to work out an arrangement with your dad. He raised you. And he would only let you go live with her if that is what you truly want."

I give her a pointed look because I want to hammer the point home. This is not what she wants, and she shouldn't do it because of the hurt.

She finally nods. "Okay."

I squeeze her hand. "Ay, can I get you to promise me something?"

"Yes."

"Promise that you'll talk to your dad, and you'll be completely honest about how you feel. You'll tell the truth that you want to be with him and explain why you hid the calls from him."

"What if he doesn't listen? What if he hates me?" she asks.

"Your job is not to worry about the outcome. Your job is only to tell the truth. Trust the love you have for each other. Okay?"

She nods. "I promise to tell him the truth."

"Thank you." I hug her tight and try not to cry again. I hope to God this makes things right. I want Ollie and Ayla to be happy.

27

Oliver

I can't seem to find my place tonight. With Ayla spending last night at Adri's, I don't think I have ever been so alone. At least not since she was born. I twisted and turned all night while thoughts of Lux plagued me constantly. I wondered where she was and how she was doing. I wanted to call and ask her. I didn't think I had the right to ask the question.

I went through tomorrow's workday, organized what I needed, and printed out the forms, but my brain and heart are all over the place, like my brain got demo'ed before a renovation. Other than work, nothing is where it's supposed to be. I keep thinking about A and how I can bring us back to where we used to be.

Chase was right. I need to fix it. I can't be without my girl.

I can't love her and hold on to this hurt forever. I'm going to miss the great things if I don't right this ship. It's my issue. I want to make that clear to her.

I can't get over what Luciana did, and I honestly can't worry about her until I fix my world with Ay. But I can't help but miss Lux's smile, our conversations, her body, or the way she touched me.

I look up, and there she is, on the TV playing in the background. There's a feature on the gossip show that Ayla and Bron like to watch.

Last night, Mateo De La Cruz's Cross Foundation held its annual gala. It was jam-packed with New York's rich and famous emptying their wallets for children in the Dominican Republic. La creme de la creme showed up, including his off-again-on-again girlfriend, popular lifestyle influencer Lux Blake, also known as Bougie Girl. She hosted the event that managed to raise five million dollars.

I freeze, my hands on my keyboard. She's wearing a barely there dress that hugs her curves and darkens in any explicit areas, leaving her long legs bare. The free-fall drop in my stomach is instant. She's smiling up at Fabian Marte, the Emperors' right fielder.

"Rumor is that she kept her distance from Mateo. She flirted with his teammate Fabian and was seen enjoying drinks with the Yankees' centerfielder, Angelo Gomez. She obviously has a type: handsome, rich, and successful athlete. Then again, why would she go there, in that turquoise killer revenge dress, if it wasn't to rub Mateo's face in it?" the male anchor says.

The female anchor chuckles. "Honey, she may have kept her distance, but his eyes never left her. He stared at her all night, and when she presented him the award, he found every excuse to touch her hand and arm."

The chef on the other side of the room chimes in. "Whoever says they don't see this reconciliation coming needs goggles not glasses. She opened the door by agreeing to the interview earlier in the day and going to the gala. Sparks were flying. Whew." He fans himself.

"I don't know. She seemed really indifferent to me," the female interjects again. "Though it's always more fun when Lux and Mateo have drama, I hope she moves on to someone who's not as skeezy as Mateo. I'll admit I'm game for Fabian or Angelo. That would make it juicier."

All three laugh while the world around me melts into a red haze. I go on my browser and search for the interview. It was posted to her YouTube channel. I struggle through watching it. Mateo makes attempts to flirt with her, practically eye-fucking her. It should've made me feel better that she stared at him with that blank look I hate so much when she directs it my way. Because there's nothing blank about it. She was over it.

I close my laptop hard enough it should shatter the screen when the footage of her with Fabian and Angelo comes up.

It hurts that she's flirting with other guys. It's only been two days. How can she move on that fast? Did I mean so little to her? I can't even picture another woman, and she's on the way to moving on.

You dumped her. Did you expect her to sit here and cry for you?

My heart sinks. Yes, I broke up with her without thinking much about it, but she lied. I wasn't the one who wronged her. But she's moving like she was waiting for the first chance. She didn't even try to convince me or talk to me. She hasn't called me even once. Another woman who can put me away so quickly. I didn't mean anything to her either. That's what I get for trusting and for opening myself and my kid up when my instincts have always cautioned me against it.

You broke up with her. You pushed her away.

The text from Adri comes through, snapping me out of my self-pity.

ADRI

We are two minutes away.

I turn off the TV. I want to talk with Ayla when she comes in. I go downstairs to thank Adri. When I get to the sidewalk, A and Bron are hugging like the world is ending, and they're seeing each other for the last time.

My gaze meets Adri, and she's shaking her head. She mouths the word *dramatic,* and for the first time today, I feel a little bit of a smile. Something is as it should be. Teenage best friends being drama queens.

We thank Adri and Bron and wave them away. I put my hand on her shoulder. "Let's go inside."

She looks up at me with red-rimmed eyes and swallows. "Okay."

We go up the stairs, and she stands in the middle of our family room like she doesn't know where to go.

"You can put your things away, and I'll wait for you here. I want to talk to you."

She nods and turns but then drops everything and turns around. "I'm so sorry, *Papi*. I didn't want to betray you. I just wanted to talk to Noris, and I knew you wouldn't like it. I wouldn't have gone away like she wanted me to—"

I hold my hand up, and she halts. There's so much desperation there, and she's really just a little girl.

"Ayla, breathe. Let's focus." My words are measured.

"But I need you to know—" she sobs.

And now I'm hurting like before. I cross the room and hug her to me. I kiss her hair and temples. "Don't cry like this. Let's sit down."

She tries to pull away. "I'll go put my stuff away."

"Leave it. It's not important right now," I say, moving us toward the couch.

When she's upset, she always gets herself worked up, and I want her to be calm. I guide her to sit and go get us water and tissues.

I wait until she drinks some water. "You've been crying a lot."

She bobs her head up and down. "I hurt you, and I'm sorry."

"You did, and I hurt you too. I'm sorry I said that you betrayed me. You didn't. That's not a betrayal. You lied to me…"

She winces and lowers her head.

"…but you didn't betray me, A. In truth, you had all the right in the world to talk to your mom. I'm sorry because I never made that clear to you. I'm sorry I was stuck in my hurt and made you feel like you had to talk to her in secret."

"I shouldn't have lied, *Papi*. I damaged our relationship. You don't trust me, and I don't even know if you want me to stay with you."

Jesus. The wave of emotion hits so hard my eyes start to sting quickly. I have to swallow the mass of emotion and clear my throat so I can speak.

"No, you shouldn't have lied, but don't you know how much I love you? Don't you know you are the most important thing in my life? How can you say you're not sure if I want you to be here?"

She stands and moves away from me. "Because you won't look at me anymore. You acted like I wasn't around, except to drive me to school, like grandma said, like a chore."

The rage flows right through me. "What? She told you that?"

She shakes her head. "She told Mom when she thought I hung up. She said that you're a great dad, but maybe you wanted a break from the chore of being a full-time parent. She said you gave up everything for me. I'm sorry you gave up everything you love for me."

I breathe because I'm not going to call that woman a bad name in front of my daughter. She already knows where we stand. Right now, I need to reassure Ayla and figure out how to proceed. My daughter is not a toy of hers to discard and pick up because of a whim.

"Your grandmother is mistaken. You've never been a chore to me. I didn't give up everything. I gave up baseball because I got hurt, and I didn't think I could go back to being the player I was before. And yes, you were on the way, and you are a billion times more important than the game. I wouldn't trade a second with you to be playing for any team. I love being your dad and coaching you."

She half smiles but doesn't come back to the couch.

"I don't want to go live with Mom, but I will if you need some time for yourself. Maybe you want to go make things work with Lux."

A freezing wave blows through my stomach. Those are not her words. I'm so angry I could punch a wall through the brick with my fists. Noris is still manipulating and causing problems for me.

"I don't want you to live with anyone but me. If you were to go live with your mom, I would follow you wherever you go because you're the only person in this world I cannot live without. My issues with Lux have nothing to do with you."

"How can you say that? You're both lying. If it weren't because of me, you would be together."

So, she saw her.

"She lied to me, Ayla. I can't forgive her for that."

"I lied too," her voice rises.

"Yes, but it's different. You're a child who wanted to talk to her mom. She lied about something she and I should have been on the same page about. I'm not angry with her anymore. We see things

337

differently. And I don't want this talk to be about that. I want this conversation to be about you and me. I'm not going to get in the way if you want to talk to your mom. But I want you here with me…if that's what you still want."

And I hold my breath because what if she tells me she doesn't want that?

She comes back to the couch and sits right next to me. She buries her face in the crook of my shoulder. "I want to stay here with you. And I just want to talk to Mom sometimes. I don't want to live with her. She asked me, but…"

"But?"

"I don't trust her."

Because she's not trustworthy. She's opportunistic, and she left you. How can someone leave someone so beautiful to chase money?

Her words are a balm for my soul. "Trust takes time, *negrita*. You have to get to know her first."

"I don't know. She left us. Is it going to take a long time for you to trust me again?"

I shake my head. "You and I are different. We have an established relationship already. A few bad days do not erase our life together. And we're human. We make mistakes."

She snuggles closer. "That's what Lux said."

Please stop mentioning her.

I don't want to hear her name, but Ayla loves her, and this is exactly what I always watch out for, what I always try to protect her from. So now we are both heartbroken because I love Lux too, but I don't know if I can trust her.

"Do you want to watch something? Spring training games are on," I ask.

She nods, and I switch the TV on. And there's Mateo, warming up to get into the batter's box. *That fucking guy.*

Ayla grabs the remote control from my hand. "We can watch another game or a TV show."

"You like the Emperors, and you like watching him." To my endless grief.

"Yeah, but he's a jerk."

I want to hug her. "You can still study him and learn from his craft."

She shrugs. "I already know how to strike him out. Pitch him down and away. He has no range there."

I laugh. "You're something, you know that?"

"I get that from my dad," she says, hugging me.

And for the second time tonight, my eyes fill before I can help it, and the tears escape the corners of my eyes before I can stop them.

28

Oliver

I leave Ayla at school, and this is the first time in three days when I can breathe better. Things are better, a little tentative, but more like the norm. She smiled and kissed my cheek before she got out of the car. I told her I love her, but as soon as I started driving, Lux took hold of my thoughts, and I found myself in Federal Hill and turning onto her street.

I've been thinking about her nonstop, and I just need to see her, talk to her. I get out of the car as soon I park it and make my way to the place we designed together, that I helped make to satisfy her needs.

She may not want me here.

But I need to try to convince her.

I stare at the door I helped install and tested with my own hands. It's sturdy like a southern oak. I remember wanting it to be almost unbreakable so it would keep Lux safe. Now it's an impenetrable barrier that keeps me away from her. I no longer have a reason to come in or the expectation of being invited. But here I am, waiting to talk to her, to explain my side. She may still not see it my way—*yet, I hope.*

Fuck yes, I hope she would be willing to give this another chance.

The door opens, and the breath leaves my body. There she is, beautiful as always, in a green ensemble that brings out her eyes. She's in one of those fitted sporty outfits that make me hot all over. Eyes that sweep over me without the emotion from days before. She's got sneakers on and looks ready to step out.

"Hi, Ollie." She doesn't look excited to see me.

What did you expect? Did you want her to look like she was about to jump you?

"Hi, Lux. I was wondering if I could talk to you."

She looks down and back at me. "I'm going for a walk. You can join me."

I smile for the first time. This is a good sign. "Okay."

We head down the block, but she's not saying anything. I need to start but don't know how to begin.

"What did you want to talk about?" she asks, and I don't think I've heard this detached tone of hers. It goes well with the blank look on her face.

"I had a chance to talk to Ayla, and we cleared the air. You were right about her having the right to see her mom and maybe not feeling like she could come to me. We are working through it, and she can see her mom—with supervision, of course."

She smiles. "I'm happy to hear that. I never want the two of you to be at odds. You make a great team."

I nod. "We are. Because of my complicated history with her mother, I let that blind me, and I reacted too harshly with Ayla…and with you."

The smile slides off her face, and she picks up the pace again. I put a hand on her arm to stop her. She stares at it until I drop it.

"Look, Lux. I've had some time to reflect on the past few days and our conversation. I don't think it's right that you kept the situation from me, but I should have handled the conversation better. I shouldn't have broken up with you the way I did. You were thinking of Ayla, and I should have seen that."

She sighs, her shoulders dipping a little. "You're right. I was giving Ayla the chance, but in truth, I should have given you a heads up and confided in you. It would have made things easier for A. I hated that I could have prevented her pain and yours. I apologize for that again."

I take a step closer to her. "Thank you. I'm glad you see it that way. I apologize for how I handled things and letting my pain talk for me."

We are walking in silence again. Her phone pings. She looks at it and hits the ignore button. I catch Mateo's name on the screen. He's still trying to sneak his way in, and that's my fault.

"You can answer if you want. I already said what I came to say."

She shifts her gaze briefly to me. "I don't need to answer."

"I saw your video interview yesterday." Now why did I say that? "Not the best subject, but you did a great job."

"Thanks. Not my favorite either. I'm tired of playing the same record."

"You looked like you were having a good time at the gala."

She stops to face me. "Are you accusing me of something?"

"No."

"Then why are we talking about this? It would be my right to do whatever I wanted with whomever I wanted, because you broke up with me."

I hold up my hands. "It would have been. You're a hundred percent correct. I'm happy you're not."

Her eyebrows knit together. "Why?"

My hand finds hers. "Because I want to ask you if you'd be willing to give us a chance again. I love you, Lux. I want to be with you."

She blinks a few times, and her eyes well. She pulls her hand from mine and presses it to her chest. "All the time you were wrestling with keeping things from Ayla because you didn't trust me not to hurt her, I couldn't understand you and your motives."

"But now you can?" I ask. Hope wells from deep in my heart. *She understands. She gets it. There's a chance.*

She nods. "Yes, because it's an instinct to protect the most vulnerable part of us, especially when we've been hurt so bad."

There's a jab at my side because I caused the pain that flares over her eyes. I reach for her, but the pain is gone as quickly as she takes a step back.

"You threw us away without a second thought. You made the choice to walk away and blame me for everything. And I get it, I fucked up, but I deserved a conversation. So, now it's me. I'm the one who can't trust you not to hurt me when something goes wrong."

"Lux—"

"I spent years waiting for a man to get it together and be faithful. I waited months for you to see me as someone worthy of officially introducing to your daughter. Then, one mistake, and suddenly, I'm not mature or suitable. I learned from being with Mateo that when something is potentially not good, I need to let it die. Because when I continue to give it chance after chance, it will only grow ugly and more hurtful. And I don't want that for us. Or Ayla."

The knot in my throat grows. I fucked up, and she's not going to forgive me.

"I understand." I begin to turn, but her hand on my elbow stops me. Her touch scars my already burning skin.

She's staring at me with clear eyes, like her words didn't slice my flesh open. "I love Ay so much it hurts, and I want to stay in her life. I don't want to be someone else who walks away from her. Can you please let me be there for her?"

The pain that twists my chest is threatening to bend me. This is the worst moment. She's doing what I always dreamed of. She's loving my baby girl and putting her first like I would, but she doesn't want me as part of the equation.

I can't let Ayla lose someone else, and I can't imagine a life without seeing Lux or having contact with her. And that's the reason I nod.

"Thank you." She turns and walks away from me, leaving me to stare after her.

29

Lux

As I walk away from Ollie, I stomp on my urge to cry. There will be enough time for that when I'm in Positano with a glass of wine. There is no way in hell I'm going let myself get photographed by anyone while crying on the streets of Baltimore. I'm done being social media drama fodder. I'll be damned if anyone calls me *Poor Luxxy* ever again.

I finish my walk, head home, shower, and wait for my ride. My skin is tingling, and part of me wishes I had called an Uber. I hate being here with the memories of Ollie and me whispering from every corner. I can't look anywhere without being reminded of his kiss, his touch, the way we rolled on the bed, the floors, and bumped the wall while tearing into each other during sex.

I shove my eyes shut, and I swear I hear the moans he extracted out of me. I push to my feet and go to my studio. I record a cryptic mini message to my followers, telling them to expect new content from a mystery location.

The Bougie Life goes international again.

I post it impromptu. I can picture Mimi's sour face when she sees it. I didn't clear it with her, and I don't really have to. I do have autonomy to post ad hoc content, but she'll hate it, especially since, thanks to what happened with Mateo, my lawyer is using a clause in my contract about inflicted emotional distress to renegotiate some of the terms of my contract. This will give me the power to make sure they can't force me to interview people I don't want to again. *Thanks, Cam, for lending me your sharks.*

The video has been up for a few minutes when the likes and comments start appearing, and what I see has me smiling.

I love when you go on location, Lux.

OMG. This is not a drill. She's trying a new spot.

I'm planning a vacation. Give me somewhere I'll love.

Tell me you're taking Fabian or Angelo so Mateo can drop dead after.

GIRL, I was worried you were backpedaling. So relieved.

Everything is a blur after that: the trip to the airport, getting a shoulder massage at the lounge, boarding the plane and downing two glasses of champagne only to knock out. I slept the entire flight and thought I would be up for dinner when I got into Positano.

Now that I'm here, I need a minute. Lying on the bed, I scroll IG for a few minutes but can't even concentrate.

My brain keeps landing on Ollie's sad eyes before I walked away from him. One of us is always walking away.

My phone drops on my chest, and it jolts me. I place it next to my pillow. Maybe I'll take a little nap. It's only four in the afternoon.

The shush of sea waves rolling over sand and crashing against the rocks slowly brings me out of my slumber. I burrow closer against the too-soft pillows while covered in sheets sprayed with lemon essence. I didn't notice the smell when I came in. It's still light outside but too bright. I reach for my phone, and the screen lights up. It's ten in the morning, and I've been asleep since four in the afternoon yesterday.

There are tons of texts messages—Adri, Lauren, my brothers, and three missed calls from Marilyn. I'm definitely not calling her back. The latest one from Maeven makes me push off the bed.

MAEVEN

Get your ass up and come eat breakfast
with me.

I brush my teeth, spray some rose water on my face, moisturize, and apply a heavy layer of sunscreen, then grab a silk turquoise robe from the bathroom. On my way out of the room, I pull back the curtains. The sun blares in my eyes. My vision adjusts and lands on the color progression from aqua to turquoise, blending into the darker shades of blue. A gasp rocks my body, and the breath catches in my throat. The Tyrrhenian gradient is unforgettable and even more beautiful than I remember.

"Get outside." Maeven yells from the table on the far left of the balcony. She's wearing a robe just like mine but in a blue that complements her brown porcelain skin. She's sitting at a table with a breakfast spread in front of her.

I open the double doors and walk out onto the balcony. The smell of the sea fills my nostrils, engulfing me in instant memories of Ollie's cologne and the warmth of his body. I force myself not to close my eyes and let it sweep over me. Instead, I shake my head to clear my thoughts.

"Good morning, Sleeping Beauty," Maeven says.

"I should be saying that to you. God, your skin is glowing so much you need a sponsorship."

She smiles up at me and sweeps a hand over the table. "Thank you. Sit. Eat."

I obey and immediately reach for what I know is a Bellini. "When did you get here?"

"An hour after you." She sips her drink and then points her glass to the outdoor couch. "I knocked, but you didn't answer. I fell asleep out here with a glass of wine. I woke up in the middle of the night, all disoriented and shit."

"I know the feeling. I smacked myself with my phone." I chuckle.

"We've been through hell. Me with shithead Mateo, and you with both your exes."

I lean back in my chair, letting the sun balm my skin. "Mateo has not been a problem for me for a while. Having to spend the day with him wasn't stressful as much as it was annoying. Well...yeah, a little stressful since I had to constantly fight to keep my face straight and avoid side-eyeing his flirting."

"Homeboy was coming on super strong. You did well, though. You were polite but didn't encourage him. You put him in his place several times, making him want it more." She laughs at the end.

"I don't care anymore. And since my contractual duties are fulfilled, I don't have to give him the time of day anymore."

She raises her glass. "Samesies. I'm free."

"What is he going to do without you? Who the hell is going to clean up his messes?"

She shrugs. "Don't know. I made recommendations. He can take them or not...either way, I. Don't. Care."

"I can't believe he's going to let you go just like that."

"It's not just like that." She sips. "He and his agent have been nonstop messaging me. Between you, me, and the Positano Ocean, they've offered me three times my salary and full autonomy. He keeps swearing he will do better and listen more."

"That's a whole lot of money."

She sighs. "Yeah, still not doing it. I can design any situation for my clients, but that fucker was burning me out."

No kidding. He has so many messes. "What are you going to do, then?"

"My friend, YES, and I are forming an athlete management agency."

"Oh, that's cool. So, you would take on clients and manage them together?"

She nods. "Yeah, each in our own lane but together."

"And her name is Yes? That doesn't sound very agent-like."

She laughs. "Her name is actually Yasmin. YES is an acronym. She's a shark, and we've been consulting each other for our athletes for years. It's time we offered a one-stop shop for clients."

"You're going to do great. Mateo's loss is her clients' gain."

"I hope so."

"Girl, please, you're like an Olivia Pope in the business. I'm not even mad at how you kept Mateo's image intact." I'm really not bitter. She was doing her job.

She rolls her eyes. "He was the most exhausting job I've ever had. I'm not breaking confidence because you were there for all his messes. He's a fucking trainwreck."

"Oh yeah."

"I have to say… Even though it made my life more difficult, I was glad you finally broke up with him for good. You deserved better," she confides.

"You really thought so?"

"Yes." She sips her drink. "You were the perfect girlfriend, a publicist's dream. You gave him credibility because you had your own life, your own followers, and didn't carry any baggage. You're the whole package."

It's so good to hear people say that. "That reminds me about a conversation with Chase."

"Chase…" She sighs.

"That's gross."

"You don't see it because he's your brother. I'm mad at myself for not jumping on him. He was a hot mess back then, but I'm an expert at wrecks. I could've fixed him."

I remember and shudder. That was a rough time all around for us. "He was in love with Lauren. He has always been."

"I could tell he had more baggage than Samsonite. But he's so delish I almost let him beat the shit out of Mateo that one time he came looking for him, just to watch him flex all those muscles." Her eyes are dreamy.

It's my turn to laugh. "You're so crazy. Do you know how scary that was? My brother would've done some damage."

"I know. That's why I stopped him. I wouldn't want him going to jail. Anyway, it worked out for the better. You met someone new…"

"And got dumped," I retort, trying to keep the bitterness from my tongue but failing.

"He made a mistake but tried to rectify it yesterday."

I look out past the downstairs terrace into the water. "I don't know what that was about."

"He fucked up. It happens. Trust me, I see it every day. Unfortunately for him, he doesn't have a Maeven to fix it for him."

"Um… If I can help it, I will never be in a relationship with someone who needs a Maeven in his life. No offense."

"None taken," she says, taking a bite of a croissant. "It's messy. But life is messy in general. I would tell you to fuck it out of your system here in Positano. I know some people here I can hook you up with. But…"

"I'm not in the mood for that—"

"You're not over Oliver," she says, conjuring images of his smile, his hands around me.

"I'm not," I admit. Painful as it is, there is no bigger truth.

"What are you going to do about it?" Maeven asks.

"I'm going to get over him."

She flips a hand over, exposing her pink stiletto nails. "How?"

"I have a plan."

Her eyes light up. "I love plans. Tell me."

"I'm going to take some time to myself. I haven't done that well. I'm going to use that time to work on my career and myself. I have yet to do a *single and traveling* series." I dig into my croissant.

"That sounds good. Like Princess Meghan before she met Prince Harry."

"God, I used to love her blog. Yeah, something like that but more me."

"I like it. Let's start this afternoon. There are a couple of spots here that are perfect for IG videos. You can do some organic content."

"Are you auditioning to be my publicist?"

She giggles. "We can add you to the roster. Right now, I'm more like auditioning to be a friend."

I smile at her. "Consider yourself selected."

"Okay, then, let's get you started in your single bougie life."

———

Oliver

Another sleepless night. Another day I'm driving on I695, but this time, I'm going in the opposite direction of Baltimore. I'm headed to Virginia with my stomach in a knot. Things with Ayla are improving. She's back to her bright-as-the-sun smile and was her usual chatty self on the drive to school. She got to talk to her mother while I was in the room. I told her she could go to her room for privacy, but she chose to stay.

"No secrets." She smiled and went on to talk to Noris for half an hour.

I was touched by her trust and a little scared because I needed to do the same. I need to be as transparent as a parent can be with her. In the conversation, she mentioned her favorite teddy, Alfonso. It was a gift from my ex-girlfriend, Marcia. Even though Ayla didn't mention her name, it stayed with me, and I found myself thinking back to her and when we dated.

We had the same argument that I had with Lux and Lyssa before. Now I want to know more. Marcia loved Ayla, but she disappeared, and back then, it was easy to blame it on her not wanting a kid or wanting to compete with my daughter, but after what happened with Lux, I just don't know. Maybe I've been wrong.

That's how I find myself in Old Towne, a city by the water, where you can see D.C. across the way. It looks like the towns in those romance movies that play at Christmas time. I'm planted firmly in front of her bakery, but part of me wants to get back in the car, drive away, and not look back. But I can't find answers if I don't ask the right questions.

I reach for the handle and open the door. Marcia's eyes widen when she sees me, and then she smiles and comes around the counter.

"Oliver." She takes a few steps toward me and hugs me. Her warmth is familiar and sweet, like she doesn't remember our last conversation together. The way she left my house in tears stayed in my memory for months.

Then again, she looks great, and when I looked her up, her business had mostly five and four stars. To be in this area, she has to be successful. Maybe it was for the best.

"How are you doing, Mar?"

"Good. Busy. Between the bakery, the husband, and the kids, I barely have time to breathe." She laughs. "Thankfully, today is a slow day."

Her face glows, and her happiness shows. I don't ever remember her being like this before.

"How's your family?"

"Really good. The two older kids are in school, and the two youngest are finally in daycare. Joe and I can finally have normal work schedules."

"Four kids? I can't even imagine how you two manage that."

She shakes her like she can't imagine either. "You don't want to know this insanity. But how about you? I was so surprised when you called me, but I was glad you did."

"You were?"

"Of course." She points at a chair. "Sit. I'll bring you some of our coffee."

When she walks away, it hits me how familiar she is to me. After seeing Noris again, I see the physical similarities between them—tall, shapely, beautiful brown skin. Have they always resembled each other?

A few minutes later, she comes back with the coffee with cream, the way I like it.

"Thank you for this and for agreeing to see me."

She nods. "I always remember you *con mucho cariño*. You and Ayla were always in my heart. How is she?"

"A teenager." I pull out my phone and share some photos.

She gasps. "She's beautiful. I always knew she would be, but she's more than that. She could be a model."

My chest puffs because she's right. But Ay is more than that. "She's actually an excellent pitcher. The ace of her team."

"She gets that from her *papi*." She smiles like she remembers, as if she's feeling the love, not like someone who walked away and didn't look back.

"Why did you say you were glad I called?" I ask.

Her eyes grow a little sad. "I meant it when I said that I remember you fondly. You and Ayla were a big part of my life for a while. We talked about the future like dumb high school kids."

I remember that. "Why dumb?"

"Neither of us were ready for that. You were not over Ayla's mom."

My back stiffens. "I didn't love her anymore."

"But you couldn't forget her betrayal or the hurt. Everything about our relationship back then was about that. I didn't love myself enough to see it."

Her confession leaves me blinking.

She chuckles. "You checked all the boxes in the beginning, and I made the mistake of holding on to that. It wasn't until later, when the time had passed and I was out of the haze, that I began to see how absent you were even as you made promises to me."

My stomach tightens, and I want to deny all she says, but I'm here to listen. "I really did care about you."

"You did. Like I did for you. But you weren't present. You were not vulnerable or open. You didn't even want to go away for the weekend together," she says, catapulting me to our last argument, when she yelled that Ayla would be fine for forty-eight hours. I just didn't want to put the effort into our relationship.

"That's the day you left and didn't look back. Ayla missed you like crazy. She still remembers you."

She dabs at the corner of her eye. "It hurt my heart not to be able to see her or say goodbye."

"You could've kept in touch." I can't keep the bitterness from coating my tongue.

She shakes her head. "That would've meant keeping in touch with you."

The skin on my cheeks begins to tingle like she slapped me across the face. I rear back. It was me. *She didn't want contact with me.*

Her hand shoots out to cover mine. "It would have been too

painful. To see you or have to hear your voice, and not have you…it would have destroyed me. I was *aficiá de ti*, so madly in love. I couldn't be near you without going back to you and risking it becoming a mess for all three of us."

"Three?" I manage.

She bobs her head up and down. "You, me, and Ayla. You were going to move on eventually. I loved myself enough to remove myself from the situation before you started seeing someone else."

I swallow the knot in my throat. "That was the last thing on my mind."

"Yeah, but hot contractors in Baltimore don't stay unattached for long." She chuckles. "It worked out the way it was supposed to. I moved down here, got a loan for the bakery, and met Joe. He's a good guy and a contractor too. He helped me build all of this."

I look around at the beautifully built shelves and the dollhouse architecture. "It's a work of art."

Her smile widens. "High praise coming from you. Tell me about you. Have you given someone the chance to love you?"

Another punch, to the chest this time. I think of Lux and the way she walked away from me. She can't trust me with her heart but still wants to be a part of A's life even if I loom in the background.

"I messed it up," I blurt out. "I wasn't open with her either. Ayla was my excuse."

She squeezes my hand tight. "Do you love her?"

I nod. "I do, and she loves my girl."

"Does she love you?"

The sadness in Lux's eyes as she walked away haunts me.

"I think so."

She leans in. "Then fight for her. You've waited for this love for too long. If you had shown me this kind of emotion, we would be in another place right now."

"I'm sorry," I say because I never wanted to hurt her.

"Don't be. Our breakup freed me to be the happiest I've ever been. Joe and I are made for one another. Since I'm happy, I think it's your turn. Don't waste this opportunity."

She's right. I can't waste my chance. I'm going to wait for Lux to come back from her trip, and I'm going to *enamorarla*, court her, until she gives me another chance. She may say no, but I won't go down without fighting for her. For us.

Twenty minutes later, I'm driving back to Baltimore when my phone rings on my dash. It's Adri.

"Ollie, I need a favor. Can you pick up Bron from school today and bring her home?"

Her tone is subdued and downright sad.

"Yeah, of course. Is everything okay?"

"No. Marilyn Blake died this morning."

My heart lurches, and I grab on tight to the steering wheel. Lux. God, her mother is dead.

"Does Lux know?"

"Chase is going to call her. Cam is sending a plane for her."

Jesus, she's going to be devastated.

"What can I do?"

"All we can do is be there for them, and you're doing that by picking up Bron. We wouldn't trust anyone else."

We hang up, and the news is weighing heavy on my heart. Lux is going to hurt, and I can't do anything about it.

How can I be there for Lux when she doesn't want me near her?

30

Lux

"You were right," I say, looking up from my phone to Maeven. "Positano is the perfect travel content place. These photos of the sunset by the bay are to die for. I just hit post, and people are already commenting."

"This is a photogenic city. Every angle is gorgeous."

"Yes, and—" I look over her shoulder and freeze. There's a cute little boutique, but my eyes are on the small blue leather jacket. It would be perfect for Ayla. I don't let myself think about it. "Come."

She trails behind. "More shopping? Sign me up."

The clerk comes around the desk. "*Ciao. Cosa posso mostrarti?*"

I smile at her and point to the jacket. "I want to see that one."

"Oh, *Americana*. Yes. What size?"

"Medium."

When she hands it to me, Maeven reaches out to touch it. "So soft."

"It is. Do you have any other colors?"

"In the back, I have an orange one. I can go get it."

"Yes, please."

As she disappears through the door, Maeven turns to me. "It's beautiful, but this doesn't seem like your style."

Her arched brow tells me there's something more on her mind.

"It's not for me."

"I know. It's for Ayla."

I nod. There's no need for me to lie. "Yeah, her skin tone is gorgeous, just like yours. It reminds me of her."

She nods. "I think a lot of things here do."

"Yeah." I shrug like it's no big deal.

"You've been texting with her for two days and bought her so many presents it's going to put whatever her dad gets her for Christmas to shame."

"She and Bron like to dress alike and share clothes."

The store clerk returns, and I pay for the purchases.

As we walk in silence down the cobble path, we stop at other stores. I pick up sweatshirts for CJ, Justin, and Felix. I even find the cutest dress for Avelyn.

We send a messenger to drop off our bags to the house and continue the walk, heading for a night festival at the beach.

We get a table at a seaside bar.

"You know I'm a straight talker, right?"

I chuckle and look at her. "I do know that about you."

"I wasn't trying to make you uncomfortable, but you *are* buying lots of presents for Ayla."

"And Bron. They're stylish girls. Ayla looks like a model, and I just love her. I want to stay in her life."

She nods, her eyes so warm I have to look away from her. She's pitying me.

She touches my hand. "There's nothing wrong with that. I just wonder if you can really do that and get over him."

My eyes fill so fast. All day today, Oliver has been in my head. I keep imagining him across from me instead of Maeven. I can't seem to zap him out of my mind. The best way is to concentrate on making the moment memorable for Instagram, or thinking of how I can replace the decor at home so I don't think about him when I see everything. I keep thinking about him and Ayla, and I keep including Bron in everything I get for her to justify it.

I dab at the corners of my eyes. "It's too recent. I'll get over it."

"You don't have to, you know? He wants to get back together."

I blink away the tears. "He didn't trust me. He dumped me like I didn't matter."

She sips her wine. "He handled it wrong. You did something that, at the time, he considered unforgivable."

The memory of that day hits me hard. My stomach turns. "I did, but he didn't really give me the chance to explain or atone."

"It's better that he broke up with you and not continue and have it become toxic. You know how destructive a toxic relationship is. I'm not on his side. I just want you to consider everything." Her empathy is so vibrant.

"I know. He's a great guy who hurt me as much as the asshole I used to date before him. For different reasons, I know, but I'm back at the place where I have no peace. Where I see him in every corner of my house because he had a hand in everything there. I miss him like I've had him all my life when it was only a few months."

"I think that's what love is. You get used to someone so fast and can't remember a time when you didn't have him."

I stare at her. "Have you loved someone like that?"

She shakes her head. "It was a conversation I had with one of my best friends. He met someone for whom he risked everything, and when that person betrayed him, his world began to fall apart."

"Oh. That's awful. Where is he now?"

The way her eyes well and she looks out to the sea tells me everything I need to know. Her friend is gone.

"Do you want to talk about him?"

She blinks the tears away and shakes her head. She takes a sip of her wine. "Someday. Not today. We're talking about you and your love."

The word sends a flash of cold through me.

"I don't ever want to be that vulnerable again."

"You love him, and that already makes you vulnerable." Her words are soft, almost a whisper. It reminds me of the way I would talk to the horse when I took riding lessons.

She's afraid of spooking me, but it's too late for that. I feel the urge to deny, but I woman up.

"I do. I think even he knows that."

"Lux, I don't think you do, though."

I frown at her. "What the hell are you talking about? I just said I do."

She regards me over her wine glass. "The way you love him is not the way you loved Mateo. You love him in a selfless way." The lilt at the end of her statement is almost a question. "You love that man deeply. You love his daughter just as deeply. You shouldn't walk away from something like that without making sure there's no way to make it work."

"Who are you? Where's the woman who plots relationships better than any novel? You taught me that it all has to make sense: the actions, the gestures, the emotional connection."

She smiles. "I mean that from the bottom of my soul. To prove it, let me ask you this. Think of the actions from the beginning of your relationship with Ollie to the end. Was there a natural progression? Did he do what he said he would do? What were his gestures to show his love for you? Did those fulfill the need within you?"

I think back to how we started. He was scared of doing the relationship thing because of Ayla. Then when I put my foot down and voiced my opinion, he didn't run. He faced his fears. He came down hard on me when I made the mistake, but he also came back to own his part, what he did wrong. That's very Ollie. He's responsible. He's a real man.

"Yes. He showed me," I say. "I'm just afraid of opening up like I did with him again. I also don't want to do the whole thing and then have it not work out because of Ayla."

"You really love that kid. And that's a great thing. But you're doing the same thing he was doing: hiding behind her. You owe it to yourself and him to try. You don't want to spend your whole life wondering."

"I'm just not ready right now. I don't think I'm letting myself heal. I want to do that."

She nods. "That's fair. You have to be sure before you take the step, and there's nothing wrong with you taking your time—"

My phone rings, and it's loud, rattling both of us. It's the ringer I have saved for Chase. I grab it and don't let him talk. "I haven't been gone that long, and you already miss me?"

"I actually do," Chase says.

I chuckle. "You have no one else to bug."

"Something like that." His voice is low, and he doesn't take the bait.

"What's wrong?"

"Lux, are you with Maeven?"

I'm about to crack a joke about him remembering her, and Lauren killing both of them, but his somberness hits me. "Yeah. What's wrong, Chase?"

"Something's happened. I hate having to tell you this on the phone. I wish you were here..." His voice goes out, and he clears his throat. "Marilyn fell down the stairs this morning. Eddha called Cam this morning, and we headed to New York. She slipped away a few minutes after we got here."

"Slipped away?"

His breath fills the line. "She died, Lux."

My heart drops, the thump so loud it sends me forward. My hand grips my phone. *She died.*

My brain races, trying to grasp all the words he just said. *Marilyn is gone. My mother is dead.*

"Oh God. I just spoke to her at the gala. She wanted to talk to me. I...Chase...God..."

Please, Luciana, I just want to talk.

Her words echo in my ears. I rejected her and didn't pick up her calls. Now I won't see her again.

Across from me, Maeven reaches for my hand. I can tell by her wide eyes that she heard everything.

I don't know when I stopped listening to Chase or when she took the phone from my hand, but within minutes, we are out of there and in a cab to the house.

Maeven is still talking to my brother as we move through the house. I head straight for the closet and take out my suitcase. I didn't get to take anything out of the big suitcase, so we are both in tandem, running around the room and throwing my shit back in the carry-on.

She is in tears as we say goodbye, and I jump in the cab to the airport. The second I'm in the backseat, in the dark, I close my eyes and breathe.

My thoughts turn to all our conversations of late. I don't know what she wanted to say to me. I can't remember loving moments between us, and every time I saw her, I was already tired before we said a word to each other. I got so used to not having a real mother that I forced myself not to need her or love her. And I didn't.

And now she's gone, and I won't hear from her again. I won't sigh when I see her or remove her from rooms so she doesn't ruin family moments.

And that's sad, and it shatters my heart because this is what I remember.

Not hugs and love, like what I see between Bron and Adri or Lauren with the boys. She would've never put me first the way Ollie does with Ay. She didn't fight for me the way he fights even her mother to make sure Ayla is okay and not hurting.

I feel so alone, but I don't pick up my phone when Lauren and Adri call. I need the silence more than I need anyone's words. As the private jet Cam arranged for me takes off, I look out the window at Positano with yearning. I didn't think I could feel worse about life than when I landed here. Turns out, it can always get worse, and my heart could be doubled over.

And then my notification pings, alerting me to a voicemail message. It's from Oliver.

My pulse speeds, and I rush to listen to it. Even at this moment, I'm drawn to him like a moth to a flame.

Hey, Luciana. I was calling to tell you how sorry I am about your mom. I know what this loss feels like, and I hate that you're going through it. I'm here for whatever you need. My heart is with you… always.

He lingers at the end, like there's more he wants to say but then hangs up. The walls in my throat close, and I have to force myself to breathe. Because if his heart were with me, I wouldn't have been here or flying alone for hours to bury my mother.

And it's that thought that forces me to start focusing on what I need to do. There will be enough time to mourn Marilyn. So, I message Mimi about pausing some of my content.

Maeven sends me a message with a drafted public statement. *I know this is the last thing on your mind, but I thought you could use it.*

I send her a hug emoji and save it to my social media drafts. Tomorrow, I will post it.

I close my eyes and start falling asleep when the notification pings. My pulse races, thinking it's another message from Ollie, but it's from Ayla.

> AYLA
>
> Heard about your mom. I'm really sorry. Love u so much. 💕

She follows it with the double pink hearts that have become such a big part of us. My eyes fill so fast and the sob escapes my throat, releasing the weight occupying my chest, weighing it down and choking me up.

And I cry because this teenage girl has managed to say the words that set my complicated emotions free.

I cry for the love she feels for me, the love I feel for her and her father. I mostly cry because Marilyn and I could've had a relationship like they do, except she stopped being my mommy long ago. And now it's too late.

———

Oliver

"Can I make you some coffee, *Papi*?"

I look up from my phone to find Ayla so close to me. "No, thank you."

She doesn't move away. Instead, she takes a seat next to me. I can't stop thinking about Lux, and I keep staring at her reply to my text. Just one word: *Thanks*.

Regret is a rippling echo because I should've said more. I should have told her that I love her, and I wish I could be with her. I should've asked if I can pick her up from the airport. I would've driven to New York to do just that.

She doesn't need that from me and most likely doesn't want it. She and her family have money, and she's flying home by private jet, and Adri mentioned Chase and Cam were going to pick her up.

She needs her family now, not the guy that hurt her.

"I'm so sad for Lux," Ayla says, bringing my attention back to her.

"Me too, *negrita*."

"I want to do something for her. I just don't know what." Her big eyes are cloudy and troubled.

I touch her cheek. "All we can do now is keep her in our thoughts and be there if she needs something from us."

"How is she going to get through this?"

The question should be rhetorical. No one has an answer, and I'm getting ready to give her the standard, "Give it time," but her eyes go liquid, and her breathing becomes shallow. "Ay?"

She shakes her head and rubs the back of her hand over her eyes, like when she was three and tried to shake a fall.

Her gaze centers on the TV, on the movie neither of us is watching, but the tears fall free and fast. The sight burns a hole through my chest. I scoot closer and put my arm around her shoulders.

"Death is never easy, *mi amor*. But time and those who love us can help make things a little easier."

"She won't ever see her mom again. She can't make it up to her."

I frown and look at her. *How much does she know?*

"What do you mean?"

"She wasn't there for her or Chase or Mr. Cam. Her dad either. I didn't have my mom, but I had you. You were always there for me. I don't think she had anyone, and now she can't make up with her mom."

"*Negrita*, life is complicated. I am sure her mom loved her too."

"But she's dead, *Papi*. She loved her, and she's dead."

"I know, and that happens."

She pulls away from me, her eyes wild and teary. Her mouth is half open. And it hits me.

This is about more than Lux's mom's death.

"Ay—"

"Anyone can just die at any moment?"

My heart thumps because how the fuck do I make this better for her? For Lux?

"Remember when *Abuela* Amada died?"

She nods.

"Sometimes God takes people with him when they have fulfilled their path in life."

"But what about their families? What about their kids? I don't have any other family. Just you."

I breathe and stay calm, not letting myself think about how much that bothers me. How, for months now, I have been harboring on this very subject. "First, you're not going to lose me. I'm not going anywhere."

"How do you know that?" she yells.

I need to be careful what I say and not speak from the place of fear. "I'm not going to lie to you, Ay. I can't swear that I know. All I can do is have faith. But I want you to remember that you have people who love you. You have your *Abuela* and your mom—"

Her lip curls. "Are you serious? You don't even trust them. And Mom walked away. I like her, but she's not you. She doesn't know me like you do or care for me like you. All she can talk about is me becoming an influencer. She wouldn't know how to talk me down from a pregame panic because I don't have my lucky socks. She doesn't even understand why me and B are so close. She's not you. No one is you. What will I do if you die?"

Tears prickle the corners of my eyes, and my heart has never been so whole and so broken at the same time than at this moment.

"*Mi vida*, we can't live thinking about death. We need to make the most of every moment we spend with those we love. We have to take advantage of every opportunity to tell them how much we love them. And if anything were to happen, you have to give your mom the opportunity to step up. And you also have so many other people who love you, like Bron, Lauren, Adri, Winter."

"And Lux. She told me today."

Oh. "What else did she say?"

"She's sad, but she said that my reaching out helped her. That I was the only one who knew just what she needed to hear."

"That's good." And I wish it didn't bug me the way it does. "What did you say to her?"

She shrugs like it's no big deal. "I told her I was sorry about her mom and how much I love her."

The pain stabs through my chest. I wanted to say that. I should have told her I loved her. She needed the words that were at the tip of my tongue on the message. Why didn't I say it?

Because you let the fear whisper to you. But your daughter knew just what to do and what to say.

"You're so smart, you know that?"

Ayla looks up at me again. "Why?"

"Because you've already got the hang of loving people and knowing what to do for them. It's so tough, but you know to tell her you love her. I'm giving you the advice you already practice."

She smiles. "That's what you always do for me when I'm having tough times. You tell me you love me and find a way to make it better."

I kiss her forehead. "I'll take that coffee."

She springs to her feet. "I'll be back."

And I'm alone to torture myself because I should have told Lux I love her. I could have been there when she arrived, but I let her down yet again. I don't know what to say or how to be the man she needs.

I need to let things be for now. She'll have plenty of people to console her.

I need to fall back and sort my thoughts. I just can't put away her kindness toward Ayla. It doesn't surprise me that she was gracious with my baby, even in her moment of pain and grief.

It doesn't even surprise me that it's not a formality. I know how much she loves her.

That's why her words haunt me. She loves my daughter but doesn't trust me. It started with me feeling like I couldn't get security from her, but it's me who can't make her feel secure because of my own fucking issues. Maybe it's for the best that things ended this way. It's like I'm never going to get it right.

The ping on my phone forces my gaze to it.

> **LAUREN**
>
> The service is set for the day after tomorrow at ten in the morning.

> **ME**
>
> Thank you. Ayla and I will be there. How's Chase?

> **LAUREN**
>
> It's complicated, just like their history…

> **ME**
>
> I get it. Have you seen Lux?

> **LAUREN**
>
> Yeah. She got in a while ago. Very sad but strong. She's been helping Chase and Cam with the arrangements and has been in communication with her dad.

That has to be rough on her. She has a complicated relationship with her dad too.

> **LAUREN**
>
> She needs our support.

ME

Whatever she needs, I will be there.

LAUREN

I know...but you have to SHOW her...

Even she knows that's where I failed. But I will do better. I will give her time and space, but I will make sure she knows she can count on me, even if nothing comes of it.

When Ay comes back with the coffee, I look up and thank her. "The service for Lux's mom is the day after tomorrow. I would like you to come with me."

She nods. "We have to be there for Lux and Bron. Yes, and for Cam and Chase. The whole family needs us."

I run my hands over her hair and nod. "We will be there for them."

31

Lux

It's a cloudy day, and that doesn't surprise me because such was my relationship with my mom. It was never bright, and that doesn't change because she's gone. We are surrounded by our loved ones and close friends. It warms my heart to see Oliver and Ayla here. Lauren said he's been asking about me and that he's here for me. And though we are not together, that fills my heart.

But no one is really here for Marilyn. The only one would have been Eddha, but her daughter took her home because the funeral would have been too much for her.

I stare at the baby-blue coffin, and the wave of regret washes over me again. Cam, Chase, and I agreed to expedite the services without seeing a need to prolong the inevitable. So, like we did when she was alive, we outsourced and paid to speed up the process of dealing with her death. And that breaks my heart.

And scares me to death.

I don't want to end up this way, where the only time peace is reflected on my face is in a beautiful coffin that will end up six feet under anyway. We will pay for beautiful grass and a flower bush to be planted.

The three of us can't bring ourselves to speak about Marilyn to the world. We said the things we needed to say when Cam and Chase picked me up from the airport, and I got to go see the body. I brought her baby-blue Manolos and the matching Zuhair Murad dress she wore when Cam got signed to the Emperors. I forgave her for not being a mom to me and for manipulating me all these years. I told her I was sorry I couldn't be the daughter she wanted and told her I was still working on forgiving her for what she did to Chase.

As in life, my brothers and I didn't leave each other alone with her, and since then, every time we have things to say about her, we say them to each other. No one else understands what our relationship with her was like. We even called Walter together. Chase held my hand as Cam gave him the details and explained the arrangements we made. Through a tear-clogged voice, he said he was all alone now as he knew none of us would be there for him. Manipulation was their way of life, and that won't stop because she's gone.

That's why, when the priest asks if anyone would like to share a few words about her, the three of us stiffen and look at each other with trepidation. Then, footsteps tap on the cemetery grass, and I'm stunned as Mateo stands in front of us, in between her photo and the coffin.

He clears his throat. "Ms. Marilyn was a caring person. She was the first one outside my circle to call me when my mother died. She was supportive and always in my corner. Somehow, she understood that my mistakes didn't define me as a person. And when I called her, she always had kind and encouraging words. On a trip a few months ago, she told me she saw a little of herself in me. Someone who, despite my best intentions, never knew how to make the right decision." He shrugs. "She told me there was a chance for redemption for everyone, and she wanted me to be happy. She wanted her kids to be happy. Whatever her mistakes, she loved the three of you. Ms. Marilyn was a complicated lady, and I hope, in death, she finds the peace she never had in life."

The knot in my throat tightens as does Chase's hand on mine.

When I look up, there are tears in my brother's eyes, sparking some of my own. When the service is finished, we say goodbye to the rest of the family, and everyone leaves but us.

We hold hands as they lower her into the ground. I didn't want to leave her alone at that moment.

"Thank you for staying here with me," I say, fighting the lump in my throat.

"This may no longer mean anything to her, but it meant something to you." Cam's hand tightens around mine. "Her best gift to me was the two of you."

I nod and lean my head against him. "I know it's just a ritual."

Chase clears his throat. "Who are you kidding? She's loving this wherever she is. The three of us with our attention fully on her. She's smiling."

And there's even a touch of warmth in his voice. When I look up, he's staring at the lowered casket. I throw my arms around him, and Cam hugs us both.

We throw the first clumps of dirt into the ditch, and thirty minutes later, we are sitting in a limo, side by side, on our way to Cam's brownstone.

"The jet is ready to take us home this evening," Cam says in the car.

Both Chase and I nod.

"Lux, Lauren and I want you to come home with us," Chase says.

I smile but shake my head. "I want to be alone."

"You shouldn't be alone. You can come home with me too," Cam insists.

"It's sweet of both of you, but I'm at peace. I just want to go to my place and be with my things. Of course I'll come over and hang out but not to stay. You get it, right?"

They nod. Chase is still frowning, and I squeeze his hand. "I'll call if I need you."

"Or if you need to talk."

I can't help it; I tease him. "Oh, you want to talk? You must really love me."

He holds up his thumb and index fingers in the universal 'a little bit' sign.

He opens his palm and latches on to my hand. "If her death taught us anything is that we need to hold on to each other and deal with everything as a unit, including Walter. I know he's a mess right now, but this is not just your problem. It's ours. Promise me, you won't try to tackle this alone."

I nod and so does Cam. A sense of peace washes over me because Walter is destroyed and his guilt is too much for me alone.

When the car pulls up to Cam's brownstone, I hold my breath because we now have to let the world in and interact with people other than those we love.

But I'm going home soon, and that's a comfort in itself.

When we go inside, Mateo is in conversation with Mimi, and though I would typically run far away from those two, there are a few words I need to say to him.

When I approach, Mimi gives me her condolences, and I thank her. Relief pours over her face when she realizes she doesn't need to stand there, and she moves on to Cam and Chase.

"I'm sorry for your loss," Mateo says.

I nod. "Thank you for standing up for Marilyn. Your words were touching and meant a lot. She was really fond of you."

"As I was of her. Luxxy, I just want you to know I still love you, and if you ever need me, you know how to find me."

He means it. It's in the way he looks at me, but if I have it my way, as grateful as I am, this will be the last time we are in each other's presence.

I give him a quick hug and move on to greet other guests.

As he's walking out of one door, Ollie walks in with Ayla and Bron. He takes a step my way when a reporter stands in my line of view and asks me for a word.

———

Oliver

The church service went by in a blur. Bron sat with Ay and I, holding on to my *negrita's* hand. They whispered and talked through parts of the service, but my eyes were glued to the back of Lux's head. She was sitting between Chase and Cam.

Our gazes met graveside, and Lux half smiled, half grimaced at me. She dabbed at her tears when Mateo spoke on behalf of her mom. He really cared for her. It was in the affectionate way he talked about her.

The three siblings were stoic through the service. They stayed behind while everyone walked away. Lux's green eyes were nearly gray, her hand firmly wrapped around Chase's arm.

The rest of us got in our cars and headed to Cam's for the repast. Bron rode in the car with me and Ay. We took the long way to the house and got stuck in traffic. By the time we got to Cam's, the siblings were there. Lux and her brothers were receiving people coming in and out to pay their respects. She was speaking to someone from the press on behalf of her family.

I see my moment to speak to her when she sits in a chair near a window in the back of the room. But my daughter and Bron reach her before I can. Bron heads toward her parents. Ayla sits next to her. They hug and pull away, still holding hands. I can't hear what they say, but my *negrita* whispers something that makes Lux nod and dab at the corners of her eyes. They continue to talk in hushed tones, with a familiarity that tugs at my chest. Soon, Lux is mirroring Ayla's smile.

At one point, both turn to me. I don't want to make this awkward by pretending I'm doing something else, so I move to stand by them.

Ayla stands. "I'm going to hang out with Justin and Felix." She leaves us to stare after her.

Lux pushes to her feet and hugs me. "Thank you for coming."

I squeeze her tight, feeling her body against mine, trying to make her feel what my words can't say. "I'm sorry for your loss. I'm here for anything you need."

"Thank you." She pulls back and sits again.

I remain standing.

She finally smiles. "Please sit. You're making my neck hurt."

I nod and take the chair next to hers. "How are you holding up?"

"Surprisingly, I'm okay. A couple of really dark days dealing with arrangements and helping Walter through it…he's not dealing with it well. We got him some help…" She sighs. "But, I have my family around me. That helps," she says.

"Being around the people who love you and care for you is the only thing that's truly comforting in these moments."

There's such emotion in her eyes as she says, "That's mostly true. Ay's messages have meant the world to me. She has the right words. Thank you for bringing her."

"We needed to be here for you. Lux, I—" I shake my head. "No, this is not the time."

Her hand flies to cover mine. "Tell me."

"When I called you, I had so many things I wanted to say to you, but I was scared and a coward. You know, for so long, I thought Mateo was a pure imbecile because he had you and didn't appreciate you. Then Noris appeared, and I overreacted so badly because I let fear and my past whisper in my ear."

What am I doing telling her all of this? She's frowning, and I don't blame her, but I can't stop. "It turns out that I'm dumber than he is for letting you go. In the end, I had you, the prize and the glory, but ended up losing it all because I couldn't control myself."

Her mouth goes slack. Then she closes it and opens it again. "You had your reasons to be angry."

"I shouldn't have thrown us away because of that. I pride myself on being calm and rational, but I screwed up so badly. But you know what's my biggest regret?"

She shakes her head.

I cover her hand with mine. "That you're grieving, and because I was so rash, I can't spend the whole night holding you, rubbing my hands up and down your back. I can't let you cry on my chest, or kiss the sadness out of your eyes, or tell you I love you with every fiber of my body until you can sleep."

Her eyes go liquid, and she snatches her hand back to cover her mouth. "Ollie, I can't—"

I shake my head. "You don't have to say or do anything. I just need you to know that."

She nods.

"Lux," Cam calls from across the room. There's a man I vaguely recognize with him.

She sighs. "I'm sorry. That's the mayor. I need to go receive his condolences."

"Go," I say, helping her up.

She walks away, but as she talks to the mayor, she looks my way.

And though she didn't say it, I see hope. I swear I will be there. I won't miss my chance when it comes again.

Chase comes to sit by me. He's more somber than I've ever seen him. "Thanks for coming, Coach. Look at Cam over there talking to politicians. He hates those people. This shit is so fucked we don't know how to act. But I'm not going over there to talk to that clown, so I'm sitting here with you."

He looks tired, like Lux and Cam.

"How are you holding up?" I ask.

"Fine, I guess. Me and Marilyn were a shit show. Now she's dead. It doesn't matter, though. We have to take care of Lux."

"We will."

Chase pats me on the shoulder. "She's been tough and probably better adjusted than me and Cam. She's always been, but she needs us. She needs you." He points at me. "You need to go ahead and step up your game and get her back."

He's giving me his blessing all over again. If this is not a sign, I don't know what the word means. "Thanks."

Chase nods. "Just don't make me regret it. I don't ever want to see anything that makes me uncomfortable."

I chuckle. "Like what?"

"Don't manhandle my sister in front of me."

I wish that was a possibility right now. "You're assuming she'll let me get close to her."

"Lauren thinks it can work."

"Did she give you ideas?" I ask.

He wrinkles his nose. "No. I wouldn't tell you anyway."

"Then why am I talking to you? I need the professional on my side."

He considers it then hooks a thumb toward the door. "Go get your intel. I'll go save Lux."

He stands and heads toward the group on the other side of the room.

I go looking for Lauren. I need all the help I can get to make this work. I don't make it ten feet when my phone pings with a message.

NORIS

I want Ayla to spend her birthday with me.

Her timing is always impeccable.

32

Lux

I don't get inside my house until late. I had to fight my entire my family to be able to come home alone. My brothers, Lauren, and Adri wanted me to stay with them. Adri's mom tried to sweeten the pot by promising to make me breakfast tomorrow. Even Winter tried to get me to go home with her and Grayson. Her Aunt Millie hugged all three of us so tight and whispered in my ear that if I didn't go home with my brothers or them, I should go home with Ollie and Ayla.

It ripped a chuckle out of me. But saying goodbye to them had been hard enough. I'm not good company, and I am not going to subject anyone to that. Plus, things are complicated enough with all the shit happening around me. I need to be alone and breathe.

My cleaning lady came by while I was in Positano. Everything looks and smells like a spa. I have Lauren to thank for that. I know she's been on top of it. My house is so beautiful, and being here is like the air is fresh and flows right through me. It's cold and quiet and should be heaven to sleep.

But I'm not tired.

My footsteps echo in the silence.

And I need two sweaters because it's so drafty.

I pull out my app and turn the lights in the house to a low turquoise. I strip out of my clothes and fill my freestanding tub. The water is almost boiling, and I dump in bath salts and aromatic oils. I pull up my hair and throw in a rubber band. I lie inside, a glass of wine on the wide ledge next to it and my phone in my hand.

I have a message from Eddha, letting me know she's resting and feeling better. I thank her and go into a chat Adri, Lauren, and I started the other day.

> ADRI
>
> I wish you would've come home with one of us, Lux.
>
> LAUREN
>
> Yeah, you're not alone. You have us, and me and the boys want to show you and Chase how much we love you.

I reply with a teary emoji.

> ME
>
> Love you too. I just need to be by myself.

As tempting as it is not to be alone, the kids and she shouldn't have to split their attention between Chase and me. I put my phone next to my wine glass and lie back against the pillows. It's eerily quiet, and normally, I welcome that. I know I'm not alone, but I can't help but feel it when I breathe the quiet and can hear my own breath. I close my eyes and let the warm water soothe my skin, relaxing into it.

Ollie's face manifests behind my eyelids—how kind he was today, how tight he hugged me. I still feel his hand wrapped around my wrist. His words echo in my heart.

I'm dumber than he is for letting you go.

I'm the one who fumbled the ball because I messed up by hiding Ayla's secret from him. They have more than made up for it. I remember walking into the church today and spotting the way he held her. When we were alone, Ayla confided that she was worried about losing her dad. It's only normal, but she said he reassured her. It felt like she was trying to earn him brownie points. She said how sad he was without me.

My phone pings. I grab it, and my heart skips a beat.

> OLLIE
>
> You okay?

I tell myself not to message back. Leave him on read and answer tomorrow. But my fingers are typing.

> ME
>
> Yeah, just relaxing.

> OLLIE
>
> Good. You need it.

> Me
>
> Thanks for checking on me.

It's really sweet of him to do that. And then my phone rings, and my fingers hover over the green icon. I answer anyway.

"So, I know you want to be alone, but Ayla made you some cookies—"

"And we're downstairs to drop them off to you. Can you come get them?" Ayla yells in the background.

Oh. My. God. They're downstairs, and I'm not dressed.

"Lux?"

"Uh. Yeah. I'm coming. Give me a minute. I was in the shower."

"I'm sorry," he says. "We can come back."

"No, don't. I'll open the door, and you guys can come up. I'll be out in a few.

I am extra careful getting out of the tub. I'm so nervous I would probably slip and fall. *How embarrassing would that be?*

I rush to my closet to grab my emerald lounge set, quickly slipping into the joggers and tank top. The long duster jacket envelops me and doesn't make it seem like I'm in pajamas. I put my hair in a messy bun, and apply moisturizer followed by lip balm.

I come downstairs to find them both standing with their jackets still on.

"Please sit."

I don't miss the way his eyes roam over me or how quickly the lust is replaced with worry.

"No. We are not here to bother you. We are only dropping off these goodies, and then we are leaving."

I smile at him but rush to take the cookies from Ayla. "Thank you for making these for me. And you never bother me. Sit."

She sits on the couch, and I plop down next to her, and he takes the opposite chair. It reminds me of the day he told her we were together and how uncomfortable she was when we were holding hands.

Except, she and I sit on the same side. I swipe a cookie and start to eat it. The sugar and chocolate chips hit my tongue, and my eyes drift closed. "So good. This is the nicest thing anyone has done for me."

Ay smiles so wide. "*Papi* made hot chocolate."

Our gazes meet, and then I see the thermos in his hand. "You did?" I push to my feet and take it from him.

"I hope you like it," he says with just a hint of shyness that makes it adorable.

"I'm going to love it. This is so sweet."

I swear he's blushing a little. "What about that?"

We all turn to look at the ginormous monstrosity of a bouquet Mateo sent me.

"It got delivered while I was away."

"So gorgeous." Ayla stands close to it and leans in to get a whiff.

Her father, on the other hand, says nothing, but pushes to his feet. "We should go, A."

"I'm a peonies kinda girl," I say, ignoring Oliver's frustration. "I once got the prettiest daisies. They became my instant favorites."

His eyes widen, and then he gifts me his signature smile, potent enough to melt the clothes off my body.

"Why don't you guys stay a while and hang out?" I find myself asking.

"Okay. What do you want to do?" she asks, the light dancing in her big eyes.

"Cookies and hot chocolate," I reply.

"And...*Vampire Chronicles*?" She's really too cute.

"You know me so well."

I begin to stand, but Ollie does the same.

"Stay. I'll get the mugs," he says. "But first, I need to make a phone call."

We sit on the couch, and ten minutes into the new episode, Ayla and I turn to each other and roll our eyes.

"We should watch old episodes. I don't like Carla with this guy. I miss the hybrid. And I bet he's missing her too. He lights up when she's around. You know?"

I nod. "It's sad because they're made for each other."

"Like you and *Papi*."

I almost choke on my cookie and have to pat my chest a couple of times. She keeps staring at the screen like she didn't just drop a bomb in my family room.

Did he put her up to this? No, that's not his style.

"Why did you say that about me and your dad?"

She turns a pointed look my way. "Because you are. He was so worried about you and was sad because you were hurting. I asked him to bring me to drop off the cookies, and he insisted on making you hot chocolate because he knows you like it."

"Are you sure that wasn't your idea?"

She shakes her head. "He loves you. He wanted to find a way to make you feel better."

We switch to watching a movie. It is about a guy who goes back to his hometown and finds out he's a dad.

"It's like Bron and Mr. Cam," Ayla says. I don't have to look at her to know she's smiling. "She was so happy when she finally met her dad."

"She wasn't the only one. All of us have been the happiest since we found her."

"She loves that she also got another aunt and Chase."

"How's your mom, A?" This time, I do look at her when I talk.

She shrugs. "Good. She got me a bunch of clothes and shoes. We talk from time to time. She's trying."

"That's really cool. That reminds me. I brought you presents from Positano. Want to see them?"

She turns the brightest smile on me. "Yes."

We go to my bedroom, and I grab the bag where I kept the stuff I brought her and Bron. I pull out the canvas bag.

"It's so pretty," she says, looking at the Amalfi Coast panorama painted on the canvas.

"The real gift is inside."

She pulls out the blue jacket first, and her eyes go round. "O-M-GEE. It's so beautiful. I never had something like this. Thank you."

She shrugs it on, and just like I imagined when I first saw it, it pops against her brown skin.

"You look amazing in it."

She throws her arms around me. "I love it."

"I got an orange one for Bron because I know the two of you need to twin it."

She bobs her head up and down. "Can you take a pic? I want to show her."

I take several photos.

"Papi doesn't like me wearing makeup, but he says the stuff you got me is okay. Can you show me what I can do to make it look even better?"

We end up going upstairs and using the lighting in my studio to make a video so we can watch it later.

When we get downstairs, Ollie is on the couch, waiting for us. He's gaze is on me, and it's like he's searching for something. I smile at him, and I swear something like relief pours over his face.

He stands. "We should probably get going, negrita. Lux needs to rest."

"Are you going to stay by yourself?" Ayla's question brings my attention back to her.

"Yes."

She frowns. "You shouldn't be by yourself. You should come home with us."

I look between them and shake my head. "Thank you, but I want to sleep in my bed tonight."

Ayla thinks about it. "I can stay with you."

Ollie's eyes widen a little, and he shakes his head. "You shouldn't impose—"

I raise a hand to still him. "She never imposes. I would love for her to stay with me tonight…if you agree."

I know I'm throwing down the gauntlet. I want to see how he reacts.

"Okay," he says, shocking me to my core when he says, "I can come get you in the morning, *negrita*."

My heart is beating so fast because he trusts me, and he came to New York. He's showing me he means it when he says he loves me.

He moves and presses a kiss to Ayla's cheek. She squeals and hugs him.

Then he steps closer, leans in, and presses a kiss to my cheek. He tries to pull back, but I hold onto his hand.

I'm not wasting my chance. In truth, I don't want to be alone. I can't think of anyone else I would want to be with but these two.

"You can stay too."

———

Ollie

I don't think I heard Lux right.

My pulse quickens, and my jaw drops. "Did you just say I can stay?"

Lux chuckles and hooks a thumb to the stairs. "You can sleep in the guest room."

The guest room in her house. She's letting me stay.

"Are you giving us…" I trail off because I don't dare hope.

But she nods, her lips still curved.

The long breath I didn't know I was holding flows right out of me.

She's giving us another chance. I lean in and brush my lips against hers.

It's soft and chaste and quick because my heart is trying to find its way out of my chest, because I don't think the happiness fits in it any longer.

When I pull back, she's smiling, and her gaze immediately goes to Ayla, whom I forgot for a minute, but her face matches the joy in Lux.

"Okay, we'll all be together."

"We are," Lux says and looks at me. "Right?"

"Yes." My voice is louder than I meant it, and we both chuckle.

We say good night, and I head downstairs while they go to Lux's room. Once I'm in the guest room, I take out my phone and shoot a message to Lauren and Adri.

ME

So...I got the opportunity of a lifetime.

Their replies are quick.

LAUREN

‼️ ‼️ ‼️

ADRI

Yes! How can we help?

ME

I don't want to impose, but can one of you pick up Ayla in the morning?

ADRI

I'll be there bright and early.

ME

Thanks.

LAUREN

I'm so happy for you guys. About time!

I text Ay next.

ME

Shhh. Do you want to go to Bron's in the morning?

She answers.

AY

Yes.

ME

What are you guys doing?

AY

Lux is already sleeping. I think she's exhausted.

ME

You go to sleep too. Adri is coming to pick you up at 7.

I set my alarm and barely sleep. I'm happy and excited. She's giving me a chance, and now we are starting with the doors open. No secrets or hiding.

I blink, and my alarm goes off.

ADRI

I'm outside.

Crap. I shoot out of bed, and when I start to head upstairs, Ay is already coming down.

"She's still sleeping. See you later, Papi."

I hug her and walk her outside. Adri is parked, and I walk Ay to the car, thank her, and wave them off.

When I get upstairs, Lux is still asleep in her bed. I stand there, watching her, taking it all in. I don't know what to do first. Then her hand shoots up toward me. I shrug my shirt and pants and take her hand, climbing in beside her. She rolls into my arms. Her body is warm from sleep. I wrap my arms around her.

Then her head comes up. "Wait, where's—?"

"At Bron's."

"So, we're alone?" She presses herself closer to me, tilting her face up with a smile.

I indulge her with my hand behind her neck, kissing her like I wanted to when she asked me to stay and throughout the night. Her tongue flicks against mine while her hands roam my back, drifting lower.

I pull my mouth from hers. "Are you sure? You're mourning, and I don't want to take advantage."

The smile blooms again on her lips. Then she laughs. "You sent our girl away only a few hours after I told you to stay on the couch. Then you take your clothes off and climb in my bed…" She takes my face in her hands. "You're sensitive, and I love that about you. I love you for it."

My chest almost caves in at the feeling coursing through my veins. I've missed hearing it from her lips. "I love you too, more than my life, Luciana." And I kiss her again. "If all you wanted me to do is hold you, I can do that. I'll always be here to support you and listen."

Her eyes fill with tears, and she nods. Then she swallows and shakes her head. "I don't want to cry. I slept so heavy last night. I had not slept since I got the call in Positano. You know why?"

I shake my head.

"It's because you're here, and I feel safe and loved and cared for. You'll never know how much it means to me that you came by. I told everyone in my family I wanted to be alone, but the truth is that I didn't want to take away the attention my brothers were going to get from their wives and kids. They need to be loved and doted on. None of us wanted anything to happen to Marilyn, but her death is as complicated as her living was for us. They need the distraction and all the love they can get."

The tears rolling down her cheeks shatter my heart into pieces.

"But you need your family too, *mi amor.*"

She nods. "I did, and you guys showed up right when the loneliness was starting to get to me."

The lump on my throat grows and thickens. I have to breathe and then swallow to be able to say the words. "And we're always going to be there. We're a unit, the three of us."

She closes her eyes, and there are so many emotions dancing in her face at that moment. When her gaze is on me again, the intensity makes my heart tremble.

"What is it?" I ask.

"I want us to be more than three. I want a big family, with all the craziness, and kids that love each other like crazy. Give me three more of Ayla, and I'll be happy."

I'm shocked into silence and can only nod. "Okay. Let's work on the first one and see how we do."

She nods. "Now, we've been apart too long, and I need you. Show me how much you love me, Oliver. I need to feel it."

EPILOGUE

Lux

The next spring

Oliver removes the blindfold, and I have to blink a few times. I know exactly where we are. I heard about this place, and it's been on my list of places to try. I never thought it would be this beautiful.

It's a garden with tall cherry blossoms in full bloom, surrounding a glass igloo. There is a bench outside and peonies everywhere. The igloo is lined with cushions and pillows. There are curtains inside, but they're open, allowing me to see everything. And I already see us tangled on that floor, naked with our lips on each other.

My hand tightens around his. "You planned a lot."

His eyes glow like red-hot embers in the night. He takes a step back and goes to lock the gate.

"It locks? You really planned for everything..." I laugh.

"You've talked about this place and even put it on your vision board. I want to give you beauty, Luciana."

"Then, let's go in there and take me high as only you can while I stare at the sky and the pretty flowers."

His smile is so big and loaded it should melt everything off my body. He takes my hand in his again, and we go inside. It's warm, with the sunlight covering every corner. The sensual scent of flowers mixed with spices infuses the room.

His lips are still on mine, and he shrugs my shawl off my shoulders. I can see everything so clearly, his brown skin, the honey tones in his eyes, the desire that rattles my core.

"Wait, don't you want to draw the curtains?"

He kisses his way down my neck. "No."

"Anyone can see us?"

"Well, if I close them, you won't be able to stare at the flowers while I fuck you like a *sucia*."

My stomach drops. "Dirty?" I repeat.

His hand sneaks between my legs. "Yes. I've been fantasizing since I saw the photos on your board, and there's no other way."

I grind my pussy on his hand and bite my lip as the sensation floods me.

His mouth descends over mine again, and I keep rubbing myself against my hands. The desire builds, and I give myself into it, closing my eyes. I revel in the feeling of his hands that I missed so much. I yearned every second we were apart to fill his hands, his cock.

My eyes fly open, and I pull my mouth from his. I still his hand. "I need you in my mouth."

His mouth drift opens, and he swallows. "I planned this for you. This day is about you, Luciana."

I smile. "Yeah, but on my day, I want to give you a treat."

I drop to my knees, reaching for his fly. The rustle of his jeans follows the slide of the zipper as I pull them over his ass and down his thighs along with his boxers. He springs out in front of my face. I nuzzle my cheek against him. He's hot, thick, and impossibly hard.

I want to tease that it hasn't even been that long. Instead, I place a noisy kiss on his tip. Ollie hums. I take him in my hand, caressing him, following the tender path from balls to tip, staring into his eyes until he shudders.

I rub my thumb over him as I grow thirsty, wanting to caress him with my tongue.

When he starts rocking against my digit, I guide the tip inside my mouth and suck it with enough pressure, then pop it out like a cherry lollipop.

He rocks forward. His hands shoot to the sides of my face, and he guides his cock back into my mouth. I run my hands up and down his thighs, hollow my cheeks, and slide up and down. Between the pressure of my tongue, low moans, and the slight gag when he hits the back of my throat, he grows harder.

That's when he pulls out. There's a dab at the tip, shimmering proof of his desire. I flutter my lashes up at him before I lean forward and lick it off.

"Fuck, you're such a *sucia*. I love it." He takes my hand and pulls me up. "I want to show you the flowers before I come."

His lips crash against mine, and we share the taste of him. He pulls my top off and sends it flying. Then, he rolls down my pants and my panties. His hands roam my body, following a trail from my tits to my pussy.

He steps back and discards his sweater and pants. He sits on the floor and extends a hand toward me.

"Get on your knees beside me," he orders, his voice rough and commanding.

My pussy pulsates, and I don't hesitate. I obey.

"Now turn that way and straddle me, but I don't want you sit on me. I want you to lie down."

My heart thumps in my chest. I don't know where this is going, but I am trembling with the need to feel him inside me. I do as he says and lie in front of him.

His hands hook on my hips, and he pulls me back, his cock sliding inside me, ripping a moan from my throat as my walls grip around him.

"*JesuCristo.*"

He rubs his hands over my ass. Then, he does that thing I've come to love when his fingers slide through my crack, and he draws a few circles over my hole. It's so dirty, but it feels so good.

The sensation shoots through my nipples and clit. I buck back, circling my hips.

His breath catches. "You got it. Now put your arms behind your back and look ahead."

I do, and there are peonies and cherry blossoms out past the glass walls of the igloo. He grabs my arms from behind. My heart pounds so hard, and I'm nervous and excited all at once, but I trust him. Because he will do the one thing I need him to do. He will take care of me.

"This position is called The Irish Garden. Now enjoy the view and the feeling."

He begins to thrust, and I feel all of him inside me, hitting all the spots at the same time. He's stretching me, fucking me, loving me so hard. My eyes begin to blur, and when I think I can't take any more, he moves closer. He holds my arms with one hand and pulls my hair with the other while grinding after each thrust. His sac slaps against me until my skin starts to shrink.

I concentrate on the blooming peonies because that's how I feel, spread out for Ollie to see all of me. My pussy pulsates hard and fast, and I burst into a million pieces with my eyes and mouth open. My moans fill the space, and I collapse on my hands as he continues to pound me while I ride the aftershock.

I'm like a rag doll as he pulls out and drags me against his chest.

"That was so good. You feel so good," he says, and that's the last thing I remember before I fall asleep.

I open my eyes, and the night has fallen. Outside our igloo, the hanging lights have come on. It's not overly bright. There's enough light to see everything but not so bright they hurt my eyes. I turn, and Ollie is awake. He's texting.

"Why didn't you wake me?"

He pulls me against his side. "You looked so peaceful. I think you needed the rest."

I run my hand down his chest. "I did. I haven't been sleeping well, and we had quite the workout."

We both chuckle.

"Dinner is about to be delivered."

"I can't believe this place. You'll have to bring me here more often."

He places a kiss on my lips. "You know I will. Maybe our honeymoon could be like this. Just the two of us away from the world."

My heart slams against my ribcage. "Honeymoon?"

He nods. "I want to marry you—if you want to, of course."

My throat swells. *He wants to marry me.* "I do, but do you think Ay is ready for that? Do you think we are?"

"I am. I don't want to spend another minute not being your husband. And Ay loves you too."

"Yeah, but this is a big step."

He turns his phone so I can see his screen.

In the green bubble, he says:

ME

I want to marry Lux.

There's a heart emoji reply.

AYLA

Let's do this!

My eyes well fast, and I turn to him. "I do, and I think this is the best time in the world, because I think by the end of this year, there's going to be a fourth Amador in this world."

———

ABOUT THE AUTHOR

J. L. Lora is a Dominican-American author. She currently lives in Maryland, pursuing her dream of writing compelling, sexy, can't-put-down stories about empowered, badass alpha heroines and take-your-breath-away alpha heroes. You can find her and or chat her up on Social Media.

Sign up for her newsletter and learn more about new releases, events, news, freebies and much more at **www.JLLora.com**.

facebook.com/AuthorJLLora

instagram.com/jllora

bookbub.com/profile/j-l-lora

ALL BOOKS BY J. L. LORA

The Trinity

BOSS

MADE

STEEL

A Love for All Seasons

THE SUMMER I LOVED YOU

THE WINTER OF MY LOVE

THE LONGEST DAY - *Prequel to novella*

THE AUTUMN YOU BECAME MINE

A NOCHE BUENA FOR LONELY HEARTS - *Prequel novella*

THE SPRING IN MY HEART

Sometimes Love Happens

SOME NIGHTS

SOME MORNINGS

SOME DAYS

WHEN YOU BREAK GIRL CODE

Short Stories

ALL I EVER WANTED — *Free Short Story* — **Epilogue to** The Summer I Loved You (online only)

TRUTH UNDER THE CAROLINA SKIES — *part of the Loving Carolina Anthology to benefit the victims of Hurricane Helene.*

BOUND BY DECEIT — part of the Hate Mates: A Dark Romance Anthology in honor and memory of Catherine Wiltcher, and all proceeds will be donated to Bowel Cancer U.K.